PENGUIN BOOKS
The Devil's Wind

Manohar Malgonkar was born in 1913. After taking a BA degree
in English and Sanskrit, he became a hunting guide but gave up
that career in a couple of years and turned conservationist. A few
years later he joined the army. After a decade in the armed forces
he tried his hand at various careers such as business and politics
before settling down to a life of farming and writing with
occasional breaks for lecture tours and travel.

Manohar Malgonkar has written ten novels, four volumes of
non-fiction and three history books. The best known of his books
are *Combat of Shadows, The Princes, A Bend in the Ganges,
Distant Drum* and *The Men Who Killed Gandhi.*

Mr. Malgonkar lives on an estate in the middle of the jungle and
devotes himself to farming and writing. He is presently at work on
a novel set in post-Raj India.

Manohar Malgonkar

The Devil's Wind

Nana Saheb's Story

A Novel

Penguin Books

Penguin Books (India) Private Ltd., 72-B Himalaya House
23 Kasturba Gandhi Marg, New Delhi-110 001. India
Penguin Books Ltd., Harmondsworth, Middlesex, England
Viking Penguin Inc., 40 West 23rd Street, New York, New York 10010, U.S.A.
Penguin Books Australia Ltd., Ringwood, Victoria, Australia
Penguin Books Canada Ltd., 2801 John Street, Markham, Ontario, Canada L3R 1B4
Penguin Books (N.Z.) Ltd., 182-190 Wairau Road, Auckland 10, New Zealand

First Published by Hamish Hamilton 1972
Published in Penguin Books 1988

Made and Printed in India by Ananda Offset Private Ltd., Calcutta
Typeset in Times Roman

To Sunita

In memory of the day we brought the dog
back and other shared adventures

Contents

Prolegomena

A British view:

"Few names are more conspicuous in the annals of crime than that of Nana Saheb, who achieved an immortality of infamy by his perfidy and cruelty at Cawnpore."

— *The Indian Mutiny*, by A. Miles and A. Pattle. London, 1885

And a French one:

"A scented sybarite, who read Balzac, played Chopin on the piano and lolling on a divan, fanned by exquisite odalisques from Cashmere, had a roasted English child brought in occasionally on a pike for him to examine with his pince-nez."

— Indian Government archives

And an American:

"*Sepoy Rebellion* (se'poi), 1857-58, rebellion of native soldiers in Bengal army of East India Co. Indian princes and the Mogul court, fearing confiscation of land by Gen. Dalhousie, may have encouraged unrest among Hindu and Moslem alike. . . . Revolt began Feb., 1857, and soon raged over N. Central India. Lucknow was besieged, and Cawnpore [Kanpur] and Delhi were captured, with Nana Sahib massacring entire British colony at Cawnpore. . . . Also called Indian Mutiny."

— From a standard reference work, 1968

Author's Note

The man who emerged as the archvillain from the so-called Indian Mutiny of 1857-1858, "a monster to frighten children with," was Dhondu Pant Nana Saheb, heir to the late Peshwa—the erstwhile overlord of the great Maratha Confederacy who had been deposed by the British East India Company's troops in 1818 and exiled from Poona to Bithoor. Some estimates of Nana's character, still current, are printed on a preceding page. Everyone from private to general, from clerk to commissioner, every trader, planter, schoolteacher, or missionary who happened to be in India at the time seems to have written his own memoirs. Every book is written in anger and in every one the principal villain is the same: Nana Saheb—infamous, dastardly, despicable, crafty demon, barbarous butcher, and arch assassin, Nana. In England he replaced Napoleon Bonaparte as the hate object of a nation.

Few Indians shared this view of him. In the villages they sang ballads extolling him as a patriot and parents privately warned their children not to believe the history taught in schools. What the British had tried to pass off as a mutiny was, to most Indians, a national uprising for achieving independence. And right enough, when freedom came, India acclaimed Nana Saheb as a hero and raised a memorial to him, at Bithoor, which bears this inscription:

> KNOWING THE DANGERS
> HE EMBRACED A REVOLT
> HIS SACRIFICE SHALL LIGHT OUR PATH
> LIKE AN ETERNAL FLAME

There were contradictory notes in the archives too. And I had heard other stories about him, current in the Gwalior court in the early years of this century, from my grandfather, Mr. P. Baburao, who was a minister there.

X

This ambiguous man and his fate have always fascinated me. I discovered that the stories of Nana and the revolt have never been told from the Indian point of view. This, then, is Nana's story as I believe he might have written it himself. It is fiction; but it takes no liberties with verifiable facts or even with probabilities.

—MANOHAR MALGONKAR

Burbusa
March 8, 1971

The Principal Characters

In Bithoor

NANA SAHEB, heir to the last Peshwa, BAJIRAO
KASHI, Nana's wife
CHAMPA, his first concubine
   GANGAMALA, their daughter
AZIJAN, his second concubine
BABA BHAT and BALARAO, his younger brothers
KUSUMA, his sister
RAOSAHEB, his nephew
AZIM, his secretary
TANTYA TOPI, his estate manager
WAGHU, his personal servant
TODD, his Eurasian English tutor

In Kanpur

SIR HUGH WHEELER ("HAMLAH"), the British Commanding
   General
JANAKI (Lady Wheeler), his "country-born" wife
   GEORGE, their son
   ELIZA and EMILY, their daughters
MICHAEL PALMER, an adventurer
The HILLERSDONS: Charles, a civil servant, and Margaret
DR. TESSIDER, Nana's personal physician
NANAK CHAND, an informer
HULAS SINGH, the town major

In Nana's fighting forces

> TIKA SINGH, Subedar of the 2nd Cavalry, a rebel leader
> NANE NAWAB of Oudh, a Muslim who became artillery commander
> NIZAM ALI, a Muslim in charge of a cavalry patrol
> JWALA PRASAD, highest-ranking infantry commander

Other historical figures involved

> The SCINDIA (JAYAJI), the Maharaja of Gwalior, a former feudatory of the Peshwa
> HAZRAT MAHAL, Queen of Oudh, last of the independent Indian States
> BAHADUR SHAH, the last Mogul Emperor, sequestered in the Red Fort at Delhi
> ZEENAT MAHAL, the dominant Mogul queen
> The MAD MULLAH, her co-conspirator, a rebel leader
> JUNG BAHADUR, the ruler of Nepal
> BALBHADRA SINGH, his deputy

Governors-General for the British East India Company

> LORD HARDINGE (1844–1847)
> LORD DALHOUSIE (1848–1856)
> LORD CANNING (1856–1858; first Viceroy, 1858–1862)

British Commanders-in-Chief

> SIR CHARLES NAPIER (1849–1850)
> SIR GEORGE ANSON (1850–1857)
> SIR PATRICK GRANT (May–August 1857)
> SIR COLIN CAMPBELL (later LORD CLYDE) (1857–1860)

PART I
BITHOOR

Chapter 1

Among my father's papers in Bithoor was a copy of Maharaja Pratap's appeal to Lord Hardinge, the East India Company's Governor-General in India. It was in the form of a printed book and on its fly-leaf Pratap had inscribed the following words:

FROM
A deposed and exiled Monarch
T O
His deposed and exiled Prime Minister.

"Monarchs!" my father would often say with contempt. "They were more like dummy calves."

I don't think dummy calves are known outside India, where, when a calf dies, its hide is stretched over a bamboo frame and propped up before its mother at the time of milking.

"That's what our kings were," my father would go on. "Skins mounted on sticks so that the great cow that is the public should gaze upon them with adoration and go on lactating freely."

He was right too. Pratap and the kings before him had long ceased to be rulers; rather, they were the prisoners of their Peshwas, or Prime Ministers, who were my father and his forebears. For a full hundred years, the Maratha king was no more than a skeletal relic, preserved mainly for display, so as to serve as the focus for the common man's loyalty. He was kept confined in the fort of Satara, subjected to discipline and to niggling budgetary controls. Here Pratap and his forefathers spent their days like frogs thrown into a deep well, cursing the reigning Peshwa and, as often as not, plotting for his downfall.

The Maratha confederacy, which, before the British came, had ruled the greater part of India, was headed by the Peshwas. My father, who bore the name of the greatest of our line, Bajirao, became the Peshwa in 1796. Only someone perversely gifted could have succeeded in squandering so vast an inheritance in so short a time or disgraced a noble name so thoroughly. He was mean, cruel, vindictive, avaricious; surprisingly well-read and shrewd in his financial dealings; and almost morbidly religious. He was, above all, a moral and physical coward, the only Peshwa held in contempt by his subjects. A popular song about him ran as follows:

> We emptied the wells
> And drained the land dry,
> To grow a tree of thorns,
> "Running" Bajirao.

It is no use my trying to console myself with the argument that Bajirao II was not my *real* father, but had only adopted me as his heir; no use because he has influenced my life more than any real father could have. My world has been abased and defiled by his misdeeds; the realization that I was powerless to undo the harm he has done is like some unsightly birthmark I bear.

Besides, among us, the Hindus, a son adopted with the proper religious ceremonies is no different from a son of one's own—someone who ignites his father's funeral pyre so that he may reach heaven and who inherits his worldly possessions. Equally, he is the heir to his father's accumulation of sins. He cannot pick and choose, accept only the pluses and reject the minuses. The whole bundle devolves on him: the house and the fields and the cattle and the family gods, and also all that is dishonourable and ugly.

And yet I owe it to myself to put down that distinction, that I was not Bajirao's natural-born son but his adopted heir. Of the eleven women Bajirao married, only one bore a son, and he died in infancy. After that there were only daughters, and, among us, daughters don't qualify as successors.

After the British deposed Bajirao II as the Peshwa at Poona in 1818 and banished him to Bithoor, among the thousands of loyal adherents who had followed him into exile were my misguided parents.

My real father's name was Madhav Bhat, and my parents named me Dhondu, which means "a stone." It was not, as many people assert, an expression of their disgust at my ugliness and want of intelligence. I may not have possessed the Peshwa family's theatrical good looks, but I was certainly not ugly, nor was I lacking in ordinary intelligence. The reason for my inelegant, low-bred name was this: Three of my mother's children had died in infancy, and she and my father had become convinced that this was due to some curse they bore. To exorcise it, they had made a pilgrimage to the Amba temple at Hardwar, where, after undergoing the prescribed penances, they had made the prescribed vow that, in order that it should not be snatched away from them, they would name their next child after the most worthless object they could think of. In the event, the pilgrimage served them well, for thenceforward their offspring survived. After me, there were two sons, Baba and Balarao.

It was therefore in fulfilment of a vow that I was named Dhondu. In practice, of course, a respectful suffix was added to this unflattering name and I was always addressed as Dhondu Pant, or "Stone Esquire."

If anything, my parents had good reason to rejoice at my coming, for my horoscope predicted that I was destined to become a king:

> He shall be crowned a king and his name shall become known in distant lands.

It is this quite unequivocal prophecy that must have induced Bajirao to adopt me as his heir: in me he saw someone destined to win back what he had lost.

How ironically prophetic it all was, for I did become king, and I believe that my name is known to more people than that of any other man living.

At the time of my adoption, in 1827, I was three years old; Bajirao was fifty-two. He decreed that I was to be called Nana Saheb after one of his Peshwa ancestors. So, all my life, I have been known by two names: Dhondu Pant and Nana Saheb.

Thus I became the Peshwa's heir. If I had not been adopted, the burden I was destined to carry through life would certainly have been lighter, for my parents were humble and God-fearing and, I like to think, incapable of malevolence. Bajirao's load of sins was immense, as was his worldly wealth. Both were to come to me.

They say there were a hundred priests at my adoption, and there might well have been, for religion was one of Bajirao's two major obsessions, the other being sex. He gave to the priests with an insane recklessness. I have myself seen how once, when the quarterly instalment of his pension was brought over from Kanpur and he happened to be at prayers beside the Ganges, he had haughtily ordered that the money should be distributed among the priests who had gone with him.

"What has once been brought to Mother Ganges cannot be taken back," he had declared, and given away twenty-five thousand pounds.

So the hundred priests must have been there, chanting *slokas* and making a din like monsoon frogs; and in a place of honour just outside the sacrosanct square must have been the British Resident, for in those days Bithoor still had a "court" and that court a "Resident."

But none of the Maratha princes could have been present, for by that time Bajirao had been forbidden all contact with his erstwhile feudatories. In any case, not many would have come even if they had been free to do so, for the simple reason that they hated Bajirao even more than they hated the British. As the Peshwa, he had made a deplorable overlord, a man who delighted in humiliating them and seizing their estates on the flimsiest of pretexts and, what was worse, someone who imagined that their womenfolk too belonged to him. He would often hold the master of some prominent family for ransom and demand that he send his wife or sister or daughter to his palace to participate in his orgies. Those who refused were singled out for reprisals.

Bajirao had a fetish for observing beautiful women undress and titivate themselves. He had fitted out one of the smaller *aine-*

mahals, or mirror halls, as a dressing-room and stocked it with a selection of rich silk and goldwork saris and jars of attars and lotions and perfumed pastes. He would politely invite his women guests to go into this room and choose whatever garments they fancied and come out dressed in them, and he would watch them by the hour through holes in the mirrors. Some of his other abnormalities were, however, less privately conducted. He would egg on his cronies to take liberties with the ladies from the highest families in the land as though they were prostitutes brought over from a brothel. He would sometimes let loose a score of men and women of mixed ages in a room that was totally dark. And the story is told of how he got his own back on one of his prominent *sardars,* or noblemen, who had lured away a favourite singing girl. He invited this nobleman to one of these orgies in the dark. When, after a time, Bajirao suddenly ordered lights to be brought in, the young man discovered that he had been making love to his own mother.

The result of such goings on was that those on whose support his kingdom had rested, his powerful hereditary chieftains, were often up in arms against him, and it was mainly through his facile tongue and his charm and good looks, and his ability to play one against the other that he had been able to keep his position as the Peshwa as long as he did—for twenty-two years. Certainly he had no natural qualities of leadership, least of all valour. He invariably watched battles from a distance and, if the sound of gunfire approached too close, just as invariably ran away, which is why they had begun to call him "Running" Bajirao.

That was exactly what had happened. In the cold weather of 1802, he had run away. Apparently he had been trying to put down a rebellion by one of his principal feudatories, the Holcar, and had run away from the field and into the open arms of the British. The trap door that had been held so tantalizingly open for just such a contingency slid into place.

The British were profuse with offers of assistance. The fountainhead of Maratha power, the greatest in the land, had come seeking their aid. They kept him in comfort and showered him with gifts, and they sent him back to Poona with a formidable escort and restored him to the *guddi,* the seat of the Peshwas. From then on, a permanent British force would be maintained in Poona for the protection of the Peshwa from the wrath of his own commanders; six thousand infantry, complete with guns and officered by the British. For the expenses of this "escort," Bajirao ceded to the East India Company a large tract of land along the western seaboard which the British had coveted for nearly a hundred years.

So Bajirao was back in Poona, held secure on the guddi by his new friends, the merchants of the East India Company. He ruled as Peshwa for another sixteen years.

The question is often asked: Why did the British let him stay in power as long as they did? Those who know the British know the answer: they never lance a boil before it is ready to burst nor pluck a fruit till it is ready to fall. Having isolated the Peshwa from his feudatories, they concentrated on the feudatories with molelike industry. They took them on one at a time, and finished them off.

Inevitably, during these years of grace as a British dummy calf my father made more enemies than ever. His lust for money became insatiable. He began to auction off the revenues of his domain with the result that the franchise holders squeezed his subjects dry. He spent most of his waking hours in sexual orgies. No one could get a hearing except through his cronies, and these were from the dregs of humanity, ill-bred and unlettered: eunuchs, sharks, adventurers, jesters, pimps, priests, and mendicants.

By 1817 the boil was ready to burst, the mango ripe for plucking. John Company, having gobbled up the limbs of the Maratha confederacy, was ready to chop off its head: the Peshwa, a man bereft of supporters and despised by his own subjects.

They went about it in the classic pattern of conquerors, in the garb of liberators. Overnight they set themselves up as the champions of the Maratha king, Pratap, and let it be known that once they had ousted the Peshwa who had usurped the king's position, they would restore it to Pratap. Meanwhile, they directed their energy and talents to preparing a charge sheet against the Peshwa so as to justify their disavowal of him.

"Only poor, gullible Pratap was taken in," my father used to say. "No one else would have swallowed such undisguised bait."

I did not remind him that he was one of the first victims of John Company's blandishments.

"The silly fool actually believed that the British were going to set him up as the ruler of the whole of the Maratha confederacy."

But the British knew very well that poor Pratap had never been nor ever would be more than an easy mouthful, someone who could be finished off at leisure by the mere serving of a marching order, which, as it happens, is what they finally did, packing Pratap off to live out his days in exile. The Peshwa, on the other hand, was quite another matter, even when isolated from his supporters and softened up by years of unceasing work. There was no question of supplanting him without an all-out war.

So they declared war. The pretext was that Bajirao was sheltering a Maratha nobleman whom the British suspected of having murdered their most energetic agent. On November 5, on the day of Diwali, our festival of lights, the "escort" maintained for my father's protection and paid for by him, revealed its true purpose and attacked Bajirao's personal guard. True to his character, "Running" Bajirao watched the battle from a distant hill, and when the sound of gunfire came close he fled.

Five British columns set out after him in full cry, slavering at the thought of the "prize money" that lay at the end of the chase, while my father shuttled from fort to fort. Many rude ballads are sung about his speed in retreat and his ingenuity in dodging pursuit. The man who had inherited the most powerful union of rulers in India had become a butt of ridicule, but no one seemed to feel sorry for him.

"This is only his just reward for running to the hat men for help," they said with bitterness. "Let him do some more running."

For five months, he dodged his pursuers and then realized that the game was up. There was, of course, still a chance for him to redeem himself, to live up to the illustrious name of the grandfather whose name he bore and who was India's most talented military genius of all times. If, even now, he had made a desperate stand and died fighting, it might have shocked the country out of its degrading resignation to a trading company's enslavement. At least it would have shamed his still-powerful ex-lieutenants, the Scindia and the Holcar, into making some sort of a gesture on his behalf. God knows no one wanted the Company's rule and they would have come to the support of almost anyone who could have provided a focus for their patriotism and resentment.

Anyway, such a drastic solution could never have occurred to my father. Anxious, above all, to save his own skin and, of course, as much of his wealth as possible, what he did was to choose carefully his captor from among the five contenders: Sir John Malcolm, "Boy" Malcolm. To him he sent an emissary under a white flag.

Bajirao had chosen well. Malcolm was businesslike but not rapacious or even vindictive. Doveton or Adams might have finished him off; "Boy" Malcolm, his appetite craving for nothing more than a military triumph, was prepared to keep him on as a life-term prince and to let him retain his personal fortune. He made Bajirao renounce all claims to his heritage, however, for himself as well as for his successors, and to undertake that he would never return to his homeland. In return, Malcolm consented to let him live with his retinue in some place that the British would assign to him and to pay him a pension of a hundred thousand pounds every year. It was stipulated that Bajirao should not style himself as the Peshwa, but that there was no objection to his calling himself a Maharaja, and that the British, on their part, would address him as His Highness. A small territory was to be granted to him as his domain.

The Company's Governor-General, Lord Hastings, was thoroughly displeased with Malcolm for agreeing to even these terms; Hastings himself, I feel sure, would have liked nothing better than to hang my father like a common felon and declare his wealth to be prize money. The only reason why he ratified the treaty at all was his conviction that Bajirao, frail and ailing and known for his sexual excesses, would not live long. He was already past forty, and none of his ancestors had lived much beyond that age.

The British chose for him this place Bithoor, a small village on the right bank of the Ganges, where, so to speak, they could keep a close watch on him, for it was only twelve miles from Kanpur,* which then held their biggest military establishment. The territory assigned to Bajirao was exactly six square miles, and, what with his retainers, there were now fifteen thousand inhabitants in it. Once he had ruled fifty million.

* "Cawnpore" to the British. —M.M.

This was in 1818. I was born six years later.

Bajirao II seems to have accepted his fall with remarkable equanimity. In Bithoor, he got himself five new wives and, as often as not, spent his nights with the women picked up from the streets by his pimps. Thanks to the magnanimity of "Boy" Malcolm, he was still an immensely wealthy man, so that he continued to live as he had always done, like a Peshwa, and his elephants were sprayed with rose-water and given their special feed of almonds and sugar every day just as they were used to in Poona, and the horse cloths of his personal guard were still bordered with pearls. Incredible as it may seem, I have always believed that here my father was actually happier than he had ever been as the Peshwa. There were no responsibilities, no quarreling feudatories, no vast armies of mercenaries clamouring for wages; only limitless leisure to enjoy life and the money to buy anything he wanted—anything except freedom which he did not seem to miss.

Shame or repentance were alien to his nature. It was almost as though, having lost an empire, he felt liberated and light; free to give the fullest scope to his most perverted cravings. The Ganges, which was capable of washing away all sins so conveniently, flowed past his palace steps. He rarely missed his daily dip.

He led an empty life; empty yet not idle, for it was sickeningly filled with sex during the hours of darkness and with religion during the hours of daylight. Contrary to the Governor-General's fond hopes, he lived for another thirty-three years.

Bajirao died in 1851, aged seventy-six, when I was twenty-seven years old. The British made no secret of how relieved they felt. Contending that Malcolm's stupidity had already cost them dearly, they lost no time in declaring that the pension would not be continued to Bajirao's successor. And then they took back even the fragment of territory that they had given to Bajirao and discontinued the titles of His Highness and Maharaja, so that I, the successor of the last Peshwa, started life as an ordinary citizen of India—an India that had become the East India Companys' private property and pieces of which could be bought and sold on the London market.

If the British were glad to see Bajirao die, the Indians did not mourn his passing either. A new generation had grown and matured—mine, a generation that had known only British rule; we were like animals born in a zoo, never knowing what it was to be in the jungles, roaming, free. Bajirao II, the last of the Peshwas, had been forgotten long before he had died.

Chapter 2

As a child in the court of Bithoor, I had everything. I was never scolded or beaten. Servants hovered around and jumped to do my slightest bidding. And yet I don't believe I was a coddled and spoilt child. Bajirao, himself an erudite man, was anxious for me to learn Sanskrit so that I could read the scriptures in the original. He engaged a Benares priest as my tutor. Also, as though to make up for his own lack of soldierly qualities, he made me learn fencing and riding at an early age.

A *paga*, or riding school, was built by the river, complete with a ring and, to one side, a series of graduated jumps. Sundays, Tuesdays, and Thursdays were the riding-school days. I was awakened before sunrise, made to drink a cupful of bitter *chiraita* water that had been brewing all night in a copper goblet as a tonic, and sent off to the paga. On three other days I went to the roped-off fencing school at the back of the house, where I was put through the moves and countermoves of traditional Maratha swordsmanship, first with a satinwood stick and then with a blunted practice sword.

My fencing master, Tantya Bhat, was the sort of person around whom legends naturally grow. Indoors or outdoors, he never went about without a sword strapped to his waist. Tall, slim, handsome, elegantly—almost foppishly—dressed, he was respected by men and sought after by women, and yet he was a shy and simple man who took life far too seriously. It was said that he had once killed a tiger with a spear, strangled a robber with a silk handkerchief, and rescued a princess abducted by bandits; that he could bring down a running black buck with a single bullet and a running man with a single stone; that he could cut in two with his sword a feather fluttering in the air.

Tantya Bhat had joined the Company's cavalry for six months to see for himself what it was that made the British invincible in war, and had come back with the conviction that the British were not invincible. There was something else he brought back from his days with the Company's army: a pith helmet. He discarded the turban and began to wear the helmet, or *topi*, whenever he was on horseback. That was how he acquired the nickname that stuck to him for life: Tantya Topi.

Several of the children of Bajirao's retainers were encouraged to use the riding school and the fencing school and to go swimming with me in the river. One of them was a girl; only, in those days, none of us ever thought of her as a girl. She was Mani, Bajirao's goddaughter, whom he was bringing up to be my wife.

Even today, I only have to shut my eyes to conjure the fencing school at the back of the *wada*, as we used to call the palace; and I can see myself and Mani and the other children, all of us smaller and lither, lunging forward and side-stepping and whirling around to fend off an unexpected attack from behind, dummy swords banging into shields at the precise split second to make the sharp, unmistakable crack of cane against rhino hide. But, every so often, no one knew how, the movements would become desynchronized and one or the other would be caught on the wrong foot. And then, over the sharp sting of pain, there would be the sudden jab of anger, causing nostrils to distend and lips to flare and words of abuse to escape our lips . . . all this to be instantly quelled by a peremptory clang of the bell, freezing us into the positions we were in, like statues breathing hard. Tantya would order us to drop swords and to make deep reverent bows to our adversaries and smile.

Occasionally there would be a stentorian yell from the sky. "Stop! *Stop!*" Bajirao, leaning out of the balcony, swayed gently like an elderly elephant pestered by flies. We would turn to face him and touch our foreheads with our sword hilts and wait, knowing what he was going to say.

"This is only for self-defence, not for killing. Being brahmins, you may not take life. You can kill only in battle—an enemy. But, of course, there are no enemies any longer. Now carry on; smile and don't curse!"

Once again we would stiffly touch our foreheads with our swords and put on obedient smiles.

In the event, the only time I found it necessary to kill with a sword it was neither in self-defence nor in battle. My victim was a woman, elderly and fat as a pumpkin, and I never remembered my diligently practised swordplay and footwork and lashed blindly, producing some meat carver's stroke no one could have taught me, for I managed to cut her neatly in two halves, right across her bulging stomach.

But when I was at my schoolwork there were neither companions nor onlookers. I was alone with Pandit Umashankar, whom I called Guruji, both of us squatting on a reed mat placed under a framed painting of Saraswati, the goddess of learning. To begin with, Guruji and I did not share a language; I spoke only Marathi and he, even though he was a master of five languages, did not know Marathi. All the same, he promised Bajirao that he would, in time, make me a *pandit,* or a learned man. He haughtily dismissed arithmetic and algebra as subjects fit only for the children of tradesmen and concentrated on teaching me languages, Sanskrit, Persian, and Urdu, all through the medium of Hindi, which I was supposed to pick up as I went along. The method worked admirably, especially with Hindi, which I learnt well enough to pass myself off as a born Kanuji—who are brahmins who come from Kanaj and speak the purest Hindi.

Monday was set aside for prayers. I had to accompany Bajirao to the river. The priests in white dhotis were already assembled on the ghat steps. Bajirao, now dressed as simply as they, would squat in their midst, his hands folded, his eyes shut tight, his face luminous with reverence. I would sometimes wonder what he prayed for, for he never uttered a sound. Or had he, at last, come to the conclusion that he was beyond redemption, that prayer could never lighten his load of sins?

Over the years he had hardened and set into his new role, that of a kept prince, and, like a kept woman who is no longer desirable, all he craved for was the goodwill of his keepers. Apart from that, what was there to seek, for he had everything that other men pined for but never attained. He lived in splendour, in a kingdom that was guaranteed and protected by others; he was in good health and virile; he had money and the pick of women. In Bithoor Bajirao floated like a giant carp in a stone pool, as though no longer aware that there was a world beyond the Ganges; seemingly unrepentant, wholly contented with the maggoty hash he had made of his life.

Seemingly, because he was tormented all the same; tormented by a ghost.

How often did I hear his screams in the middle of the night?— weird animal howls emanating from the wing of the wada over-looking the river. And once, rushing into his room, I had seen him, haggard-faced and with staring eyes, pointing a trembling finger at the patch of moonlight on the fluttering lace curtains and whim-pering like a dreaming dog. There was a woman in his bed, a girl who could not have been more than seventeen, cowering and look-ing fixedly at where he was pointing. I was overcome by guilt as I looked at the girl and then realized that she was naked, her body ghostlike and almost transparent in the dimness. I fled in panic and shame, keeping a hand pressed against my mouth to prevent my-self from making a sound. I don't think either of them realized that I had been in the room.

And because of Bajirao's unceasing efforts to exorcise the ghost, many people had come to know about it. It had shown up soon after he had become the Peshwa. It was the ghost of the fifth Peshwa, Narayan, whom Bajirao's father and mother had caused to be murdered. Narayan, his bloodied hands clumsily stuffing back his spilling guts into his split-open stomach, would appear in Bajirao's dreams, and rant at him for having sold his kingdom and become a British *hujria,* or body servant. After a while, Bajirao had rushed off to Pandharpur and had set the priests there to rid him of the ghost, and the priests had succeeded in working their magic, for from then on, the murdered Peshwa had ceased to haunt him. In gratitude, Bajirao had ordered the building of a riv-erside embankment in Pandharpur, which bears his name. But in Bithoor the ghost had come back. Since the British had forbidden him to go back to his land, Bajirao had sought their permission to go on a pilgrimage to Benares, and there performed the penances prescribed by the priests and distributed alms. But the ghost remained. On his return, he planted trees, built temples and bathing ghats, gave extravagantly to orphans and widows, performed endless *poojas,* his private devotional services, underwent stringent fasts, and fell at the feet of ash-covered sandhus and soothsayers and astrologers. The ghost stayed with him for the rest of his life and, I am told, was with him at his deathbed.

"Your house will be ashes and your clan perish!" the ghost would rant. "Your palace will be burned down by your protectors, your line will end with your successor!"

"Why should it end?" Bajirao would scream. "Nana shall have numerous sons—sons of his body! I shall find wives for him—fecund girls from the highest families. I have already chosen the girl he will marry."

Then Bajirao would hear the prolonged laughter that was like a jackal's howl. "Marry!" the ghost would chortle. "He can marry more women even than you have. But if ever a marriage is consummated, the wife shall die—not a single woman can live to bear his child!"

This was where Bajirao would find himself awake, sweating and pleading for mercy.

I have never myself seen Narayan's ghost, and yet my entire life has been warped because of its curse. For it happened as the ghost said it would. The first two women I married did not long survive the marriage. The third—the third is still alive; alive, I am quite convinced, only because I have never been a husband to her, knowing that I would only be killing her.

But at the time I am speaking of, in 1841, the curse, so far as I was concerned, had still to prove itself. Bajirao, who implicitly believed in it even then, called in his most trusted priests for a consultation and, predictably, they came up with a pat solution to nullify the effect of the curse.

"There is a perfectly sound precedent to circumvent such prophesies," they told Bajirao, and then read out to him the story of Patali-putra. "He too bore a similar curse. So he was first married to a vine, the *patali,* and after that to the girl his parents had chosen for him. His children lived to found a great dynasty."

So that was their solution. "Get Nana Saheb married to a patali sapling; sacrifice the plant in place of the wife."

In the state he was in, Bajirao would have been prepared to try out anything. It does not seem to have occurred to him that the ban was not so much against marriage itself as upon marital relations, and that it was not restricted to just one wife but applied to as many as I married.

And so, a few days before my seventeenth birthday, I was duly married; married with the fullest Vedic ritual to a plant in a tub. At the time of the wedding, the patali was lush with clusters of leaves that were pink at the edges and sprouting pale-yellow buds at the joints. That same night the union was pronounced to have been consummated after a ritualistic sprinkling of my seminal fluid upon the bride. Every morning I inspected the plant, which was kept on a special pedestal in the main courtyard so that it should get the proper amount of sun and shade. I watered it every day and once every week I loosened the soil and put in handfuls of farmyard manure around the roots. For a month the vine flourished. The leaves became dark green and the yellow buds turned into orange flowers. Then one day the flowers withered and the leaves curled and the stem drooped. Nothing could revive it; neither the droppings of goats nor the round-the-clock prayers offered by the selfsame priests who had performed the marriage. It was exactly forty-nine days from the day of the wedding that the vine was finally pronounced dead. In the event, the vine turned out to have survived consummation longer than either of my wives.

The priests gleefully pronounced that their plan had succeeded. The plant had been accepted in sacrifice in place of the wife. But Bajirao himself thought otherwise; he stared long at the stump of the patali and shook with helplessness. That very evening, he abandoned his long-cherished plan of marrying me to Mani, the girl he had always spoken of as my wife-to-be. As a compensation to me, he himself selected a healthy young woman from one of the courtesan establishments of Lucknow and presented me with my first concubine, Champa.

So the girl I had always thought of as my future wife, Mani, suddenly went out of my life, and another whom I had never seen before, Champa, began to sleep in the room adjoining mine. Even though, to be quite honest, I have always believed that Champa was the best thing that could have happened to me at the time, the fact remains that I never forgave Bajirao for ruling that Mani was not to be my wife.

Mani was the daughter of Moropant Tambe, who, like my own natural father, had followed Bajirao to Bithoor. Had Mani been around when Bajirao adopted me and had she been a boy, I am sure he would have unhesitatingly chosen her as his heir. She was like someone in a fable, a symbol more than an actual person; harsh, unbending, audacious, and yet with a tenderness that was wholly feminine; cold and deliberate in spite of her fiery temper, and impishly impulsive too; a supple, athletic, hard-grained creature of the wind and the sun with the boldly sensuous configuration of a stone goddess, she was yet all woman who could make your heart turn to water with a mere look.

As children, we were always together, and even though I shall never admit that she was better than myself at riding or swordsmanship or swimming, I will concede that she brought to these activities such gusto and style that she invariably seemed better. Bajirao adored her and saw to it that she was brought up as a princess.

Was it any wonder that I grew up almost hating her, not knowing that this hatred might be a perverse manifestation of tender feelings? I was jealous of her, even though, to be sure, I was always careful not to show my jealousy openly. Only at unguarded moments did my suppressed dislike of her come to the surface, as for instance on that occasion when I was taking one of the elephants to the river.

The elephant, named Airawat, was being taken for his bath and I had persuaded his keeper to let me ride him unassisted. Airawat was a dignified, mature animal who could have been controlled by a small child, and he was ambling behind his keeper, not minding me sitting astride his neck, when I heard shouts from behind and the sound of running steps.

"Stop! Stop! I'm coming for a ride too!" It was Mani.

I don't know what made me say what I did. "Elephants are for princes to ride on," I yelled over my shoulder, "not retainers' children." I prodded the spot behind Airawat's ear for more speed, knowing that Mani would come running after us.

The silence behind me made me turn back and look. I think Mani was waiting for me to look back. She stood scowling, a compact, reed-thin figure like a polished black pole in the sand.

"You wait, *Prince* Nana! For every one of your elephants I shall keep ten—you wait!" Her voice was shrill with the suggestion of held-back tears. Before I could apologize, she had turned and fled.

I don't know how many elephants Mani did come to possess when she became the Rani of Jhansi, but she certainly had many more than I ever had.

But when I was seventeen, Mani was not yet the Rani of Jhansi, just a nimble and sturdy bundle of mischief and arrogance who seemed to delight in showing me up as someone who was slow and clumsy and a little ludicrous. My hands itched to slap her pert, grinning face. And yet, the moment Bajirao revealed that she was not to be my wife I experienced a sudden sense of loss as though something to which I had been grafted was being severed, leaving a raw wound that would remain with me all my life. I have never doubted that if Mani had become my wife, my life would have been altogether different—richer, rewarding, exciting. She might not have made me a quiet, properly subservient Hindu wife; but she and I would have made a matched, formidable team, cancelling out the pluses and minuses in our personalities and rounding them off.

That was one thing Bajirao should not have done to me; he should not have done it to Mani either. She whose life he sought to lengthen did not live long, but burned up quickly, like a roaring flame. The husband that Bajirao found for her was old and feeble, for all that he was a ruling prince and fabulously wealthy. Bajirao did not know that he also suffered from a queer perversity which made him masquerade as a woman and even pretend that he suffered from the pangs of menstruation. Mani, hobbled by the bonds of marriage to this obnoxious creature, made him a devoted and dutiful wife and—by what sexual artistry or magic it is difficult to say—even induced in him the spark of maleness necessary to have marital relations with her so that she bore him a son. This son died in infancy and the enfeebled father died soon afterwards, but not before adopting another's child as his successor. Again Mani fell into her new role with gusto, the role of the diligent foster mother and the protector and regent of her husband's principality. Then the Devil's Wind stirred and she reached out to embrace it and became the grandest rebel of us all.

"From now on you must regard her as your younger sister," Bajirao told me on the day of her betrothal.

I looked at my sister, now dressed in bridal red and wearing the bangles and necklaces of diamonds and pearls that Bajirao, as though to make amends, had given her as a wedding present. She looked very demure and slightly sanctified, as brides do. I longed to fold her in my arms and cover her with kisses, defy Bajirao and his absurd ghost and defy the world. For a moment our eyes met, and Mani smiled brightly and blushed and turned her head away. I never saw her again.

So Mani went out of my life. Left to me was a concubine, Champa, named after a delicately scented, velvety flower, for all that she was as much a creature of the earth as a rock lizard, with a skin the colour of ancient copper and the texture of grained silk. She was a mature, fully developed woman, with a body toughened by the demands of professional dancing and professional sex.

I yelled at her to get out of my room and never come again. She went without a word but came right back as soon as I was in bed. I hurled abuse at her as she stood patiently clutching the bedpost, which made me get up and slap her hard and shove her bodily out. The moment I had put out the light, she had crawled right back. Then, almost as though I was working off my rage, I ripped off her clothes and tore into her body, only to discover that she was reaching out to absorb my clumsy assaults. Her hot mouth sought mine in the dark and her fingers ranged all over my body to reawaken passion when all I wanted was to lie back and sleep. Legs coiling like snakes held me fast; nipples slippery as sucked betel nuts brushed tantalizingly against my skin. Resentful in the knowledge that I was being prepared as a victim for her lust and yet once again in the grip of desire, I was conscious of the sense of revulsion brought on by the smell of her skin that was like sour wine, by the mouth which had been so shockingly depraved in its search breaking out into a repetitive half-breath, half-word, English obscenity just seconds before the final shudders.

Within a matter of days, I realized that I could never match Champa's range of passion, and after that I surrendered and was content to be led; surrendered and was rewarded. With Champa I discovered sex as though I were the first man on earth and she the last woman. Soon I began to shiver with desire for the very things that had made my flesh shrink, the controlled pressure of her fingers, the heady, warm smells of her body, the feline purring breaking into its incantation of obscenity as though to mark the attainment of some goal, and the convulsive shudders as though something within her had burst.

How much longer did it take me to regard Champa not merely as a woman who had sold her life for a backward place in mine? There may not have been love in our relationship, but there was no deceit either. She was my very first mistress, and what that meant was perfectly understood by her. She worked at her role with zest and made of it a complete success. She was devoted but not demanding, tender but not mawkish; she never presumed or took for granted. She was there whenever I needed her and yet she never intruded in my life away from the bedchamber. And when I told her that Bajirao had found a wife for me, she was far more excited than I.

I needed something like Champa just then; and it was my good fortune that she was there.

Did I, without knowing it myself, want to punish my bride for not being Mani, or did I expect her to be another sexual athlete like Champa? How well I remember that first night: the bed smelling of roses because of the petals strewn over it, and somewhere in the distance the *sehnais* playing. The frightened, cowering girl in my bed stared at me as though I were a wild animal come to devour her.

She did not scream, she did not even resist. What I had lived out in trembling anticipation as an experience in sheer ecstasy turned out to be a trial of perseverance. This was no Champa, to whom sex came as naturally as to an animal of the jungles, but a terrified child, ignorant and unaroused. Her skin was cold and covered with goose pimples, and her shrinking away from me was an insult to my newly discovered manhood. I did not even know that something had ruptured until later that night when, as I lay exhausted but unfulfilled, I heard her sobbing into the pillow. I got up and lit the big Birmingham lamp. Where the rose petals had been were patches of dark blood. This I had anticipated and I tried to assuage her fears with a tenderness I did not feel. But the flow of blood did not cease for a long time. By the morning she had burning fever. Within two days she was dead.

For days I did not want to touch another woman. Then, gratefully, I went back to Champa.

Within a few weeks, Bajirao sent out emissaries to find another wife for me, and held out an offer of a lakh of rupees to the father of the bride.

"Maharaj should have waited," Champa said to me. "Given them time to forget."

"Forget what?"

"They know about the curse—that you have only to marry a girl to kill her."

So the curse was already widely known. It was therefore not surprising that, in the whole of the Gangetic plain which is the stamping ground of indigent brahmins, not a single one seemed to be willing to offer his daughter to the heir of the Peshwa and walk away with a hundred thousand rupees.

But not for long. The greed of brahmins is as proverbial as their poverty, and the smell of the hundred thousand, lying unclaimed and rotting, must have made their nostrils twitch till they hurt. Barely two months had passed before the emissaries returned, complete with a family carried in three separate palanquins: father, mother, and marriageable daughter—or, indeed, a daughter long past the marriageable age, for she was already seventeen and could never have found a husband because her father was so destitute. Bajirao approved and the marriage was quickly got over, and the parents stayed on only long enough to collect the reward and then disappeared without a trace as though anxious to shake off pursuit.

My bride's name was Girja. At the time of the marriage, the

priests decreed that she must perform a pilgrimage to Ujjain on the full moon of the month of Magh before I could have marital relations with her. I have a feeling that it was their device to spare Girja the fate of her predecessor. I on my part was more than willing to respect their prohibition; I was nineteen and my love life was so adjusted that the period of waiting was no special hardship.

For four months, Girja shared my bed. We talked and read books and played chess, and she sang and strummed the sitar for my entertainment. We got to know each other very well and, I think, to like each other too. And there is no reason why, given time, we should not have learned to love each other.

Girja, a grown-up girl and strong as an ox, must have begun to worry about my coldness. In the middle of the night I would wake up to find her clinging to me with desperate eagerness but pretending to be asleep. I would gently slide out of the clinch, myself pretending to be turning in my sleep.

Then came the month of Pousa, the one before Magh. The nights were warmer after the end of the rains. The moon waxed bigger and cleaner in the rain-washed skies. Girja would lie beside me sighing and drawing my attention to the fact that she would soon be going on her pilgrimage. On the very day before her departure, I told her about the curse. She stared hard at me and cuddled close and kissed me gently on the mouth and broke into girlish giggles.

"It's no laughing matter," I admonished.

"Oh, but it is! I thought only people who live in dark forests believe in such things; not those who live in palaces and are full of the wisdom of books." She gave a loud groan and then, very deliberately, blew out the light.

When you are nineteen, it takes so little to make you ashamed of your superstitions; and a young and voluptuous girl mocking at you, a bride aroused and demanding to be taken can topple the most ironclad of resolutions. And so it happened that night. And afterwards, as she lay fast asleep with her head pillowed on my shoulder, I saw that her cheeks were wet with tears. I nudged her awake and again we made love.

The next morning, Girja left on her pilgrimage. A dozen maids and an elderly niece of Bajirao went with her together with an escort of fifty soldiers. Of course there was no question of my accompanying her, since the British would never have let me travel to Ujjain, which lies in the domain of my father's erstwhile feudatory, the Scindia. From the tower of the wada I watched the procession till it became a line of ants and disappeared into the forest on the hill.

Who does not know the Magh-mela at Ujjain, when beggars and holy men from all parts of India gather there, the sick and the maimed in the hope of getting cured, the others to acquire merit? On the day of the full moon they plunge into the thin stream of the Sipra to wash away their dirt and diseases and sins. Girja performed her ablutions and set out on her return journey. On the third day nine people from her party took ill with cholera. They established camp in a wayside mango tope where, by the next morning, all nine were dead. But by then more had been affected. Among them was Girja. That was where she died, in a wayside hut among the mango trees. Only her ashes were brought back to Bithoor, where I immersed them in the Ganges.

Years later, Dr. Tessider, my physician, told me that it was certainly the consequence of drinking water from the Sipra River. It seems that many doctors are now convinced that cholera spreads through water. I had the consolation, if that was what it was, that my second wife had not died of injuries inflicted by me.

To forestall Bajirao's efforts to find brides for me, I told him that I did not want to marry again.

"No?" He arched his eyebrows in mock surprise. "For how long?"

"Never."

He clucked his tongue. "What about the succession?"

I did not tell him that there was nothing worth succeeding to, that the heritage of the Peshwa had been already lost by him. "I could adopt a son," I said.

He shook his head very slowly. "I have a feeling they will make difficulties." "They" in such conversations always referred to the British—the East India Company.

"But they allowed you to make an adoption."

"I don't know. They let me adopt a son; not a successor."

That was the first time the full realization came to me that, in signing away his vast possessions, Bajirao had not even stood firm for a hereditary princedom such as was conceded to even the lowest ranking among his feudatories.

"Of course they have promised that, at the appropriate season, the question will be reconsidered," Bajirao explained. " 'At the appropriate season,' in their language, means when I am dead."

"All the more reason not to worry about the succession, then."

"They've not said no definitely; it all depends on their goodwill."

Goodwill. How we pushed and pulled that word around in those days, like vultures tugging at a dead calf. We lived with it and went to sleep with it, holding it caged tenderly in our thoughts. It was the one abiding aim of my early days and of Bajirao's last days. We cringed and smirked and suffered agonies for it; we intrigued, cowered before their meanest functionaries, pandered, entertained, bribed, and were mercilessly exploited.

"Anyway, why create an extra complication?" Bajirao asked. "If you have a natural son, your case will be so much stronger."

So "they" had kept the whole thing dangling, and it all depended on my putting up a "case"; meanwhile, we had to build up goodwill. It cost us a lot of money, this process of manufacturing goodwill: Persian carpets, diamond rings, cases of brandy, English carriages and saddlery, and the gifts of "Oriental" swords, which meant swords with jewel-encrusted hilts.

"But I cannot marry again."

"Why ever not?"

"Because they die."

"One of them might give you a son before she dies." To Bajirao, it must have seemed nonsensical to be worrying about what happened to a wife after she had delivered a successor. But I had the most effective answer to block that line of thought.

"I can't bear the thought of touching a woman—my limbs turn to molasses."

"Oh, that's bad! I'm sure it will pass off."

"When it does, that would be the time to think of marrying."

He broke into a smile. "I don't agree. You should have someone in store—a virgin, ready and waiting for you to recover."

"The way things are, she'll remain a virgin all her life."

"You mean you've become impotent?"

"That's what I have been trying to tell you."

"Ungh!" he snorted and asked, "What about Champa?"

"Champa is a mistress, not a wife. If I were to marry her, I'm sure I should never have anything to do with her. I would always feel it would be like making love to a dead woman—or at least a woman on her deathbed."

He kept shaking his head. The argument must have seemed so perverted to him. He, Bajirao, would never have let it influence his mind. If anything, he would have slept with a woman on her deathbed just to find out whether such a macabre act of copulation held a special thrill. He narrowed his eyes and said, "Well, perhaps you should wait a while—give yourself time to get over this. But I should have thought the most reliable remedy for your state would be a new woman. Get a new mistress. The Chinese ones are the best equipped for . . . for arousing jaded appetites. There are quite a few of them in Calcutta."

"Oh, no, I'm quite happy with Champa."

"Then why are you in this state?" he asked sharply. "She should know what to do. Get rid of her; get someone younger. How old is she?"

I made no answer, knowing that this was Bajirao's way of taunting me for being attached to the same woman for so many years. He himself acquired a new one every few months and indeed always had one or two held in reserve. For the moment, it was enough that I had given him a shock; the skin on his cheekbones had tightened and gone pale and the corners of his lips twitched.

"And don't, for heaven's sake, mention your . . . er, disability again," he admonished. "That sort of detail is vital to them, and they have informers everywhere."

"Not here, surely."

"Here too. What do you suppose Todd is?"

"Toad Saheb! You mean, while he teaches me English he also snoops? But he's your servant, not theirs."

"I pay him; all the same, he's their servant. That class knows only one loyalty: race. And you must never call him Toad Saheb —never!"

Todd, at this time my English tutor for six years, was a first-generation Eurasian who suffered inwardly because he was not pure white. With his mottled, yellow-grey skin, luxuriant black hair curled in tight ringlets, a thin, accountant's mouth under a bulbous nose that, because of his fondness for red wine, looked as though it had been fried in deep fat, he was a plump, pompous man who dressed with fussiness and treated the house servants as a form of untouchables. They, on their part, retaliated by calling him Toad Saheb.

I must explain that, for them, it was easier to say "toad" than "todd" because in our alphabet the vowel o has only one sound, as in "rope" or "soul," and, when they discovered how much Todd resented being called Toad, they gave up trying to pronounce the name correctly. To get over this particular difficulty, Bajirao had ordered all of us never to call Todd by his name but by his calling, Guru Saheb, which means "the honoured teacher." But Todd on his part had never given up looking for insults: it was bad enough having to make a living by working for a "native," but he was not going to stand for that native's menials making fun of his name.

And here was a new facet of this prickly man: an informer of the Honourable Company. No wonder Bajirao pampered him outrageously.

"Also that sewer-rat Nanak Chand. He too is a spy." And Bajirao snorted.

The name called for snorts; it was later to become the most despised in Kanpur, almost a byword for treachery. But even in the days I am writing of, my breath quickened and saliva spurted in my mouth at the mere mention of it, for Nanak Chand was one of the most repulsive of God's creatures; more like a foetus overgrown than a man, with an enormous, round face supporting the only visible sign of maleness, a wispy moustache of which he was immensely proud, soft, spongy hands and an oily yellow skin like that of a rotted melon. He was employed in the firm of Bathgate and Potter in Kanpur and he often came to Bithoor trying to sell us English saddles and cases of Madeira or claret on behalf of his principals. He had a habit of straying off into corridors and I had several times seen him gossiping among the servants and sharing their hookas. Was he pumping them for information? Finding out how many mistresses Bajirao had and how few I had? What else was there to report?

"Nanak Chand?" I said almost to myself.

"Him we know. There must be several others. You must always be on your guard."

I made my bow and left Bajirao's presence, not even thinking of Todd or Nanak Chand. They were both his problems. As for me, I had gained a respite, perhaps a year at the most, but even that was something. After that, I would have to get married again. Bajirao, tormented by the thought that the Peshwa's line would be extinct, would go on finding brides for me. Anyway, I had thought of a remedy for that too.

In 1846, when I was twenty-two years old, Champa gave birth to a girl.

"The holy Ganga's blessings!" Bajirao declared. "We shall call her Gangamala, the Garland of the Ganges."

Even though my daughter was concubine-born, Bajirao ordered an elaborate public celebration for her naming ceremony, complete with a fireworks display by the riverside, followed by a *nautch* party for his special guests. He invited all the Kanpur officials and their wives and gave away gold snuffboxes to the men and attar cases to the ladies, each one inscribed with the words:

A memento of the naming ceremony of
Gangamala
Daughter of Dhondu Pant Nana Saheb
28th October, 1846

The gold boxes were more than just goodwill builders; through them, Bajirao was making it known that I could father a child, in case what I had told him had been carried to the British by someone like Todd or Nanak Chand. The celebrations, the gifts would be talked about, and in due course a line added to the record piling up in some building in Calcutta—and it was important that the line should be favourable.

Chapter 3

I myself had no hand in selecting the wet nurse for my child, and neither had Champa. Bajirao sent men round to Lucknow and Kanpur to look for one, and from among the five or six lactating mothers who were rounded up, his senior wife had chosen Azijan. It seems that the man who had fathered her child had never been seen after the act of fathering. Azijan had dumped the baby at a temple door and she swore that she didn't even know whether it was a boy or a girl.

The court physicians pronounced her milk to be sweet and nourishing and plentiful, whereupon she was sent to live in the small bungalow behind the stables to which Champa had shifted for her confinement. Even though I had visited Champa several times since the birth of my daughter and must have seen the wet nurse before, I had not noticed her till that day in December, nearly two months after the naming ceremony.

Champa had dozed off. I lay beside her, idly looking out of the window that opened out onto a side veranda, when I saw Azijan; but of course I did not know her name then. It was weeks before I found out.

I saw a young woman in the first blush of motherhood, a baby at her breast, a rapt expression on her face as though the act of suckling caused her both pleasure and pain. She did not know I was watching and, after a time, shifted the baby's hungry mouth to the other breast. In the sunlight, her bared shoulders shone like oiled teak. She was bending slightly forward, perhaps to facilitate the flow of milk, and her lips were parted; and her breasts which were the same colour as her shoulders, not lighter as in most women, were set well apart and had the classical mango shape so that the reddened nipples pointed outwards.

I don't know how long I was looking before I became aware that Champa had raised her head to see what I was looking at. She leaned against my shoulder and said in a sleepy, contented voice, "Isn't she beautiful!"

"Not half as beautiful as you."

"No, but don't you think she's the loveliest thing you ever saw?"

I shrugged and quoted a proverb. "At seventeen, even a she-ass looks ravishing."

The tremor that passed through the body pressed into mine, the sharp, snakelike hiss that escaped Champa's lips, made me realize my mistake. She was admiring our daughter.

"*Ohé,* you cast-off dung basket!" she screamed at Azijan. "Are you too dumb to see the child's gone to sleep? Go and put her in the crib—at once! *Jao!*"

After that, even though I went to Champa's bungalow every afternoon, Azijan did not appear in the veranda. One day, about a week later, when Champa was resting, I slipped into the adjoining room where the baby's crib was kept and demanded a glass of water.

It was brought by Azijan, in a copper goblet so full that, as I took it from her, some of the water spilled over. She stood very close to me as I drank, close enough for me to feel her breath against my chest and to smell her sun-warmed young body. I drank about half the water and handed her the goblet and our fingers touched. And the smile on her face was so impudent and the look in her eyes so provocative that I drew back my hand and threw the water over her face and body. I watched her turn and go away, pouting and smiling, walking with that peculiar animal grace that only those who are habituated to carrying heavy loads on their heads seem to master.

Champa was lying on her stomach. There was a fold under her navel and her buttocks stuck out. In my own mind, I could not help comparing her figure, limb for limb, with Azijan's. I was still peering at her closely when I found that she was looking at me through puffy, half-awakened eyes.

"When are you coming to live in the wada?" I asked.

"Soon."

"It has been so long—months."

"It takes ages to . . . to become normal after childbirth. Everything seems to suffer damage, inside and out."

"You look more seductive than ever," I assured her.

Champa stretched her limbs and yawned. Then she called for a glass of water. It was brought by Azijan, whose sari was still wet from the water I had splashed over her. As Champa drank, she stood by her bed, looking demure, her eyes downcast.

Suddenly Champa scowled and flung away the cup. She caught Azijan by her hair and held her close. She sniffed hard and thrust her head between her breasts and under her arm, making snorting sounds. Then she picked up her slipper from the floor and hit Azijan on the face with it, hard.

"Pubic louse!" she screeched. "How dare you suckle my child on those filthy tits smelling of somebody's tobacco? I'll have you flogged if you don't wash your stinking body every day! Every day, you hear? Before the sun is up! Pig's spawn—go and have a bath at once—all over wash—and come and show me how clean you have made yourself." Again the slipper was raised and slammed hard into the upturned face, again and yet once more.

Most women look beautiful when they are angry; only hatred makes them look ugly. And I could not bear to look at Champa's face; so contorted it was with hatred. She was hating herself and trying to lash out at something that had happened to her—the widening of the hips, the fold under the chin, the pimply dark circles around the nipples and the mottling of the flesh over the thighs. The triumph was Azijan's; she stood straight as a soldier, not defiant but somehow contemptuous, intuitively aware that she was making her mistress suffer by being just what she was and what Champa would never again be. She did not utter a sound or even flinch against the blows, but the pitiless, scornful eyes were causing far more hurt than the limp, velvet slipper.

When I went to see Champa two days later, there was a new wet nurse sitting in the veranda, and she too was suckling my daughter. I kept my eyes averted.

Champa was dressed in a bright-red sari and wore flowers in her hair, and her whole body was reeking of some smothering perfume as though she had had a bath in pure attar. She told me I must not come to the bungalow again.

"Why not?"

"Because I am coming back to the wada."

"Oh, good. When?"

"On the new-moon day."

"But that's nearly a month from now."

"You have to be patient."

"I've been patient for far too long—months of celibacy."

"Poor you."

"Why does it have to wait for the new moon?"

"It is the auspicious day."

"How can a moonless day be auspicious?"

"Well, then, it's a secret."

"Good or bad?"

She pouted, bringing furrows on both sides of her nostrils, and shook her head and smiled, as much as to say that it was both good and bad.

"Tell me, anyway."

"All right. Here!" And she held her wrist close to my nose.

"Oh, that smell; it's far too strong."

"It's called youth paste, see?" From under the bed she pulled out a brass container and opened its lid. It was full of a dark, tarry substance speckled with bright flecks. "Powdered pearls and peacock's fat and secret herbs. A *hakeem* brought it all the way from Damascus."

"That's a long way to bring anything from."

"It's made for Queen Zeenat; a regular massage for a month makes your body youthful."

"Has it worked on the Queen?"

But Champa wasn't listening. She went on in a dreamy voice, "When I was seventeen, my body was like a whip, hard and supple. At the dancing school I was the one chosen to lead—always, and men paid double to see me, gambled and fought for my favours. They said my figure was like Apsara—heavenly."

It was sad to see that she had taken my flirtation with the wet nurse so much to heart, but she was so earnest about the whole thing that I could not even make a joke of it. I agreed not to come to the bungalow and not to see her till she came back to the wada.

Then she brought up the other conditions. I was not to have a lamp in the room but to wait for her in total darkness. She would slide into my bed at midnight. She would not say a word to me all night, and I was not to light a lamp.

"But that means I can't even see you," I protested.

"There'll be plenty of time, afterwards."

"There's no other prohibition, is there—only that you won't utter a word and that I must not light a lamp?"

"None."

"That's a mercy; otherwise there'd hardly be any point in having you in bed—after all these months."

She pouted again. "Don't be vulgar," she admonished. For someone brought up in what she called a dancing school, which was only another name for a high-class brothel, Champa was, in many ways, a real prude.

I lay naked in the dark, trembling despite the wine I had drunk as a precaution against overeagerness. As the clocks in the hall of mirrors were striking the hour, she came and lay down beside me. And it was just as she had said: the miracle had happened. She was what she said she had been at seventeen, like a whip. The suppleness of her limbs, the texture of her skin, the responses of her body, even the sounds of gasps and moans were different, as was the rhythm of the final ecstatic shudders. The nose-filling smell of the youth paste was the only thing recognizable; that and the one English word repeated like a stutter that I had learnt to accept as a sort of punctuation mark, signifying culmination.

I paid her extravagant compliments; told her that she had never been like this even on that night when she had first come to me, six years earlier. I told her that she was like a tigress hungry for love and indulged myself to the utmost in the obscenities of love talk. When I begged her to let me light a candle so that I could gloat over her restored figure, she silenced my protests with a kiss that left me exhausted. Smothered in the soft, velvet night, we made love as though two animals of the jungle, male and female, had come together by a process of natural selection and were discovering each other. I dropped off to sleep like a tired child, pillowing my head against her fragrant shoulder.

I slept late, and awakened with an awareness of happiness. Sleepily I reached out for Champa and then, even before my eyes opened, I must have recoiled or registered disenchantment in some other way. And as I stared at her, she could not have failed to notice the shocked expression on my face, nor to hear the cry I could not prevent from escaping.

For Champa was exactly as I remembered her: a matronly, comfortably stout, square, pleasant-faced woman in her midthirties; not the slim young woman whom I had compared to a tigress, a tigress who could yet constrict her body like a snake and whose tongue was like the tip of a bullwhip.

"So it wasn't you!" I stammered, and my voice came out like a croak.

She grimaced and shook her head.

"Who, then?"

"You will see."

"When?" And I knew by the way her smile changed that I had hurt her by my eagerness.

"She'll be with you every day from now—your new concubine," she said. "Don't be impatient."

I tried to make amends. "I'm not impatient. And I don't want another concubine. I want you."

"Me? I'm thirty-two, and that's hiding three years. You are twenty-two."

"I don't care."

"Who ever heard of a mistress thirty-five years old?"

"I love you."

"I love you too; that's why I found you someone—someone nearer to your own age, who'll give you all you want."

"You've always given me whatever I wanted."

"Don't tell lies so early in the morning."

"It's the truth."

"That's not what you were saying last night."

I blinked and the backs of my hands began to sweat. "You mean you were here—in the room?"

"Here—in the room," Champa answered as though she was deriving some pleasure from my embarrassment. "I didn't trust your hungry tigress not to let you light a lamp so that you could gloat over her odd-shaped tits."

"It was a cruel joke."

"Darling, it wasn't a joke. I wanted you to have just what you were pining for, so that I could retire. I wanted to make things easy for you."

"But you are not going?"

"I am."

"Where?"

"Oh, not far—back to the bungalow. I'm a mother now," she said with a touch of pride, "not just a concubine."

"I'll come and see you every day."

"I know you will. What father can resist the call 'Baba'?"

"Is that what I am going to be called?"

"Unless you'd rather have her call you 'Appa' or 'Dada.' "

"No. 'Baba' is fine. How soon do you think she'll be able to say it?"

Champa did not answer, and she was smiling smugly again. She got up and went in. When she came back, she was holding Azijan by the elbow.

It was not fair, this seeing them together, one on each side of the bedpost.

"Do *mujra* to your master," Champa ordered.

Azijan bowed stiffly and touched her forehead with her fingers, three times.

"What's her name?" I asked Champa.

It was Azijan who answered. "The slave is called Azijan."

"Where does she come from?"

Again it was Azijan who spoke. "The place of the slave's despicable origin is Fattepur."

"Why does she speak like that?" I asked Champa.

"Elegant talk," she explained. "I taught her to say things a properly brought up mistress should."

I remembered that in the early days Champa too had been punctilious about daytime courtesies. "She's made a good pupil," I commented, remembering that she had even been let into the secret of our most intimate signals.

"A whole month I've been doing little else. Taught her to scrub her body and had my maids rub pearl paste into her to get her clean and soft. She was wild and vulgar and she stinks like dog shit and she is used to being felled only by grooms and sweepers. I don't know how she hasn't caught some disease, but she hasn't. I have had her examined. I have made her fit to be a king's bedmate."

"Thank you," I said.

"But she won't last," Champa pronounced viciously. "She eats all day as though she has never seen food before. She'll grow fat and pendulous and you'll throw her out and she'll have to learn groom talk all over again—for no one else is going to look at a drag-bellied sow."

And with that final, feline baring of claws, Champa was gone. I was alone with my new mistress. Eagerly I pulled her into bed.

Does a curse carry its own compensations? For, fated to be unlucky with the women I married, I have been singularly fortunate in my mistresses. Azijan ate sweets all day and yet retained her slender, supple figure, and soon she became as devoted to me as Champa herself, which, as will be seen, is a high compliment. Admittedly, she was not very faithful—she could not be—but her lapses were so infrequent and discreet that it was easy to connive at them.

And this may be the proper place to bow my head in gratitude and fold my hands to the gods for their gift of Champa. I have read of retired mistresses of Chinese noblemen becoming absorbed into their families as indispensable and honoured members. In India, Champa was that rare phenomenon. She was indeed indispensable, and no one could have held a place of greater respect in my tightly circumscribed world. Not my wife, she yet was the partner of my joys and sorrows, a nurse during my illnesses, a jester during my ill humours; she ordered the meals and supervised the washing of the windows and the swabbing of the floors and saw to it that my guests were well looked after. No longer my mistress, she remained the mistress of my household, the woman who held the keys of the safes and storehouses and worried about wastage. My brothers addressed her as *Tai,* or elder sister, and brought their problems to her, and neither Tantya nor my secretary, Azim, ever sat down in her presence or could bring himself to tell the latest campfire joke.

Even though, to me, her special attraction lay in her womanly ways—the little coy, disarming gestures of the hands and the subtle play of the eyebrows, the twisting of the nose and the pouting of the mouth and the fluttering of the eyelids which are so essentially Indian—she betrayed none of the weaknesses inherent in femininity, such as tears and tantrums and sulks. It was almost as though, having withdrawn from a life that was dominated by sex, she had rejected femininity itself, or at least shucked off its special armour plating and the weapons of offence; or as though she had changed her sex and inwardly become a man, someone equipped with greater powers of understanding and forebearance and an altogether tougher mental fibre. In China there would have been a special corner in the household shrine for someone like Champa. The most I can do is to acknowledge my debt.

Meanwhile, as soon as Bajirao had discovered that Champa was pregnant, he had sent agents to find another bride for me. Pretended impotency no longer served me as an excuse to remain unwedded. But by this time everyone in northern India must have heard about the curse. The agents went farther and farther south. Months passed and then a year. At last a camel rider came with news. A bride had been found in the Deccan, in a small village called Sangli, which must be at least a thousand miles from Bithoor.

This unfortunate girl was brought all the way from her homeland to be married. Her name was Kashi and she was, they said, only ten years old. I first saw her during the marriage ceremony, as the curtain held between us was lowered and the priests were chanting, "Beware, the golden moment arrives," which is the last verse in our wedding service. A sickly, black-haired creature with large, petrified eyes and skin mottled as though feathers had been plucked from it, stared back at me. She reminded me of a crow brought to a snake house for a python's meal. I quickly shut my eyes and concentrated my thoughts on Azijan, who must be, I knew, already in my bed, waiting.

"Kashi shall be brought up as a queen," Bajirao decreed, and proceeded to engage tutors and companions for her proper upbringing.

Kashi and I never slept in the same bed. She lived in a distant wing of the wada, which I seldom visited, so I saw her but occasionally. All the same, during ceremonies and festivals, we had to sit side by side as man and wife and offer prayers together, for, in families such as mine, conventions are inviolable. A wife is a wife, a husband a husband, and the two are tied together in one bundle that only death could untie. It was almost a master-and-slave relationship. God knows I did little enough to live up to my obligations as the master; all the same, Kashi made a perfect slave, industrious, diligent, and, above all, loyal. Her unswerving loyalty makes me squirm with guilt—unless that was her way of punishing me, some intuitive, feminine form of revenge.

Chapter 4

I was in the billiard-room, practising rebound cannons when, above the chiming of the clocks in the hall of mirrors, I heard a thin wail rising from the *zenana,* the women's wing, and knew that Bajirao had died. He had been ill for hardly a week. The priests, who were waiting by his bedside, began their chant. *Wasansi jeernani yatha vihaya . . . ,* "As we cast off worn-out garments, so does the immortal soul." He was seventy-six years old, this man whose soul had shucked off its abused shell.

The red ball stopped rolling and came to a halt close to the opposite edge, almost in the exact centre; the white was about a foot from the right-hand centre pocket. It was a challenging shot and I walked all round the table before deciding how I would bring it off. I was chalking the cue when I heard the commotion from the riverside. My manservant, Laghu, rushed in, babbling that Tantya Topi had thrown himself into the river and had drowned. I ran to the ghat and found that half a dozen boatmen had jumped in after him in an attempt to save his life but he kept fighting them off. I threw my billiard cue at them and dived in. "Hit him hard!" I yelled. "Never mind if you break his skull."

Others threw more sticks from the embankment to the swimmers. They got close to him and struck him till he ceased to struggle. Then they fished him out, limp and blood-soaked.

When he regained consciousness, they brought him to me. The blood had caked on his temples and cheeks and his eyes stared unseeingly as in an opium daze. His shoulders heaved with the effort of breathing. "You don't understand!" he groaned between convulsions. "The master is gone—it is futile to go on living."

What did I not understand that he, Tantya, did? He was not even a distant relative, merely a retainer. His grief, when I felt none, made me livid with anger. "Listen to those women bawling!" I yelled. "Not a tear among the lot. You're even worse—you're a disgrace to your maleness! Shave your moustaches and put on bangles!" Then I ordered the doctor to give him opium. Tantya did not wake up for a night and a day.

I felt no grief; all the same I went through the full ritual of mourning. I shaved my head and moustaches and considered myself in a state of defilement for thirteen days. I fed relays of brahmins and ordered unceasing prayers for the pacification of Bajirao's soul. I even announced that I would make a *mahadana,* the grand almsgiving that is customary after a king's death in which his successor must give away five elephants, five horses, five pearls, five *seers,* or about ten pounds, of gold, and five *kroshi,* or about ten acres, of land. I did not want to deny this star-crossed man, in death, the afterglow of royalty that still clung to his name.

Only on the day of the ceremony did I discover that, while I had the means of giving away the first four gifts, I could not give away the land because I myself did not possess any. I was bluntly told by the Commissioner that even the land on which the wada stood and the grounds surrounding it were mine only for life, that they all belonged to the Company.

Raghunath Vinchurkar, the present head of the Vinchurkar family who once were one of the lesser feudatories of the Peshwa, happened to be in Bithoor at the time and, on hearing of my predicament, came to see me and suggested that I should gift the land from his holdings in the south.

"There should not be the slightest imperfection in the ritual of the mahadana," he told me.

"But I have to give away only what is mine," I pointed out.

"Your forefathers gave us whatever we have; it is still yours."

As it happened, it was not even true. The bulk of the territory held by the Vinchurkars had been appropriated by the Company. Their present, relatively modest holdings were a British gift—or, more correctly, Lord Elphinstone's gift; Elphinstone who had urged on his superiors the view that the family's unswerving loyalty to the Peshwa was no reason to penalize it. It was characteristic of Elphinstone, who, driven by his own unquestioning loyalty to his masters, had been largely instrumental in seizing the Peshwa's kingdom, to have recognized its force among his erstwhile enemies. So, grudgingly, the Company had given back to the family a small part of what it had confiscated, and out of this denuded holding the head of the family was now offering me ten acres to enable me to perform the last rites of the last Peshwa in proper style.

I looked at the man—a ghost from the past come to attend a funeral. He was dressed in conventional mourning white, head and moustache shaved as after the death of a parent, the thin face aglow with eagerness, hands folded as though he were begging instead of offering. Here was a man whom Bajirao had impoverished more than enriched, humiliated more than honoured, coming forward to perform yet another service for him. It was a despicable demonstration of self-abasement; and yet it brought me to the verge of tears. I, who had little knowledge of what Bajirao had scuttled when he had run to the British merchants for protection, suddenly saw a glimpse of that other India, which, for all its turmoil and misery, had yet been a richer, nobler land. And before me stood a citizen of that lost world, his face red with anger because he had been done out of making yet another sacrifice for his worthless master.

I did not accept his offer. Instead of land, I gave away money to the brahmins, which they avidly accepted. But Vinchurkar's gesture and Tantya's misery cut through my indifference and left a mark. In later life I have often wondered if the seed of resentment I carried was not the outcome of a sense of guilt for not feeling sufficiently poignantly about the heritage of the Peshwas.

For me the next few years were marked by a foredoomed and quite undignified wrangle with the officials of the East India Company over my pension and privileges, to say nothing of the petty squabbles with some of the members of my family. Bajirao was survived by several of his wives, and each had numerous hangers-on. Clever British lawyers soon got at them and provoked them to demand a share of Bajirao's wealth, even though they knew that the terms of Bajirao's will were quite unambiguous. The lawyers made a lot of money but they did not win a single case.

The first few sentences of Bajirao's will make his intentions clear:

> This is written for the purpose of making known to Her Majesty the Queen of England, the Honourable East India Company and to all men: That after me, Dhondu Pant Nana Saheb, my eldest son . . . shall inherit and be the sole master of the guddi of the Peshwa, the dominions, the wealth, Deshmukhi, family possessions, treasure, and all my personal property. And he, Dhondu Pant Nana Saheb, shall inherit the rank of the Peshwa.

It made sad reading, for he had only wealth to bequeath and nothing else. The rank of the Peshwa which he sought to bestow on me was not his to give: the British had not allowed it even to him; and the original guddi, the seat of the Peshwas, had been broken and burned by Elphinstone when he planted the British flag on his palace in Poona. *Deshmukhi*, the right to collect tribute from his vassals, no longer existed for the simple reason that there were no longer any vassals. And as to his "dominion," even in his day it had been whittled down to a sort of landlord status over a microscopic holding: the six square miles around Bithoor that had been allotted to him by his masters.

At the time, I did not know what I later discovered: the British, as early as 1841, ten years before Bajirao's death, had decided to give me nothing. The facile assurance that the question would be considered at the "appropriate season" into which Bajirao had read so much was merely a device to stop him from making a nuisance of himself. By then they had discovered that Bajirao had managed to bring with himself a large part of the Peshwa wealth. What did his son need a pension for?

Perhaps it was a question of viewpoints, occidental against oriental, realistic against emotional. To be honest, the pension was not an important consideration; the extra eight hundred thousand rupees, or eight lakhs, would not have made much difference to my way of living, as it had not made to Bajirao's. What my two principal advisers, Tantya and Azim, wanted me to strive for was the

title of Maharaja and all that it entailed, including the right to rule
Bithoor. And since the pension and the title were believed by us to
be inseparable, we thought we should ask for the lot. I later
learned that if I had restricted my claim only to what we considered important, the British might have conceded it: outlandish titles meant nothing to them; it was the money they jibbed at.

"How can the Company-*bahadur* say no, Malik?" Azim argued.
"They are men of honour who keep their word and call themselves
the 'Honourable' Company. They've even kept the Mogul Emperor
on pension. He gave them nothing, because he had nothing to give.
Your father signed away half of India to them. All my British
friends assure me that it is only your due."

That was precisely the impression I had gathered from all *my*
British friends.

"The yellow-faced ones just have no option, Malik," Tantya
Topi assured me. "They're thieves, but they are businessmen first
—too clever to go against public sentiment."

From opposite viewpoints, both had arrived at the same conclusion. Azim, plausible, persuasive, clever, tactful, was an admirer
of the British. He aped English ways and often dressed in their
clothes; he had even mastered their revolving dances, which
he sometimes performed for our amusement. Tantya, guileless,
haughty, outspoken, a brahmin by outlook and a soldier by pro-
fession, despised and distrusted the servants of the Company. One
I had appointed my *Dewan,* or minister, knowing that I would have
to live all my life in amity with our overlords. The other I had made
the manager of my estate, because I trusted him and respected
him. Both, for reasons of their own, had come up with the same
advice.

It had not even occurred to us that the British might make
difficulties. They had permitted six hundred lesser rulers to retain
their territories and titles; I, who was the heir to the biggest of
them, demanded less than what most of the others had. Besides,
my personal friendship with the Company's officials was a matter
of record; I got on better with them than almost anyone else
among the princes. We had taken it for granted that the Company's Governor-General would, without even a formal request from

me, continue in my case what had been conceded to Bajirao. Lord
Hardinge, whom we distrusted, had gone, and in his place they had
sent Lord Dalhousie, from whom we expected justice if not the
sort of magnanimity such as Elphinstone and Malcolm were capable of. I wrote a polite letter to Dalhousie announcing that, since
Bajirao had styled himself as "His Highness Maharaja Bajirao," I
had ordered my own seals to be cast with a similar inscription.

Dalhousie's reply was prompt and curt: "The Governor-General
in Council recognizes no such person as Maharaja Dhondu Pant
Nana Saheb."

"Dalhousie is new," Azim commented. "He does not know the
background."

So we sent a representation to Calcutta, explaining the background and pointing out that the Governor-General's predecessors
had led us to believe that such a request would not be turned
down. I still remember Dalhousie's reply:

> In thirty-three years, the Peshwa has received the enormous sum
> of more than two and a half million sterling. . . . Those who
> remain have no claim whatsoever on the consideration of the
> British Government. They have no claim on its charity either.

Tantya was livid. "What can you expect from traders!" he
snorted. "All they think of is profits!"

Even Azim was provoked. "We had not asked for charity—only
what was ours by right. Dalhousie is even worse than Hardinge. If
only Malcolm were . . ."

"They're all alike," Tantya pronounced, "Whores! Grab-grab-
grab!"

Tantya Topi lived in a world of his own, a world that was pure
because there were no white men in it. Every time he shook hands
with one he would wash his hands as tho gh to remove contamina-
tion, and Dalhousie he loathed almost as a matter of principle because he happened to be the Governor-General—as it were, the
biggest white man. But then Dalhousie seemed to take a sinister
delight in arousing hatred. In our minds, he had taken the form of
an enormous giant who spat fire and gave out blood-curdling
honks as he went about swallowing kingdom after kingdom as

though they were his natural food. His ambition was to clear India of Indian rulers and he all but achieved it with his Doctrine of Lapse.

The Doctrine of Lapse was an instrument of confiscation so crude that it might have been devised by a child, so tyrannical as to resemble an act of God. If a ruler died without a son, Dalhousie simply "annexed" his domain.

This was about the time, the winter of 1851, when the Maharaja Holcar sent a tiger cub for my animal park. This cub, which I named Sheroo, grew to be an enormous tiger and used to follow me about like a dog, and many people who visited my house have written about his endearing pranks. I now mention Sheroo's arrival only to pin-point the time, because it was while the Holcar's equerry was still in Bithoor that I used the expression "The God who rides a buffalo" to describe Dalhousie.

The God who rides a buffalo is Yama, the Lord of Death. The Holcar's equerry must have reported my words to his master as a piece of gossip he had picked up in Bithoor, and the Holcar, in turn, must have repeated them to *his* friends so that, in no time at all, in most Indian courts it became Dalhousie's second name. But I was quite shaken when one day Todd told me that it had reached Dalhousie's ears and that it had made Dalhousie chortle with laughter. Todd seemed to be offended that the Governor-General had taken the whole thing so lightly.

"His Lordship is blessed with a truly English sense of humour," Todd said into his beaker of port.

Ordinarily I would have told him that Dalhousie was Scots, not English, but I kept quiet and concentrated on his nose. The nodules on it were darker than the port.

"Any other man in his position would have appointed a commission of inquiry to find out who first dared to refer to the head of the government in such slanderous terms." The red nose dipped into the beaker. The level of the port dropped. Then words came again. "Kingdoms have been wiped out for less. And then your Rajas go wailing about justice and honour!" The nose quivered and emitted a thunderous snort.

My shoulders shook with the now-familiar rage of slaves, but I must have managed to smile all the same. Azim jumped up and topped Todd's glass with port, and, by way of dismissal, I ordered his palanquin to be brought to the porch. As Todd gulped down his wine, a servant came and announced, "Toad Saheb's palanquin is ready."

It was years since anyone had called him that—in his presence, at least—and we could see him swell with anger. Then he hurled the glass of wine at the servant and stamped out of the room without so much as a glance at us.

For a moment, no one said anything, and then Azim said, "Only that white pig could have reported it—no one else knew."

"Is there no way of getting rid of this spy, Malik?" Tantya asked.

"If there were, I would have done it long ago. No Indian can dismiss a white man."

"Give him money, enough money for him to go and settle in England. He will grab the chance, for he has never seen the land he claims to be his own," Azim suggested.

I shook my head. "They'll smell through it at once."

"But he doesn't do a stroke of work since he stopped teaching."

"Malik knows much more English than Toad," said Azim.

"It is easy for a drunk to have an accident."

"No," I said very firmly. "I forbid accidents."

"We could try a little pull-push," Azim offered, closing his eyes as though he were thinking out his plan.

"Yes? What sort of pull-push?"

"If Malik were to write privately to the King of Oudh, I'm sure His Majesty would offer to . . . to do something."

The very next morning I sent Azim to Lucknow to explain my predicament to the Nawab. And a week later, Azim came back with the news that the Nawab had already set some scheme in motion, but that we would have to wait a while for it to cook. It was not till nearly a year later, in the autumn of 1852, that Todd himself came to see me and, after a good deal of prevarication, asked me for a letter of recommendation to the King of Oudh who, it appeared, needed an English tutor for his children. I gave Todd a glowing letter and, when he came to tell me he had got the job, presented him with a carriage and pair as a parting gift.

But, as I said, this pull-push took a long time to work.

Meanwhile, my affairs had further deteriorated, which may well be the reason why Todd had decided that there was no future for him in my employ.

For, as though to bring home to me how remiss I had been in so much as putting a claim for Bajirao's pension and titles, Dalhousie had followed up his reply with an order summarily withdrawing a special privilege that all of us at Bithoor, members of Bajirao's family as well as the retainers, had enjoyed for the past thirty-three years: the exemption from the jurisdiction of the Company's law courts. Its effect was that I was soon deluged by all kinds of vexatious lawsuits instituted by those who professed to have some claim on Bajirao's estate.

Upon that I sent an appeal to London, to the directors of the Company. They blindly endorsed Dalhousie's actions. As a last resort, I sent Azim to London to put up a personal appeal. He was snubbed and insulted by such of the directors as he succeeded in getting to see and fleeced by middle men who professed to have influence with those in power. Indefatigable and courteous as ever, he even managed to obtain an audience with Queen Victoria, who was both polite and sympathetic. But it seemed that in England, the Parliament was even more powerful than the monarch, and the East India Company far more powerful than the Parliament.

So Azim came back, swinging his arms, as we say, because they held nothing. He came back a changed man, given to prolonged silences and fits of anger. He no longer boasted of his familiarity with the sahibs or their ways, or admired their punctuality or imitated their mannerisms. For days he avoided seeing me, so that in the end I had to send for him. He stood before me like a guilty man, with bowed head and with the palms of his hands tightly pressed together as though his wrists were tied with cord—the classic posture of the courtier waiting to be admonished. He wore plain clothes. Gone was the swashbuckling, scented emir gowned in Lucknow brocade and festooned with flashy jewellery. The only thing remarkable about his appearance was his beard, which he had cut in a precise triangle and dyed orange.

"It's the funniest beard I have ever seen," I remarked.

He gave a weak smile and did not say anything.

"The dye is Turkish, the cut is French," Tantya explained.

"So he went to France and Turkey both?"

"And Italy and Russia . . ."

"Only a little bit of Russia," Azim interrupted. "The Russian army."

I did not want to talk about his mission, so I asked him if he had been able to buy me all the things I wanted.

"Yes, Malik," he answered, and his gloom lightened.

Crates kept arriving for months, containing chandeliers, statuary, a grand piano, a billiard table, a machine for making ice, double-barrelled shotguns by Westley Richards and Jeffery; English saddles, French china, tapestry such as I had seen in a painting, and four paintings by Claude Lorraine.

"I was determined to get Your Highness better things than the Governor-General's palace has," he explained.

We still avoided talking about his mission. We had lived with the thing too long, and now that it was over, even in failure, it was, in some ways, a relief. As Azim thawed, he spoke of his experiences more freely. I and Tantya and Champa would listen raptly, like children to fairy tales, for he was the only Indian whom we knew who had travelled beyond the seas and seen the white man in his own country. He told us they were not all like the Company's men here. Admittedly, they were reserved. But once you got to know them, they were hospitable and even generous. Whatever they were, they were not arrogant or pugnacious.

Tantya had tipped me in advance, so I asked, "Tell us about the women."

He glanced at Champa and gave me a reproachful look. "Let me tell you about my journey through the great Ottoman Empire," he said.

"About the women he will tell us later," Tantya said.

Azim told us about his visit to Constantinople and his excursion into the Crimea, where the British and the Russians were at war.

"Why are they fighting?" I asked.

"When have the British needed a cause to start a war?" Tantya asked.

"It seems they did not want this one," Azim said. "I was told in London that the mobs made them declare war."

"Mobs!"

"People in the streets. They were so incensed by Russia's insulting behaviour towards Turkey that they forced their rulers to go to war against Russia."

"To insult other nations is the prerogative of the British—how dare the Russians usurp it?" Tantya said.

"I saw the fighting too," Azim said importantly.

"In a Turkish bordello?"

"*Toba-toba,* Malik!" He slapped his cheeks gently at such a scandalous suggestion.

"He says he went over to the other side too," Tantya said.

"Yes, I saw the fighting from both sides."

"Both sides?"

He told us that in Constantinople he met a British journalist, Sir William Russell. Azim was greatly impressed by Russell.

"Oh, what a *shareef*—a real gentleman; cultivated, educated, courteous. Here even a half-pay captain feels insulted if you don't fold your umbrella as you pass him in the street. This man who was a 'Sir' treated me as an equal. We ate at the same table."

"How did you meet this 'Sir'?"

"He had taken a room at the same hotel, Misserie's."

"Don't fib. Good-class Englishmen don't live in hotels where Indians are admitted."

"Hunh!" he snorted. "In the realm of the great Sultan, the English don't claim special privileges, nor are they granted any."

"He really was a 'Sir'? Or have you made all this up?"

"A real nobleman; the Turkish people called him 'Milor.' "

"And what did they call you?"

Azim sniggered, and Tantya answered for him. "It seems they called him an Eastern Prince."

"So the Prince and the Milor ate and drank together," I said. "What happened then? Both went in search of girls—of *bibis?*"

"We sat and talked—talked late into the night," Azim said. "Sir William is a journalist, and he was going to the front. I asked him if I could go with him. And he agreed."

"To the British lines?"

"And the French too; the French and the British are allies."

This came as a surprise to me. Here in India, the French and the British were like cat and dog, traditional enemies. That was

why the first British had come to the Peshwa's court: to prevent
the French from winning over the Peshwa to their side.

"Sir William managed to get a pass from the British general for
me to go through the lines and over to the Russian side."

"Your Milor must be a very influential person."

"Journalists are very powerful in Europe."

"What're they like—the Russians?"

"The Russians? Ah, the Muscovites!" He stroked his beard lov-
ingly. "Bigger made than either the British or the French, and their
officers look like gods and drink like fishermen. They were
pounding the British with guns—such powerful, trouble-free guns!
They laughed and joked as they loaded the guns—the British and
the French only cursed and swore; they cursed everything, the
food, the rain, the mud. . . ."

"It is their national characteristic to curse the weather,"
Champa said.

"And then I knew that even the British could be beaten—defeated in battle," Azim was saying in a voice that sounded like a
creaking door.

"We shall beat them here too," Tantya declared.

"That is the only answer!" Azim said. "War."

Was that the measure of the change that had come over him?
He had gone to England a staunch admirer of the British. Now he
was talking of going to war with them. "The British are doomed,"
he went on in the same voice. "The Russians will bring them to
their knees. Then we can rise and finish the job here. Revolt!"

The word dropped in our midst like a shot in the forest. For a
few seconds we were all silent. What had been held suppressed had
bobbed to the surface. The thought held us captive. In my mind,
the East India Company's battalions were marching on and on, towards the sea, where their ships were lined up to take them home;
and their bands were playing slow, funeral marches. The horizon
fell back and opened out, and the Ganges became the Godawari
and then the Krishna, a thousand miles away.

Then a sound broke through like the cawing of a crow, harsh
and abrasive. Azim was rumbling on. "In Bombay, when I held
out my hand to a white port assistant, he flung it away in disgust."

My dream broke. The English were not in orderly retreat. They were here, and they were so powerful that a lowly officer at a port could spurn to shake hands with a true nobleman like Azim; Azim, who, in the Sultan's kingdom, had been accepted as the social equal of a Milor.

"It could never have happened in the domain of the Sultan," Azim said.

"Nor in the domain of the Peshwa, forty years ago," Tantya said.

Forty years. What had they done to us? I felt hot with anger and I found myself repeating Azim's words. "In the realm of the great Sultan, the English don't claim special privileges, nor are they granted any." It was good to think that there was such a place on earth, somewhere.

That was when, as though to lighten our despondency, Azim began to tell us about the women of Europe. "There is not a single town I visited where I did not have a woman," he boasted.

"That only means that every town in Europe has a brothel," I taunted.

Azim pretended to be outraged. "Buy it? Never!" he snorted. "Not once. And some of them were women from the highest families. One was a countess, a real Milor's wife."

Azim had the bold good looks of his Afghan ancestry, and he always dressed like a nawab going to receive an address of welcome; and his manners, for all that his parents had never even owned a donkey, were those of a Lucknow grandee, so that his mere presence gave tone to the most glittering gathering. He had taught himself to speak Persian, French, and English with great fluency and possessed a voice that seemed to lend these languages a special richness. In his own surroundings, of course, he was believed to be quite irresistible to women; all the same, I was not prepared to believe that he could have had such success with white women.

"Hi-toba! Malik," he protested. "But they're not the same at home. There they're not white women, but just women. At first it is sheer curiosity, they eat you with their eyes and undress you in their minds, and they can't wait to have a tumble to find out what a brown man is like in bed. It's the curiosity of the fish for the hook—they just cannot let go. I had so many offers of marriage—

yes, from women so beautiful!" He rolled his eyes and smacked his lips to make a wet sound. "Soft, like champak flowers and, aah, so passionate—aaah!"

At the time we had all laughed this off as an instance of Azim's propensity to sound off about his quite fatal charm for women, but not for long; for, in the autumn of the year 1855, all the way from a place called Houndsditch, came Miss Sylvia Bolten, lugging a box which, she told everyone proudly, held the latest in wedding dresses. It seemed that Azim had promised to marry her and here she was in Kanpur, waiting impatiently to become his *begam*. One day she came seeking my intervention.

A big-made woman with bright yellow hair, square wrists and big hands that might have been made for banging a town crier's drum, and thick ankles. She was certainly no champak flower, and I could see why Azim was reluctant to keep his promise. I gave her tea and promised to do what I could.

Azim already had two begams and, although his religion allowed two more, was in no hurry to squander away his quota, since, now that he had risen in life, he wanted to pick his wives carefully and also demand from their parents extortionate dowries. I sent for him and asked him what he proposed to do about Miss Bolten.

"But she's so exceedingly plain, Malik!" he groaned. "Otherwise I would certainly have offered to make some sort of an accommodation."

"She wants marriage," I reminded him, "not accommodation. Says she has letters to prove that you promised marriage. If the British decide to hold you to your promise, you know I can do nothing to help."

"If all the women one promised to marry were to come chasing . . . ," he began, but I cut him short. "This one happens to have engaged a lawyer," I told him. "Jonas Pilchard."

That made him sit up. "Pilchard! *Hi-toba!*"

"They'll quite likely hang you for this."

Ever since the days of Impey, the judge who had hanged Calcutta's richest banker because he had complained that the Governor-General took bribes, the thought of white judges dispensing the Company's justice made every Indian quail. "*Toba!*" Azim said again, and nervously tugged at his beard.

"Is there really a place called Houndsditch?"

"Yes, Malik."

"And what were you doing there?" I asked, and, when he did not answer, added, "Go and see the lady. I'm sure something can be arranged—a cash settlement. I'll treat you to it."

But when Azim went to Kanpur to see Miss Bolten, he discovered that a sepoy guard had been placed at the gate of Watson's Hotel, where she was staying, with orders to turn away all "native" callers.

He nosed around among his friends and discovered what was happening. The British community was up in arms, but not against Azim. They were scandalized that a white woman should have come all the way to India to marry a "native" and were determined to prevent her from doing so. It was a matter involving the prestige of the ruling race, and a deputation of Kanpur ladies had been sent to Miss Bolten to explain to her the shocking impropriety of such a union.

"I never suffer one of them to enter my bungalow from the front gate," Mrs. Scobie told her, "but insist on their using the servants' entrance; and then I make them wait in the back veranda." Mrs. Scobie was the wife of the Resident Magistrate and the senior lady of the station.

But Miss Bolten had remained obdurate and, it appears, was quite rude to Mrs. Scobie. That very evening an urgent meeting of the community was held in the Assembly Room. Here a suggestion was made to have Miss Bolten certified insane by the brigade surgeon, but when someone mentioned that she had engaged Jonas Pilchard as her lawyer, it was unanimously decided to extern her on merely moral grounds. If she could be declared by the Resident Magistrate to be an "undesirable person" (under a regulation normally invoked to get rid of disease-ridden prostitutes), there would be no difficulty in having her forcibly shipped back to Calcutta and thence to England.

"Of course she qualifies," Mrs. Scobie had told the Assembly, and her husband had mumbled assent.

But Jonas Pilchard acted before the R.M. could, and spirited away his client to the neighbouring kingdom of Oudh, which, at the time, was still ruled by its nawab, and where the Company's edict did not run. So Miss Bolten established herself in a bungalow in Lucknow placed at her disposal by a friend of her lawyer's, a Captain Frazer. Within two weeks, she married Frazer and, as we shall see, on the disbandment of the Oudh army, came to Kanpur as a proud military wife, the peer of Mrs. Scobie herself, vigilant in her efforts to preserve and protect the purity of her race.

Chapter 5

In February 1856 something happened that rocked our world. We saw the death of a kingdom. Dalhousie had "annexed" Oudh; annexed it on a pretext so unsubstantial as to be nonexistent; it made the death appear the result of natural causes. There was no war, no belligerence; on the part of the King, Wajid Ali, nothing but the most abject self-abasement. Anyone less pugnacious than Wajid Ali would be difficult to imagine. He and his ancestors had run Oudh dry to pay the price of British friendship, for the Governor-Generals, almost as though to provoke them into some semblance of disobedience and thus provide an excuse for war, had gone on raising the amount of Oudh's tribute. Lord Dalhousie was no believer in such subtleties, no respecter of treaties. He merely "served" an order on the King telling him that his country had been taken over.

Wajid Ali broke down as he read the order, and his subjects mourned as though someone in their family had died. His Majesty and Nawab one day, he was bundled off to Calcutta the next as a private citizen. Dalhousie's minions marched in, disbanding, dismantling, desecrating.

Admittedly, this had happened before. This time the shock was greater because Oudh was the very last Indian kingdom, and also because the kingdom was so close to us—the other bank of the Ganges had been Oudh. It was like a neighbour's house going up in flames. The eclipse was now total; the moon eaters had finished their job.

Every Hindu believes that an eclipse happens when the demons,

Rahu and Ketu, swallow the moon or the sun, and that they regurgitate their prey only when they are propitiated by mass prayers and fasts. No fire is lit in the house nor food eaten, and men and women crowd the holy places to beseech the demons to disgorge their prey. But the Dalhousies of the company were not like our propitiable moon eaters; they never gave up what they had swallowed. Prayers, fasting, mourning meant nothing to them.

The seizure of Oudh brought us face to face with the reality of the Company's rule. It made us lift our eyes from our little fishpond world and look around. And suddenly, like some complex mathematical equation that only in its final step yields a simple, uncomplicated answer, the solution emerged in one word: revolt. The forces were already at work.

A body of traders with the appetites of caterpillars and with their consciences armoured in tortoise-shell, who yet called themselves the "Honourable" East India Company, had conquered the whole of India. All the same, they had been careful to preserve the fiction that the Moguls, not they, were the real masters. I must confess that this was precisely what the Marathas too had done. Whether we were fighting Mogul armies or restoring a defeated emperor to his throne, hacking away the limbs of the empire or subduing Mogul enemies, we had never disowned their sovereignty and, above all, we had never shown disrespect to the person of the Emperor. And by and large, the British had followed our example. Alamgir, the lord of the universe, no less, still lived in his fabled palace in Delhi and there held daily court in the marble hall which bears the inscription: *If there be a heaven on earth, it is this, it is this, it is this*. His Majesty Bahadur Shah, a shrunken old man in his eighties and only half alive, was both Padishah, which meant Emperor, and Gazi, which meant holy warrior. Before his throne everyone, including the white merchants, had to wait barefoot and with bowed heads for a grudgingly granted audience.

But the dummy calf, as my father would have called it, had ceased to serve its purpose; the time had come to abolish the phantom court. The new masters had decided to come out into the open. They wanted the palace vacated, the Emperor packed off to some obscure village; they wanted the people of India to know that they, not the descendants of the Great Moguls, were the Padishah.

Left to himself, I have no doubt that Dalhousie would have enjoyed evicting the Emperor and his dependents from their ancestral home, the Red Fort. But the directors in London, severely shaken by the uproar in the Parliament and the press caused by Dalhousie's galloping annexations, had advised caution. They had no wish to arm their rivals and detractors with yet another scandal in India.

Dalhousie, contemptuous of caution as ever, put into effect an alternative plan. The heir apparent had died in 1849, and in his place the Governor-General, no doubt with some such development in mind, had refused to nominate another. The pretext was that, among so many royal princes from so many different mothers, it was difficult to decide who was the most senior. Now Dalhousie made a pact with one of the contenders, Fakiruddin, that he would recognize him as the heir on the understanding that, upon succession, Fakiruddin would vacate the Red Fort and renounce all the titles that the Moguls had adopted.

Who let out the secret? Fakiruddin himself, a known opium addict, or some official of the Company, for a sizeable bribe? Anyway, within months it was common knowledge that the monarchy was to be abolished; that with the death of Bahadur Shah, the family of the Great Mogul would be thrown out of their ancestral home and last refuge, the Red Fort.

Then the counterplotting had begun. Behind the moat and behind the rose-pink walls and behind the latticed windows of the innermost court, plans took shape. And at their centre, amidst the lotus pools and the fountains endlessly spraying rose-water was, unbelievably, a woman. A woman soft and plump and faded and compelled by the enormity of her abdomen to walk with a peculiar, straddling gait; for, like some monster queen white ant, this queen was believed to be blessed with a state of continuous pregnancy. Zeenat Mahal, who has been compared to a scorpion and a she-leopard, was ruthless, selfish, and utterly unscrupulous; but, for all that, she was a Mogul queen, even if one of several dozen, and, as such, had claims to the blind reverence of millions of the Mogul's subjects. They took up her cause. Zeenat's private vengeance was to become the rallying point.

And at her side, emerging as it were from some nether world at the rubbing of a magic lamp, stood the sinister, satanic figure of Ahmadulla Shah, the Moulvi of Fyzabad; the firebrand patriot who has become familiar to the world as the Mad Mullah. His shadow fell everywhere.

To the outside world, Zeenat, for all her genius for intrigue and her fiendishness, was merely a voice behind a veil, but the voice could make your skin prickle, and those who have heard it have likened it to the squawk of a Singapore cockatoo, sharp and strident and invested with a quality of alarm. A harem maid, singled out at random by some transmuted functionary to provide a night's warmth to the frail, dope-dazed Emperor, had sprung a surprise on him by giving him his very last, unhoped-for son. That was in 1838, eighteen years earlier, but Zeenat still held the old King tethered by the same nose ring, pandering, by her simulated pregnancies, to his illusions of vitality regained. Even after an implausible number of false alarms and miscarriages, Bahadur Shah, now in his eighties, still clung to the hope of fathering another son by this woman of miraculous fecundity. He drooled at the sight of her and whimpered like a scolded child when she denied him her favours. And Zeenat, for her part, played him like a fish brought within reach of the gaff, tormenting him and making him give in to her most outrageous whims.

Zeenat cared little for the lost glories of the Mogul empire and still less about the conquest of India by the hat men. Her only reason for detesting the British was that they had refused her request to recognize her son, Jawan Bakht, as the Emperor's heir. If they had, there is little doubt that Zeenat, on her part, would have cheerfully signed away all that the British were asking for and more. She even prevailed upon her unfortunate husband to represent to the Company's Resident, Sir Theophilus Metcalfe, that Fakiruddin was ineligible to become a king because he had been circumcised.

"No one whose body has been in any way mutilated may sit on the throne; that is Mogul tradition," the old King wailed. "Jawan Bakht alone among my sons is uncircumcised."

Did that, we all wondered, mean that the six Great Moguls, from Babar to Aurangzeb, all devout and some quite fanatic Muslims, had not even been circumcised? If true, Zeenat's argument had great weight, and at that the British would not have bothered much about its validity if it had suited their purpose. But a practical difficulty supervened. Jawan Bakht was the youngest among at least a score of royal princes. Metcalfe had no option but to turn down this very convenient request. That night Zeenat swore vengeance against the Company.

This tantrum in the royal harem rapidly blossomed into a determination to resist the usurpation of the King's palace by the hat men. And then it was realized that any such resistance would be futile so long as the hat men held power. So it flared into something infinitely bigger—a struggle to throw out the traders and to resuscitate the empire of the Moguls.

And from there, Moulvi Ahmadulla, the Mad Mullah, had taken over and guided Zeenat's hand.

It was the Mullah from Fyzabad, the mysterious fakir who went about preaching death and destruction in the name of the Emperor, who might be said to have been the brain behind the revolt. Wherever he went people seemed to become aware of the omens they had not noticed before. The Ganges had flowed red, there had been a rainbow ring around the moon, the tower of the big church of the hat men in Bombay had collapsed. There were rumours of a sinister mass treachery: beef bones had been ground into the flour supplied by the Company's commissariat department, and sugar needed pig's blood to make it white. It was the Mad Mullah who sent across India the messengers bearing the *chapatis*--the flat wheatcakes which were the common man's food. And with the chapatis travelled the rumours.

And he it was who set the date, a date which was truly inspired for it had the power of making every Indian react as though to a piece of terrible news: the twenty-third of June, 1857. It was the day of the centenary of the battle of Plassey, when Clive's victory had begun the Company's rule.

By the time Oudh was liquidated, the Mullah had given up all subterfuge. A man of religion, he ceased preaching religion. All he did was to call upon his listeners to "kill the *firanghis* [the foreigners] as though they were cobras and mad dogs—to exterminate their race." It was, we all knew, only a matter of time before some junior British official would have him arrested and pass sentence of death.

The British, as I have said, had been waiting for the Emperor to die before announcing the dissolution of his empire. Their spies at court brought them daily bulletins about the shades of difference in Bahadur Shah's health. No one expected the old man to last long, and at that the British were in no hurry. Meanwhile, there were record bags to be shot of duck and partridge, weekly hunts after the jungle jack, and glittering receptions at Metcalfe Park, the Resident's palatial house in Delhi. The very first strawberries to be grown in India were being served at the Resident's table, and the marble platform of Safdar Jung's tomb made an excellent dancing floor.

But there were others who were in a hurry, desperate to bring things to a head before Bahadur Shah expired. For what they planned to do, an emperor was altogether indispensable.

Early in 1856 Fakiruddin, the Prince Dalhousie had chosen as the heir apparent, died. One evening, after a palace dinner, he complained of a stomach-ache, and even though two important officials, one a physician and the other a miracle-worker, were rushed to his side, he died within the hour.

It was murder. The physician and the miracle-worker were both Zeenat's trusted lieutenants. None of us who were familiar with Mogul methods of doing away with rivals could have been deceived and the formula was, if anything, conventional: a kitchen maid ordered to put a few grains of dhatura root in the victim's food and then, while he lay writhing in agony, two agents rushing in and administering additional poisons instead of palliatives, or even strangling him to death.

But the British, even though they had spies inside the Red Fort and a Resident just outside, did not appear to see Zeenat's hand in the death of the heir apparent. The Resident, I am told, did not even put off his scheduled week of pigsticking at Najafgarh. On his return, he called for reports on all the remaining princes so that he could select a new heir apparent. At this stage, the Emperor and Zeenat once again pressed the claims of Jawan Bakht. Sir Theophilus very firmly and not very politely declined. What other prince he had recommended to the Governor-General will never be known, because before the British announced the decision, the revolt had begun, and afterwards the question of a Mogul successor had ceased to be relevant. In any case, there were no princes left. A man called Hodson had killed three, and Sir Theophilus himself had helped to finish off the rest—as many as twenty-one of them.

Thus, in the beginning of 1856 signs were already in the sky. There were forces at work which were going to engulf the country in war. But we quickly turned our eyes away from the signs, pretended we had heard nothing, seen nothing. The British, on their part, were going about as though swallowing moons were a commonplace affair, something that must not be allowed to interfere with everyday life. We too had to join this game of pretence, make out that, whatever indignities were heaped upon us, we would never retaliate but would only sit up and ask for more.

Chapter 6

This day there were no portents in the sky; there should have been. It had the green-and-gold sparkle of early spring and the air was heavy with the scent of mustard blossom and boiling molasses.

I was going to Kanpur to make my formal call on its newly arrived military commander, Major-General Sir Hugh Wheeler, K.C.B. Beyond the fact that he was an old man, certainly in his seventies, that he had a very pretty Indian wife much younger than himself, that, except for a two-year stint with one British column or another in Europe, he had never been out of India since he had first arrived as a boy of seventeen and was thus more Indian than British, and that his name was held in the highest esteem by the Indian soldiers, I had known very little about Hugh Wheeler.

Conscious that such calls on the Company's seniormost civil and military officials were the merest formality and that neither they nor I had any particular wish to make one another's acquaintance, I had not bothered to take the customary precaution of asking my astrologer to find out a specially auspicious time for my visit. If only I had had some inkling of what impact the meeting was fated to have on the Wheelers and myself, I would have turned in my tracks and waited for a less malignant hour. Something should have warned me—perhaps a cat crossing my path as I stepped out of the house, or a vulture perched on the gatepost. As it was, there were no danger signals.

By now the formalities of these meetings had become routine. The General or Commissioner received me on his porch steps and led me into a reception room where chairs were arranged in a precise horseshoe. He would sit on the central chair and make me sit on his right and we would inquire after each other's health and talk about the crops and the weather. The moment our talk flagged, an aide would distribute betel nut folded in neat little packets and sprinkle rose-water over all present, after which we would walk back to the porch and say good-bye. All this, however, made up only one half of the ceremony of calling. The other half took place a week or so later, in Bithoor, when the General or Commissioner returned my call. Introductions over, we seldom bothered one another.

But this time Hugh Wheeler stood at the gate to receive me. Instead of stiff bows and handshakes, there was a warm Indian embrace; instead of the pantomime of betel nut and rose-water, a musical entertainment. But before we sat down to it, the General introduced me to his wife and children. Lady Wheeler told me that she had ordered a special dinner to be cooked by high-caste brahmins, and that I must call her Janaki. It was taken for granted that I would stay on for the evening meal. Before the evening was over, it was arranged that the return call would take the form of the family spending the coming week-end at Bithoor.

Hugh Wheeler, Sir and K.C.B., had already served in the army for fifty-four years. In my mind I see him as an old war horse, caparisoned in gaudy harness as for a ceremony, pawing the earth at the sound of bugles in the distance, but wheezing and grunting too. He was the seniormost general in the entire army and his war record read like the battle honours on some regimental banner. Among the sepoys, or Indian soldiers, his zest for warfare had earned him the proud sobriquet of "Hamlah," or "Attack."

Six years earlier when, after a row with Dalhousie, Sir Charles Napier had quitted the office of the Commander-in-Chief, everyone was certain that Wheeler would succeed him. But Dalhousie had refused to countenance someone like Wheeler, who, according to him, had "gone native," as his military chief.

Wheeler had never forgiven Dalhousie. "Compared to Napier, he was a tick, a bedbug," he told me. "Napier was a real sharcef, a gentleman. I'm surprised that the Duke of Wellington backed up this villain Dalhousie, knowing that everyone hated him—Indian and British alike."

"And Dalhousie was made a Marquis," I reminded Wheeler. "And the Company voted him a special pension of five thousand pounds a year."

"Pooh—pooh! They just had to throw him a piece; after all, he'd added five million to the Company's revenues. What's five thousand a year when he had swallowed up Oudh and no less than seven of your Rajas? You know what was burning Dalhousie, don't you? What was behind this Doctrine of Lapse?"

"No, I don't," I told him, even though, of course, it was common talk among us.

"Because Dalhousie has no son of his own, and no heir. Under English law, his estate and titles must lapse after his death. So this was his revenge."

"His revenge added five million pounds a year to the Company's revenues."

"Hah! And made fifty million enemies! You know what Napier used to say of him? 'Weak as water, vain as a pretty woman—or an ugly man.'"

Rejected by Dalhousie, Wheeler had gone on marking time, convinced that when the post fell vacant again and with Dalhousie gone, they could hardly ignore his claims. But that was just what they did do when, in 1856, the new Governor-General, Lord Canning, promoted General Anson to be the C.-in-C. in Bengal.

Now in Kanpur, and already in his seventies, Wheeler still spoke with undiminished hope of realizing his life's ambition, which was to become the Commander-in-Chief, the *Jangi Laat*. I remember he once told me in all seriousness, "George Anson's is a political appointment. C.-in-C.! Anson's never led a squadron in the field, not a company. What does he know of war? 'As much as a spinster!'—that's what the Calcutta 'Englishman' said, 'Not much more than a spinster.' They can't keep him on for more than a year or two at the most. Besides—besides, Anson's health is to be measured in grains rather than ounces." His eyes which were bright blue twinkled with some inner vision of glory.

As he often did when speaking to me, Wheeler had lapsed into Hindi, and the expression he had used meant that Anson's health was failing.

"And then the only man between me and the Jangi Laat's post is

Patrick Grant. Grant. He's the one to be feared now—feared only because he has the right connections. Married to Lord Gough's daughter. But I won't have it, I tell you; I shall never take it lying down. I'll send in my papers on the spot and lodge a protest before the Board of Control."

The haunting fear that he might once again be superceded made his whole frame shake. "But how can they?" he demanded in a querulous voice. "Grant—fifteen years my junior. I was a captain, commanding a squadron, when he joined up. How can they? After Anson it has to be me."

And so old Hamlah waited for Anson to die or to be retired, meanwhile striving hard to hide his age, which he believed was his principal handicap; hide it or at least prove to anyone who might be looking his way that he was in full bodily and mental vigour. He dyed his plentiful hair and whiskers a discreet grey, strapped in his stomach with a wide canvas belt under his breeches, swore and drank heartily, and regularly rode to hounds.

It was almost as though Wheeler himself did not know that his main handicap was not his age but the general belief that he had "gone native." The fact that he had been posted to Kanpur itself should have made it clear to him that he had reached the end of the road, because with the extention of the Company's dominion beyond Delhi, Kanpur had become the least important of commands; this was no stepping stone to the Jangi Laat's position, no matter how many Jangi Laats died or retired.

Fifty-four—or at least fifty-two—Indian summers had burned his skin a dark cinnamon shade, and monsoon upon monsoon had layered his habits and thought processes with mildew so that the pink-faced boy from an impoverished Cornwall rectory who had been sent out into the world to fend for himself had been laid to rest under them. No matter how hard he rode to hounds or how tightly he corsetted his sagging belly into his scarlet uniform, he would never be made Master of Fox Hounds as his predecessors had been, nor voted the President of the Doab Club. For was it not common knowledge that the moment he got home every day, the sahib was instantly transformed into a nawab? He could hardly wait to change into a loose muslin *kurta* and flowing pyjamas and smoke his hookah sitting cross-legged on a mattress flung on the floor and leaning against a sausage-shaped bolster. And did he not, in his bungalow, for all that it was called the Flagstaff House and flew the Union Jack, eat curried meats with his fingers at three meals a day and speak only Hindi to his family? And did he not, from time to time, send for a native band from the bazaar because he was passionately fond of Indian music and—most shocking of outrages—invite natives to Flagstaff House dinners? And had it not reached even the Governor-General's ears that his wife entertained the Indian guests with her vulgar dancing which she performed to the music of the *tabla?*

"Does she really dress like a bazaar nautch girl?" Mrs. Scobie once asked me in shocked tones. "With her navel showing?"

It was all quite true. If his years in India had made Wheeler himself more Indian than British, his wife, alas, was irremediably Indian—country-born, as they said. As a young girl, she had taught herself to dance, and I, who at one time was considered a good judge of dancing, can testify that she had taught herself very well indeed. She was close to forty when I first met her, and yet it was a delight to see her dance. Her style was more campfire than classical, and her repertoire limited, but what she lacked in style and technique, she made up for in the quality of gusto and abandon and a god-given fluidity of movement. To see her dance the *tandav* was to see a little storm let loose on the stage.

Janak. Wheeler not only loved to dance to the drums, but she went about barefoot in the house, wore saris, chewed *paan,* stained her lips red and the palms of her hands and feet saffron. And what the ladies of the Doab Club must have found even more unforgivable, she was very beautiful, someone who, on the verge of middle age, could carry off the scanty and revealing dancing costume that left a wide expanse of flesh exposed between the breasts and hip-bones. That, and also the fact that she was just as proud of being Indian as they were of being British.

"Such airs for someone who's only country-born," Mrs. Scobie and the other women would snort, with a mixture of contempt and indignation.

"Country-born" meant Indian, just as "country-bred" meant born to Indian mothers from English stock. Both were terms applied to horses as well as to human beings.

Never, not even among the brahmins of Tanjawar, who are the most rabidly orthodox among us, could there have been a caste system as rigid as the one that prevailed in the Company's cantonments. The greenest of the "griffins," as the new arrivals from England were known, was far more acceptable than a country-bred Palmer or a Skinner, for all that the Palmers controlled chains of prosperous counting houses and the Skinners not so long ago had commanded proud regiments. And as to those who were merely country-born, they were the untouchables of the order, never to be permitted into the drawing-rooms.

"I learnt to dance in a Pindari camp," Lady Wheeler once told me, "to save myself from being sold into slavery. I was taught to milk buffaloes, clean stables, groom horses, brew arrack—so that I should fetch a good price. I can still milk a buffalo." It was difficult to imagine anyone so dainty and birdlike as a maid-of-all-work.

Her father was a prosperous moneylender in a village near Saugar. One day a band of Pindaris raided the village. They shot Janaki's father and the other village elders and set fire to their houses. Then the leader of the band, the notorious Jamal, rode up and down the village calling out the amounts of ransom each householder had to pay.

"I stood in the middle of the street clutching an ax," Janaki told me. "I spat at his horse and then hurled the ax. It severed the horse's leg."

The result was that Jamal had ordered her to be seized and taken to his camp, where, after a little initial chastisement, she was put to do menial work. For two years Janaki had milked the camp buffaloes and patted cakes from their dung. At the same time, she had also learned to dance. A temple girl whom Jamal had kidnapped earlier on and kept as his mistress taught her the few routine dances she knew. There was a drummer in camp but no other music. Once when Jamal had come to his mistress's tent he had found instead the slave girl dancing. He had promptly made her his second concubine.

This was the time when Lord Bentinck had launched his campaign to root out the Pindaris, and the two-company column that was ordered to beat out the Chambal Valley for Jamal was commanded by Wheeler, who was then a captain. For eight months, from October through May, Wheeler's column had quartered a landscape that might have been ploughed over by some gigantic machine; miles and miles of stunted thorn-bushes covering deep fissures that went turning and twisting as in some patternless maze. The robbers were always reported to be just one march ahead, and often Wheeler came upon mysterious footsteps in the soft sand of the dry stream beds which closer inspection revealed to have been their own. They never saw a Pindari.

At last it had dawned on Wheeler that in that country, which was impossible for riding, with as many ravines as a teak leaf has veins, his was a hopeless task; he would never succeed in catching up with Jamal to bring him to bay. Also, his time was running out. In June the operation would have to be halted for four months while they waited out the monsoon in some convenient camping ground.

And then, one afternoon in late May, while the column had halted for its midday meal of dry rations, when the *loo,* the summer wind, blew like an invisible flame and curled the leaves on the *ber* bushes and raised gusts of scorching sand, a woman had burst into their midst, brandishing a blood-stained ax and yelling incoherently.

"I killed the louse as he was sleeping off his opium tea," Janaki once told me proudly. "And then I ran."

That very day the leaderless band had surrendered. Janaki stood beside Captain Wheeler and helped him to make up his mind about who was to be shot on the spot and who sent off under an escort to the fort at Agra. That evening she danced for Wheeler and later shared his bed. For the four months of the monsoon interregnum and then for another eight while the column still roamed the Chambal Valley, Janaki continued to live in one of the tents adjoining Wheeler's almost as a part of the Captain's baggage, to be sent for whenever the sahib desired her presence in the main tent. But this was not every night for, to be sure, Wheeler, like other old-time officers of the Company's army, never went on a campaign without a few of his more favourite bibis. But by the time Wheeler returned to his base at Allahabad after his protracted campaign, Janaki had moved into the main tent and the other bibis had vanished. In Allahabad, Wheeler, now promoted to Major, announced his decision to marry Janaki. She made him a dutiful, devoted, and, I like to think, faithful wife, for all that she was at least thirty years younger than he.

In Allahabad, Wheeler engaged a tutor, a half-caste from Martine's school, to teach his wife English, but soon discovered that the tutor had begun to speak fluent Hindi, even though Janaki had not mastered more than a few phrases of English. Old Hamlah had then given up his unequal struggle and sent away the tutor and resigned himself to speaking only Hindi at home. And even though the General's three children, George, Eliza, and Emily, spoke flawless English, they were far more at home in Hindi and always, so they told me, found it more natural to think in Hindi.

But if the Doab Club and other British Clubs were closed to Janaki, Flagstaff House, the moment she became its mistress, in turn became closed to the British colony. Except for purely official functions, they were never asked to the General's house, and at these Janaki made jokes within their hearing about the thickness of the women's ankles or the lengths of their noses or the number of dresses they wore one under the other like skins on an onion. They, in their turn, looked the other way whenever she passed and never, except in the General's hearing, spoke of her as "Lady" Wheeler.

The Wheeler children were country-bred and, as such, of a higher caste than their mother. But that did not make them *pucca,* or pure. They were the in-betweens, the Anglo-Indians who were specially provided for in the numerous subordinate services but, by a recent directive from London, barred both from the army and the civil service. As a consequence, George, the General's son, could not be absorbed into the Company's army even though his father had spent his life in it and aspired to become its chief. With his influence among the older servants of the Company, Wheeler had, a couple of years earlier, managed to secure a cornetcy for his son in the King of Oudh's army, which then was a specially preserved grazing ground for the country-breds, with uniforms even more flamboyant than those of the Company's regiments and perquisites far exceeding those available to the Company's officers.

Unfortunately, with the dissolution of the Oudh kingdom, the army had been disbanded, and the thousand or so Anglo-Indian officers employed in it, to say nothing of the fifty thousand Indian sepoys, had become jobless. Luckily, Wheeler was still in a position to provide for his son. He brought him over to Kanpur as his aide-de-camp, which was more or less a sinecure appointment in his gift, and which did not have to go to an officer in the Company's permanent cadre.

"I don't know what I'm going to do once the old man retires," George Wheeler used to complain.

The General's two daughters, Eliza and Emily, regularly went to the balls at the Doab Club, but their escorts were generally from among the country-breds. Lady Wheeler, of course, could not normally have entered the club, but at the military functions occasionally held there she took the head of the table and sat in a spiteful silence, pecking at her food because she detested boiled mutton and spiceless vegetables. Defiantly she chewed paan while the others drank coffee.

God knows that Hugh Wheeler, for all his seventy-odd years, was a remarkably vigorous man, a soldier venerated by the sepoys and whose military record was superior to those of all the other generals who were aspiring to be the next Commander-in-Chief. And admitting that he was long past his prime, advanced age by itself was no bar to high office in the Company's army. Some were even older, and in the case of General Perkins, it was well-known that it took two men to assist him to mount his horse. It was just that, even though old Hamlah was of the right caste, he had disqualified himself by marrying that "ghastly dancing girl from some robber's harem." The new crop of the Company's officers and, even more so, their ladies would never have suffered a country-born to be the mistress of the Jangi Laat's gleaming palace in Simla.

The festival of Holi came and the earth put on its gaudiest garments. The summer followed. Windows and doors were shuttered with mats of scented grass. All throughout the long day people remained indoors and came out only during the cool of the nights. It must have been at the end of May or in early June that I finally got a chance I had been waiting for for a long time: to rid myself of the attentions of Nanak Chand, the Company's informer.

One day he asked to see me alone. It was very hot and I was sitting on a reed mat on the floor, dressed in a brief dhoti and nothing else. It was dark in the room because of the shutters. He came slithering in and squatted on the mat next to me, very close, and the reek of some cloying attar filled my nostrils. Then, leaning over, he began to whisper. His breath was hot in my ears, and droplets of spittle fell on my shoulder.

"I bring a message, a secret message," he was saying. "This is your last chance—I alone can do it."

I pushed him away and fanned the air vigorously. "Say what you have to from a distance," I told him, "and finish saying it in one minute."

He told me, in a thick, dramatic whisper, that he had the ear of the Chief Commissioner, Moreland, and that if I paid him, Nanak, a lakh of rupees, he would intercede with the Chief Commissioner to support my claim for Bajirao's title of Maharaja.

"The pension they'll never allow. The title—they might change their mind, if you are prepared to pay. But only I can do it—no one else." He smirked self-importantly and saliva made wires in his mouth. Then he twirled his moustache.

How often have I spoken of my restraint? Not today. I lost my temper altogether and made a mortal enemy. I seized Nanak Chand and shook him so that his head wobbled. Then I called out to Laghu to summon my barber, and while Laghu and I held Nanak down, squirming and whining, the barber shaved off the right half of his moustache.

Needless to say, he never showed his face in Bithoor again, and I had so hoped that he had gone out of my life forever. But I was wrong. He struck back the moment he got his chance, at last revealing himself in his true colours. The earthworm you had squeamishly prevented yourself from treading on had been a cobra all along.

Chapter 7

On a day dark with monsoon clouds, the Mad Mullah's agent presented himself before me, bearing a letter with the Queen's seal. Zeenat, the letter said, had decided to hold a ceremony of formal mourning for the heir apparent's death and had invited the erstwhile vassals of the Moguls to Delhi to offer their condolences to the Emperor in person.

"Couldn't Her Majesty have thought of a more credible reason for this gathering?" I asked. "The Prince died six months ago."

"This ritual is sanctioned by custom," the agent explained. "Many of the princes are coming." And he proceeded to rattle off their names.

I would have liked to go but feared that, if I asked for permission, they were certain to send one or two spies along to find out what everyone was up to. But there was no objection to my sending a representative. So I sent Azim, and with him I sent the customary presents to the Emperor and to his favourite consort and five seers of the best Lucknow hookah mixture to the Mullah.

It was at this meeting that the broad strategy of the revolt was decided upon. The rasping cockatoo voice emanating from the lavender veil announced that the Queen's personal seal, the white lotus, would be the symbol of the revolt and that it would be used in secret communication among the leaders, almost as a code sign. And the Mad Mullah explained his plan for spreading discontent through the distribution of chapatis.

"The Mullah is an amazing man," Azim told me on his return. "Quite frightening."

"What does he look like?"

"Immensely tall, with limbs that are all bone and no flesh, face like a falcon, eyes hooded as though the light hurt them, beard the colour of fire. Wherever he goes, the people flock to see him, and when he speaks, his voice is like the cry of the butcher bird."

"And the chapatis?"

"They are to be passed by hand, from village to village. Each village that receives one has to bake four more and take them to four villages, and so on. They carry divine blessings, both from Mecca and Benares—that is, for the Muslims and Hindus alike, and anyone who fails to pass them on draws a curse upon himself and his family."

"What is their message?"

"That word will come to you—something big is going to happen."

"But aren't chapatis distributed to get rid of some pestilence, such as smallpox?"

"The hat men, the Mullah says, are a pestilence worse than smallpox."

"I doubt if they will mean much to the people."

"Malik, the Mullah is convinced his message will go round the country with the speed of the telegraph the white men have installed. 'The essence of a rumour is its ambiguity,' he says."

In the event, the method worked quite well. By leaving everything vague and mysterious, it aroused universal curiosity, and by avoiding the appearance of a religious behest, it embraced both the Hindus and Muslims.

"And when the word is received, what are the people to do?" I asked.

"There are not more than a hundred thousand white men in the whole of India," Azim said as though he were quoting someone else's words.

So the plan was born, the date set.

There are not more than a hundred thousand white men in the whole of India.

The words had the unambiguous ring of a hunting song, the

round figure a nakedness, as of a nest of lizards exposed on a vast rock. A hundred thousand . . . a hundred thousand among a hundred million . . . so few white zeros bobbing up among so many brown zeros, waiting to be swamped.

I myself, brought up as a vegetarian and brahmin, to respect learning and culture, someone taught to believe that all life— human, animal, even insect life—was part of a great single divinity and therefore sacrosanct, had the vegetarian's instinctive squeamishness at the shedding of blood. I shrank from the brutalities that lay ahead. Even though I realized that a good many Englishmen would have to die, and that many times that number of our own people would also have to die, I fervently hoped that the carnage would not be excessive; that somehow, only just that number of white men would be slaughtered for the remainder to be persuaded that their best course was to leave our land for their own. And, to be sure, there were a number of Englishmen I would not have liked to leave our shores either: families such as the Wheelers and the Hillersdons and the Morelands, or the half-whites such as the Skinners and the Herseys. My loyalties were hopelessly intermixed, and my hatred far from pure.

I am not making up excuses. Lest my motives be misunderstood, let me make it clear that even at the time I was, as I am now, wholly convinced that we were morally right. Ours was going to be an uprising against oppression, an attempt to drive out the men who had come to our shores in the garb of traders, to buy and sell, and then, like some Arabian Nights pirates, taken out the weapons concealed in their cloaks and turned upon their hosts and made them slaves. In our struggle to take back what was ours, there was no room for a feeling of guilt. On a purely abstract level of thinking, even if we had to kill every single white man, woman, and child in India in the course of our fight, morally we would still be justified. If the situation were reversed, I have not the least doubt that this was how Englishmen too would have felt; and I am not at all sure that this is not precisely what they would have done too.

Thus, if anything, my hesitancy was a weakness of mind, or an offshoot of some stump of chivalry, or a purely brahminical humanitarianism. And it was perhaps just punishment for being thus insufficiently committed that I came out of the whole thing as a monster to frighten children with.

But there were several on the opposite side too who suffered from the same uncertainties. Prolonged living among Indians had erased their racial arrogance and insularity. This was the country of their exile if not adoption, and, in a twisted way, they had learned to love it and, in a few cases, become fond of its inhabitants. Men like Hillersdon and Wheeler were, in a sense, my opposite numbers. However resolutely they fought to put down our revolt, they could never bring themselves to match the unqualified hatred of the Coopers and the Hodsons; as though deep in their hearts, they were never free of a doubt that they were fighting for the perpetuation of a great wrong, the enslavement of a gullible and hospitable race.

"The Queen and the Mullah are certain that the people will follow their erstwhile masters blindly," Azim was saying. "The princes must come forward now."

The ruling princes were the Maharajas who had been allowed to remain as the vassals of the Company. Now they were like jungle animals waiting for a game drive to begin, paralysed with fear. Before their very eyes, Carnatic, Nagpur, Satara, Jhansi had been liquidated because their rulers had failed to produce sons, and Oudh, whose King had many sons, because Dalhousie believed that God wanted him to do so. So if human error and incapacity to produce sons were not enough, God could always be relied upon to provide a pretext for annexation. It was just a matter of time before their own turn would come. Another Dalhousie, and there would not remain a single ruling prince in the country. The princes saw the hundred thousand white men not as insignificant dots lost in a mass of brown, but as a gigantic crouching figure towering above the Himalayas: Dalhousie.

Did not Zeenat and the Mullah know that the princes were far too demoralized to be of any use to either side?

These princes were the descendants of Shivaji and Bajirao and Tippu. Where there had been tigers were now sheep—sheep waiting in neat, British-made pens, nervously eyeing the figure with the ax to make the next move, hoping they would be spared just this once. And yet, being sheep, planning the vengeance of sheep, hoping that someone else, some other herd of sheep would stampede and trample down the butcher with the bloody ax.

"Her Majesty has a special request," Azim was saying. "She wants you to visit the Maratha princes and to prepare them. And the Mullah more or less said the same thing."

"More or less? What were his exact words?"

"Well, he actually said that— In fact, I was to repeat his exact words to you."

"Yes?" I prompted.

"That rather than bear the Peshwa's name, you should announce yourself as someone spawned by a dung beetle, if you did not now rise to the occasion."

"Strong words."

"The Mullah never minces his words—not even before the Queen."

"Why can't the Queen write to them herself—or that mad man?"

"They're writing to the Muslims and the Rajputs; and even to the King of Persia and Kabul and Russia. But they felt—we all felt —that with the Marathas, your word would bear more weight."

The logic could not be faulted. Several of the Maratha princes were, after all, created by my ancestors; and while all of them, at one time or another, had accepted the Peshwa as the head of the Maratha confederacy and that confederacy itself had accepted a loose sort of Mogul supremacy, they had never taken their orders directly from the Moguls. Many of them still professed to respect the traditional bonds, and tradition has a way of surviving almost intact among those who are consigned to live in the past. It was quite true that I had a better chance to win them over than either Queen Zeenat or the Mullah. But what was logic to sheep?

Anyway, I wrote and told Zeenat Mahal that I would go and see as many of the Maratha princes as possible and send messengers to those I could not visit. And then I sent a few discreet presents to some of the British officials and followed this up with a formal application for permission to go on a pilgrimage to pray for a son. The new Collector, Hillersdon, who was inclined to be friendly, assured me that my application had been forwarded to Lord Canning

with a favourable recommendation. After that, there was nothing
to do but wait.

And during this period of waiting I fell in love, boyishly, roman-
tically, and quite hopelessly. It was like going into an opium daze,
warm and cold; it could make you shiver both with pleasure and
pain.

Chapter 8

The game of pretence continued; the tempo of life went on undisturbed. The rains were plentiful, the summer, as summers go, was remarkably mild, and there was a bumper harvest. The mother of rivers flowed full to the brim between fields of sugar cane and mustard.

At thirty-two, I had settled into the role of a pensioner—a man with money who had nothing to do—even if a pensioner hounded by scores of lawsuits filed by claimants to a share of the Peshwa's estate. I engaged two lawyers, Jonas Pilchard in Kanpur and David Little in Calcutta, and placed them on a retainer to fend off all suits. For the rest, I studied scriptures and English. I ordered the building of a marble embankment along the river in memory of Bajirao, made numerous additions to my private zoo—and waited for permission to proceed on my pilgrimage. I kept open house for the Europeans in Kanpur and Lucknow. Many people sought invitations to come to Bithoor, others just turned up in small and large parties to spend the day looking over the temples and the bathing ghats and going round my zoo, which they assured me was the best kept in India.

Those who came for week-ends included my physician, Dr. Tessider; the Collector, Mr. Hillersdon; and a Mr. Lang, a lawyer who had come from England to plead a case against the Company and who was to play a most unexpected role in my later life; Mr. Martin, the Deputy Commissioner; and Mr. Potter of Bathgate and Potter. Both Lang and Martin have written about their visits to my house.

My most cherished guests were the Wheelers, who, soon after their arrival, had become intimate friends. Janaki and my Champa were both on the verge of middle age and, after only the minimum of sparring that convention demands, declared themselves sisters and began to behave like elderly aunts, going into conspiracies over the General's and my affairs. They would talk late into the night, munching *chilgozas* and pistachio nuts while the General slumped among the bolsters in his favourite balcony, puffing at his hookah and sipping brandy poured over crushed ice. The son, George, and I played billiards, and it was all arranged that, after his father had retired, George would take over from Tantya Topi as my estate manager. The two girls and their escorts filled the house with noise, singing, playing the piano, or inventing games which involved a lot of scurrying about in dark corridors and occasioning squeals of laughter.

How I longed to participate in those games, how I kept listening to the sounds and building up romantic situations around Eliza and Emily and feeling jealous.

There is a certain kind of woman who, the very first time you see her, bruises your heart in some way. You are held captive not so much by her physical charms as by some magnetic attraction which has no meaning for anyone else. But for you it is there in the way her face puckers when she laughs and in the way her eyes light up and her lips pout; in the way her hair falls over her shoulders and the way she taps her feet to music or preens before a mirror. Whatever she is doing or not doing, you want to go on looking at her, and when she is not around, you want to go on thinking of her.

This is what happened to me when I saw Eliza. But my feelings were so private that I never revealed them to anyone, and I was especially careful to conceal them from Eliza. The Wheelers must have come to Bithoor perhaps a dozen times in all, but not once did I betray my infatuation. Vast mountains and oceans stood between us: religion, race, conventions, prejudices. On the contrary, since I was aware that Lady Wheeler was trying to find suitable husbands for her two daughters, I had told her that she could bring over their friends any time she cared to.

One of these was named Michael Palmer and he claimed to be a grandson of the famous William Palmer of Lucknow, who was popularly known as "King" Palmer. He rode hard, drank and gambled and swore to excess, his manners were abrasive, and his morals execrable. In appearance he was a mismatched blend of the East and the West: a muddy skin, sharp, overemphasized features, sunken eyes in which the pupils were colourless as water, thick blue veins like tapeworms under his skin, and an Adam's apple like a mango seed stuck in his throat.

All this encased in the uniform of an army that had become defunct; gaudy, tight as a bandage, glittering with gold braid and stiff with padding; high blue-velvet collar and yellow facings, narrow overdraws piped with scarlet, silver buttons bearing the insignia of a deposed nawab, long, slender boots shining as though made of glass.

And yet he was not ugly. His oddities forced themselves upon you so that he was someone you could not lightly forget. The kingdom of Oudh had been the natural breeding ground of his type. He had no money and he had lost his job because the Oudh army in which he held a commission had been disbanded. He had come to Kanpur with the idea of starting a riding school, but had brought his ill luck with him too. His stable had caught fire and his three trained horses, all he possessed, burned to death. Already heavily in debt, he had no means of raising the money to buy a horse and make a fresh start in life; without a horse, he was like a man without legs.

And now, as my house guest, he had spent an entire evening playing cards with Mr. Potter. Needless to say, he lost. Bob Potter, to my knowledge, never lost money—in cards or in any other venture.

All this I discovered later. Until then I knew Michael Palmer as just another young man trailing behind the Wheeler girls. Lady Wheeler had brought him over.

There were perhaps a dozen at dinner that night. I sat with them while they ate, and afterwards left them to billiards and cards and their hookahs and brandy to go and dine with my family. I had nearly finished eating when Azim came and told me that the elder

Miss Wheeler desired to see me. When I looked up in surprise, Eliza was standing in the corridor, beckoning urgently.

"I'm sure Michael has gone to shoot himself," she told me when I went out. Her voice was trembly and her face white.

"Michael?"

"The angry-looking boy. . . . He's out in the garden, near the *tulsi* plant. Oh, please hurry!"

I was about to say something flippant when the look in her eyes stopped me. It was a desperate look, a look of split-second urgency, like that of a leopard about to spring. I have seen it in the eyes of wounded animals and of women in love.

I turned and ran, grabbing a flower vase which stood on a table. At the other end of the courtyard, I saw him as a dark shadow against the marble of the tulsi pedestal, and in the shadows I saw a gleam. Then the shadows fell into place and there he was, a man holding a pistol barrel against his temple.

I checked my stride and froze, knowing that the slightest sound I might make would cause him to tighten his finger on the trigger. I held my breath and waited, not knowing what to do. A second passed, and then another. Slowly, I counted ten. Then I raised the flower vase high and recited the gayatri mantra, which takes about five seconds. Then I let the vase go. He whipped round as though jerked by wire.

"I'm sorry I startled you," I apologized.

"Startled!—hey-hey!" he barked as, rather clumsily, he tried to hide his pistol. "Fudge, my dear sir—I say fudge to you!"

I gave him time to compose himself and then went up and placed a hand on his shoulder. "I don't want a dead body on the tulsi pedestal," I said. "It's a family shrine in a brahmin household, the tulsi."

"Body! Fudge, sir! I was merely intending to water your plants."

"I could show you a more suitable place for that too. Instead, will you join me in a glass of wine?"

"Your claret is too good to say no to."

"Perhaps we could have a game of cards," I suggested. "Just a few hands to while away the time before the nautch begins."

"I am sorry," Michael Palmer said with gravity, "but I don't gamble with strangers."

"I accept IOUs dated a year ahead," I said.

I could feel his muscles tighten under my hand, but he relaxed almost at once and allowed me to lead him into the house. And in the balcony adjoining my bedroom we played cards. After half a dozen deals, I suggested doubling the stake, to which, after a little hesitation, he agreed. But the very next hand he picked up he threw the cards on the table and sat staring belligerently at me and sniffing through his pinched nostrils.

"I can read Hindi," he said hoarsely.

I had suspected as much, and said nothing.

"These cards are marked. Hindi figures worked into the designs of the backs."

"So they are. You were the wrong person to have tried them on."

He sat breathing noisily for a time and demanded, "Did Miss Wheeler set you to do this?"

I managed to keep a blank face. "Which Miss Wheeler?" I asked.

"Then why are you going to . . . to all this trouble?"

"Reasons of economy," I explained. "A dead body on the tulsi shrine would have necessitated a purification ceremony. It would have set me down at least a couple of thousand."

"I need three," he said very softly.

"These Benares priests might have charged me even that. Besides, a suicide would have quite ruined the evening. There is a very good dancing girl coming on."

"I never accept charity," he said defiantly and shaking his head. "Never!"

I shook my head too, almost in imitation. "I never give in charity. Indeed I have a reputation for investing wisely."

He laughed, showing yellow, uneven teeth. Before he could withdraw into his shell, I called for a bottle of wine and began to shuffle the cards.

"And will anyone know?" he asked.

"Not unless you tell them."

He picked up the hand and said, "Something seems to be amusing you."

I shook my head. "No."

"Then why do you keep smiling?"

"It's just my card-playing face: to keep you from guessing what I'm thinking."

After that we played in silence, as professionals do, with set expressions. Below the stairs the musicians were tuning their instruments. Two or three people strayed into the balcony and stood watching us, impressed by the high stakes. And in their presence, I lost the sum of three thousand and four hundred rupees to ex-Lieutenant Palmer.

The dancer that evening was a girl from Tellicheri. Her colour was the glistening purple of a *jamun* berry, and she could not speak any language any of us knew. But her feet and hands and eyes spoke, as did her fingers and toes. They told stories of brave men and bold women and demons and gods and made you become involved in them. My guests sat entranced, nodding in appreciation, and even Wheeler, who normally began to snore after the opening *Nandi* or song of invocation, kept awake.

I saw Eliza and Palmer slipping away, one after the other. The tandav, the last dance, was at its most frenzied when they returned, from opposite doors, and then sat without looking at each other.

It was long past midnight. The dance was over and my guests had gone to bed. Before turning in myself, I was standing in the veranda of my room, gazing at the temple lights mirrored in the river and thinking of Palmer's little drama. One thing kept worrying me. How, I kept asking myself, had he been so sure that I would rush to his rescue merely because Eliza had asked me to?

There was a sound behind me and I turned. Eliza emerged from the shadows, her head held stiff as though she were walking in her sleep. She flung her arms around me and held me close. I was aware of the heady odour of her skin and clothes, and her body, pressed hard against mine, fluttered like that of a bird. I felt the moist pressure of her lips against mine, fleetingly, and then, without a word, she was gone, leaving me with the impression that I had imagined it all.

That was how our first kiss came about, as a by-product of the little drama that Michael Palmer had put on to raise some capital. I never told Eliza that he had had no thought of shooting himself.

But, from what happened later, I think I succeeded in conveying to Palmer himself the idea that I knew.

Gambling, drink, a certain slackness of the moral fibre; these are not the attributes of a stayer. And yet I was surprised when, a few weeks later, Dr. Tessider told me that Palmer had fled.

"Disappeared under a heavy cloud," Tessider said mysteriously. "Oh, no one knows where." He did not know much more, or was not prepared to tell.

What cloud? I wondered. It was not money, because as the man who was a partner in most of Kanpur's banks, I would have known if he had left any debts unpaid. Had he then put up some Raja to complain about his Resident's impositions or seduced some very senior official's wife? Very little else constituted "heavy cloud" under the Company's *raaj*. About a week later Azim told me something more about it.

"He was expelled because Mr. Scobie challenged him to a duel."

"Scobie? The Resident Magistrate?"

"He took Mrs. Scobie to Noor's hotel. The R.M. broke open the door of their room and found them."

It was incredible. How could someone so self-righteously proper as Mrs. Scobie, the keeper of Kanpur's conscience, have been so foolish as to allow herself to be taken to so well-known a place of assignations as Noor's hotel? "I don't believe it, do you?" I asked.

"Scobie Sahib has asked for a transfer, and Mrs. Scobie has gone to Calcutta."

So it was the truth. Inwardly I thanked Mrs. Scobie for removing Michael Palmer to some distant place and I hoped I would never set eyes on him again. Whoever the Wheelers now brought to Bithoor, Michael Palmer would not be among them. Perhaps I could now create opportunities to see Eliza by myself, to show her a new clock or an old shawl or the latest fawn or panther cub in my animal park and gaze at the wonderment on her face as I had done before Michael Palmer had turned up.

But I was to meet Micahel Palmer again, riding a jet-black horse and wearing another uniform and a captain's stars.

In October came Diwali, the festival of lights, an occasion for the most elaborate of poojas, for giving thanks to the goddess of wealth for her gifts. I sat amidst the flickering oil lamps and the fragrant smoke of incense and tried to concentrate on the mechanics of the ritual, folding my hands and mumbling words of prayer and adding flowers to the growing pyramid as the priest directed. All the same, every now and then, my eyes strayed.

The idol was buried deep under the offerings; the real goddess sat beside me, primly but not withdrawn, on a wooden board that touched mine. Tradition dictated that a husband and wife must sit side by side for this pooja and that the husband should offer flowers and the wife tulsi leaves in turn. Not once did my wife glance in my direction, but sometimes, when, quite accidentally, our hands, mine with the flower and hers with the leaf, touched, she could not help smiling to herself and her face reddened.

Now, married nearly ten years and still, for all I knew or cared, a virgin, this mousy creature had blossomed into an implausibly beautiful woman. I also knew that, as the result of the course of training Bajirao had laid down and with which I had not interfered, she could talk with authority on any subject that a cultivated person might be interested in and could ride and shoot and play the sitar and sing and, as I knew from personal observation, could make herself look seductive or unapproachable as the occasion demanded. Indeed, I have often thought that this was how Menaka, the seductress that the gods sent down from heaven to make great saints break their vows of celibacy, must have looked and behaved as she went about playing havoc with their saintliness.

On that Diwali day of 1856 I again thought how my wife's sheer physical beauty gave added validity to the family curse; that it was not merely a heavily underlined passage in my horoscope, but a continuing challenge, as though some spiteful godling were trying to test out just how long I could keep myself from making a sacrificial offering of my wife.

The curse I had inherited from Bajirao had acquired a sharp double edge. Here was a problem with no solution that I could provide. What, I kept asking myself, was I ever going to do with this woman who was married to me and yet was separated? If I was saving her from death by not sleeping with her, was I not, by the same token, killing the woman in her? Kashi was made to be a mistress, not a wife—a mistress or, even more fittingly, some professional seductress to arouse and assuage the repressed sex hunger of saints.

"You are the father and mother, knowledge, wealth, . . ." the priest was mumbling. The hands with the flower and the leaf collided. My wife set her teeth and assumed her unapproachable look and her shoulders went rigid. Even a saint's ardour would have shrivelled. I shut my eyes and thought of the way Eliza's mouth curved when she smiled, and the dimples that played on her cheeks when she laughed.

The very last time the Wheelers came was in late November 1856, when the weather should have been cold enough for fires but was oppressively hot because of the low-hung clouds. I cancelled the indoor entertainment I had arranged and took them on a boating picnic.

For me, this week-end had been flawed by the presence of a new young man whom Janaki had brought over, a Lieutenant Delafosse, of the 2nd Cavalry. He was a combination of rude health and courtly manners and high spirits, and he went for Eliza with the unblinking directness of a cock sparrow at mating time. And Eliza, as though Michael had never existed, gave every impression of encouraging his advances. They went off in a small boat and in the evening sang duets at the piano. Throughout that week-end I hardly saw Eliza when Delafosse was not around, and I was desolate because I knew that I was not going to see her for at least two months.

"The field manœuvres start next week," Wheeler had said importantly. "And then come Christmas and New Year. But we'll be here in January. On the ninth, or certainly on the sixteenth—*inshallah*, if Allah wills.''

That Monday evening, after the Wheelers had gone, Delafosse, who had asked to stay an extra day, was still my guest. He had retired immediately after dinner, mumbling something about practising his Hindi because he was studying for an examination.

In the relaxed mood that comes over one after one's house

guests have gone, I was lying on my stomach on a reed mat in the balcony of my bedroom. Champa was gently massaging my limbs. The air hummed with mosquitoes and the Ganges looked a dirty copper colour.

"This new boy," Champa began. "Janaki was pushing Emily at him. It didn't work."

It was only too plain that it hadn't. "He fell for Eliza," I said.

"Drooling and sniffing, trying to entice her into dark corners."

"She too seemed to enjoy it all," I commented dryly.

"A girl Eliza's age needs a man, not a schoolboy."

Over the stab of jealousy, I managed to say, "Poor Delafosse. He's only just come out. Couldn't have seen a woman for months. He's only going for what he can see."

"What do you mean?"

"Who knows what Emily's like underneath, with all that muslin they drape themselves in. Eliza at least wears a sari when she comes here. One can see what one is getting—or not getting. Like fruit under glass."

And after that I must have made some appreciative sound, for Champa asked, "What did you say?"

"Nothing. I was just thinking that Eliza's figure was like yours when I first saw you."

That must have touched some raw nerve. The fingers kneading expertly into my back lost their rhythm for a moment. "And you think they fall for that figure just because . . . just because it is under glass?"

The hum of the mosquitoes, the massaging of the limbs, the cracking of the different joints of the body had made me drowsy with sleep. I had shut my eyes and I was seeing Eliza. "Because they're pinned down," I said. "What they see is like one of those stone carvings from Sarnath—a woman who has never worn clothes. The figure has a thrust."

"Thrust?"

"Um-hun. A kind of buoyancy. Animals have it because their bodies grow without laces or buttons. And the skin—it has the sheen of oiled wood, something you long to run your fingers over."

"But she's so dark," Champa pointed out, and I could detect the note of disapproval.

The woman I was looking at with closed eyes was dark by the standards of northern India, where to be fair is to be beautiful. Her skin was the shade of copper our peasant women acquire by going about near-naked in the sun all their lives. In Eliza, of course, it was the gift of the mixed parentage, like the sapphire-blue eyes. "The white men are not blind," I said. "They too know it is the perfect shade for that figure—like fine rosewood."

"Janaki would be thrilled if she were to marry an Indian," Champa said.

I did not say anything. Champa's tone had told me that this was merely a preliminary gambit. And right enough, she came out with it.

"Why don't you?"

"Why don't I what?"

"Make Eliza your wife?"

"Don't talk nonsense!"

"She's always trying to get you to look at her—wearing saris while she's here, and then turning those cowy eyes at you, as though there were some secret shared."

"There is—was. I was able to help Michael Palmer. That boy with the mad look. Eliza was in love with him."

"Oh, that lizard! How could anyone fall in love with him? Anyway, she can't still be in love with him. He's married to Bellamy's widow."

That made me sit up. "What did you say? Palmer married!"

"To a woman old enough to be his mother, Janaki says. But she came with an indigo plantation."

It was as though, inside my head, knots were being unravelled, some clogged vein that had obstructed thinking had opened. Now what Champa was saying made sense. And then again, where did Delafosse fit in?

"What shall I tell Janaki?" Champa asked.

"Was it her idea or yours?"

"Mine. But when I broached it, Janaki was thrilled."

"And her husband will want to shoot me; it will quite ruin whatever chance he still has of becoming the C.-in-C."

"Oh, Hamlah!" Champa snorted. "Why should anyone worry about the old fool?"

"He happens to be her father, and he'll want her to marry an Englishman. This Delafosse."

"What'll she do with a mere boy?" Champa laughed. "Anyway, she's told her parents she won't marry a white man."

My heart was beating faster. The moon broke through the clouds and the Ganges became a sheet of silver. "But why not?" I asked.

Champa did not know. And yet how simple the explanation was: colour. Eliza was dark and that made her Indian. She thought like us and was governed by the same drives. She was Janaki more than Hamlah and if it had not been for those hallmark eyes that all the Wheeler children had inherited, I would have suspected that her father too was Indian.

"It's not good for you to go on being without a wife," Champa said.

Her words had a sobering effect. "Wife," I said. "I do have a wife—a woman whose good looks hit at you like a laburnum in springtime."

"I mean a wife you can have children by."

"So that she dies, so that I can have another wife, so that—"

"Nothing will happen to that Eliza. She's like her mother: thin, but strong as a she-buffalo."

"A strong curse can kill strong buffaloes."

"What is a curse in their religion? The Issahies don't believe in our superstitions."

"They have their own. You should see them squirming if they happen to see the new moon through glass. And didn't you know that old Hamlah, every time he's here, secretly visits Dassaba, wanting to know what the future holds in store for him?"

"Hamlah is like a monkey stung by a scorpion—mad, because they won't make him the Jangi Laat."

A breeze started and dispersed the mosquitoes. I filled my lungs with the warm air and waited for Champa to come back to the main theme.

"What shall I tell Janaki?" she asked.

I had been thinking out my answer. "Nothing just yet. I'd like to talk to Eliza first."

"Whatever for?"

"I want to tell her about the curse."

"No curse is going to scare that one away."

"Maybe not. But this is something I want to go right. I don't want to take chances—build anything on deception. I want Eliza to . . . to do whatever she wants, with open eyes."

Champa gave a rude laugh and made a rude sound. "When a cow starts shifting her tail to one side, it is the time to send for the stud bull—not for talking," she quoted a farmyard proverb.

"Oh, stop that cattleshed bawdiness!" I snapped.

"The girl is just dying to jump into your bed. You should pull her in. What's the use of just going on drooling?"

"What do you mean 'drooling'?" I asked angrily.

"It was quite disgusting, the way you went on about her figure. Describing it limb by limb, as though . . . as though you were taking her clothes off, garment by garment. . . ."

And that sparked one of those sudden quarrels during which we both said things intended to hurt and which ended only when I got up in a huff and darted into my bedroom. I had changed and got into bed when I heard the purposeful tinkle of Champa's bangles. She was standing in the open doorway, a finger to her lips, the other hand beckoning me to follow her. I turned to one side in an effort to ignore her, but she came and leaned over me and pulled me out of bed. It was not what I thought she had in mind.

"There's something you must see," she whispered. "Quick!"

At the end of the corridor leading from the Indian-style drawing-room, beyond the main guest suites just vacated by the Wheeler family, were the two bachelor rooms with tiny overhanging balconies where, in the hot weather, my guests usually preferred to sleep on rope cots. One of these rooms was still occupied by Delafosse. Champa led me up the stairs and to the terrace at the top of the house from where you could look down on both these guestroom balconies.

Delafosse and Azijan were lying on a carpet spread on the floor of the minute, bed-sized balcony. They were naked, cuddled so tightly together that they looked like a single, two-coloured animal with many limbs aborted by some undersea monster and washed up by the tide. Apparently they were both fast asleep. Even in the moonlight, their separate colouring stood out: the boy, long and skinny and white; the woman, soft and voluptuously curved and dark. Her leg and head and arms were thrown protectively across his body; spent, innocent, passionless.

Guiltily we crept back, and, in my room, sitting on the bed and still holding Champa's hand, I suddenly began to laugh. So Delafosse had not been bowled over by Eliza or anything like that. All he wanted was a woman.

"Practising Hindi!" Champa hissed.

"The best way to learn a language," I said, still laughing. "While you're making love."

"She's been here too long, the bitch! Ten years! You should have kicked her out long ago."

Ten years. Was it really ten years since Azijan had crept into my bed that night of the new moon?—crept in like a black panther seeking a mate.

"Shameless bitch! She just can't leave a man alone. Dung beetle!"

It was painful to see how someone normally so incapable of viciousness as Champa could nurse a grievance for ten years.

"She must be driven out, now. Dragged from her embrace and disgraced and driven out!"

I did not say anything.

"And you have to get someone else. I already have a girl in mind. A half-white—"

"Oh, can't you shut up about that!"

Champa reacted as though I had slapped her. In a hurt voice, she explained, "I don't mean your Eliza. There is another, in Lucknow. One of the King's girls."

"But whatever are we going to do with poor Azijan?"

"Poor, hunh! Have her flogged, naturally!"

"No," I said firmly. "We'll find some groom to marry her."

Champa gave me an angry look. But we had already had our quarrel for the day and we did not start another.

But Azijan, when confronted the next morning, spurned the idea of marrying. If only I could give her some capital, she told me, she would like to open a dancing school in Kanpur. "I have in mind a house behind the Golaghat bazaar," she said.

"Is Delafosse going to keep you as his bibi?" I asked.

"How can I be any one man's bibi now—after being with Malik for all of ten years?"

Not sure I was being complimented, I said with sarcasm, "It will be conveniently close to the cavalry lines, won't it, this dancing school?"

"Soldiers make the best patrons of dancing schools," Azijan said evenly. "Particularly cavalry soldiers."

A woman who has been your mistress for ten years has special claims. So, all unknown to Champa, I gave Azijan ten thousand rupees as a parting gift. It would prove to have been a good investment.

And so the wonderful year passed, scarcely leaving a ripple on the surface. Yet, there was already such turmoil underneath that everyone was aware of it. The signs were unmistakable. The Wheelers and the other white families suddenly stopped coming to Bithoor. And whatever I had been meaning to say to Eliza went unsaid.

I must now mention a small incident that took place right at the end of the year, though; something which, though trivial in itself, was to change the course of my life.

Jayaji Scindia, the Maharaja of Gwalior, had visited Calcutta to pay his respects to the new Governor-General, Canning. He had studiously avoided passing close to Bithoor on the way out. On the return trip, however, he paid me a visit, which meant that he had obtained the Governor-General's permission to see me.

The first Scindia had been a slipper-bearer in the service of my great-grandfather, the first Bajirao, and the meteoric rise of the Scindia family had been almost wholly due to Bajirao's support and benevolence. During the last hundred years, Bajirao's descendants had lost everything they had, but the Scindias, even though they had been deprived of their independence, were still as influential and wealthy as ever. They ruled a vast territory and still maintained a sizeable army.

I did not trust the Scindia—few of us did. He was far too friendly with the British, who were constantly heaping new honours on him and had recently taken to addressing him as their "ever-trusted ally." The fact that he had been allowed to come and see me at all made him doubly suspect, for the British were very strict about not letting ex-Indian rulers get together. Who knew? He might even be acting as their agent.

So I refrained from asking him what must have been uppermost in both our minds, and he for his part gave no indication that he was on to anything. As far as Jayaji Scindia was concerned, the coming year, the month of June in that year, and the twenty-third day of that month, might have had no special meaning.

And yet, on the last day of his visit, I think he gave me an unmistakable hint as to how he would act in the coming conflict.

He had brought me a *sasanpatta*, which is a sword of a special design that is traditionally presented by a military commander to his monarch. In return, I gave him the robes of the commander-in-chief that custom prescribed. We treated each other to sickeningly elaborate banquets and to all-night nautch performances. We sat on the same mattress and offered betel nut to each other and gazed reverently at the Ganges and made desultory conversation. It was on the last evening of his visit, just as I had dismissed the hookah *burdar* signifying that we were about to retire, that the Scindia asked me if there was any service he could do for me.

I laughed, and I could not resist the temptation of having a dig at him. "Your Highness should have asked Lord Canning what service you might perform; he is your master."

"You too are my master."

"A master who is emasculated—a master who can demand no service."

"He might ask. I speak in the hearing of Mother Ganges. There is such a thing as tradition—bonds of loyalty."

"The new masters are no respecters of old bonds. Tell me, did you not actually have to obtain Canning's permission to pay me a visit—me, whom you call your master?"

"Yes, and it took a great deal of persuasion."

"There you are. Lord Canning is your master. Not I."

He was polite enough not to remind me that Canning was my master too, but in my bitterness I gave him no credit for his courtesy. I laughed again and said, "You cannot serve two masters. You will never bring yourself to do what the British might disapprove."

That was the nearest I came to asking him which side he would be on.

He drew on his hookah pipe for a long time before answering, as though he was weighing his words. Then he as good as told me which side he would be on.

"No one can like these men; no one wants them. Yet we must never forget that they are both powerful and vigilant. We who are tucked away in the remoter parts have no idea of their power, their resources. In Calcutta I was shown a carriage as big as a house running faster than a horse—and it ran on boiling water . . . and mills that weave cloth: cotton goes in at one end and cloth comes out at the other—folded. They have factories where a single machine does the work of a hundred men. It was incredible—it was also frightening."

"And arsenals?" I suggested. "Surely you were taken round the arsenals too, as their most trusted ally?"

"Yes, arsenals, filled to the roofs with ammunition, for soldiers who are ready for battle, night or day. . . ."

"Indian soldiers."

"But haven't they won all their battles with Indian sepoys? No, no, it would be quite suicidal to cross them openly. That I shall never do—that I would urge my friends not to do," and he stared at me over the stem of his hookah pipe before going on. "No one who opposes the British openly can survive. And yet, they're gullible too. They can never fathom our minds. I don't find it difficult to keep them happy and still get my way."

So that was what he was going to do. He would not oppose the British, and yet he would not give them much help; and he would give us all the help he could without appearing to do so.

I remember that night as though it were yesterday. Jayaji and I sat on the same mattress in the balcony overlooking the Ganges, and I had a feeling that we were both acutely aware that the river bore witness to our thoughts and words. I had been sorely disappointed that this powerful and influential Prince had been so visibly awestruck by the showpieces of British power, and yet I must have been impressed by his worldliness too. Whoever won or lost, the Scindia would never lose. How else can I account for what I then said to him on the spur of the moment?

"Yes, perhaps there is something you can do."

He was suddenly alert. "Anything, anything at all."

"I want you to keep something for me."

"Certainly," and he bowed his head slightly.

"An elephant-load of gold."

He took a deep puff of smoke and exhaled. "What does the master want done with it?"

"Nothing. Just keep it for me, with yours, in case something goes wrong."

He nodded several times and said, "You are very wise. But then I have always admired your farsightedness in these matters— money matters."

"And I yours in 'all matters. You won't tell the British, will you?"

He frowned and gave me a look to tell me that my question had been in bad taste. "I brought out two hundred elephants," he said. "Who is to know that I go back with two hundred and one?"

So I sent off one of my elephants with the Scindia, loaded with some of Bajirao's heavier gold pieces, to be tucked away in the Scindia's vaults.

Chapter 9

The Christian New Year brought the first whiff of trouble, and after that the days were full of omens.

The Company had introduced a new rifle and a new cartridge. The cartridges, made of paper, were smothered with grease, and to break them open before loading they had to be bitten.

In the barracks at Dum Dum someone told someone else that the grease was made from the fat of pigs and cows. And suddenly a wave of panic and indignation shook the land.

"*Toba!* This is treachery!" Azim pronounced.

"The cartridges are an instrument of conversion," Tantya said to me with complete conviction. "The hat men, having conquered the country, are now making the people Christians. Soon we'll all be Issahies!"

To a Hindu, the cow is a sacred animal, the mother of the universe; to a Muslim, a pig is the filthiest of God's creatures. A Hindu would rather starve to death than eat beef and, similarly, a Muslim would rather die than touch pork. A Muslim who tasted pork would never attain heaven; a Hindu who tasted beef would instantly lose caste, a fate worse than death. And now both the Hindus and the Muslims in the Company's army were being compelled to put into their mouths cartridges dripping with the fat of cows and pigs.

The sepoys were self-professed mercenaries; for a pittance, they served an alien master's army. They would just as readily have served other foreigners such as the Chinese or Africans. Soldiering to them was no more than a means of earning a livelihood. They worked only for "bread and salt," as they were wont to explain; and in exchange for a specific quantity of bread and salt, they gave back a specific quantity of loyalty. And that was the entire basis of their allegiance.

And now the white man had come out with this cunning device to force them to accept Christianity, so that they would no longer be working for pay alone but would be bound irrecoverably to their masters. They protested, courteously and hesitantly.

"Gross insubordination!" their officers thundered. The protesting sepoys were paraded and "broken" and sent to jail for life so that their comrades should be terrorized into obedience. The cartridges, the orders went, must be accepted.

To be sure, the British had run into our religious taboos several times before, and, while on those occasions too they had been just as severe with those who had dared to offer protest, they had later quietly withdrawn the offending orders. Now, having made themselves undisputed masters, they were no longer prepared to make concessions.

Fifty-one years earlier, George Barlow had introduced equally misguided reforms concerning uniforms. Turbans were to have leather cockades, caste marks were banned and so were beards. To a Hindu, the mark on his forehead is a badge of distinction, something to be proud of, and to a Muslim a beard is the very hallmark of masculinity. And as to the cockades, who could say what leather they were made of? It might be cowhide or pigskin. Then too the sepoys had offered the mildest of protests. The British answer had been to muster the men on parade and mow them down to a man. All the same, the orders regarding the reforms were rescinded.

The sepoys were recruited in India for service in India. The terms of their engagement never visualized that they would be made to march with the Company's flag to distant parts of the world. All the same, in 1824, when the Company decided to invade Burma, they were ordered there. The sepoys of the 47th Regiment thereupon represented that the act of crossing the sea would make them lose caste and instead offered to go to Burma overland. They too were paraded and their "ringleaders" shot and the others given deterrent prison sentences. But in 1852, when

Dalhousie declared *his* war against Burma, no sepoy was made to cross the sea against his will; their prejudices were respected.

But not this time. This time they were determined to force the issue. The Dharma Sabha of Calcutta, vigilant as ever to guard the sanctity of the Hindu religion, was equally obdurate. It sent around a circular to all Hindu religious organizations to declare as an outcaste any sepoy who had used the new cartridge.

"At last the Sabha has woken up," Tantya pronounced, "after being quite deaf and dumb in the past. There are thousands of missionaries roaming the land, all of them paid by the Company to preach Christianity. We Hindus practise our religion in our homes and temples, and the Muslims in their mosques. But the missionaries stand on platforms in market squares and denounce our creeds in the most violent and abusive terms. . . ."

"Ye shall roast in hell," Azim intoned in quaint missionary Hindi and in a parody of some missionary's voice, "if you make stones into your gods and naked scoundrels into your holy men!"

"And everywhere the missionaries are setting up schools."

"But that's to teach people English," I pointed out. "So that they may have a plentiful supply of petty officials who know English."

Azim differed. "In all these schools, the study of the Bible is compulsory. And every morning the little children are confronted with the question—every morning they're asked, 'Who is your God? Who is your redeemer?' Yes, every morning. They see the offers of employment and the packets of sweets that come with the copies of the Testament. They see the other children giving the right answers. Before long, they too learn to give the right answers."

"Thousands are being converted—thousands! It's quite frightening!"

"Not thousands, surely?" I questioned.

"Malik, whenever there's a famine, the starving orphans are herded together and given food.. They're also invariably made Christians."

"That they are given food is the important thing," I said. "Surely, you wouldn't rather they were left to die than made Christians?"

Both my advisers gave me stony looks, signifying that that was just what they would have preferred.

It must have been within a week of this conversation that General Wheeler dropped in, "after a long day with hounds," as he explained. He was flushed and winded and his moustache red with dust. The hounds had killed closer to Bithoor than Kanpur, so he had decided to spend the night in my house. "All I need is a bath and a drink," he concluded.

The somewhat elaborate explanation made me think that what he wanted was more than a bath and a drink. And right enough, later in the evening, he came out and asked me if I had heard the rumor from Dum Dum.

He lay sprawled on a mattress, wearing a pair of pyjamas and a kurta which I had lent him, and he was drinking brandy and smoking a hookah. He looked more like an opium-eating nawab than a British general unwinding after a workout.

"Everyone is talking about it," I told him. "They say that the sepoy is being forced to lose his caste."

"*Bukhwaz!*" he pronounced. "Rubbish! Why *should* anyone want to do that?"

"So that they should all become Christians."

"You don't believe it yourself, do you?"

"Well, no."

"There!" Wheeler gave a snort. The tufts of hair jutting out of his nostrils quivered. "No one wants Jack Sepoy to lose his caste. But how in Allah's name is he to be made to understand that, tell me? The fact is they don't trust our new breed of sahibs. It'd never have happened in the Duke's time, or Bentinck's. But what sepoy will venerate this shit? Dammit, sir, I don't myself."

"You feel the sepoys have no confidence in their officers?"

"They've nothing in common any more—they live in different worlds!" Wheeler said, and I remember his face had become flushed with anger. "They mistrust each other. It could take a small thing to change mistrust into hatred. The cartridges might do it."

"Are they really offensive?" I asked.

Wheeler expelled a puff of smoke. "Obnoxious! Disgusting! Smothered in rancid fat."

"Cows' and pigs' fat?"

He gave me a belligerent stare. "The Commissariat department buys tallow by the ton. I defy anyone to tell what part is cows' fat and what part pigs'. It's all mixed—and it's all filthy!" He drained his glass and added, "Damned if I'm going to issue them in my command."

"You won't?"

"Many of us have written to George Anson that the cartridges should be withdrawn, or at least the loading drill changed—break the things with fingers instead of teeth. As for me, I'd rather resign than compel my sepoys to bite them."

"What about your officers?"

The answer was a loud snort. The General closed his eyes and began to smoke.

It was good to know that at least in his command the sepoys would not be ordered to accept the cartridges, or be blown up from the muzzles of guns if they refused. In this, at least, old Hamlah was, if anything, more on the side of the sepoys than of the new crop of officers. He had nothing but disdain for the racial insolence of the majority of the Company's servants. "The trouble is," he went on, "the trouble is they haven't fought together. What do they know of Jack Sepoy—what he's done for them?"

For my part, I had nothing but contempt for what Jack Sepoy had done for his masters. It was Jack Sepoy who had defeated the Peshwa and the Scindia and Tippu and Holcar and nailed the Company's flag to the four corners of India. But I did not say anything.

"Contact between officer and man is confined to the parade ground," Wheeler went on, "because women from England have started arriving in droves and the officers have given up their bibis and harems—everyone knows what invaluable service the harems did. The bibis were the link between sahib and sepoy." He drank some brandy and wiped his moustache with the back of his hand. His eyes closed and the hookah pipe slipped out of his hand. After a while, without opening his eyes, he said, "You still haven't told me a thing."

"What do you think I can tell you that you don't already know?" I asked. "You have spies everywhere."

"I want to know about the sepoy's side, about his loyalty to his salt."

For a moment I hesitated, and then decided to answer his question truthfully. He must have known all about it in any case, and was merely seeking corroboration. "A sepoy's loyalty to his salt is to be measured exactly against the quantity of salt. No more, no less."

"Hunh!" Hamlah snorted.

"They're saying that the Company cannot expect from them more than a twelfth part of the loyalty it commands from its British soldiers."

"What's that again?" Wheeler was leaning forward, twitching his eyebrows.

"The Company has three hundred thousand sepoys, but only about forty thousand white troops. And yet it spends twice as much on the white soldiers—one white soldier costs you as much as a dozen black ones. That's the proportion of loyalty you can expect."

"Damme, sir, Jack Sepoy never did measure his loyalty in terms of rupees!" Wheeler snapped. His whiskers quivered with indignation.

"He does now."

The General expelled his breath in angry snorts. "And at that he's far better off than he ever was," he taunted. "The Indian Rajas never even paid him a regular wage."

I was stung by his taunt and could not let it pass. "When you are dealing with mercenaries, you learn to think only in terms of rupees," I said, and realized that my voice had gone trembly. "Jack Sepoy may not have received regular pay in our employ, but we gave him *jagirs,* land grants. And there was no limit to how high he could rise—to commands of battalions or even armies. Now the best of your sepoys, someone who may be as good a commander as Bajirao or Hyder, can never rise above a *subedar,* a sergeant. That's your highest-paid Indian—the ablest and the bravest veteran must serve under a baby-faced white boy with milk teeth—"

"They should never have abolished jagirs," Wheeler growled.

"The Company has consigned all Indians to a life of serfdom," I went on. "Just as no sepoy can rise above a sergeant, a civilian cannot rise above your newest 'griffin.' Only forty years ago, their fathers were ministers and governors—they themselves can never rise above clerks."

I stopped, realizing that Wheeler had made me say things which I had trained myself never to say in the presence of a white man, but then it was difficult to think of old Hamlah as anything but Indian. He poured the last of the brandy from the bottle into his glass and blew on the hookah bowl with great concentration till he got it glowing.

"Take care or you'll singe your moustache," I said.

He pulled his head back. "Is there anything else you think I should know?" he asked.

"You knew it all; and for my part I have already said more than I should."

"I was hoping you'd tell me something about June twenty-third. No one does."

And suddenly my heart was beating faster. I had to take a deep breath to control my agitation. "Twenty-third of June?" I said. "What happens on the twenty-third of June?"

"That's what I'd like to know. And remember you are speaking in the hearing of Mother Ganges."

I laughed, almost in relief. How many lies had I not told in the hearing of *Ganga-mayi*, Mother Ganges; I, a fourth-degree brahmin who had studied all the Vedas had long ago ceased to consider myself on oath just because the mother of rivers bore witness to what I was saying. I would have told a thousand lies rather than reveal to a British general what the twenty-third of June 1857 meant to us.

"It's the anniversary of Plassey," Wheeler prompted, "the hundredth anniversary."

Who did not know that? In our minds, the date was emblazoned in scarlet letters that stood higher than the Himalayas. Plassey!

The period of mourning was to last for a hundred years. We knew it in our bones; we had been told about it in the dying pronouncements of *satis*, widows who cremated themselves on their husbands' funeral pyres, and in the prophesies of our saints. When the hundred years had elapsed, the Company's rule would end. The Devil's Wind would rise and unshackle Mother India.

Many of us who did not believe in miracles or prophesies knew that the Devil's Wind would not be a gentle breeze but a great tornado. And there were a few like myself who shrank from the convulsion that confronted us, fearing that all our sacrifices might be in vain.

"Plassey?" I shrugged and yawned. "You British have such long memories. Indians don't think of hundredth anniversaries. Only of annual feasts. The average Indian wouldn't even know where Plassey is."

General Wheeler closed one eye completely and then opened it and closed the other, and gave a loud belch.

"Would you like another glass of brandy?" I asked.

"I see my good friend Azim has kept a bottle by my bedside," he answered. Then, aiming with his hand, he said, "Look at the river! Ganga-mayi. At this time of the year so placid that a bird may walk on it. At such moments it is so easy to think of the river as a person, someone holy, full of dignity—peace; the wife of Lord Shiva sleeping so trustingly, oblivious to the sins of her children."

He knew a lot about our religion, old Hamlah, and I had a feeling he was again trying to put me on oath. So I said good night and left him to his brandy. In the morning, before I had awakened, Wheeler had gone.

Azim told me that after I had retired Wheeler had put on a robe and gone to see Dassaba, my astrologer. I naturally assumed that what Wheeler wanted to ask Dassaba had something to do with the anniversary of Plassey. But I was wrong. It seemed he was far more concerned about his promotion. The question had acquired urgency because it was reported that General Anson had again taken to his bed.

Chapter 10

In March my permission to travel came through. Mr. Hillersdon, the Collector of Kanpur, sent it on with a little note in his own writing to say that he wished me success, meaning that he hoped I would succeed in getting a son.

I had a feeling it was already too late. The time for a leisurely ramble through the country, sounding out the Maratha princes, had already gone. The rumour that the British were plotting a mass conversion of the army through the new cartridges had spread with the speed of a monsoon breeze. Everything had come into the open too soon. The British had been alerted and were nervously watching, sniffing the air. A visit to the princes was out of the ques ion.

And right enough, a messenger came from the Queen to tell me not to go off on a long journey that might find me stranded and away from my post when the storm broke. The Mad Mullah felt that we might all be called upon to assume our respective roles in the revolt much sooner than we had bargained for. Instead, I was to proceed to Lucknow, barely forty miles away, and see how things were shaping up there.

So to Lucknow I went, feeling a little as though I were proceeding on some adventurous journey. In all my thirty-three years, it was my first beyond Kanpur, twelve miles from my home.

Lucknow. Barely a year earlier it had been the capital of a court renowned for its flamboyance and profligacy, for its barbaric riches and corruption and debauchery, for its musicians and dancing girls and artisans and painters, for the beauty of its women and the ele-

gance of its men. Now it was merely a property of foreign merchants, a city without a soul. The King had been bundled off to
Calcutta and his court dismissed. Left in Lucknow were Queen
Hazrat Mahal and a large number of elderly ladies from the royal
family, including no less than a dozen former queens, the wives of
Wajid Ali's predecessors. They lived by selling their jewellery to
sharp-nosed Armenians so that they could buy their daily needs
because their sumptuary allowances had been stopped. There were
also the ex-courtiers, buzzing about like bees around a smoked-out
hive, administrators removed from their jobs and noblemen driven
out of their estates.

Hazrat Mahal, the Queen of Oudh, was a girl from Fyzabad,
and a protégée of the Mullah. It was widely believed she had risen
to be the favourite queen solely by virtue of the Mullah's blessings
or machinations. And I was now the bearer of a personal message
to her from the Mullah telling her that her place was in Lucknow,
not at the side of her deposed husband.

So we had these two queens backing the revolt, Zeenat of Delhi
and Hazrat of Oudh, and both were guided by the Mullah. In the
event, the Queen of Delhi never left the Red Fort; the other,
Hazrat, took an active part in the fighting.

In Lucknow there were no visible scars, for the kingdom had
been taken over without a declaration of hostilities, "annexed" as
Dalhousie termed such unresisted takeovers. All the same, Lucknow was a raw, quivering wound. Everyone I spoke to, from the
Queen down to the man who swept my rooms, was bristling with
grievances. They felt cheated, abased, humiliated. The white merchants had not only taken over their kingdom but had destroyed a
way of life by methodically breaking down its framework. The
ministers and the heads of departments were replaced by the Company's writers and factors, and the Talukdars who owned vast estates were made subordinate to young British career servants, their
castles razed and their estate guards disbanded and driven out.

There were incidents every day. A white soldier beat up the ex-
curator of the museum for neglecting to fold his umbrella while
passing him in the street, and a subaltern horsewhipped a banker
for demanding the repayment of a loan. Soldiers strutted like na-
wabs, itching for a fight, and their womenfolk rode in gaudy

carriages which had so recently belonged to the King, demanding that the streets be cleared before them. The King's elephants had been sold for their ivory and the deer in the park for their meat, and the tigers and bears in his zoo shot down for their pelts.

And they still talked in angry whispers about the forcible taking over of the palace of the dowager queens by the Chief Commissioner, Coverley Jackson. He had had the women dragged out because he wanted the palace for his own residence.

"A year ago Jackson would not have been permitted an audience with the Queen Mother," Sharfuddin, the ex-Chief Justice, wailed. "Now he throws her out of her house."

Dalhousie may have approved; his successor, Canning, was shocked. Jackson was hastily recalled and the palace given back to the ex-queens.

Then there was the affair of the *Kadam Rossool*, or the Prophet's Footmark. The shrine, immensely holy to Muslims all over the world, was commandeered by the new rulers and converted into a military storehouse, a place to keep boots and saddlery and boxes of ammunition.

"How would they like it if some foreign merchants were to convert their St. Paul's Cathedral into a tannery?" Sharfuddin asked in shocked tones.

Having deported the King and taken over all he possessed, the Company had disclaimed all responsibility for the maintenance of the King's dependents.

"The royal princes, my husband's cousins and uncles—they're actually starving," Hazrat Mahal told me with a dramatic catch in her voice. "I hear their children howling like raving jackals. There!"

The Mullah's letter had opened all doors, and the Queen received me as a member of her family, without her *burqua,* or veil.

Hazrat Mahal was a creature bred and shaped for dalliance; perfumed, voluptuous, coquettish, her lips seductively sucking an imaginary grape, and the quick, signalling eyes and the dancing eyebrows of a courtesan lining up customers. She was, when I first saw her, like some juicy hothouse fruit which should have been eaten yesterday. Her skin had the pale gold pallor that can be acquired only in a harem, where the light of the sun never penetrates; and under that skin, it was difficult to imagine some sort of a bone structure—only layers of the softest down.

And yet, before I left Lucknow, I discovered that, under all that droopy, sun-starved languor, under the outer covering of helpless femininity, was a core of hard flint, harbouring a burning fanaticism planted by the Mullah. Despite a natural aversion to her type of cellar-grown beauty, I was altogether won over. Here was a woman who would be cool in a crisis, who would not be swayed from her objective, no matter what happened.

Lucknow to me was a revelation. It was like looking at a woman raped. Admittedly, what had happened to Lucknow had happened to other places, to Allahabad and Delhi and to my ancestral Poona. But I had not seen those cities and, in any case, there it had happened long ago and the scars had been covered over with new tissue. Here I was witnessing the process of a British takeover in the raw, the deliberate and methodical tearing down of what had taken centuries to grow, and replacing it with something that had been concocted by alien minds to conform to some mercantile dream and dictated by utility. Everything that was familiar, the good and the bad, the cherished, despised, sheltered, nursed, honoured, and venerated, was dug out and left to die; old arts, crafts, old customs, an entire social structure had been hacked down. The crudest of unlettered British tradesmen were elevated above the grandees and intellectuals of Lucknow. It was not the spectacle of one rule being replaced by another so much as the uprooting of a civilization.

"Their greed is insatiable—frightening," Hazrat said in a charged whisper. "They've confiscated everything: palaces, parks, menageries, museums, rareties—they threw on the streets the entire book collection, two hundred thousand volumes!"

It was all very sad. And yet in a way it was gratifying. Here conditions were just right for our purpose, better than in any other part of India I could think of. Here the resentment had not had time to cool off. Here, above all, the leadership was in the capable hands of the ex-Queen.

The Chief Commissioner who had replaced Coverley Jackson, Sir Henry Lawrence, had assumed his office only a few weeks earlier. I had heard many favourable reports of Sir Henry and sent a messenger to him expressing my desire to see him. But I was told that the Chief Commissioner was too busy to see me, which of course I did not believe, for I could see him every day going for leisurely rides in the city's parks, and he even presented a cup at the race meeting which I attended. Azim was told by his British friends that I had caused affront to the Chief Commissioner by the size of my retinue and the flamboyance of my equipage and, even more so, by the enthusiasm with which I was received wherever I went.

The size of my entourage was not really large; including mahouts, light-bearers, grooms, bandsmen, palanquin *bhois,* personal servants, and escort, they could not have exceeded two hundred. I had, I think, no more than a dozen elephants and perhaps fifty horses. The previous year the Scindia, on his visit to Calcutta, had taken with him at least two thousand men along with his two hundred elephants, and no one had objected to the size of *his* retinue. It was just that, a few weeks before my arrival, when Sir Henry Lawrence had made what was scheduled to be his grand official entry into the capital, Lucknow had received him with empty streets and shuttered windows. Even the beggars of Lucknow, who can never be kept away from even a funeral because they hope that someone will throw them a handful of coins, had vanished.

That was what had made him angry. For me, the streets were crowded, and often the people would beat drums to clear the way and throw flowers in my path.

In place of my courtesy call on Sir Henry, I went to see the Financial Commissioner, Martin Gubbins. Gubbins was a small, jackal-faced man with shifty eyes and a nose that might have been pressed thin in the pages of an account ledger; and his habit of turning his head this side and that brought to mind a lizard eyeing two flies on opposite walls. In Gubbins I detected the first signs of jitters among the British. All the time I was in his office he behaved as though I might get up and do a Maratha war dance on his table. And he never met my eyes.

I was too intent on observing the way Gubbins' head swivelled from one side to another with a thin, audible snap, to have registered any positive impression of his feelings towards me. Later I learned that he had disliked me and distrusted me and found me "arrogant and presuming." He himself was such a weedy, colourless man that it would have been almost impossible for anyone not to feel inwardly superior to him. For my part, I felt that I had got over a chore that was distasteful to both. If I had not gone through the motions of a formal call on the local head of the Company's administration, I would have been instantly singled out as someone "arrogant and presuming."

I had to cut short my visit to Lucknow. While I was there someone hurled a clod of earth at Sir Henry Lawrence as he was riding past the palace. The world of the merchants was abuzz, planning instant retribution. That the city had received them with a sad, mourning face was perfectly understandable to them; that someone among the thousands of Wajid Ali's subjects should have had the gumption to make some kind of a positive gesture to express his resentment was an unforgivable act, deserving of swift and exemplary punishment. They talked of seizing hostages and of imposing collective fines.

That same evening I received a curt note from Commissioner Gubbins that it would be advisable for me to return to Bithoor without delay.

Bad news awaited me in Bithoor: I was told that the Mullah of Fyzabad had been arrested.

"Have they put him to death?" I asked.

"They have passed sentence of death."

Daily we awaited news of his death so that prayers could be offered for his soul. In a few days we learned that he had been arrested while on a visit to Fyzabad, which was his home town. Here it was almost natural for him that, upon entering the jail where he was to be kept before being executed, he should demand hookah and rose-water. The chief jailer and the wardens rushed round to comply and treated him as their honoured guest. They also went on putting off the date of his execution on one pretext or another till they could arrange for him to escape.

Two months later the Mullah appeared again and instantly became a far more effective instrument of ferment than he had been before, for now he was believed to be endowed with truly magical powers. For him the walls of British jails collapsed and bars melted and doors opened, and indeed he was virtually indestructible, for had he not survived a sentence of hanging? He began to style himself "The Khalifa," or the Prophet's heir, and commanded his listeners in the name of Allah to "kill the firanghis as though they were cobras and mad dogs—to exterminate their race." Whereas before he had only ranted at them and called them names, now he was the voice of God.

Did it ever happen? Can there be such a summer as the Indian summer, with the heat so intense that you have to drape a wet sheet over your head to be able to breathe freely, and your hands and legs smart with the particles of hot sand whipped against them by the loo—the loo, our dreaded summer wind.

It was the month of May and it was very hot; the loo singed the young leaves on the trees and birds opened their beaks wide in voiceless cries and suddenly dropped into the dust and lay still and dogs scurried about with lowered heads and bared fangs.

Imagine such a time as the high point of our summer season, then, and assess its effect on the brains of those who were forbidden even a drop of water to wet their lips with, for this was the month of Ramzan, when Muslims are permitted to eat or drink only during the brief interlude of darkness. The peculiarities of the lunar calendar had brought the Ramzan and the loo together, and the rulers had added to this brew the new cartridge.

The rulers, for their part, comported themselves with elephantine indifference, seemingly unaffected by the pressures building up around them. Pork and beef, fasting, caste prejudices—these were merely the aberrations of a primitive race and not to be taken seriously. The summer itself could not be dismissed so lightly, though; but, at that, if your water-carriers were well trained and kept the shutters of fragrant *khas* grass on your doors and windows constantly wet, the heat was not unbearable. Their day began before dawn, but ended at nine a.m., when they went indoors and sealed themselves in. They would emerge only in the late afternoon, dressed for clubs and messes. Normal social life was not disrupted. It had made inroads into the warm, scented nights and become more romantic, more permissive. Work on parade or in offices was something to be got over quickly, before the sun rose high, and the rest of the long day spent indoors, reading novels, playing cards, or just resting. The evenings were for music and dancing and flirting, for love and laughter under the falling stars. Everyone said it was such a pity that the delightful riverside balls at Bithoor, which had been such a feature of Kanpur summers, had to be given up because of some absurd rumour from Dum Dum, for, as I have already related, since the beginning of the year, Bithoor had ceased to figure in the social life of Kanpur.

And in the midst of this dancing and novel reading, laughter and flirting women, had come a telegram tapped out by some petrified clerk in Delhi:

> THE SEPOYS HAVE COME FROM MEERUT
> AND ARE BURNING EVERYTHING
> WE HEAR SEVERAL EUROPEANS DEAD WE MUST SHUT UP

This telegram was received in Kanpur on May 14. The revolt had begun four days earlier, in Meerut, some two hundred miles to the northwest.

The sepoys of the 3rd Native Cavalry had begun it. God knows they had had enough provocation. It was almost as though their officers were putting them through some test to find out how far they could go on bending human material before it would snap.

Meerut had about five thousand troops, the bulk of them Indian. The British elements consisted of one battalion, the 60th Rifles, and a battery of artillery; the Indian, two infantry battalions and the cavalry regiment. The weapons of the entire garrison were normally kept in a central armoury, which meant that, except while they were on duty, none of the troops, British or Indian, were armed.

On April 23, Carmichael Smyth, the Colonel of the cavalry, ordered a parade to demonstrate the new drill by which the cartridges could be loaded without biting. He detailed ninety of his best men to carry out this demonstration. At the actual parade, however, all but five of these men, firmly but most respectfully, declined to handle the new cartridge on the plea that its mere touch would defile them.

This, Carmichael Smyth pronounced, was mutinous conduct and

ordered the offenders to be tried by court martial. The court sat for a week and found all eighty-five guilty as charged and dealt out uniform sentences of ten years' "rigorous imprisonment." Then the mechanics of military justice required that, before they were sent off to the jail, these sepoys must be ceremonially broken. A garrison parade was ordered and the public invited to see it.

So, on May 9, under a livid sun, and when the heat was like a fire lit under the earth so that you could not have stood on the parade ground with unshod feet, the whole of the Meerut garrison, British and Indian, was lined up to witness the spectacle of soldiers being "broken." The offenders were stripped of their equipment and uniforms and made to stand in their breechclouts while the blacksmiths called up from the city riveted fetters on their wrists and legs.

The fettering took hours. I have heard that there were cries of "Shame" and groans and much gritting of teeth among the watchers, white and brown alike, and oaths and curses and even tears among the victims. At last the ceremony was over. The parade was dismissed; the guilty marched off to the local jail, soldiers no more, but common felons.

For the rest of the day and through the night the officers sat in conference and decided to disband the Indian battalions and drive away the sepoys by force. The precedent for such a solution had already been set in a place called Barrackpore. Two battalions, the 19th and the 34th, had refused to accept the new cartridge. The ringleaders, as the spokesmen were termed, were given life sentences and the battalions called on a parade and disbanded while British riflemen and gunners stood by with loaded arms to mow them down if they resisted. Already it had become the boast of many a zealous commanding officer that he had dealt out deterrent punishments to the sepoys for merely "talking" about the new cartridge.

But here in Meerut, where the Indian troops outnumbered the British three-to-one, a parade-ground ceremony for the mustering out of an entire brigade must have been viewed with misgivings. Here subterfuge was called for. So the general and his battalion commanders devised a plan. The next day was a Sunday, and it would cause no comment if they were to hold a church parade exclusively for the white troops. Then, instead of going to the church, the troops could be marched to the armoury, where they would quickly seize the entire stock of the garrison's arms and ammunition. After that they could deal with the sepoys from a position of strength.

The church parade never took place. Even as the British battalion, the 60th Rifles, and the horse artillery were falling in before their barracks preparatory to marching off to the armoury, a cook boy ran into the cavalry lines, yelling that the regiment's arms were being confiscated.

In their own "lines" the sepoys had not slept either, knowing that some treachery was afoot, for throughout the night they had heard the sound of hammers beating ceaselessly in the smithies. "The blacksmiths are fashioning three thousand pairs of fetters!" the rumour went.

So the cook boy gave the alarm and the cavalry sepoys ran; ran as they were, naked to their strips of waistcloths. Some went to the jail and unfettered their comrades, others rushed to their officers' bungalows to wreak their vengeance, and many began to loot the bazaar shops. The 20th Infantry, somewhat more disciplined, even in a state of panic, marched straight to the armoury and got there only seconds before the church parade. The third Indian unit, the 11th Infantry, stood steadfast at their posts and waited for their officers to come and give them orders. They waited in vain. Such officers as had not been massacred by the sepoys were hastily preparing an all-white defensive position, and a few had taken to their heels.

So the revolt had begun, on Sunday, May 10, 1857.

They were like stampeding cattle and indeed some were like mad dogs. In throwing off their yoke, they threw away all restraint. There was no purpose in what they proceeded to do and no sense. They looted the Meerut bazaar and set fire to the shops; they hunted down their officers as though they were wild animals, and some went berserk and broke into their officers' bungalows and butchered their wives and children. By eight o'clock the fury had begun to ebb. They then took it into their heads to march to Delhi, fifty miles distant.

In Delhi the garrison was entirely Indian; only the officers were white. Here, as everywhere else, the sepoys were ready to rise and were only waiting for the word. To them, the first garbled reports of the Meerut outbreak were like a signal. They instantly turned upon their officers and killed all they could lay their hands on and then decided to finish off all the Christians in the city as well. The Christians of Delhi were converts, brown men like themselves. They massacred them all the same. After that they waited on the bank of the Jumna to welcome the Meerut sepoys. Here, in the burning sand, the two garrisons combined and then marched into the Red Fort in search of a leader. The bent old Emperor, immersed in the act of composing his daily couplet, blinked at them in annoyance.

"A kingdom awaits you, O Lord of the Universe!" they were yelling.

The Emperor, they say, trembled like a leaf about to fall, realizing that this was an ultimatum as well as an invitation, and bowed to the inevitable. That same evening the city's town criers proclaimed the restoration of Mogul rule: "The land has returned to Allah, the government to Bahadur Shah!"

Now that it had happened, my first feeling was of a numbness mixed with regret. Something irrevocable had been done. The plunge had been taken; now the fight must go on till victory was won.

What happened in Meerut frightened me and made me realize that, for me, the issues were not altogether clear cut. I could not, in my own mind, separate the national struggle from personal involvements. I was on intimate terms with many British and Eurasian families, and it was well known that I had more friends among the whites than among my own kind. This was because, owing to my princely lineage, my own people tended to treat me with excessive formality; the British, with certain reservations, treated me as one of themselves. Could I now stand by and watch the men and women who had sung and danced and laughed in my house slaughtered by howling mobs? They had done no harm to me, or indeed to India. Why should they have to be sacrificed for all the wrongs piled up by the East India Company over a hundred years?

The Meerut sepoys had forced the issue with an abruptness none of us were braced for. Any day now, any hour, the storm would break in Kanpur and Lucknow. Then I too would have to come out into the open. I could no longer sit back, playing the aloof observer, dispensing wisdom, airing views about who was right and who wrong, and inwardly hoping—always hoping—that somehow the day of reckoning might be put off.

My grievances, such as they were, had had time to cool off, and the men who had wronged me, Dalhousie and his arrogant, self-righteous colleagues, had gone away. I had had too little contact with the new Governor-General, Lord Canning, to have generated any friction, and as far as I was concerned the moon eaters were represented by a handful of fun-loving functionaries stationed in Kanpur. I was no sepoy, a mercenary living on a pittance and in daily dread of being forcibly converted to Christianity. I had created a snug little niche for myself as a man of wealth and learning, respected among his own people, who yet preferred the society of the British, for whom he kept open house; cultivated and tolerant if somewhat eccentric, since, even though he served meat and wine to his guests and sat at table with them, never ate with them nor accepted return hospitality; the Indian potentate who was free with his carriages and lavish with his brandy, who prided himself on the number and variety of dancing girls in his employ as well as upon the rare specimens of wild animals in his private zoo. Apart from my own retainers, Englishmen were the only people I had any intimate contact with. I did not wish them ill.

Meerut was not so much a declaration of war as a plunge into barbarity. It was more; it was like the inmates of a madhouse breaking loose. No one had expected that the revolt would be merely a matter of sepoys and tommies shooting each other down in just sufficient numbers for one side or the other to cry halt, but now I could see the horrors of Meerut as the pattern. I shrank. "Yield not to impotence," so the Geeta admonishes, for in war, people must die. And yet would it have been a surrender to impotence if someone had tried to save the women and children from being butchered? What would I myself do if I saw a mob chasing Eliza or Emily, or clubbing the Hillersdon children who called me "uncle".

The man whose children called me uncle came to see me two days later, offering to place those children in my hands, and other white children and their mothers as well. "We've decided to entrust the women and children to your care," he told me.

Charles Hillersdon and I could have been intimate friends if he had not been the Collector of Kanpur or I the Peshwa's heir, for I had more in common with him than with any other man, white or brown, that I can think of. I liked to think that he was my exact opposite number, a cultivated English brahmin, less interested in hunting and shooting than in abstract learning, the man who wanted to get to know people more than to govern them or even to be a demigod to them; the sort of man who dreams and talks of his dreams. In his middle thirties, and thus perhaps a couple of years older than I, he was, in a small way, already known as an "Orientalist," and to that extent regarded by his compatriots with suspicion.

We had exchanged the customary official calls when he first arrived, but the relationship had not terminated right there, as it had with his predecessors. He was making a study of Kalidasa as a dramatist, and I rather hesitantly asked him to come to Bithoor and take whatever books he fancied. He brought his wife and two children, a girl of about the same age as my daughter, Gangamala, and a much younger boy. So, rather than sit huddled up among books, we had gone boating. After that the Hillersdons came regularly. As I have said, if he had not been the custodian of the secret files that were kept on my doings, we might have got to know each other much better. But as it was—that is, despite the somewhat stilted, magistrate-and-accused relationship that governed our behaviour—we had become fairly friendly.

My first thought was of Eliza, that she would now be brought suddenly closer. And then the thought was swept away by an awareness of the topsy-turviness of things, the abrupt shifting of the balance of everything, even though the man sitting in the opposite chair did not seem to be affected by it. He was wholly relaxed and disarmingly frank. Another man in his place would have talked around the subject, making mental notes of any slips on my part to use as pointers at my real intentions, or to intimidate me and perhaps even to buy me by offering to give me something of what I had been clamouring for since Bajirao's death. Not Hillersdon, who was acting as though he had come to borrow a book, not to make a bargain. To him, I was someone he could trust; the fact that I was an Indian and therefore someone whose sympathies might be presumed to lie on the side of the enemy made no difference to what he had come to ask.

"Who thought of this?" I asked.

"There's a committee, with Wheeler as chairman. We—I'm on the committee—all felt it would be the best course."

"Are you free to reveal to me what made the committee take this decision?"

"I don't know whether I am free, but I'll tell you all the same. We don't want a repetition of Meerut; wives and children in scattered bungalows for hooligans to slaughter. So they're going to be sent to a safe place."

"Suoh as Bithoor."

"Such as Bithoor—and I wish we had more of them handy. Don't you see? Whatever white men we can muster will have to bear the brunt of the attack. We don't want the women on our hands too. I can't imagine their being more safe anywhere else, can you?"

"Frankly, no. What I wanted to know was why you—the committee—thought they would be safe here."

"Because of you. If you take them under your wing openly, it is not likely that any sepoy will molest them. That's all."

"All?" I asked.

He smiled and his eyes narrowed. "Look, I know I'm the Collector here and supposed to keep an eye on you; and that that makes it difficult for you to tell me what you have in mind. Let me say it for you. We know that if the thing does break out here, your escort is not going to remain unaffected. So it's not as though you were going to be able to protect these families by guarding them with troops. In the last analysis, it is you, the person—your name, your ancestry, your influence. If you declare openly that the safety of the British women and children has been guaranteed by you, they'll be as safe here as they can be anywhere in India today."

"And that's all there is to it?"

"But naturally."

"I have a feeling that you have still left the crucial question unasked."

"What question?"

"Am I or am I not going to declare myself openly to be on your side?"

"Don't be silly," he laughed deprecatingly. "At the moment it is not even relevant. It won't do for our purpose, anyway. Let's get this straight. If you were to come on our side openly and then the sepoys rebelled, the whole reason for their abiding by your word disappears. It'll only work so long as you are either able to remain uncommitted or are openly in their camp. And, naturally, we take it for granted that you will do everything in your power to prevent the thing from breaking out here at all."

I was grateful for Hillersdon's confidence that a sense of decency would prevail because of me; that whatever my name and ancestry meant to the people of India was insurance for the British against barbarity. And I was struck by the clarity of reasoning. He had told me, very bluntly, that I would prove less useful as an ally than an enemy. As an ally, I could never guarantee that their women and children would remain unharmed; as a neutral or even as an enemy, I could.

"We'll send you word," Hillersdon said, "to bring your entire escort to Kanpur and take back the women and children. Bring your guns too—we want to make the whole thing as impressive as possible. Let the people of Kanpur see that Nana Saheb has come personally to escort the British families to Bithoor. You'll come yourself, won't you?"

"Yes, I'll come myself," I promised.

"Fine." He got up and put on his thick cork hat. "I knew I could depend on you for this."

"Remember me to Margaret," I said.

"Yes, I will. She's going to have her baby sometime in September, by which time all this will have blown over—*inshallah!* She, for one, will be glad to know she is coming to Bithoor."

PART II
KANPUR

Chapter 11

Soon after Hillersdon had left, I had sent men to hire a dozen riverside houses and paid extortionate rents for them in advance. I had these houses vacated, cleaned, and staffed. After that I waited for word from Kanpur.

On May 19, two bodies floated down the Ganges—white bodies, mangled and bloated out of shape and yet recognizable as those of a man and a woman. They floated sluggishly, obscenely, like abandoned waterbags, bobbing slightly as the fishes tugged at them. Somewhere up the river there had been a massacre. Late that night I received the call from Hillersdon.

I left Bithoor at five the next morning. Even at that hour, the slight coolness that comes before dawn had passed and the sky gave a copper light, as though reflecting a distant fire. The anxious citizens of Kanpur, already astir, if indeed they had slept at all that night, crowded the rooftops to see a mile-long cloud of dust advancing from the west.

That cloud was us, a straggly column deliberately extended to give the impression of size, for all it contained was two hundred horsemen and six hundred foot soldiers that comprised my entire guard. A mile away from Kanpur, I heard the morning gunfire, followed by the bugles blowing reveille. It was oddly comforting to see that the cantonment was awakening to another normal day, to be reassured that nothing terrible had happened during the night.

The road from Bithoor, or the Delhi road, enters Kanpur from the west, at Nawabganj, and the first buildings you see are the public offices: the court and the treasury and the jail. After that the main road gets lost in the tangle of bylanes of the civil station, dotted at random with the white bungalows of the senior civilians. When the trees are in leaf, you cannot see one bungalow from another.

I halted my column at Nawabganj, and Tantya and I rode to Hillersdon's house. Hillersdon was out but had left a message to say that he was taking his family to the Entrenchment and that he would be back at eleven. Meanwhile, I was to treat his bungalow as though it were my own.

It struck me that something had gone wrong, but I could not put my finger on it. "Where has the sahib taken the mem-sahib and the *babas?*" I asked the servants.

They waved their hands towards the east. "It's near the race course."

By now it was very hot and the light had an eye-searing whiteness. Our horses cowered and turned their heads away from the sand-filled wind. Tantya and I went in and sat in the drawing-room. The servants, a semblance of routine restored, took up their chores. Every few minutes, water was splashed against the scented-grass shutters. Only for a few seconds after this, a cool breeze came through, to dry the sweat on our bodies. We drank endless glasses of thin buttermilk, which Hillersdon's wine waiter kept bringing. Even as we were gulping it down, it spurted out of our skin through every pore.

Hillersdon returned with British punctuality. We heard him stamping his feet in the veranda to shake loose the dust on his boots, and then he strode in and for a few seconds stood blinking against the darkness. He looked hot but businesslike, his face brick red below the line of the topi and pale pink above. He greeted us and ordered a beer for himself. Then, very formally, he thanked me for my troops and told me there had been a change in the plans. "Now we'll need your troops for guarding the treasury. There's a lot of money there—a hundred thousand pounds."

At first I thought I had heard him wrong, and then, suddenly, everything became clear. *They* no longer trusted me, and Hillersdon was doing his best to break it gently. And in the wake of this thought, came another. Was this a calculated manoeuvre to separate me from my soldiers?

"Is gold more precious than women and children?" I asked.

"Sir Hugh is making special arrangements for the families," he said. "Inside the Entrenchment itself."

"And Janaki. Will she be happy with this change of plans?"

"Lady Wheeler will naturally fall in line with . . . with whatever the authorities decide for the other British families," Hillersdon said dryly.

This was the very first time that Hillersdon—or someone like him—had, while speaking to me, referred to Janaki as "Lady" Wheeler, or spoken of her as belonging among other British ladies. In a sense, it was the measure of the astonishing change that Meerut had brought over the community—a sudden and seamless closing of the ranks. The home-breds and the country-breds were one, and even a bandit's ex-mistress who had become white by marriage no longer an outcaste. . . . Meerut—or the two bodies that had come floating down the river.

My thoughts were running wild, conjuring devils out of shadows. I stared at Hillersdon with resentment, the bald man with the two-coloured face who was a philosopher and scholar, who could not have harboured an evil thought in his mind, was no longer a friend. We had argued about the shades of meaning in the Rig-Veda and about the origin of the Rajput races and he had sent his children boating with me. Now, somehow, there was distrust. Did they think the bodies had come from Bithoor, that I was at the back of whatever killings had taken place?

Ordinarily I would have asked him. Not today. I could see he was not being sincere and any familiarity on my part would have looked misplaced.

He was, at any rate, all politeness. "Margaret laid on some fruit," he told us, "knowing you wouldn't eat anything cooked by our boys. So a sort of meal is ready. She specially ordered Lucknow *karboosa* melon and Langra mangoes. I told her you might stay on."

"Why did you think I would stay on?"

"I thought you might like to be close to your men till they were settled in. It would also give us more authority over them—if you were here, in our camp, as it were." Abruptly he shouted an order to his butler to bring out the fruit and turned to me again. "Margaret, for one, would have felt far more at home in Bithoor." He grinned.

"More secure too," I pointed out.

"The responsibility for the protection of the families is now the General's."

"Hamlah must be furious," I commented.

"Furious?"

"To be told to guard families instead of—leading armies into battle."

"He's still the District Commander."

"Yes, but of a truncated district. Isn't it true that Sir Henry Lawrence has taken personal charge of Lucknow—detached from Wheeler's command?"

Hillersdon wiped his head with a handkerchief. "The fact is," he said somewhat awkwardly, "the fact is that Sir Henry Lawrence wanted to have unfettered powers in Lucknow. The Governor-General agreed. There is no question of truncating commands."

I shrugged. "That's not what the sepoy believes, Jack Sepoy. And surely it is not the practice to reduce the authority of generals when wars start—to be demoted."

Hillersdon's face reddened. "Sir Hugh is a soldier out and out; ever willing to bow to his superiors, whatever his private feelings. His task is now to guard Kanpur, and he feels that the women and children will be safer in the Entrenchment, guarded by our own troops, than they would be anywhere else."

He was speaking very plainly now, and looking hard at me as though to study my reactions. "It's up to you," I said. "You and Wheeler. I personally feel convinced it's a mistake."

"Oh, but we're expecting extra troops—a whole regiment of cavalry. They're already making the arrangements for housing them. Hadn't you heard? The advance guard has already arrived."

"Fifty men from the 32nd Queens and two hundred from the Oudh irregulars," Tantya Topi said.

"There you are, then."

These reinforcements had come from Lucknow, and on arrival they had been marched all around Kanpur, escorted by a dozen gaudily dressed trumpeters blowing lustily at their instruments, almost as though to ensure that the maximum number of citizens should see them go past.

"The remainder'll be here within a week," Hillersdon was saying. "Till then, we need your men—for the treasury."

"You're welcome to them, such as they are," I told him. "They're not trained for fighting, and their weapons are, well— primitive. My guns, as you know, are saluting guns, only good enough to make loud bangs. Yes, you keep my soldiers and make them guard your gold. But I wouldn't expect much more from them than that."

"I understand perfectly," and Hillersdon grinned. "You mean that your men are not going to side with us against the rebels if there's an outbreak here too. *If*," he added with emphasis, and then, as though the thought had just occurred to him, asked, "Are they going to break loose on the day of the Id, you think?"

Id was Ramzan Id, the first day after the month-long fast for the Muslims. It would fall on May 24. "Is that what your spies have told you?" I asked.

He laughed. "That's the bazaar *gup*. Anyway, you wouldn't know for certain, would you?"

"No."

"I thought not," he said, smiling still, "and I told Hamlah that."

To this day, I don't know what made me say what I then did. Was it the contempt in his tone, camouflaged in well-mannered laughter, the taunting assumption that I would never know what was being planned by my own people that stung me into showing off, to demonstrate that I knew far more than I did?

Or again, was it the delayed reaction of the morning's happenings, my discovering that I had been done out of the role I had imagined myself playing in the coming conflict? The arrangement of events I had gone on building upon had collapsed even before the revolt had begun. I had fervently believed that I was going to be the voice of reason, the key man held in esteem by both sides, the mediator and the negotiator; someone who would go down in history as the man who had tempered a revolt, who had helped his own people to achieve freedom from foreign conquerors with only the minimal bloodletting; the man who, above all, understood and practised old-fashioned chivalry, for had he not given asylum to the women and children of the enemy?

I don't know what prompted me to say it, but this is what I did say: "Tell Hamlah from me that I shall give him advance warning. This I promise."

I can still hear the hiss of indrawn breath that came from Tantya Topi, and I can see Hillersdon raising his dust-encrusted eyebrows as a paleness came over his brick-red cheeks. Hillersdon quickly said, "Yes, I'll tell Sir Hugh that."

"But of course it is possible that my master may not himself know anything about the plans," Tantya said in a voice that held a warning for me.

"Oh, yes, I'll know. I'll stay on in Kanpur and make it my business to find out."

"Ah, here come the melon and mangoes," Hillersdon said in a relieved tone.

Hillersdon invited me to use his house while I remained in Kanpur, and I gratefully accepted. He drained his glass of beer and excused himself. We heard the jangle of spurs and the creak of saddlery as he mounted and trotted off, and then we heard the quickening pace of his horse as he spurred it into a canter. Tantya ate mangoes delicately, avoiding my eyes. The servants splashed water against the shutters. The humidity rose.

At four o'clock I ordered the horses, and Tantya and I rode to the race course. I wanted to have a look at the Entrenchment from a discreet distance, discreet so as to avoid the suspicion that we might be spying. It was a long way off from Hillersdon's house in the civil lines, at least seven miles. More than an hour's hard riding every time Hillersdon came to his office, I reflected.

Kanpur is a city of distances. A palanquin with the most agile bhois took all of two hours to go from the old cantonment to the "native" lines; and the Delhi road is at least three miles from the river.

As it turned out, we could have ridden right into the Entrenchment without anyone's taking the slightest notice. The confusion was so great that the whole thing resembled a cattle fair more than a military stronghold. For every white man capable of bearing arms there must have been at least half a dozen extras—elderly men, women, and children—and for every white face I encountered there were at least twice as many Indians, all of them of the menial class known as the *jaswaras*. Gathered into Christianity from the spillover of the outermost fringes of the caste system, they now formed a class of serfs who knew no other life than that of a parasitic dependence on their masters. Like tickbirds on the backs of water buffaloes, the jaswaras had become the adjuncts of white men—grooms, cooks, water-carriers, table-boys, dog-boys, sweepers of lavatories, children's wet and dry nurses. There was also a full complement of cattle, donkeys, horses, dogs, birds in cages, and sullen, silent cats.

Was it then that I named the Entrenchment the "Fort of Despair"? I don't remember. But I do remember saying to Tantya how utterly insecure it looked as a place of refuge and how chaotic the conditions would be if it was subjected to a siege.

"The hat men are terrified," he said gleefully. "Utterly helpless."

The sepoys of the native lines which lay on the other side of the race track saw all this too and so did the sharp-eyed Gujars, the notorious criminal tribe of the Doab who, barely a generation ago, had lived by plunder. Stray bands of Gujars converged around the enclosure like crows around a wounded bull; they leaned on the fence rail and flung conventional obscenities at the jaswaras passing in and out.

The Entrenchment was a cruel joke. It was not only in the wrong place, it was in the wrong country, among the wrong people; people who, all these years, had been kept in their places only by force of arms. The Company's men had been living as conquerors in a hostile land, a few among vast numbers. They had been living as masters, and it was not possible for them to coexist in any other role. The only thing that had enabled them to hold their own —force—had collapsed, and suddenly they were vulnerable.

The sun was already setting in a sky made blood red by a raging dust storm when we turned back. Near Mogul Serai, we passed a knot of cavalrymen on their way to see the Entrenchment. I asked Tantya to find out from them where Azijan's school was. He frowned and gave me a reproachful look so that I had to repeat my order.

"But it is—it's a house of ill fame," he protested.

"That's where we're spending the night."

The soldiers laughed uproariously as they gave us directions. We made our way to the back of Golaghat bazaar, to Azijan's so-called dancing school, which, I knew, had already become the most popular soldiers' brothel in Kanpur.

Tantya had to bang long and loudly with the hilt of his sword before the door behind a strong iron grille opened. A lamp appeared, and behind it a face, creased and scowling. An old voice squawked abuse at us and told us to be off.

"Go away, soldiers! This house is closed for cowards! The whole bazaar knows it. *Thu!*" she ended off with a spitting gesture.

She was about to shut the door when Tantya rattled his sword hilt against the grille and yelled in his parade-ground voice, "Shut up, crow's mate! Open the door at once! Don't you know who seeks admittance? Or have your eyes grown scales? The Peshwa himself, Nana Saheb of Bithoor."

The woman stared at us for a moment and then darted in. Within seconds, a dozen or so faces were pressed against the grille, babbling excitedly and giggling. Then they all fled away, as birds do when the shadow of the hawk falls. The grille swung back, and there was Azijan, bowing us in.

We followed a servant holding a lamp and passed through a room and then a courtyard open to the sky before coming to a room redolent with the smell of musk and incense. I later learned that it was called the *sheesh-mahal,* or mirror room. Its floor was fully carpeted and along the walls were bolsters covered with apricot-coloured velvet. On the walls were the mirrors in gilt frames, now reflecting the light given by two ornamental brass lamps with pink globes. On the wall hung a picture carpet, which, from the way it gleamed, must have been a genuine Heriz. It was good to see that Azijan was doing well. We removed our shoes and sat down on a mattress. One servant brought hookahs and another glasses of sherbet. After they had gone Azijan asked professionally, "Does Malik desire music or paan?"

"He desires information," I told her.

"Not even a Malabar *malish?* I have a girl whose feet are as soft as champak buds."

"Some other day."

"Could I have a paan, please?" Tantya asked shyly.

" 'Paan' here does not mean betel leaf," I told Tantya. "It means a girl for the night."

His face reddened. "No, I mean a real paan—folded betel leaf."

Azijan opened a brass box and began to prepare the paans. I said, "What is all this about cowards?"

"The Company's sepoys; this house is closed to them."

"Surely there are other houses."

"They're all closed to the men in uniforms—my girls spit in their faces."

"And who are the heroes?"

"The sepoys of Meerut; the sepoys of Delhi."

"And here?"

"Emasculated, one and all. They drink *bhang* all day and sleep like pigs; in the evenings they swagger through the bazaar, twirling their moustaches, ogling women. But before the sircar they're as sheep—they would sell their own mothers to the hat men for grains of salt." She handed Tantya his paan.

It was past nine and the loo had subsided a little. I was already feeling drowsy, but there were many questions I wanted to ask. I sent Tantya off to where our servants were camped to have our evening meal brought over.

"Shall I press Malik's feet?" Azijan asked.

"Please." I stretched out against the bolsters and sucked at the hookah pipe while Azijan expertly kneaded my limbs to take away their fatigue. By the time our dinner arrived, nearly two hours later, I had heard enough rumours to set off a dozen revolts. The wonder was that nothing had happened so far.

Each side watched the other and interpreted the signs; both were in the grip of panic, jumpy, suspicious, preparing to sell their lives dearly; both convinced that the other side was plotting to destroy them.

For instance, the sepoys had not only swallowed the story put out by Wheeler that an additional British cavalry regiment was arriving, but had built upon it and come to the conclusion that the regiment was going to be used to disarm the 2nd Cavalry.

"But don't they know it is all bukhwaz—bluster?" I asked.

"There are no troops—white troops—within a thousand miles."

"Oh, yes, there are," Azijan pronounced. "Tika Singh himself told me. He's the Subedar of the 2nd Cavalry."

"What exactly did he tell you?"

"That the *goras,* the white troops, who are coming here are to be housed in the 2nd's barracks. They are coming without either horses or arms."

"Why?"

"Because they don't need them," Azijan said dramatically. "They'll be given the horses and the muskets of the 2nd Cavalry."

"And what happens to the 2nd Cavalry?"

"The same thing that happened in Barrackpore—the same thing that would have happened in Meerut if the sepoys had not acted in time. They will be disarmed, they will be fired upon—massacred by the white troops."

"But surely Tika Singh and his *sowars,* the troops—they are not meekly going to surrender their horses and arms?"

"This time the British have been very cunning. They are already covering the Indian barracks with their artillery."

"Is that what Tika Singh told you?" I asked.

"Everyone knows it. The whole bazaar saw the redcoats trundling away their guns from the depot."

The same people must have seen the guns placed all around the Entrenchment, as Tantya and I had, but the obvious explanation did not fit in with what they wanted to believe.

The gentle kneading of my arms and legs and back had a soporific effect, but I was abruptly jolted into wakefulness. "All the sepoys are to be massacred—all," Azijan told me in a whisper.

"But how?"

"The main parade ground is packed with explosives. They'll call a big parade and light a fuse somewhere. Not a sepoy will be left alive. They say the big parade is for the twenty-fifth, for their Queen's birthday."

These were the grotesque gifts of panic. The British had convinced themselves that the sepoys would rise on the twenty-fourth because it was the day of Ramzan Id; the sepoys had convinced themselves that the British were holding the big parade merely for the purpose of blowing them up.

"And are they planning to do anything about it?" I asked, trying to sound casual. "Knowing they have only five more days to live?"

But it was clear that Azijan did not know. She resorted to invective. "They're eunuchs!—emasculated. We spit in their faces. *Thu!*" She expelled a jet of saliva into the brass spittoon.

"This Tika Singh, the 2nd's Subedar. I'd like to meet him. Can you arrange it?"

"Me?"

"Only you could do it."

"And would it be wise for Malik to meet him? The hat men watch him all the time. Two men follow him wherever he goes—two Christians."

"Tell him I want to see him," I said. "And now let's have some music."

The singing was altogether rustic, but it was curiously soothing. My eyes closed and my thoughts began to unravel. Two dates: Id and the Queen's birthday. It could start on either day, but only because each side believed that the other was up to treachery.

It was long past eleven by my watch when Tantya and the servants turned up with our food, the cook disconsolate because he had been unable to bake any chapatis. The flour available in Kanpur was believed to be polluted.

"They say they've mixed the blood and bones of cows and pigs in the flour," Tantya explained.

"There is no doubt about it!" Azijan cried out. "Everyone knows it. And they're selling it cheap. But who'll buy that filth? No one except the Issahis and the jaswaras, who mind neither pork nor beef."

So here was another rumour, yet more evidence of British duplicity, something which fitted in smoothly with the greased cartridges. Now the Company was attempting wholesale conversion of cities by adulterating wheat flour with the blood and bones of cows and pigs. Hadn't the Portuguese in Goa done the same thing—converted entire villages by throwing beef into the common village wells? These were the recognized devices of proselytization.

"They'd rather starve than eat that *atta*—the flour," Azijan concluded.

"Luckily, you can smell it—smell it in the shops from the

streets," the drummer interposed. "I had to hold my nose. It smells like the swill baskets behind British regimental kitchens."

Did not Mr. Benjamin Disraeli taunt us that revolutions are not made with grease? How little does he know of the East, where, in the proper climate, even a smell can be transformed into a powerful explosive.

I flung a handful of coins on the carpet, which the drummer gathered up. The musicians made their bows and left. Tantya and I ate our dinner in silence.

Chapter 12

We left Azijan's house soon after the morning gun. At the fork near the civil station Tantya and I parted, he proceeding to Nawabganj to see how our men were doing, and I to the Collector's bungalow. The sun was rising as I entered its gate, but Hillersdon was already there, having ridden the seven miles from the Entrenchment. He came out onto the porch to receive me and led me into the sitting-room. The moment we were alone he asked me if I had been able to find out anything.

"I haven't seen anyone to find anything out from," I answered.

"You spent the night in the dancing school behind the cavalry lines."

"A musical evening."

"Tika Singh also frequents the place."

"And who is Tika Singh?" I asked.

"The Subedar of the 2nd Cavalry."

"He certainly wasn't there last night. The house was closed for business."

"I gave Sir Hugh your message. He was deeply touched. He told me to tell you that he had never for a moment doubted that you would rise to the occasion—do everything in your power to help your friends."

Were friends in the ranks of the enemy still friends? And was there still anything I could do for them? I had been thinking about it hard earlier that morning as Tantya and I cantered over the road that ran beside the Ganges, for I have always believed that I was able to sort out my thoughts best while on horseback. The motion of the horse seems to shake loose the inessentials; the fractions cancel each other out and the answers come out in whole numbers. But today my thoughts were just as hopelessly tangled as ever. I said, "What happens if there is no rising in Kanpur?"

"Is such a thing possible?"

"There's a chance. The three of us—you, Wheeler, and I—can bring it off if we make that our principal aim: to keep Kanpur unaffected."

Hillersdon shook his head in perplexity. "I don't understand. You mean just go on pretending nothing is happening in Meerut and Delhi and Fyzabad? How can we?"

"Why not?"

"Because we cannot isolate ourselves; whether it is Meerut or Delhi, it is still our business."

"How does it become *your* business?"

"Well, the Company's business."

"But surely, even as you are a loyal Company official, it is to your advantage to keep the trouble from reaching Kanpur?"

"Let's get this straight," he said very slowly. "Tell me. Does this mean you have decided to come out openly on our side?"

I did not take umbrage, for this was a familiar blind spot among the Company's servants. They themselves were fiercely proud of their unswerving loyalty to their race, their religion, and above all to their employers. And yet a similar drive among the Indians was unthinkable to them. They took it for granted that, because they belonged to the same religion, the Indian Christians would side with them as a matter of course, and they could not understand how anyone who had been accepted by them as a friend might think of putting patriotism or racial loyalty above the obligations of friendship.

As simply as I could, I explained my position: "Once the sepoys here rebel, I have no choice. I shall join them. Not only that, but I shall work for them. But till such time as they do rebel, I am un-committed. Till then I can go on helping friends. So the thing to do is to prevent its happening here. . . ."

"Oh, but Sir Hugh is doing his best to prevent a rising here."

"That medicine won't work—not any longer. Bluster will not hold them down. On the one hand, you intimidate the sepoys by telling them you're bringing over thousands of white reinforcements; and then, while doling out their wages, you make them line up even without their side arms in case they start a knife war. They know you are both afraid and trying to instill fear. You cannot burrow into an Entrenchment and still remain masters. Your discipline worked only through fear; when you are yourself afraid and show it, how can it go on working?"

He could not have liked what I told him. "You forget Jack Sepoy's personal devotion to Sir Hugh," he reminded me.

"That was the one thing that might have worked—the emotional hold that Hamlah had over the sepoy. But you have gone and destroyed that hold. Every sepoy knows that Wheeler is the seniormost and believes him to be the ablest, the most deserving. Then you go and make him an object of pity by snatching away half his command. They cannot venerate an object of ridicule—cannot go on respecting someone dropped by his own side."

"Dropped is right," Hillersdon said, almost to himself.

"It's a link that you need at the moment; not extra cavalry. And that's what I am offering to be, your link with the other side. They trust me. The question is, do you trust me?"

"It's so difficult to say," he said softly. "Distinguish between friend and foe."

I ignored the veiled reproof. It could not have been his personal opinion anyway, but a collective one, of his community. I went on with my argument. "We can create understanding—greater tolerance—by removing the causes of fear."

"But is there still time?"

It was a shrewd question. He wanted to know what I knew about the sepoys' plans for the twenty-fourth, for Ramzan Id.

"Yes, there is still time. In fact, I can assure you that they will not stage a rising on the day of the Id, that they may be prevented from rising at all unless there is some provocation, however indirect." And then I told him about the cheap flour being sold in the Kanpur bazaar.

"Good God!" he exclaimed and thumped his forehead with his palm in a purely Indian gesture. "But that lot of atta has nothing the matter with it. It was held in the Commissariat stock during the last monoon and got wet and began to smell. So we decided to sell it to the public—cheap—through the bazaar shops. You know how your merchants were fleecing the poor by taking advantage of the shortage. We thought we were doing a good turn, that they would only applaud our efforts to bring down prices."

"They're not applauding; and you'd be doing a lot towards allaying fears of mass conversions by withdrawing the stocks."

"I shall do so at once, the moment I get to the office. What else?"

"The Queen's birthday parade. It must be cancelled."

"Oh, no! Sir Hugh'll never agree to do that. His officers have been pressing him to keep everything normal, by keeping up appearances, by—"

"That's the day it'll start, then—the twenty-fifth. You can tell Sir Hugh that."

"You mean it?"

"I do. You will never get them to assemble on the parade ground; they're convinced that they are going to be mowed down once they're all gathered together."

"But what a preposterous supposition!"

"No more preposterous than the one about Id," I reminded him. "So I have kept my promise: told you it won't start on Ramzan Id, nor, if you cancel the parade, on the twenty-fifth. The panic will subside even further when they hear you have forbidden the sale of the rancid flour."

"I'll tell Sir Hugh that," he promised, "tell him all that you said."

"Tell him also that, with luck, we may be able to prevent a rising here till the whole thing blows over."

Hillersdon gave me a hard, uncompromising look as though to remind me that our hopes for the eventual outcome of the conflict would never coincide. He wanted it to end in the perpetuation of the Company's rule, I in its extinction. And yet, I saw no reason why we should not work for a limited common objective: to spare our environs from the savagery of war by regarding Kanpur as a sort of self-cancelling factor, which would not make a difference to the fortunes of either side.

It was perhaps an impossible objective, and, in a way, it was an utterly selfish one. Even so, for the moment it suited us both: Hillersdon and Wheeler would have welcomed a breathing pause; I held secret hopes that the revolt would have achieved its purpose while our breathing pause still lasted.

Hillersdon put on his topi and called out to his syce to bring his horse to the porch steps. He strode out, keeping his legs well apart because of the spurs he wore, his riding boots creaking. In the doorway he stopped and wheeled round.

"General Anson is dead," he announced in a metallic voice.

I shot up from my seat. "What's that! The C.-in-C. dead? Does that mean Hugh Wheeler has become the Jangi Laat?"

"The new Commander-in-Chief is Patrick Grant," Hillersdon said in the same tinny voice. "Sir Patrick Grant." Then he turned on his heels and went out.

"Tell him I'm sorry!" I shouted after him. "Tell Sir Hugh how disappointed all his friends will be." I slumped into the chair, surprised at myself that when the world itself was being rocked, I should feel so strongly about Hamlah's fortunes. It was as though something I myself had longed for all my life had been snatched away. I remembered Wheeler's telling me in an anguished voice, "But how *can* they? Grant—fifteen years my junior! I was a captain, commanding a squadron, when he joined up. How can they?"

They could, and they had. They had truncated Wheeler's legitimate command and left only Kanpur under him; and now they had promoted Grant, years his junior, to the position which was his by rights. It was too much to bear, I kept thinking, particularly if you were in your mid-seventies.

Within the hour, the town criers were beating their drums at street corners. The sale of the rancid atta was forbidden. All stocks were to be destroyed. The merchants would be compensated for their losses.

And when, towards noon, Tantya returned from his round of inspection, he told me that the men of the 56th Infantry had been jubilant that the parade for the Queen's birthday had been cancelled.

"Why have they cancelled it?" I asked.

"It seems the Jangi Laat is dead; that's why."

"Were they saying who the new Jangi Laat is?"

"They don't know the name; all they know is that it is not Hamlah."

"Poor Hamlah!"

"They were saying that they have cut off Hamlah's nose—that he has been reduced to a lieutenant, that he is working under captains."

There was little more I could do by staying on in Kanpur and I decided to leave in the afternoon. But about midday a camel rider came with a letter from the Entrenchment. Hillersdon and Wheeler would appreciate it if the Raja of Bithoor would make it convenient to stay in Kanpur till the twenty-sixth.

So they wanted me to be around till both Id and the Queen's birthday had passed. I scribbled a reply to say I would stay on.

That evening, Tantya and I went riding through the cantonment and the city. The change was quite startling. All the bazaar shops were open and doing brisk business. People laughed and joked and sang snatches of song. The nervousness had abruptly vanished.

On our way back to the civil station, we were riding through the grove of ancient banyans when we passed a figure standing between two suspended roots, a figure motionless as a jungle animal lying in wait for its prey to appear or a professional thug readying to strangle a passing traveller with his silken scarf. We might have taken it for a tree stump or an anthill had it not been for the gleam of buttons and buckles. Tantya wheeled his horse and yelled at the top of his voice, "Stand still, there! Who are you?"

"Tika Singh," the voice came like a sharp clap against a drum. "Subedar of the 2nd Cavalry."

"Your business?"

"I am charged by the sowars to see the Peshwa."

"And what do the sowars want?"

"To seek an assurance from the Peshwa that, when the time comes, he will be our king."

My whole body must have stiffened. The horse reared, and I shivered as though touched by an icy hand. Was that how men were called to become kings? Tantya, who had asked the questions so far, glanced at me.

"Hasn't the time already passed?" I asked.

"For the cavalry, it will never pass."

Again it was my turn. My voice trembled as I said, "Cannot we go on as we are—accept the result of whatever happens in the rest of the country?"

"It is the way of the eunuchs—eunuchs and the infantry—not of the cavalry."

"There is only one cavalry regiment, three of infantry."

"Three thousand sheep. But they'll follow. Only there must be provocation."

"Such as the flour?"

"Yes."

"But that is over."

"Yes, they read the signs correctly. But they will do something else that will provide the spark. We only have to bide our time."

The banyan leaves fluttered in the breeze; sweat poured from the backs of my hands. "What is the Peshwa's answer?" Tika Singh demanded.

"The Peshwa has no choice," Tantya said very distinctly. "His heritage made the choice. He is yours. Your king."

"Your servant," I said, but even to myself I sounded hesitant.

"I salute my king." There was the sound of heels being clicked and then silence. The arch made by the white roots was suddenly an empty space, a dark tunnel through the limbs of the trees. Had he really been there? Or had we imagined it all? We spurred our horses as though anxious to get away from a haunted place.

The twenty-fourth passed. Muslims celebrated Id. Goats were killed by the hundred and the scent of spiced meats and attar hung over the bazaar. British officers shared the meals of their men in time-honoured fashion, clumsily dipping their hands into the common bowls of steaming curries and licking the gravy off their fingers, laughing and joking as though this were their own festival.

And then passed the twenty-fifth, the Queen's birthday. The gorged men slept like pythons, for, instead of having to go on parade, they had been given a holiday—a holiday or a day to be observed as a day of mourning, for had not their beloved C.-in-C. died? Not even the customary salute of twenty-one guns was fired lest it might alarm the sepoys. On the twenty-sixth Hillersdon came to thank me and to say good-bye.

"So we've surmounted the crisis," he said jovially. "We even cancelled the gun salutes for the Queen."

I remembered Tika Singh's words and said, "What's the guarantee that there won't be other scares—some slip that might set the thing going?"

"No danger of that; none at all," Hillersdon told me with assurance. "Sir Hugh and I have personally talked to every single officer —bound them over to be careful. 'Treat every sepoy as though he were a boil on your palm,' Sir Hugh has warned everyone."

I recognized Hamlah's phrase, bodily lifted from Hindi. "And how is he?"

"Sir Hugh? Quite his old self. Oh, this has been a great tonic for him. The old man's full of what he calls his 'josh,' again."

"Is that why he has sent back the Lucknow troops?" I asked. "Because he believes that he can handle the situation all by himself?"

Hillersdon was visibly taken aback. "Troop movements are something I am not supposed to know anything about. . . ."

"Or talk about," I corrected him. "But troops are not pawpaw seeds you can hide in your fist. When soldiers march over a bridge, they can be seen, counted. Everyone saw the fifty or so horsemen of the 32nd Queens and the two hundred men of the Oudh Irregulars go back. So Wheeler has cut his fighting strength in half."

"Just about."

"What is the thinking behind it? Or is it merely a dramatic gesture?"

"Something of both, I should imagine. He is confident that his mere presence can do a lot. That's why he is camping there out in the open, in a tent—so that he can be seen. And I must say there's a—what shall I call it?—a guardian-and-ward relationship between him and the sepoy. It is his greatest boast that, in his fifty-two years with them, he has always been strict but just, and above all he has respected their rights and prejudices. Yes, I do believe that Hamlah's *roab,* his influence with his sepoys, will prevent them from doing anything rash unless . . ." And he stopped.

"Unless one of your own people goes and does something rash to provoke them," I completed his sentence.

He nodded. "That's the danger, and Sir Hugh himself realizes it. He told me that a single injudicious step might set the whole thing ablaze. Well, Sir Hugh is the man in charge, and that is his decision; that is how he reads the situation." And, apparently afraid that I might ask some more awkward questions, Hillersdon got up and put on his topi.

Shortly afterwards, I returned to Bithoor.

How accurately Wheeler had read the situation was soon to be proved. And yet how incredibly foolhardy was his way of handling it! It was almost as though only half of his brain were functioning clearly and the other half had been deranged. Wheeler, the military commander, had assessed the situation brilliantly. Was it the emotional Oriental in him who harboured the delusions? Even if he had not awakened to the fact that his influence among the sepoys had dwindled to the vanishing point, that to Jack Sepoy he was now an object of ridicule and not of worship, surely he must have known that in demanding circumspection and prudence from his compatriots he was going against the grain of racial characteristics. How could he bank on not a single white man's taking what he had called "a single injudicious step"? It was a hope built on the false premise that all those under him would, like himself, respect the rights and prejudices of the sepoy.

Did not Hamlah realize that he was demanding the impossible —that by habit and temperament the white officials were incapable of exercising restraint in their dealings with Indians? They had too long been accustomed to treating the sepoy as an inferior animal, a *suar* or pig, and a "nigger," someone who, above all, had to be firmly kept in his place—and you could never be too firm. How could the same men now learn to treat the sepoy as though he were a boil on their palms? It was only a matter of time before the slip for which Tika Singh and his followers were waiting with such growing impatience would occur.

The last days of a burning May passed without incident. On the thirty-first a dust storm hit the city and brought the monsoon visibly closer. "Two weeks and the rains will be here," I remember saying to Azim. "If Kanpur can hold on till then, we might escape the storm altogether."

Azim gave me a cold look and said very evenly, "Then we should all pray that the monsoon should never come."

That very evening we heard that the sepoys in Lucknow had risen.

Now it appeared inevitable. Even I, who had been weighing in my mind the chances of the British offering no provocation till the advent of the monsoon, gave up hope. The Devil's Wind was now uncontrollable. And yet, old Hamlah's roab over the sepoy seemed to be holding out. Even after they had heard about Lucknow, the sepoys went about their business as though nothing had happened.

But the "single injudicious step" on the part of his officers that Hugh Wheeler had been dreading was taken two days later, on the night of June 2. Tantya Topi, who had stayed on in Kanpur with my troops, rode over to Bithoor the next afternoon to tell me about it.

Chapter 13

Tantya's voice sounded unnaturally calm, and his eyes flashed with excitement. "His name is Cox," he told me. "Last night he got drunk and sat in the middle of the road in front of his bungalow and fired at the nightly patrol of the 2nd Cavalry going on its rounds—he fired several rounds, swearing obscenely all the while, yelling that they were dung worms and pig's spawn. . . ."

"Never mind about that," I said sharply. "Was anyone killed?"

"No, but he shot the horse of the patrol commander, a man called Nizam Ali. I know this Nizam Ali; he is a *dafedar*, a sergeant, and a good—"

"Yes, yes. What happened then?"

"The patrol fled back to the lines and lodged a complaint. Every single man had seen Cox—seen him and recognized him. They're saying in the bazaar today that the hat men have posted snipers in the streets to hunt down sepoys. All shops are closed today in protest."

"And what is General Wheeler doing about it?"

"Hamlah has announced that he is going to have Cox punished, and has ordered a trial by court martial. But of course the sepoys know it is all a farce."

"Farce?"

"One thing the sepoy knows is military law. This Cox is a cash-iered officer of the Company and as such no longer subject to military law."

"And what are the sepoys doing about it?"

"They're waiting to see what the court martial is going to do.

Tika Singh came to see me this morning. A meeting is going to take place in Azijan's house."

Cox, I kept repeating to myself, Cox. No one even seemed to know his full name. Was this bit of flotsam, this reject from the Company's army, which was an army famed for the latitude it gave to its officers, going to plunge Kanpur into war?

"It all depends on the court's decision," Tantya said in an edgy voice.

And it was exactly what Tantya had predicted and what Tika Singh had hoped it would be. The court assembled on June 4 and went through a mock trial. The verdict was "not guilty." Cox, the court held, was stupefied with drink and therefore not responsible for his actions, and his firearm had been "discharged by accident."

"Our firearms too will have to be discharged by accident," the sepoys wailed.

"If a sepoy had fired at a patrol of redcoats, he would have been hanged."

"Fire?" Tika Singh asked. "For refusing to bite their filthy cartridge, our men have been blown from the muzzles of guns."

"You're all eunuchs—castrated—sheep!" a familiar feminine voice jeered. Azijan, wearing a fancy riding habit and brandishing a sabre, had become the cavalry's mascot.

And even Wheeler must have seen the Devil's Wind rising, realized that he would have to fight it out. He ordered all the white families into the Entrenchment. What the British had always termed their "steel framework" had been dismantled. The sepoys were on their own.

Long after midnight Tika Singh led a hundred men to the Commissariat yard and seized a dozen pack elephants. They rode the elephants to the treasury, which, they knew, held more than a cartload of gold coins. Predictably, my men who were guarding the treasury welcomed them. After looting the treasury, Tika Singh and his men marched to the jail and released the prisoners.

But not everyone in the cavalry was behind the rebels, nor, at this stage, were the two infantry battalions. Two of the seniormost Indians in the cavalry, Bhavani Singh and Zaffar Ali, together with about fifty troopers, made for the Entrenchment instead, and offered their services to Wheeler. Many later died in the defence of the Entrenchment, and Zaffar Ali, as we shall see, was hanged like a common felon.

As to the two infantry battalions, the 46th and the 53rd, they had been on some routine overnight parade on the night of the fourth, and it was not till after sunrise that the parade was over and the officers had gone back to the Entrenchment and the sepoys to their lines.

The sepoys were cooking their breakfasts when Tika Singh and his followers and their gorgeous mascot came, riding on elephants, yelling obscenities and jingling their pockets which bulged with gold *mohurs*.

"Rise! Rise if you are the true sons of your fathers, rise!" Azijan kept exhorting them from the leading elephant. "Show us who are the men and who the sheep; who the lions and who the dogs!"

The men of the infantry battalions were too tired and too sleepy to respond even to so rousing a challenge. They turned their backs on their tormentors and some hurled back their own obscenities at them. Now Wheeler (or did someone else act without the General's knowledge?) took a fatal step. If Wheeler himself had ridden over to the infantry lines, as Hearsey, the commanding general at Barrackpore, had in a similar situation, it is inconceivable that the sepoys could not have been still held back. Instead they were, quite literally, pushed over the brink.

For, as they were neatly assembled in long lines before their outdoor cooking fires, waiting patiently for breakfast, the guns in the Entrenchment suddenly opened up on them, just as Azijan had predicted they would. For a moment they did not know what was happening, and then, when a shot fell in their midst, they broke.

They broke, and they went berserk. A few, like children clinging to the knees of ranting parents, ran to the Entrenchment. The remaining mass followed their cavalry comrades. Wheeler's far-reaching guns had built the last span of the bridge.

And so it began, on June 5, 1857.

The prayer-room was cool and dark and nearly soundproof. I was at my daily pooja and lost in the soporific recital of the *arayanakanda* when a shadow fell over the array of idols facing me. I glanced back in irritation. My brother Balarao stood in the doorway, looking very shaken. I knew it had begun. I hurried through my pooja and came out.

The others had already assembled on the open terrace at the back of the house, which overlooked the Delhi-Kanpur road. The sun was high in the sky, creating a blinding glare and the heat was like a flame held against your skin. On both sides the road was absolutely empty, a ribbon of dust stretching away into the distance and vanishing in heat waves that created the impression of flowing water. The young roadside trees planted by the Company's road-makers threw sharp, blue-black shadows. No one said anything. We waited, staring into the distance, knowing that we could no longer hide from the confrontation of our times.

We had to wait a long time. It was past noon when we saw the dust rising in the distance. Immediately afterwards the head of the column emerged through the floating heat waves; the men in gaudy uniforms kept pouring over the horizon as through a hole in the sky, column after column marching in step.

They came closer. Now we could hear them, the trumpets and the yells. My knees felt weak and my whole body trembled, and a nerve in my temple throbbed. For one agonizing moment I thought they were going straight on, to Delhi. And then I saw them wheel round, and I don't know whether the sudden numbness I experienced, as though all sensation had seeped from my limbs, came from relief or from disappointment. Now I was face to face with what I had dreamed of all these months.

They came yelling, trumpets blowing, drums beating.

"The land has returned to God! The rule has returned to the Peshwa!"

I stood with my hands resting on the scorching marble of the balustrade. I needed the support.

"Victory to our King, to Nana Saheb, the Peshwa!"

Thus I became the Peshwa.

There was little fanfare. The mood was sober, of awakening to a crisis. The ceremony of my assuming ruling powers was brief and confined to essentials. The robes of the Peshwa were draped on me by Azim, and my brother Baba strapped on my sword.

Then I stood in the balcony to be "seen," my hands folded to the people standing below, while the priests recited excerpts from the edicts of Manu enunciating the duties of a ruler. The saffron banner of the Marathas was unfurled. Champa slid into the background and Kashi came forward to stand by my side and participate in the ritual. She it was, this stranger who was my wife, who placed a garland of white *mogra* flowers round my neck. A cheer went up from the crowd. Such a cheer I have never heard again.

In the hall of mirrors I nominated a council of war and with them hammered out the broad outlines of our aims. Tika Singh and Jwala Prasad (the seniormost officer of the infantry) were made generals and placed in charge of the cavalry and infantry, respectively. Azim and Tantya became brigadiers on my staff, and my two brothers, Baba and Bala, became my advisers.

In the early evening we started for Kanpur, myself now leading the procession on an elephant. I was racked by a feeling that I was trespassing, for Kanpur to me had always represented British territory. Savda Kothi, a large house standing in a garden, was placed at my disposal by its owner. The first report I received on entering this house was that the white families gathered in Wheeler's stronghold had already dispersed.

The moment Wheeler and his colleagues had seen the sepoys taking the Delhi road they had jumped to the convenient conclusion that they were heading for Delhi. The possibility that they might be going only as far as Bithoor to invite me to become their king seems never to have occurred to them. The result was that they had assumed that the crisis had passed, that vigilance and privations were no longer called for. Many white officials had taken their families back to their bungalows, where they began to make their own arrangements for holding out. Some ordered Indian clothes so as to escape detection, and some hired boats in which to make their way down the river to Allahabad. There could not have been more than a couple of hundred men still in the Entrenchment, and they too were careless, convinced that the danger had passed.

All in all, conditions were ideal for a surprise attack, which, by general agreement, we decided to launch the next morning.

Then I did an incredibly foolish thing, something I find hard to explain, though my conscience told me then that it was right. I secretly sent word to Wheeler that we were going to attack at ten-thirty the next morning.

I sent him word because I had promised to do so, and I shall never admit that my love for his daughter had anything to do with it. Somehow it seemed important that the gesture be made—made before I became locked in as a part of the opposition. It was my last concession to a friendship I truly valued.

Alas, how misguided it all was—a clear manifestation of the precept of Manu that, in wars, the enemy must be destroyed as quickly as possible and in the largest numbers possible. In the event, it did no good to either side. More sepoys were killed than need have been, and those I sought to save by my warning fell victims to mob fury and other grotesque drives of war hysteria.

For Wheeler heeded my warning. He recalled those who had strayed away from his stronghold and issued rifles to every man capable of firing one. He shored up the defences and carried in all the stocks of foodstuffs from the neighbouring officers' messes.

All night the bugles from the Entrenchment blared, calling "All Hands to Arms." Once again the hat men and their women ran to the stronghold, furious at being dragged away from their comfortable and well-staffed bungalows. None expected to have to stay behind the walls for long, and many did not even bother to take a change of clothes. A few, as will be seen, chose to disregard Wheeler's call.

The white men in the Entrenchment, including noncombatants, such as musicians, clerks, shopkeepers, surveyors, and others, numbered perhaps five hundred, and their women and children another five hundred. In addition, there were nearly three hundred sepoys who had joined their masters, and certainly about three hundred servants, thus bringing the total to sixteen hundred.

From the roof of one of the barracks, we could see much that was going on behind the walls of the Entrenchment. The accommodation consisted of two long, single-storied buildings, only one of which had a proper masonry roof, the other being thatched with straw. Did not Wheeler realize that, what with the continuous small-arms fire that he would be subjected to, it was merely a matter of time before half his living accommodation would be ashes?

Or did he too believe that he would not have to remain caged for more than a day or two?

At ten-thirty a silence fell over the Entrenchment, as though not a soul within was alive or all escaped through some secret passage. The surrounding wall, which was about shoulder-high, threw back the sunlight like fragments of flint. Behind us, Kanpur was shrouded in smoke, and we could hear yells and screams and sporadic gunfire: the Gujars were ravaging the city. Men and women came screaming out of the smoke, clutching children and bundles, only to be brought to an abrupt halt by the sight of the soldiers drawn up in formations for an assault and a strange dark man watching the proceedings from the back of an elephant, myself, a long brass telescope glued to one eye.

Did I say soldiers? They were like drunken apes. They strutted and struck indecent postures and laughed and swore and quarrelled and played girlish pranks. They had been rounded up after they had spent the night burning their officers' bungalows, where, like some concealed weapon of war, the officers had left behind crate upon crate of European spirits and wines. The sepoys had drunk like thirsty men gulping water and now they were rendered boneless.

Wheeler had removed all the guns to his Entrenchment. All the same, from old barrels in the artillery junkyard and the decorative guns on the lawns of the officers' messes, we had managed to assemble a battery of nine guns. Since, however, no one knew much about how guns were loaded or fired, they had been appropriated by enthusiastic amateurs. A few lucky shots fell right within the enclosure and Tika Singh delightedly announced that a corner of the outer wall had been demolished.

But our elation subsided as the day progressed. One of the guns blew up and the others became red-hot. The labourers impressed into service to bring water from the river—which was two miles away—fell out in groups and disappeared. Even I, unversed in military matters, could see that our gunners had no idea of what they were doing, that this was hardly the sort of pounding that would soften up desperate men who had been weaned on wars and who, thanks to Hamlah's foresight, possessed all the rifles and ammunition they could use.

Through my telescope I saw a sepoy fall down, and then another. Within an hour, perhaps fifty had collapsed where they stood. It was liquor, not sunstroke. At noon our shelling stopped altogether. Tantya and Tika Singh, after riding off importantly in opposite directions, came back and conferred and advised me to call off the attack.

I gave the necessary order and the attack was called off. In the evening we met to discuss our future strategy.

"We'll starve them out," Tantya said. "That's the best way."

"They'll eat their own dead and survive," Azim pronounced, as though from superior knowledge. He had grown up in an English household and was familiar with the ways of the white man. "It is thirst they cannot endure. Let their water run out and they'll come out raving."

"The thing to do is to concentrate on burning down that thatched building," Jwala Prasad said with military logic. "That will instantly halve their strength."

Here were three men, decent human beings who never failed to offer prayers to their gods or turned away a hungry man from their doorsteps, dispassionately weighing the alternatives for the best means of destroying fellow human beings. They were the professionals, and I knew that this was precisely how the white men too would have debated the alternatives had our positions been reversed—debated them and come out with the most effective answer. Yet I, the amateur, felt sickened by these inhuman impulses and had to cloak my uncertainties behind inane remarks. "War means killing"—I kept soothing my conscience with Manu's words.

They discussed the enemy's stock of food. It seemed that Wheeler had placed orders for large quantities of flour, rice, sugar, and for cattle and goats and fodder, but the contractors, even though they had made a show of energetic compliance, had supplied little or nothing. Wheeler's desperate call on the officers' messes, had yielded wines and tinned delicacies but little else.

"On the strength of those, they're going about as though they're on a picnic," Tika Singh said angrily.

"I have myself seen soldiers running off into corners with bottles and tins," Azim said.

"How long are they going to live on rum and chocolates?" Tantya asked.

"So long as they have water, they will not budge," Azim reiterated. "Water! That second well is like a thousand additional rifles, a hundred twenty-four pounders! That's why Hamlah chose that site—because of the two wells."

But within a couple of days, we learned that the second well was not being used for drawing water but had been converted into a common grave. That left them with just the one well, and from this too water could be drawn only at night, because it was visible from the roof of the nearest barrack and within range of our rifles. And even at night the squeaking of the pulley brought on the instant fire of our sharpshooters.

Every day our observers brought reports of the plight of the people in the Entrenchment. There were many deaths, particularly among children, they felt, because the bodies they had seen wrapped up in blankets were small. Wheeler had appointed a man to be the well captain, charged with the task of conserving water. The well captain was a man called John McKillop. The ration of water had been reduced to a cupful a day. John McKillop had had a soldier flogged for drawing water without his permission. All animals were ordered to be shot because there was no water to give them.

How much of this was true, how much wishful thinking, I could not say, but for this last we needed no outside testimony. We could see the dead animals, transformed into mounds of quivering bluebottles, and their stench hung around the Entrenchment like another wall.

Tantya brought more inside information. Water had become so scarce that children were given pieces of old water bags to suck, and bits of leather to chew to stave off their hunger.

It was about this time too that a fat bullock strayed near the outer wall and was felled by a volley from within. A dozen white soldiers rushed out and began to drag their prize away. Our snipers quickly opened up on this group and killed one man and shot another through the arm. But by that time they had managed to sever a leg from the bull and carry it inside. The dead soldier lay bloating beside the dismembered bull. They made another foray in the evening, but whether to take away their comrade or another leg was never discovered, for a brisk fire drove them back.

The heat was like a tiger let loose. The air you breathed seared your nostrils and our sepoys fried eggs by the heat of the midday sun. A hundred water-carriers brought us water from the river in an unending chain. How long could the enemy hold on, dependent as they were on the water from a single well stolen during the hours of darkness? Even in the underground *tykhana* of Savda Kothi, with all the openings covered over by thick mats of khas grass kept wet by relays of watering women, I found sleep impossible. How long could *they* endure their miseries?

The kitchen chimney of the barrack nearest to the Entrenchment offered a convenient and relatively sheltered observation platform, and sometimes I would post myself in the place of the sniper on duty there. I would crouch behind the masonry like a hunter covering a game trail, my rifle at the ready, anxious to see what was going on behind the wall and yet hoping that no target would offer itself, for everyone knew that I was good with the rifle and had shot many tigers and won many competitions. Also, two of my bodyguard and several idle spectators would perch on the branches of near-by trees to see the shooting. From this hideout, one morning I saw a scene that brought home to me the real plight of our enemies.

I saw a pie-dog, tail tightly curled and ears torn by many fights, stomach bloated with carrion and body hairless from a mange brought on by a surfeit of rotted meat, straying close to the wall of the Entrenchment where the blackening bones of the dead bull still lay beside the vulture-cleaned skeleton of the white soldier. For a time I watched the dog as it listlessly tore away at the cartilage around the bull's knee and then, when it turned and began to gnaw the skull of the soldier, idly, without thinking about it, raised my rifle and brought its bead against the dog's chest. For a few seconds I waited, holding my breath, knowing that I was being watched, before squeezing the trigger. The dog fell and as it rolled over, its legs stiffened

Even as I was lowering my rifle, from the corner of my eye I saw a red-faced soldier leap over the wall and come loping to where the dog lay, and suddenly a dozen or so bewhiskered faces bobbed up above the wall. The soldier picked up the dog and, holding it against his chest, scrambled back over the wall while his comrades cheered with hoarse voices.

It made my stomach churn. If they had started eating dogs, how much longer could they hold on?

And when, shaken by my thoughts even more than by what I had seen, I returned to Savda Kothi the jubilant faces of my staff told me that something particularly horrifying had happened.

George Wheeler, the General's son, had died.

A wave of weakness came over me. It was like hearing about the death of a close relative, for I had taken a brotherly interest in him. He was going to settle down in Bithoor after his father's retirement and, at heart, was closer to our side than theirs.

And now he had died fighting for those he inwardly seethed against. Had they not treated him as an outcaste because of his mixed blood—snubbed him and ostracized and openly despised him? A general's son, he had even been refused a commission in the army. In death, had they at last accepted him as one of themselves? Would they have buried him with the others, if another well had been handy—a grave set apart for the country-breds and the country-borns?

The news had been brought by two maidservants who had escaped from the Entrenchment. "They've brought us much valuable information," Tantya told me. "Everything that is happening in their camp. It seems that the sepoys who have gone over to their side are not even being given food and water; that mice have become a delicacy; they used to mix flour with water and give it to the children as milk, but now there is no flour and little enough water. . . ."

Tantya went on babbling. I wasn't listening. I was thinking of George Wheeler's special cue kept in the rack in the billiard-room, picturing the Wheeler family whom I had seen only in moments of happiness now stricken with grief, Janaki and Eliza and Emily and the trembling, red-faced, white-haired father.

It seemed that George was in the outer trench when a bullet hit him. They had carried him to his room, bleeding profusely, but Dr.

Cheke, who had extracted the bullet from his hip and dressed the wound, had pronounced him out of danger.

"They'd just given him the skin of a dried lime to suck," Tantya was saying, "and it seems he was sitting up, blanched but grinning. His father and sisters were there too, trying to do what they could. Then a shot had come, almost searching him out. One moment he was there, whole, and then they were staring at a headless trunk. The others didn't even feel a jar!"

The news of George Wheeler's death was like a tonic to the sepoys. They gloated and gave thanks and made crude jokes about the sufferings of their masters who were now their prisoners. My staff got down to its routine business. I sat in a stupefied silence while they discussed how the sufferings of the enemy were to be intensified and their end speeded up.

They talked animatedly about burning the barrack with the thatched roof. It seemed that they had discovered a man who could take charge of our guns.

So far the trouble had been that, even though we had been able to assemble nearly a dozen assorted guns from the discarded barrels and wheels that the British had left behind in the artillery yard, we did not have anyone who knew much about how to aim or fire them. That was one thing the British had retained as their exclusive preserve, artillery; no Indian was ever trained in the art of gunnery. Today they had discovered a man who was said to be an expert in gunnery, a man called Nane Nawab.

"A nawab?" I asked, for "nawab" means "lord" or "king."

"He is related to the kings of Lucknow," Azim explained. "He is Aga Mir's son."

Aga Mir, I knew, was one of the ministers of Oudh and reputedly a very rich man. "What is he doing here?" I asked.

"He was on his estate when the Lucknow sepoys rebelled. As he could not get back to them, he has come to offer us his services."

"And does he really know anything about gunnery?"

"He was a battery commander in the King of Oudh's artillery."

Nane Nawab was presented to me. He was soft-spoken, dignified, handsome.

"How long will it take you to burn the thatched building?" Tika Singh asked him.

"It all depends on what state the guns are in," he answered. "I can only try."

"The Master will give a present of ten thousand rupees and a brocade shawl," Azim offered.

"For me, the command of the artillery will be the biggest present; all I ask is the opportunity to serve."

I signed the order for his appointment, and after that they began to discuss their plan in detail. Now and then I kept nodding assent.

My own thoughts would have shocked them. I was by no means disloyal, for I wanted our side to come out victorious and for the victory to be quick and total. I wanted all, or nearly all, the white men to pack up and go and leave us in peace. And yet I did not want those in the Entrenchment to undergo further privations and suffering. And I was thinking of the hairless dog I had killed. Was it already transformed into stew—served in apportioned spoonfuls?

And yet, one thing I must confess. Once the revolt in Kanpur began, I ceased to think of Eliza with longing, and I scrupulously refrained from asking for news of her. The races had claimed their own, leaving no common ground. Perversely, I would often catch myself wishing that a stray bullet would kill her instantly so that she should not suffer. Eliza's presence in the Entrenchment did not influence my slightest action. It was as though she were already dead; so completely had she gone out of my life. Whatever I had felt towards her was too tender to survive the hatred we had succeeded in building up, and I, who had been accepted as a sort of king by one side, had no business to be in love with the daughter of the enemy king.

Chapter 14

In the summer everyone slept outdoors, in gardens or courtyards or on rooftops, and that night, as I lay on the terrace of Savda Kothi, I fought a savage insomnia. In the orb of the summer moon, which I could have sworn was radiating heat, I saw the circle of the death well, and crowding around the well were the men and women with swollen faces, waiting for their turn to jump in. Somewhere in the blue-gray shadows of the night loomed the hairless dog and the red-faced, grimacing soldier who had carried it away as a mother monkey carries her baby. I could have identified that soldier in a parade of thousands; his features were so indelibly etched on my memory. Was he suddenly a hero to his comrades? Was he given an extra helping of the stew?

At intervals I called for water and drank, but my thirst remained. A black shawl over my head did not shut out the world. Against my eyes were glowing embers changing into spots the colour of a peacock's feathers—vivid, concentric circles of green and blue and yellow. They had decided to try and burn the thatched barrack tomorrow. Who would burn to death—who escape with livid patches of pink skin to remind them of their ordeal?

The bugles, theirs and ours, mercilessly heralded another dawn. I had not slept a wink. The new day held a hint of moisture, as though it had rained a thousand miles away. I forced myself into wakefulness and doused my head with lime-scented water, cold from the earthenware jars. The chores of a king who had been called to preside over chaos stood waiting, stamping their feet.

By the time I had bathed and finished my pooja, my advisers had assembled in the hall below the stairs: my brothers, Baba and Balarao, Tantya and Azim, Tika Singh and Hulas Singh, the Town Major. All had urgent business to discuss.

Our sepoy strength was fast diminishing, owing to desertions. Would I make an announcement giving all ranks increased rates of pay and guaranteeing family pensions? I signed the order and asked, "But where is the money for all this?"

"We'll borrow it," Azim said.

"And who will lend it?"

My counsellors smiled sly, meaningful smiles, and Balarao said, "Hulas Singh has rounded up two bankers."

The two bankers were brought in, looking like fat sheep being nose-led into the slaughterhouse. With bitter smiles on their faces and many sighs, each of them undertook to give us ten lakhs of rupees.

Our supplies had been running low because the city's warehouses had been plundered and set on fire. The *kotwal,* or chief of police, who had been responsible for procuring food during the British days, had fled. After that I had appointed three different kotwals in as many days. The fourth one was Hulas Singh, who had rounded up the bankers. Now he also produced contractors who, without protest, undertook to bring in the supplies we needed: fuel wood, flour, sulphur, lead, saltpetre, . . . a hundred other things.

How these supplies were procured I shall never know—perhaps it is not good for kings to know how their orders are put into effect. All shops and most dwellings had been shuttered and the population had, as it were, gone underground. Whose house would be looted next?—whose husband tied to the doorpost and tortured till he confessed where the family trinkets were buried?—whose daughter or sister raped or abducted? No one wanted to expose himself to chastisement. From the orderly routine of a town that had grown up as a backyard of a British military encampment, the people had been plunged into disastrous self-rule. Did self-rule mean only turmoil—a reign of terror by drunk soldiers and savages? Had not their liberators suddenly revealed themselves to be frenzied beasts?

We did our best to restore normalcy. We declared martial law after the British pattern and established a court of justice. We made announcements by beat of drums that looters would be publicly flogged and arsonists shot. We initiated a system of patrols and exhorted the shopkeepers to open their shops.

As in Delhi, the Christians of Kanpur had become a legitimate target. To have killed a black Christian was almost as patriotic as to have killed a white man, and it involved so little risk. The white man shot back, the Bengali Christian didn't. While the Gujars looted and burned indiscriminately, the sepoys concentrated on the Christian community. No wonder that the Bengalis in turn were ranged solidly against us and were praying for our downfall.

"Wait till the British column comes!" they would darkly threaten.

No one could have saved the Christians from mob fury and we made no attempt to do so. About three hundred of them who had taken shelter in what was known as the mission compound were dragged from their houses and slaughtered. Near Generalganj some Christian families had barricaded themselves in a large house. The house was set on fire and all of them burned alive. The drummers and the musicians of the various regimental bands, who were also Christians, had congregated in a church. When a mob of sepoys surrounded them, they announced that they had decided to renounce their religion. Within the hour, they were made Muslims.

"Is a British column really on the way?" I asked Hulas Singh.

"I have sent spies to Benares. We will soon know. In the Entrenchment they know nothing about it."

"If it is, when do you think it'll get here?"

"It all depends on when the rains break. Let us pray that the monsoon starts soon and that . . ."

"Yes?" I prompted.

"And that there is no division among ourselves."

"Why should there be division?"

"It is rumoured that the British have sent a lakh of rupees to Nane Nawab to work against you—to make the Muslims defect; and that they have offered to make him a real nawab once they have re-established their rule."

"Rumoured? Where did you pick up this rumour?"

"One of my trusted informants brought it. Nanak Chand."

"Nanak Chand!" I groaned, remembering the slimy creature who used to come snooping to Bithoor and whose moustache I had had shaved. "He was a British informer."

"They trained him, and I have found him most reliable," Hulas Singh said. "Besides, it is what the British have always done in the past, tried to divide the two communities."

"And Nane Nawab? He is not a community but obviously a man who can think for himself."

"A man who can think for himself can also be ambitious— someone who can think of himself as a king," Hulas Singh said mysteriously. "One good thing is that he is so rich that a lakh of rupees means little to him."

"And also that his father, Aga Mir, was hounded by the British —it was they who forced the King to dismiss him."

Hulas Singh's answer was a shrug, so much as to say that he did not know whether a father's hatred descended to the son, or whether just because a man happens to be wealthy he would spurn a hundred thousand rupees.

The question had no answer, and, in any case, I had other callers waiting to see me. So I dismissed Hulas and called Nizam Ali in.

Nizam Ali has already made his appearance in this story: he was the dafedar in the Company's 2nd Cavalry whose patrol had been fired upon by Cox and whose horse had been killed.

I had promoted him to major and given him the task of rounding up the white families that had gone into hiding in and around Kanpur. He had shown himself to be one of the most loyal and dependable of my officials, for his years in the Company's service had built up in him a quality of dog-like subservience to whoever happened to be in authority over him. He had done his job well, if with unnecessary severity, and by now had acquired the reputation of being the exterminator of white men. Only a week earlier he had killed Edward Greenway and his friend Hollings and a dozen other men who had barricaded themselves in Greenway's country house near Najafgarh, but he had brought back to Kanpur Mrs. Greenway, her daughters and grandchildren, as well as several other women and children who had been sheltering in the house.

I had admonished him then. "Why did you have to kill all the men?" I asked.

He gave me a reproachful look. "They were all dead when I took the house. They fought to the last man."

"No one fights to the last man."

He tried reason. "In any case, Malik, that's what they do to our men. They don't take prisoners, and in the end it saves complications. I am only doing the job Malik entrusted me with—as best I can."

He was expecting approbation; I was censuring him. I had heard reports that Greenway and his friends had surrendered and that Nizam Ali had lined them up against the riverbank and shot them himself. I asked him if it was true.

"Hi-toba! What rumours these are! They must be spread by my enemies who are jealous of the Master's trust in me. The same people who are also saying that the white women I have brought back are for the Master's harem."

I squirmed, because that too was being said; that my orders to Nizam Ali were to kill the men and bring back the women, and that for each woman he "presented me with" I rewarded him with a fistful of gold mohurs. It was, of course, true that Nizam Ali had brought back more than a couple of dozen women to Kanpur— and we had made them prisoners. They were not recruited into my harem, if only for the reason that no one but a sexual pervert would have derived the least satisfaction from cohabiting with any of them, for they were, without exception, old and wrinkled and in a state of shock.

It is difficult to be stern in the face of excessive zeal, and I had salved my conscience by saying, "But there is no point in killing men who have surrendered."

"I would never do such a thing, Malik," he had assured me without blinking. "Never!"

"We'll see," I had said, showing that I really did not believe him.

How little does one know of one's fellow men? I had not realized that this man who had already acquired a reputation for ruthlessness was also systematically plundering the houses of the white men, and that the only reason he had brought the women back to Kanpur was that none of them had caught his fancy.

Today I gave him an encouraging smile as he stood before me at attention, stiff as a dried mackerel. I must have been still thinking of Nane Nawab. Was he planted in our midst by the British to subvert the Muslims? Here was another Muslim; and, admitting that he did not possess either the dignity or the breeding, you could at least take his loyalty for granted.

Tall, his smallpox-ravaged face shining like hammered copper, his nose like a raven's beak, his eyes hooded, his hands fine-boned but with fingers horny as claws, his moustache and beard trimmed and oiled with professional care, the swab of cotton soaked in attar and stuck in his ear giving out a faint perfume, Nizam Ali was like a character in a play. He gave me a smart salute.

"The slave has a favour to ask," he said.

"Yes?"

"That Malik should permit him to retain a prize of war that he has acquired in his name."

Did I, in my own mind, contrast the servility with Nane Nawab's correctly professional manner—elevate the slave asking a favour above the other man who had pointedly said that the only favour I could grant to him was command, not money?

For a moment I tried to make some sense of what Nizam Ali had been saying and then asked him to explain what he meant. So he came out with it: He had taken over John Bathgate's riverside house at Akbarpur. "It is called Imli-kothi—Tamarind House. I have sent my servants to look after it—so the Gujars don't loot it," Nizam Ali concluded.

I knew that Bathgate had been killed and that his servants had fled, and it was quite true that his splendid country house with its treasures would have been looted if there was no one to guard it. Even in the mood I was in, of wanting to show some appreciation of Nizam Ali's services, it looked to me like an act of barefaced confiscation. The new master was seeking to regularize its burglary. "The cobra never digs a hole for itself," I quoted a proverb, "but always takes over a ready-made hole."

It was lost on my visitor. "I don't understand, Malik," he mumbled. "If I had not made haste to occupy it as soon as it—as it fell vacant, it would have been looted and burned."

"That is one way of looking at the thing."

"Now all I live for is to entertain my Master in this house—they say it has better things in it than the Residency at Lucknow."

He was not seeking my permission so much as telling me that he had appropriated Imli-kothi. I reminded myself that one had to make allowances for the kind of loyalty and devotion to duty that Nizam Ali had shown. I knew that several other senior officials of mine had taken over the vacant bungalows of the British and were living in them; Nizam Ali had at least told me of his acquisition.

"Someday perhaps," I half-promised. "When this thing is over."

"I only live for that day," he said very earnestly. "To receive Malik in my house."

After I had dismissed Nizam Ali, Azim came in with a sheaf of impressive-looking letters written on parchment. They were addressed to all the emperors and kings whose recognition and help we sought. Many of these rulers, I later discovered, existed only in our imagination, but that day I signed appeals to the emperors of China, Russia, and France, the kings of Spain and Rome (we called it "Room" in our unworldliness), of Siam, of Kabul and Kandahar and Iran. I also made urgent demands on the Indian rulers I personally knew or had heard of: the Nizam of Hyderabad, the Maharajas of Gwalior, Indore, Lahore, Kolhapur, and Jaipur.

It was nearly dark and I was about to go in for my evening prayers when I heard the report of a cannon and thought it was the gun fired for the night's curfew to begin. Then I heard the buzz of excitement among the guards at the gate and rushed onto the balcony to see what was happening.

In the west was a vertical pink line against the apricot sky. Then the pink became smudged over with grey, as a plume of smoke rose from the centre of the Entrenchment. Against the hazy white line of the Entrenchment wall fluttered a black bird which might have been a wounded crow but which turned out to be a rider galloping towards where I stood. The guns began a thundering volley, concentrating on the pink blaze as an aiming mark.

"Nane Nawab did it!" the horseman was yelling to the guards at the gate. "He filled a shell with burning rags and camphor balls and lobbed it right on top of the thatched roof. Now they're burning—roasting alive!"

The sepoys cheered wildly. The thatched barrack was on fire.

"Nana Saheb *ki jai!* Nana Saheb *ki jai!*" they began to shout. But suddenly I realized my mistake: they were saying, "Nane Nawab *ki jai!* Nane Nawab *ki jai!*" And a cold shiver went down my body, for "jai" means "victory," and ordinarily one says "jai" to a king or to a country, never to a battery commander.

The thatched building, we learned later, was being used as a dormitory and a hospital as well as a storehouse. The women and children and the sick and the wounded were kept in the verandas and the outer rooms, and the inner rooms were allotted to the gunners and the sepoys as their sleeping quarters. When the roof began to burn, everyone who could had rushed to lend a hand to evacuate the building. All the women and children and the patients who could be assisted to their legs were rescued. But nearly forty patients who were bedridden were left to die. Some of the gunners in the inner rooms and the sepoys who had "littered down for the night" were burned to death. All medical stores had perished and so had all the tinned provisions.

The loss of virtually half of the roofed accommodation added greatly to the miseries of the survivors. Those who had hitherto taken shelter in its shade during the day now had no escape from the sun. All day as all night, they had to remain in the open. Many died from sunstroke, merely because they could not find any shade to lie under.

The next morning, at a small ceremonial parade held on the artillery parade ground, I presented the promised shawl and a bag containing ten thousand rupees to our battery commander. Nane Nawab turned up wearing a sword belt studded with precious stones and riding a horse draped in glowing brocade. If he was trying to show that the rewards of the Peshwa meant nothing to him, he had certainly made his point very well—unless of course he was trying to demonstrate to the Peshwa that the lakh of rupees he was said to have been offered by the British could not have tempted him to change sides.

It was all very bewildering, for now he had demonstrated

beyond all doubt that he was an enemy of the British, by burning their barrack. But, by the same token, he had become a hero to most of us and particularly to his brother Muslims. I could not help remembering the yells of the previous evening: "Nane Nawab *ki jai! Nane Nawab ki jai!*"

His face revealed nothing, and my proffered gifts he accepted with the utmost professional courtesy.

Chapter 15

We burned down the thatched barrack on June 13. It was not till the seventeenth that the first batch of sepoys came out of the Entrenchment. They came out in the night, cringing like mice approaching waiting owls or like cockroaches straying into a colony of tiger ants, paralysed with fear. Can there be human beings more degraded than rejected traitors? These sepoys had turned their backs on their race and religion and had gone over to the white men who had enslaved them. Now they had been thrown out because they consumed precious food and water and, even more, because they were no longer trusted.

The first lot to come out were ceremoniously humiliated. We had their heads shaved and faces painted with ochre and we paraded them through the bazaar riding on donkeys in a back-to-front position while children ran behind them pelting them with fistfuls of cow dung and other filth and the women hurled obscenities. But more and more sepoys and servants kept coming out and we could not keep up the tempo of our retribution. We locked them up in a cattle pound and gave them a daily ration of a handful of dry gram and half a coconut shell each of water, which was certainly much more than they were accustomed to in the Entrenchment.

From them we learned that Wheeler had issued an order forbidding the presence of any "native" inside the Entrenchment.

"Is he going to drive out his wife, then?" Tantya demanded.

The number of deaths, we discovered, was larger than we had thought. Hillersdon had died, "his entrails torn out by a round shot," and so had his pregnant wife; and Mr. and Mrs. Atkinson, who used to talk with nostalgia about the frosty winters of their native Midlands and who had been planning to grow Langda mangoes in England; Major Lindsay and his wife; Major Prout, Sir George Parker, Captain Halliday, Lieutenants Jarvis, Eckford, and Leveson. The well which had been set aside to serve as a common grave was rapidly filling up. John McKillop, the well captain, had died while trying to draw water for a lady who was in the grip of labour; Henry Jacobi, the watchmaker who had come regularly every Monday to Bithoor to wind and set the clocks, and Cox, the infamous cashiered officer who had started it all, and the padre, Reverend Haycock, and the schoolmaster, Gill.

"Nearly two hundred and fifty have died," Hulas Singh, who had been keeping the tally, told me, "almost a third of their number."

It may have been a third of their number, but not of their fighting strength. The dead were mostly women and children, and the resolution of the survivors had, if anything, multiplied tenfold; they were like some wild animal stunned into insensibility by pain and therefore incapable of further suffering.

Also on the seventeenth, came the first shower of the year, a rain hardly heavy enough to settle the dust. Nonetheless, it had announced the advent of the monsoon, when it would rain in torrents. Then the mud walls of the Entrenchment would be washed away and the guns would sink where they stood. We waited for the rains, our eyes turned to the skies, our noses sniffing the air for signs of moisture.

Three days later Hulas Singh came with disturbing news. His spies had returned from Allahabad with the report that a strong British column sent from Calcutta had arrived there on the ninth.

So the rumour going round the bazaar was true. Did the Bengali clerks, I wondered, possess some secret source of information, or had they, with the dry-eyed objectivity of the uninvolved, assessed the situation more correctly than either ourselves or those in the Entrenchment—for we knew that Wheeler and his colleagues, like us, had had no knowledge that a relief column was on its way.

If the column had reached Allahabad, it meant that Benares had already fallen. I tried to calculate how long it would be before they would reach Kanpur. About two weeks, I thought. The British, for all their unwieldy baggage trains, which included double-fly tents for the officers' bibis and as many crates of wine as of ammunition, moved with astonishing speed. They would be here by the twenty-third.

June 23, the hundredth anniversary of Plassey. It was a day we had dreamed of, pinned our hopes upon.

"If the monsoon strengthens, they'll be held up till October," Hulas Singh said. "If not . . . well, any time after the twenty-third." He too must have been thinking what I was.

It was unbelievable and yet it was happening. A handful of British soldiers were advancing unopposed through a vast, hostile land. They could not have moved a mile if the Indians had withheld help, for their baggage was transported by Indian coolies, their guns dragged by commandeered bullocks, their boats manned by Indian boatmen; their cooks, water-carriers, sweepers and boot-blacks and grooms were Indian. Even if all their servants had merely deserted them, they would be stranded where they were, helpless as a bogged-down elephant. And they could have been pinned down at a hundred places along the way, in defiles and at river crossings and in marshlands. What had happened to my countrymen that they were helping them instead of hindering them?

"How strong is the column?" I asked.

"They say anything up to two thousand white men and an equal number of Sikhs."

"Sikhs?"

"Yes, from the Punjab."

"Are you sure?"

He smiled. "With the Sikhs there can be no mistake, because of the beards and the hair buns."

How had they won over the Sikhs, when, barely ten years earlier they had been at war with them and British redcoats had proudly collected the scalps of Sikh soldiers to send home as souvenirs? The headiest word in the Sikh language was "Chillianwala," a village where they had wiped out an entire British column.

The ghost of a superlatively ugly, diminutive, one-eyed man with a beard like a dagger blade stood before me: Ranjit Singh, whom the Sikhs venerated as we Hindus of the west venerated Shivaji. Were not the Sikhs desecrating Ranjit's memory by fighting to preserve the rule of those who had made slaves of them?

"They say that the column has other sepoys too—'loyal sepoys,' they call them. And of course, all the camp followers are our own people."

Anger, or was it the fear of the avenging column, made me feel weak, and there was a buzzing in my head. Hulas Singh was saying something and I had to make a special effort to concentrate.

"They say they are monsters."

"Who are?"

"The commander and his deputy; they say that such savagery has never been seen."

In a land that had seen the invasions of Mohamad Gazni, Nadir Shah, and Allauddin Khilchi, such a statement could only be an exaggeration. "What do they do?" I asked.

"They kill for sport; they burn for fun. They don't spare anyone —not old men or women or children. They go in parties, looking for people to kill, for villages to burn."

"Like our Gujars?"

"Malik, the Gujars leave you alone if their ransom is paid; not these men."

In wars, there are always rumours about the excesses of the enemy, and I did not altogether believe what Hulas Singh's spies had told him. At this stage I called in my other advisers and we discussed our future course of action. If the rains came on time, the column would be delayed for months, and that would give us time to finish off our business here and go to the aid of our comrades in Lucknow, where the white garrison under Sir Henry Lawrence had holed up in the Residency. By the end of the monsoon, we should have overcome British resistance in all the major centres, and after that we would have become too powerful to worry about their military skill or ferocity.

And thus we waited, staring at the nearly white, cloudless skies for signs of the monsoon, praying for the torrents that would both flush out our quarry and delay the relief column. And every day that followed we received fresh reports of the horrors let loose upon the countryside by the men on the march. We could no longer delude ourselves that they might be panicky rumours.

"This is calculated savagery," Azim said in shocked tones. "They mean to terrorize the entire population."

"It will at least open the eyes of the turncoats," Tantya said without conviction.

Hulas Singh disillusioned us on that point. "The turncoats just have to be even more brutal than their masters. If they don't outdo them in savagery, they're marked as disloyal sepoys. The Sikhs sang songs as they watched their victims burning alive."

We heard the names of the commander and his deputy: Neill and Renaud. Soon these names were like wounds on our brains. To this day, saliva spurts in my mouth and my stomach muscles coil at the mere mention of them.

And I squirm with shame whenever I am reminded of my initial squeamishness. Did I not, in sending word to Wheeler, show myself to be a "loyal sepoy"? If the white men had not been concentrated in the Entrenchment with plentiful supplies of arms and ammunition, the sepoys could have made short work of them in their bungalows, as Nizam Ali had proved; Nizam Ali, who had so systematically destroyed the few remaining merchants and planters hiding on their estates.

We heard that Major Renaud had made a practice of killing villagers merely because they happened to be looking the other way when his column passed, and that Neill's orders to him were to slaughter all men and take no prisoners.

Slaughter all men; take no prisoners. It was like a mantra given by a guru to an eager disciple, a motto to live by.

Every morning, as I sat in my prayer-room, I would try to seek consolation and reassurance in the words of our own sages. *Satyam-eva-jayate,* the Lord Krishna had pronounced in the field of battle: truth alone triumphs. And again, *yato-dharma-stato-jaya*: the right cause always wins. I would repeat the words to myself endlessly, as though they possessed some magic powers; believing that, if repeated often enough, they would cause a collision of stars and work miracles on earth.

Satyam-eva-jayate . . . yato-dharma-stato-jaya.

Whose was the right cause? Ours—we who were fighting to liberate our motherland? Or theirs—they who had enslaved us and turned our country into a business settlement, pieces of which could be bought and sold on the London market? Freedom fighters or a gang of sharp-witted desperadoes who had gobbled up a whole subcontinent and were now exploiting it for the profits of its shareholders? Where lay the truth, the truth which alone triumphed? On the side of the pirates and slave traders or that of their victims?—on the side of the robber or the householder?

If a foreign invader, such as Bonaparte, had conquered Britain and if the British had risen to set their land free, would the British people and newspapers exhort French generals to burn British villages and hang British soldiers as though they were felons? This is how I argued.

Satyam-eva-jayate . . . yato-dharma-stato-jaya.

How many thousand times did I repeat that incantation which had been revealed by God himself? There was no bolt from the heavens. Reason stood like a black rock, invincible against the power of thought waves. Bonaparte was dead, and now there was no one left to threaten to enslave Britain. The picture of the British fighting to liberate their land from an alien conqueror was too far removed from reality to stand up as a working analogy, an argument too fatuous to be convincing. The British had proved themselves to be world beaters; in the art of waging wars, they were the professionals and all others clumsy amateurs. That was the abiding truth. The philosophy of the Geeta might bring solace, but not victory. The right also had to have battalions and guns more powerful than its enemies; truth could never triumph merely because it was the truth, not unless it had resources greater than those possessed by untruth.

How could we win when our own people were fighting against us in ever-increasing numbers?—backing up the giants of untruth, living up to a new code of conduct revealed by a new god: *Slaughter all men; take no prisoners.*

Chapter 16

We were going to attack on the morning of the twenty-third. The night before the attack pandits chanted verses from the Geeta and sprinkled Ganges water on the Hindu sepoys to render them immune to bullets, and the mullahs made the Muslim sepoys touch the Koran.

To our certain knowledge, there were now no more than three hundred men left in the Entrenchment who were capable of bearing arms. We were at least two thousand, for even though our ranks had been depleted by desertions, a few days earlier the remnants of the sepoys of Azamgarh, about a hundred miles to the east of Kanpur, had come to join us. We now had more troops than ever before.

But did our numbers represent our strength? That was the question of the moment. The rumours were thick that the Muslims were on the point of renouncing my leadership. The historic blight of my country was eating into our ranks, to divide us assunder.

It was believed that the mullahs, while making the Muslim sepoys touch the Koran, had also secretly enjoined them to reject a kaffir king and choose their own king. A deputation of sepoy leaders had approached Nane Nawab in the middle of the night. What had transpired at the meeting was not known, but the Hindu sepoys had made up their minds to be on their guard against any treachery. All eyes were on Nane Nawab. Would he suddenly turn his field guns on us instead of the enemy?

What with the rumours and the anticipation of the attack, few of us could have had much sleep that night. At dawn the attack began. It was planned to take place in two phases—that is, a diversionary advance by the cavalry, followed by the two infantry wings attacking from opposite sides.

What actually happened was this. The cavalry went into action as planned but was not backed by either of the infantry wings. The British trained all their guns on the advancing line but held their fire till the horses had come within stone-throwing distance. Then they suddenly opened up with all their massed weapons. The line of prancing horses broke and withered like paper burning. Horses suddenly crashed to the ground, thrashing their legs and turning somersaults, and died with horrible human screams. Many of them fled riderless in all directions, some actually galloping madly at the mud wall and vaulting over it to be picked off neatly by the grimacing red-coated soldiers.

It was only after the cavalry advance had been broken up that the Kanpur infantry, who were mainly Hindus, swung into action, almost as though they were participating in a different battle. Their skirmishing parties advanced behind bales of cotton which they kept rolling before them. Again the British guns waited, opening up only when they were within a hundred yards. The bales of cotton caught fire, creating a belt of smoke beyond which no one could see anything. This was the time when our second wing of infantry was scheduled to go into action. But this wing was formed by the Azamgarh troops, who were mainly Muslim. They stood fast where they were and indeed behaved as though they were partisan spectators, for I actually heard them cheering lustily when the cotton caught fire and our troops fell back in disorder.

Thus we celebrated Plassey, by a plunge into ignominy. A handful of white soldiers had once again defeated thousands of blacks. The residue of the centenary of Plassey was a writhing mass of wounded men and horses engulfed by smoke and flames and their heart-rending screams.

I called a hurried council and ordered the attack to be called off. Bugles sounded the retreat, even though the attacking troops had already scattered. The Azamgarh battalion still stood on the flank, still in formation. I spurred my horse and rode towards them, and the others uncertainly followed. A stillness suddenly came over the battlefield.

I had no idea what I was going to say to these men who had betrayed us in the field of battle. A reprimand of any sort would have brought the hostility into the open and might have resulted in a battle between our own troops. How could I, at such a moment, hope to patch up what had been festering for a thousand years—ever since the first Muslims had invaded our land and destroyed our temples?

Then I saw from the opposite direction, from where the bales of cotton were now spurting bright-red flames, a man riding towards me on a horse that kept veering sideways and was spattered with blood. "'Nane Nawab!" a murmur went up and down the bright-red ranks of the Azamgarh infantry. He came like a wounded bird spiralling, flailing his dying horse with frenzy, and hurled himself from the saddle as though he were a trick rider, just as the horse stumbled and fell. He took off his turban with a flourish and placed it on the ground in my path, and then flung himself down in the dust. This man who had fought so bravely and had been entreated by his coreligionists to be their king, was putting himself at my mercy, asking me to punish him first for whatever had gone wrong with the attack.

I jumped off my horse and pulled Nane Nawab up and embraced him tightly. Then I picked up his turban, brushed the dust off it with my sleeve, and placed it back on his head.

We stood facing each other, surrounded by a charged silence. How long did we wait before the cheer broke out from the ranks: "Nana Saheb *ki jai!* Victory to Nana Saheb."

I am convinced that the dramatic gesture on the part of Nane Nawab and my own impulsive response to it did more to heal the breach between our troops than anything else we subsequently did. For in the battles that were still ahead of us, there was no backsliding in the ranks of either faction.

That evening we made plans for another attack on the Entrenchment, which was fixed for the twenty-seventh. Meanwhile, everything that could be done to remove the distrust from the minds of both the Hindus and the Muslims was to be done. Nane Nawab and Azim undertook to talk to every single Muslim sepoy before then, and my brothers, Baba and Balarao, offered to do the same as far as the Hindu sepoys were concerned. All four set off with great hopes and solemnly promised me that they would make everyone swear on his holy book that he would either take the Entrenchment in the next attack or die.

"We shall attack with such fury that not a single man, woman, or child will be found alive when we have finished, and not a stick or stone to remind us of our humiliation."

And with that we dispersed for the night.

Once you have seen men struck down by modern weapons of war and reduced to mounds of torn, blackening flesh, horses disembowelled and fleering in violent protest, such sights are branded with fire upon your brain. Your vision is crowded by the dead or dying: fingers clawing the stone-hard earth in a shudder of death, as though to drown pain by greater pain; the mouths of men and animals forced open by unbearable agony and the blood flowing in spasmodic gouts from holes in contorting bodies . . . these remain in focus, blurring the gleaming, flower-decked gods in the prayer-room and the majestic presence of the mother of rivers. The screams of the dying are like shards of steel wedged deep in your skull.

Added to these was the torment of a defeat inflicted by an enemy inferior in numbers.

Is the capacity to erase at will these horrors that are inseparable from the conflicts of men the distinguishing mark of the warrior? The British, I know, have mastered it, which may be the reason why they have emerged as the master race—invincible because they have become immunized to the horrors of war. Many of their soldiers have told me that, in defeat as in victory, they are able to laugh and joke even while they are counting the cost; that an issue of rum to the men and brandy to the officers enables them to overcome all mental suffering and whets their appetites for the next day's battle.

I thought my head would burst. In the loneliness of my room I wanted to scream at the walls and to tear down the curtains and bedclothes with my hands. Was I going mad? Shame, remorse, self-reproach were like demons taunting; I could not escape them. Against my tightly shut lids, I saw circles of hot light which grew and grew as from a stone cast in water. If only I could, with some miracle of prayer, undo what had been done that day—the anniversary of Plassey.

Satyam-eva-jayate, I told myself. Truth alone triumphs. We could not lose. But would even an ultimate victory—the headlong flight of the British—mitigate the torment of my mind?

I got up and ordered a palanquin. I told the bhois to take me to an address in Golaghat bazaar: Azijan's house.

"A few hours of merciful oblivion brought by a woman's feet," is as near as I can come to defining Malabar *malish,* for it will bring you a night's uninterrupted sleep. It is said to be required training for a Kathak dancer. All I can say is that I have found it unfailingly effective. I drop off to sleep like a child.

Ideally, it must be performed in the open air, which is how they do it in Malabar. You lie naked under a tree on banana leaves spread in the sand. From an overhanging branch, a rope is suspended just above you. The girl, also naked, rubs warm coconut oil over your body. Then, supported by the dangling rope, she begins to knead your limbs with her bare feet. After a while, you notice that the movement of her feet has a rhythm, and you realize that she is dancing over you. The rope which she is clutching permits her to control the pressure of her feet.

From time to time she pauses to pour more coconut oil over you and to help you turn over. At times you feel her feet are as hard as knots of coir rope, at others soft as petals. Suddenly you go rigid as her heel digs into some hidden centre of pain. It lingers, like a fly around an open sore, probing and caressing alternately, with a sure, sensual touch. The pain has gone and exquisite relief taken its place, and the process of drawing off the pain has been so delectable that you long for the same spot to be worked over again, so that you may savour the coming of relief with greater involvement. There are overtones of sounds and smells: the girl hums to herself, and her feet, squelchy with oil, make soft, sucking sounds; the hot oil mixes with your sweat, yours and hers, and a sweet heady odour surrounds you. After a while you don't feel any pressure at all, only an over-all tingling sensation such as might be produced by being stroked by a hundred feather dusters. Then a blankness descends, a state of not being.

But you are not allowed to doze off—not yet. Again the heel converges around the tender spot, tantalizingly. A stab of exquisite pain follows, and then the thrilling sensation of pain being erased. You are fully awake, almost physically aroused; somehow you have, in spite of your supine state, become a participant in the dance of sleep. More oil splashed; a nudge, and obediently you turn over. The dance resumes. You lose consciousness, to be turned over again—and yet again. The process is repeated till the feet sense that your body has acquired the requisite state of limpness that will ensure prolonged sleep. Before she steps off, you have already lost contact, with her as with the world. She then sits beside you, fanning the air with a banana leaf and keeping off the insects.

Here in Kanpur, all this was done in the courtyard of Azijan's house. But the girl, her body the colour of wet charcoal, was from Malabar and knew her business well. I must have fallen asleep within an hour. When I awoke, the *koels* were already calling among the trees—a cascade of cooees that was like a series of echoes. Azijan and the black girl were still in the courtyard, both with smudged, unslept faces. With the awakening, the ghosts of yesterday came snarling back. But I had been given a night's sleep and my brain no longer felt confused. I knew what I had to do. It might not be the right move; but it was a decision, a positive step.

Grudgingly, I submitted to the scalding-hot bath that the two women gave me. The sun was still behind the charred trees of the civil station when I was back in Savda Kothi. I sent for Azim.

"Bring old Mrs. Greenway here," I told him.

For the past week or so they had taken to shooting at sight anyone approaching the Entrenchment wall. Mrs. Greenway was a white woman, dressed in European clothes, and she was going to walk up to the wall in broad daylight. As an extra precaution, she carried a child in her arms, one of her own numerous grandchildren.

"They're not going to fire at a woman with a child in her arms," she told me.

All the same, one of the sentries nearly did. Mowbray Thomson, who was the officer on duty along this section of the wall, has described how he saw a man raise his rifle and knocked it down as he recognized Mrs. Greenway. Mrs. Greenway gave him my letter, which said:

> To the subjects of Her Most Gracious Majesty Queen Victoria:
> All those who are in no way connected with the acts of Lord Dalhousie and are willing to lay down arms shall receive a safe passage to Allahabad.

I had made the distinction deliberately, to show that I respected the British queen and had nothing against her subjects, that our quarrel was specifically against the Company's officials in India, and even in their case, we were going to be spiteful only against those who had participated in Dalhousie's malpractices. In my own mind, I was quite certain that not many people in the Entrenchment thought very highly of Dalhousie and that fewer still would have claimed to be associated with his territorial burglaries.

I had also charged Mrs. Greenway to give a personal message to Wheeler, that I, as his personal friend and well-wisher, implored him to seize this opportunity of leading his people to safety; that the sepoys had been so infuriated by the tales of savagery on the part of Neill and Renaud that they had sworn not to spare anyone once they broke into his stronghold.

The mood of the sepoys, I felt, was something like what it had been just before they had risen: explosive, desperate; it was almost as though they were looking for signs in the sky, some stray act of injudiciousness on the part of someone or other.

From the topmost room in Savda Kothi, I could see many of their barracks and the clusters of tents that surrounded them. I spent the entire morning and afternoon in this room, going from window to window, trying to look for signs myself. What were they thinking, saying to one another? The heat of the day drove them indoors and the barracks looked deserted, lifeless. I heard the distant rumble of thunder and prayed that the rains would hold off till Wheeler had made up his mind and taken his men and women out —and that he would do it quickly.

Late in the afternoon the sepoys began to emerge from their barracks and tents, like termites pouring out of holes. Was there some change in the pattern of their movements—a new bustle as though something had disturbed them?

In the evening I was told that Mrs. Greenway had returned, that Wheeler had said yes. He wanted me to send emissaries for discussing terms the next morning.

The next morning! I cursed. Why not that very night? But there was nothing I could do; anyone going towards the Entrenchment at night would have been fired upon without challenge. I could not even send a message enjoining hurry.

Early the next morning I sent Azim and Jwala Prasad. The British, I learned, had formed a committee of three to negotiate terms, consisting of two military officers, Captain Moore and Captain Whiting, and a civilian, Mr. Roach, who had been the postmaster. They haggled over details as though time were of no consequence. It was well past noon when the British proposals were brought to me.

They would vacate the Entrenchment and proceed to the river, where we were to keep the boats for their journey ready. We were to send them carriages and palanquins to take their sick and wounded to the boats. Each boat had to have six sheep to provide meat on the journey. The British were to be permitted to retain their personal weapons and also to carry with them sixty rounds of ammunition per man.

"We can never agree to this!" my counsellors protested. "How will we know if they take only sixty rounds? They might take hundreds!"

I brushed aside these objections and accepted all the terms. My only condition was that they must hurry—if possible, leave the Entrenchment that very evening. We began to make frantic efforts to collect the boats and to put them in a state of readiness.

The refugees numbered about seven hundred and fifty, and to accommodate them we needed at least fifty boats. An easy enough task in normal times, it now presented insuperable difficulties. Many boats had been destroyed or damaged and many others dragged ashore and hidden under mounds of straw. Hulas Singh sent for the most prominent boat contractor in Kanpur, Budhoo, and ordered him to get us the boats. At first, Budhoo protested that it would be quite impossible to lay hands on so many boats at such short notice, but after Hulas Singh threatened to have him strapped to a cartwheel and the cart trundled through the streets, he hurried off to see what he could do.

Within the hour, the boats began to arrive. I was told they were in varying states of disrepair. Hulas Singh, resourceful as ever, rounded up all the carpenters in the vicinity and put them to work to make the boats navigable.

Azim came back from the Entrenchment to tell me that my insistence on expeditious departure had nearly made them break off the negotiations. They had again gone into a huddle and come out with the answer that a committee should be formed to go and see for itself whether we really were assembling the boats. If the committee was satisfied that the boats were being assembled, then they would vacate the Entrenchment the next morning.

"Oh, God!" I groaned. "Not another committee!"

The committee wanted an elephant to take it to the ghat, Azim told me, and an escort of mounted troops.

I cursed again, but immediately sent the elephant and the escort.

This one was a committee of four: Captain Atholl, Captain Turner, Lieutenant Gould and Lieutenant Delafosse—the Delafosse who had been my guest at Bithoor when the Wheelers were last there and who had spent his last night there in Azijan's embrace. I was told the committee inspected every single boat and appeared to be satisfied with them all. Their only complaint was that the boats had no roofs.

At the time I was greatly irritated by this new demand, but quickly realized that it was reasonable. The journey might take anything up to a week and few would have survived it if they had had to make it in open boats, exposed to the direct rays of the sun. The trouble was that not many of our boats are built to take roofs, and in the case of those that were, the frameworks had been dismantled because of the imminence of the monsoon.

On my behalf, Hulas Singh undertook to have the boats adequately thatched before the next morning, and then and there sent off guards to round up more carpenters and to forage the town for straw and bamboo and cordage. His methods must have impressed the committee, for they went back and gave a favourable report on our preparedness.

Something like a thousand workmen, bamboo splitters, carpenters, blacksmiths, and rope winders, toiled throughout the night to prepare the boats. Meanwhile, I fumed and swore. There was nothing to be done till the next morning. How often in later years have I not tormented myself with the thought: what would have happened if Wheeler had heeded my entreaties and started his exodus that very evening? Should I not have insisted on their clearing out even though the boats had no roofs?

It was quite dark when an emissary from the Entrenchment arrived with what I was told was a treaty for me to sign. He was an old man with untidy white hair matted stiff with dirt and sweat, his chin encrusted with dried-up saliva. In the light of the candles, his face had the colour and texture of groundnut shell. He wore no shoes, his trouser legs were cut off at the knees, and his coat was missing one of its sleeves. He stood with bent and trembling head while I read through the paper he had brought.

"Have the poor wretch given some food," I told Balarao in Hindi, but just as Balarao was taking him away, a phrase in the treaty caught my eye.

"What's this about hostages?" I asked.

"They want three hostages," Balarao explained. "Only for the night, though."

"Oh, all right. Send Jwala Prasad, he's been there before; and you decide who the other two are." I called for pen and ink and signed the two copies and gave one to Balarao for the emissary. "Give the man some food," I said again.

That was when the man spoke. "Don't you recognize me?" he asked, in a voice that was like a sick crow's, faltering, wheezy.

I stared at the bent, trembling man in rags, a frog from a dried-up pool. I shook my head. "Should I?"

"Yes," he squawked.

"I'm sorry. The face is not even vaguely familiar."

The man cleared his throat and quoted a Hindi aphorism. "Mother, motherland, and tutor; these one can never forget."

"Toad Saheb!" I cried out.

"Toad Saheb," he repeated, and his cheeks were wet with tears.

Todd, foppish and dandified and haughty, with polished boots and oiled hair, had become this mangy and wasted creature. I sprang up and put my arms around him. I made him sit beside me and ordered his meal to be brought to him and a bottle of wine.

I am grateful that, when he returned to the Entrenchment, Todd told everyone that I had treated him with the utmost kindness.

Chapter 17

"The hat men are leaving!"

The cry had an intoxicating ring. We had been clumsy and had made many mistakes, and yet we had done it. Kanpur was liberated. If they could achieve even this much in Delhi and Lucknow and Bombay and Calcutta and half a dozen other places, we would have won the war.

The twenty-seventh day of June. A still, breathless dawn. I remember it was a Saturday because, for me, it was a day of fasting. It was the day we had fixed for our death-or-victory assault. We had achieved our objective without military action.

Before dawn sixteen elephants, about two dozen bullock carts, and certainly no fewer than a hundred palanquins had been sent to the Entrenchment. I had sent my personal elephant, Airawat, for Hugh Wheeler and his family. I later learned that the General was too ill to climb into the howdah and so had to be carried to the river in a palanquin. Janaki and the girls rode the elephant.

"The yellow-faced ones are leaving!" everyone told everyone else. Tomorrow there would not be a single Englishman in Kanpur. Right had won and the people who had done the wrong were being driven out. Good had triumphed over evil. It was almost obligatory for everyone to turn out to see the rulers departing. No one must miss it.

Everyone went. The bustees and the bazaars emptied and the people filled the streets and the embankment. Everyone was dressed in festive garb, as for a holiday; and yet, as always, the most colourful were the sepoys in their red-and-blue uniforms and plumed turbans and gleaming buttons. They strutted about importantly, shouting orders. It was their day; they were the victors who had brought it all about, the heroes.

But, standing well behind the throngs and lining the high bank of the river were other sepoys, whose uniforms were not familiar in Kanpur. The russet-and-green facings belonged to the 6th Infantry, the yellow-and-black to the 37th. The 6th had come from Allahabad, the 37th from Benares. Both battalions had been driven away from their stations by Neill's column. They were assembled on parade and ordered to lay down their arms, and after they had done so, were fired upon by British troops. For a moment they didn't know what was happening, and then they had begun to run. Some had died in the shooting and some others who had fallen down wounded were summarily dispatched by their assailants, but a large majority had escaped. And when these men had returned to their homes, they had discovered that their villages were charred ruins, their families maggoty skeletons dangling from the village pipal trees.

Hatred, like all passions, needs an outlet, otherwise it goes on growing, feeding on itself; and these sepoys had had no opportunity to work off their rage. They had suffered without being able to retaliate. And now, when they had come to Kanpur with high hopes of participating in a murderous assault, they found that there was nothing left for them to do but witness the orderly departure of their intended victims. The Kanpur sepoys had finished the job on their own.

It is not as though I was unaware of this resentment; and yet, on that morning, I did not expect it to erupt, for I believed that they too would be glad that the thing was over and done with and pleased at whatever we had been able to achieve. We had liberated Kanpur and forced our particular contingent of rulers to surrender. Now we and the new sepoys who had come to join us could go on to Lucknow and Delhi, where all of us would have ample scope for wreaking vengeance. Meanwhile, they could, as the others were doing, gloat over the spectacle of their enemies' going away under a white flag.

Satichaura ghat, where the boats were assembled, had once been a cremation ground. About a hundred and fifty years earlier, two widows had burned themselves here on the same day, and since then it had been called Satichaura, or the embankment of the satis. A temple had been built to their memory and there were stone steps along the bank to facilitate bathing. It was more than a mile from the Entrenchment and nearly three miles from Savda Kothi.

I had deputed Balarao, Tantya, Azim, and Nane Nawab to supervise the embarkation, but this was merely to invest the occasion with what I considered the appropriate degree of formality, and I had sent a personal message of farewell to Wheeler as well. Tantya and the others were squatting on a carpet spread on the platform of the Hardeva temple and thus had a full view of the boats moored below. The flight of steps going down to the river was packed with the men and women of Kanpur who had turned out to see the exodus of their masters.

Everything had gone off smoothly right till the last moment, in a spirit of tolerance and even good humour—and then there was pandemonium: screams and war cries and the crack and whine of bullets. Even from their vantage point, Tantya and others had not been able to see exactly how it started, and once it had started, they too had to make a dash for it and hide in the temple because of the withering fire coming from the boats.

I was in the grip of a wave of depression which invariably descends on one whenever something really big has been achieved at great cost. I was restlessly pacing up and down the veranda of Savda Kothi when I became aware of the distant roar of the crowd, a sort of humming sound, rising and falling, interspersed with reports of rifle fire. Within a few minutes, a trooper came galloping from the riverside, yelling, "There's massacre on the river! They're killing the white men!"

"Then go and tell them to stop the shooting!" I yelled at the man, and then, as though I had stumbled upon some inspired solution, called up another four or five messengers and sent them off with the same order: "Find Tantya, Nane Nawab, Azim. . . . Tell all of them that it is my order. The firing must be stopped, at once. At *once!*" I was shouting at the top of my voice.

After the messengers had gone, I was overcome by an acute sense of helplessness. What had I tried to do and with what results? And what was now left for me to do? Berserk men did not obey orders. They had gone too far to be turned back. It was futile to try. I knew my commands would have no effect whatever.

Then I shook off my mood and decided to go and see things for myself. My own elephant had still not come from the river, so I called for another and rode over to the ghat with all possible speed. The streets were deserted and not a sound was to be heard. It was only after I had passed the infantry lines that I could hear odd musket shots, but there was no sustained fire. What did it mean: that they had obeyed my order, or that there were no more white men to kill? Tantya and the others saw my elephant from a distance and came hurrying over, babbling with agitation and waving their hands. They told me that the sepoys were still shooting but that there was no return fire from the river.

"Why are they still shooting then, if the enemy is not shooting back?"

"Many of the hat men are still alive—they're feigning death."

"But they're not killing our men."

"They say that every single one must be killed since their people have killed our people."

"They?" I yelled. "Who's they?"

"The Allahabad and Benares regiments have formed committees —of their senior officers."

"But they can't go on killing. There are women and children among them—they've never done anything to us!"

"We told them that."

"And what do they say?"

"That there's no means of telling the men and the women apart at this distance—all bobbing heads."

"Which they shoot at."

"Yes."

I groaned and cursed loudly. "Go and tell them to stop firing at once. Tell them we'll make the survivors prisoners—deal out punishments later."

Tantya and Balarao looked at each other uncertainly, so I said, "You go, Azim, they'll listen to a Muslim. Take Nane Nawab with you."

The leaders of the new lot of sepoys were firmly in command here and had installed themselves on the platform of the Hardeva temple. I saw Azim and Nane Nawab make their way through the crowd and reach the temple. They were courteously received and made to sit down. There was a good deal of shaking of heads and waving of hands in disagreement. Then all the members of the committee looked in my direction and further discussion followed. Within a few minutes, Azim and Nane Nawab returned, their faces glum.

"They've agreed to stop firing, but only on one condition."

"Condition!"

"That the male prisoners will be handed over to them."

"And what do they mean to do with them?"

"Shoot them."

"What kind of condition is that?"

"They'll spare the women and children."

"How can anyone agree to such a condition?"

"That's as far as they are prepared to go," Nane Nawab said.

I cursed, and then flinched as a rifle cracked from twenty yards away. There were shouts of "*Maro! Maro! Sampko maro!*—Kill the snakes!" Half a dozen more shots followed. The men in uniform sitting on the temple platform were looking in my direction. It was clear that they meant business.

I shut my eyes tight and shrugged, and that was that. As I opened my eyes, I saw that Azim and Nane Nawab had hurried off to communicate my acceptance.

I got off the elephant and went to stand on the highest step. The smell of sulphur hung in the hot air. The riverbed was strewn with grey ash. The water was the colour of sugar-cane juice and thick, like oil, and the boats like charred wreckage washed up by the storm. Some boats were still smouldering and some had become entangled. The water around the boats was a mass of human bodies, some still twitching and some stiff in grotesque knots. The blood looked purple in the mud and brown in the sand.

The shooting had stopped. I could clearly hear the groans and whimpers. One by one, the men and women stood up in the river, some holding children. They were all looking at me, somehow aware that I had stopped the shooting. Someone raised a hand as though in recognition. I knew that they all believed that I had saved them from death and were thanking me. I could not bear it.

Everyone was looking at me. I am sorry, I said to them, but without uttering a sound. This is not how I wanted it to end. Forgive me, I am sorry, sorry, sorry. I have not saved your lives. I have compromised, borrowed a little time for some, perhaps saved a few. I don't know. I am sorry.

Sweat broke all over my body and misted my eyes. I turned about, only to realize that the sepoys too were staring at me, waiting for me to go. Slowly, I made my way to the elephant, placed a foot in the crook of his trunk, and was gently hoisted onto the howdah.

That was the sum total of my intervention. The firing had stopped. About a hundred and seventy half-dead men and women were fished out of the water, some with grisly burns and bullet wounds. Nearly sixty were men, the rest women and children. The men were roped together and made to stand in a long line against the riverbank. The women marched off to one of the barracks to be made prisoners. From here, a week later, they, as well as the women and children who had been rounded up by Nizam Ali and had been held captive in one of the outbuildings of Savda Kothi, were removed to the Bibighar.

A commodious building patterned on a harem, with trellised windows all around and a central courtyard and its own well, it was called Bibighar because it had been built by a Captain Brandon for housing his bibis, or Indian mistresses.

Bibighar: it means love nest, and yet what terrible thoughts it evokes! In common with names like Waterloo, or Panipat, or Balaclava, it has its inherent violence, a power to shock. Its ruins will ever serve as whetstones to sharpen racial hatred.

I made inquiries. It was quite impossible to get a clear and coherent account. Everyone agreed that it had gone without a hitch right up to the moment of embarkation, but no one could say how the shooting had started.

The refugees came to the river in a long, untidy procession of bullock carts, elephants, palanquins, and bamboo litters interspersed with groups of hobbling, haggard men on foot, their bodies encrusted with grime, their clothes in tatters, their legs stork-thin or grotesquely swollen.

"As though walking in a daze," Balarao said, and added, "but their heads jerked from side to side in nervous twinges."

Some of the sepoys had impulsively come forward to assist their former masters and talked and joked with them and helped to carry their belongings and their children. But not all the sepoys were so friendly; some stood well back, scowling, and a few jeered.

Standing on the lowest step, Major Vibbart, who had been supervising the embarkation, allotted each person his place in the boats. The boats were bobbing up and down gently and looking, because of their thatched roofs, like floating haystacks. There were forty of them, lined up in pairs in knee-deep water. The sick and the wounded were first put into the boats and then the women and children. After that came the men who were still able to walk. Balarao and Azim between them recognized some of the officers: Moore, Mowbray Thomson, Seppings, Glanville, Jenkins, Todd, and Delafosse. Wheeler came last, in a palanquin carried by four sepoys. He looked bent and old, a shrivelled ghost of the swaggering Hamlah, untidy tufts of sandy hair sprouting out of his nose and ears. He had to be assisted to his feet and as he walked to the last boat, could take only one step at a time even though he was leaning heavily on the shoulder of his younger daughter, Emily.

By nine everyone was in the boats. There was an expectant hush as the boatmen waited for Vibbart to give the signal to start.

And then someone fired a shot. No one could say where it came from, from the bank or the river, or whether it was near or far. And before its report died out, someone shouted an order, loud but not clear. Perhaps it was Vibbart telling the boatmen to start.

After that the confusion was sudden and indescribable. Scattered shots, screams, frenzied yells, smoke, and then the crackle of fire. Some saw the boatmen throw away their oars and run scrambling for the shore. Panic spread. The soldiers in the boats grabbed their rifles and jumped overboard and began firing at the boatmen. The boats heaved and rocked and turned around and fell on their sides or became entangled. Bullets thudded into the boats and whined overhead. More and more men jumped out of the boats; some took positions and opened fire while others struggled to set the boats free. On the ghat there was a general stampede.

"Within minutes, the enormous crowd had vanished," Nane Nawab told me, "leaving a few twitching bodies. At this time I saw that high up on the bank the sepoys in green-and-russet uniforms were crouching behind bushes and boulders and taking aim."

Some piece of wadding from one of these muskets, British or Indian, must have lodged in the straw of the thatched roof of a boat. Suddenly one or two boats were burning, and the rising wind spread the fire from boat to boat. When the smoke was at its thickest, Tantya and Azim put their heads out to see what was happening. The sepoys on the bank were now maintaining a sustained fire. They would take careful aim, fire, and reload and get up and fling themselves into new positions. Some were running along the banks, screaming "*Deen! Deen! Sampko maro!* Kill the snakes!" and trying to keep pace with the few boats that had managed to get unstuck and were drifting down with the swift current.

That was all I could elicit. I don't myself believe that the British started it. If they did, it was the act of some obscure soldier losing his nerve and firing at the boatmen who were running away. It is more likely that one of the sepoys from Benares or Allahabad began it, almost without conscious volition, like a kitten pouncing on a disappearing mouse.

Of the forty boats, only three got away. They were energetically pursued by parties of sepoys running along the bank and firing upon them whenever they drifted within range. Two of the boats were overtaken that very day and their occupants brought back to Kanpur, the men to be shot by firing squads, the women and children to be made prisoners. The third boat was captured three days later when it had run aground on a sandbank near Surajpur and everyone in it put to death on the spot. As it happened, however, a dozen men from this boat had earlier gone ashore to forage for supplies. As they were camping in a small temple for the night, a sepoy patrol had found them and surrounded them. The sepoys stopped the outlets of the temple with straw and set fire to it and literally smoked out their victims and shot them as they came running out. All but four were killed.

These four men were the only male survivors of Satichaura.

They were two privates, Sullivan and Murphy, and two officers, Captain Mowbray Thomson and Lieutenant Delafosse.

Wheeler was not among the survivors, and none of the Wheeler ladies were among the prisoners. One or two sepoys swore that they had seen their boats burning.

Chapter 18

The next two weeks are a blur in my memory, a jumble of events I cannot disentangle.

On the night of Satichaura the rains broke. When morning came it was still pelting hard. At last the monsoon was with us. During the day I shifted my residence to Noor Mohamad's hotel. Savda Kothi was right in the middle of a vast, insanitary military encampment, over which stench hung like a vapour, and by now I had also become convinced that it was an ill-starred residence. That same evening the women and children held prisoners in its compound were removed to the Bibighar.

Victory, such as it was, brought new allies. The neighbouring Rajas came and joined us with their hastily raised contingents. Also, more and more parties of sepoys from the distant cantonments were still drifting in. But our number did not necessarily represent our strength, which was almost equally divided between Muslims and Hindus. Since the arrival of the Benares and Allahabad battalions, the rift between the communities had again widened and the Muslims were talking of choosing someone other than Nane Nawab as their king.

·"Not that a single Hindu will accept a Muslim king," Hulas Singh pronounced loyally.

"And what about the Emperor and the Queen? Are they going to accept a nonentity as king here merely because he happens to be a Muslim?" Azim asked.

"What is this talk of kings?" I protested. "I am no king either, merely the Peshwa—a sort of viceroy." It was a way out; the distinction had always been merely technical.

We all agreed that it would be a good thing to emphasize that distinction; to make it known that the Emperor of India was a Muslim and that I, a Hindu, was merely his nominee for administering a part of the empire. So we decided to hold a durbar at Bithoor at which I would be formally installed as the Peshwa. The *joshis* consulted their calendars and pronounced that the following Tuesday, June 30, would be auspicious.

I welcomed this opportunity of escaping from the problems of Kanpur and decided to stay away for at least a week. To act in my place, I nominated a Council of Ministers, with my brother Baba as its president. He was to be assisted by two Hindus and two Muslims. I suggested Tika Singh and Hulas Singh, and Nane Nawab and Nizam Ali.

That was when I was told that Nizam Ali had gone. "No one has seen him for days—nor any man from his squadron," Hulas Singh said. "They've all gone."

"Gone?"

"Every one a rich man, it is said," Tika Singh said virtuously.

"They should all be shot as deserters," Tantya pronounced.

"They say that Nizam Ali operated on the British system of prize money. All loot was pooled together and shared according to rank."

"So the whole squadron has vanished?" I asked.

"And some people are saying that Nizam Ali has abducted a white girl—many people saw him riding off with her."

"Where has he gone?" Tantya wanted to know.

They all shook their heads. No one knew.

I began to laugh. "I know where he is," I told them. "In Akbarpur. He's got himself a house there. Imli-kothi, John Bathgate's house."

God knows it was not unusual for me to be told at these meetings that our troops were deserting in large numbers, most of them going off to their villages to put away their loot, but somehow I had not expected Nizam Ali to desert us. I had always thought highly of his devotion to me, and his flitting away like a renegade just when I was about to make him a councillor came as a bitter disappointment to me.

We turned to other problems. The moment the revolt had broken, all public offices had shut down. The officers had run away to the Entrenchment and the clerks, who were mainly Bengali Christians, had not ventured out of their homes for weeks. "Issue a proclamation calling upon all officials to resume work without fear of recriminations," I ordered.

Hulas Singh simpered and folded his hands. "Shall I speak what is in my mind, Malik?"

"I want complete honesty," I said. I had still not realized that no ruler can expect complete honesty from his courtiers.

"They're not afraid of *us*—that's not the reason they're staying away. They're frightened of what will happen to them if the yellow-faced ones return and find them working for us."

"The British will never return," Tantya thundered. "Those who fear they will be back are defeatists and should be publicly flogged. The rats!"

"In that case, we will have to flog them by the thousand," Azim pointed out. "The clerks are not the only ones who are running away."

"Who else is running away?" I asked.

"The city people."

"But where are they going? Where can they go?"

"Into the villages, to lie low; hide from the wrath of the sahibs."

"Cowards!" Tantya said with venom.

It seemed that everyone wanted to run away from Kanpur, which, rumour said, had been singled out for the most terrible punishment. "What were you saying?" I asked Hulas Singh.

"The best riverside mansions are being offered for a thousand rupees."

They must have cost at least twenty times as much to build. Somehow we had to stop the panic. We put our heads together and decided to issue a proclamation which we fervently hoped would turn out to be true.

So, that evening, from the street corners, the red-bloused drum beaters announced: "The yellow-faced and narrow-minded race have been driven away from Poona, Delhi, Satara, as from Kanpur. The Company's rule has ended. The land has returned to God!"

To be sure, we had no news from any of these other places. But who knew, it might just be true that they too had succeeded in driving out their white populations—that the land really had returned to God.

In the rain-washed, early-morning light, Bithoor was a rose-pink cliff, or a castle in a mirage. On the flagstaff on the tower of my house flew a tiny saffron triangle. The people had erected arches at every turning and decked them with mango leaves and flowers and messages of welcome. The houses had been cleaned and spruced up and the streets painted over with designs drawn in powdered chalk of many colours. Women stood before their doorsteps, wearing bridal saris and jewellery; they cracked their fingers against their temples in blessing as I passed. They were not welcoming me, they were celebrating the return of freedom; no foreign conqueror, however mighty, would have been awarded this kind of welcome; it was spontaneous, straight from the heart. It was all very heady.

And then through a gap between houses, I happened to glance at the river and saw in the shimmering distance a plume of smoke as though a village were burning. Had Major Renaud already arrived there?

The dogs recognized my elephant and began yelping even before the sehnai players above the main gate broke into a *bagesari,* which was my favourite raga. My daughter, Gangamala, who was now nearly eleven and had taken to behaving more primly than my eldest aunt, broke loose from a line of women and came running down the drive, holding her sari up well above her knobbly knees, and the elephant, without so much as a break in step, picked her up with his trunk and deposited her in my lap.

In the afternoon I was installed as the Peshwa. Priests chanted mantras as I sat on the guddi of the Peshwas, which, even though Bajirao had had it made in Bithoor itself, was said to be the replica of the one burned down by Elphinstone. Before me was the sandalwood box containing the saffron breechclout of the saint Ramdas, which had been adopted as the flag of the Maratha kingdom and which had come down to our family as its most treasured heirloom. My wife, Kashi, looking like some fairy princess in white and gold, sat beside me.

First we honoured the Emperor, Bahadur Shah, Ghazi and Padishah, for whom a salute of a hundred and one guns was fired. A tray piled with gold mohurs and a sword and robes of brocade were dispatched to Delhi as my tribute to my sovereign. After that twenty-one guns were fired—for me, the Peshwa, the Viceroy of the Emperor in Kanpur as well as in Poona.

That night my dreams were of Poona, the capital of my ancestors, which I had never seen. I woke up early and went into the animal park. Some of the younger deer flicked their ears and tails and ran away, but the spotted doe from Canara, Lanka, came forward as soon as she heard my whistle, proudly escorting twins, miniatures of herself. I was holding one of the fawns in my arms, and its mother was nudging its face to soothe its fears, when I heard a discreet cough behind the fence. It was Tantya Topi and his face looked glum.

"There is trouble in Kanpur," he announced. "A Muslim butcher killed a cow."

A Hindu cannot think rationally about a cow, just as a white man cannot think rationally about a black man. In a Hindu raaj, a cow must be protected. And one of the very first pronouncements I had made was to ban cow slaughter. Tantya told me that my brother Baba had demanded that the offending butcher be produced before him and ordered his right hand cut off. That had made the Muslims furious. A protest meeting had been held in the Pearl Mosque.

I cursed my brother, and Tantya and I mounted our horses and cantered off in the direction of the rising sun. Baba and the others were waiting for us in the porch, their faces dark with care. Had the Muslims already hit back, I wondered—burned a temple or killed a brahmin?

As it turned out, however, the tension had subsided. Nane Nawab and Azim had gone round meeting prominent Muslims. A durbar was called for the next morning, at which the leaders of the community would wait upon me to present their grievances.

"I am not going to rescind the order banning cow slaughter," I told them. "It is one thing I shall never do."

"Their main complaint is that very few of them have been given high offices or ranks. If Malik were to announce a few promotions and grants of land to some of those who are most deserving of recognition . . ."

"No one can say there has been discrimination," I said. "That is one thing no one can accuse me of."

"Malik, it is just a device to keep some of the prominent Muslims on our side. . . ." Azim, himself a Muslim, conceded, smiling.

"You mean bribe them—give in to blackmail."

"When in difficulties, even the God Hari has to go down on his knees," Tantya quoted.

So we all agreed to placate the Muslims at the next day's assembly by doling out gifts according to a list prepared by Azim and Nane Nawab. But even after this was settled, I got the impression that this was not the real reason why I had been recalled in such a hurry. My advisers were glancing at one another as though hoping that I would myself raise the subject. My breath suddenly constricted and saliva welled in my mouth. "What else?" I asked, trying to sound offhand.

"They say the British column is only a few days away," Azim answered.

"Good!" Tantya said. "The time has come to show them what we can do."

"What do you think we had better do?" I asked.

"We'll catch the column before it gets here, where there's some natural obstacle."

For a few minutes we discussed tactics, and with a decision made, everyone seemed a little less depressed. I said, almost as though to change the subject, "I hope the public offices are functioning again."

They all looked at one another and then shook their heads.

"The city is emptying fast," Hulas Singh said very softly.

"What's the going price of a riverside mansion?" I asked.

"Oh, not more than a hundred rupees—but there are no takers."

I could then see why it was so imperative to placate the Muslims with gifts of land. This was a time to present a solid front, no matter how much it cost. We had boastfully announced that the yellow-faced ones would never return. Now we had to eat our words and prepare our men to face the avenging column.

Chapter 19

Neill and Renaud: the names had become as familiar as those of our twin mythological moon eaters, Ahi and Mahi. It was their declared policy to instil fear by terror. They selected at random what they termed "guilty villages," to be cordoned off and set on fire— anyone who tried to escape was shot down. They organized volunteer hanging parties to hunt for "guilty men," which term included anyone whose behaviour seemed even remotely suspicious to any member of the party; men were speared like hogs merely because they happened to be looking the other way, or for attempting to run away, or merely for looking agitated. By now these hunting parties had developed a competitive spirit, and bets were laid openly as to which one would spear the highest number of *pandies* on a given day.

Reports of these barbarities came to Kanpur every day, and while, to be sure, they produced the intended effect of striking terror, they also served to arouse a desperate frenzy. Those who had lost their wives and children in the destruction of guilty villages and in other acts of chastisement, craved at least one burst of retaliation before they in their turn fell victims to the white man's wrath.

God knows my control over the sepoys was never very firm. But at that, before the enemy's campaign of terror gained momentum, they had obeyed me in all essentials. Even though the British in the Entrenchment had made it a practice to shoot all prisoners out of hand, I had not ordered a single execution. But once the sepoys discovered what the other side was doing to its captives, it became increasingly difficult to curb their anger. Restraint became a sign of impotency. Children made ribald jokes about the masculinity of the sepoys and women swore that there had not been a pregnancy in Kanpur for months. At first in ones and twos, and then in droves, the sepoys had gone away to join the newly arrived men of the 6th and 37th, who, in any case, had never placed themselves under my orders.

"Both Neill and Renaud are heading for Kanpur," Azim told me. "They say their strength has been doubled. Fresh British troops have arrived, and more Sikhs."

Tantya twirled his greying moustache. "The more there are, the more we can kill."

They came. An instrument of chastisement that was more like a column of sightless ants which cannot be turned away from its course; elemental, an act of God. People fled in terror, abandoning their fields and homes.

The astrologers set July 7 as a good day for the start of a military campaign. On that day, at the precise moment prescribed, I dispatched Brigadier Jwala Prasad with two cavalry regiments and three infantry battalions to intercept the British column. Five days later, on July 12, Jwala Prasad came upon the enemy a few miles beyond Fattepur, which lies at a distance of fifty-one miles from Kanpur on the Allahabad road. "Fatte-pur" means "victory town"; it was a good place to offer battle.

Jwala Prasad, thinking that the force he had encountered was Major Renaud's advance guard, went precipitately into attack. What he did not know was that the column had been joined by the main body of the British force and was now under the over-all command of a general who had mastered the art of warfare: Henry Havelock.

Added to this fatal miscalculation was the shock of discovering that the enemy could maintain an effective and sustained fire against our troops long before they came within range of our weapons.

The explanation, we soon learned, was the Enfield rifle, which had a range twice as long as the "Brown Bess" our men were armed with. The cartridges the sepoys had rejected were now killing them from a range which they themselves were unable to match.

At least two hundred of our men were killed when Jwala Prasad decided to withdraw; all this slaughter the enemy was able to cause even before our men could open fire.

This was the battle, the battle of Fattepur, that started the Havelock legend. And rightly so, for there is not the least doubt that he was a commander of exceptional ability; a skilled tactician who could read a military situation as other men read a printed page. He was also audacious, resourceful, crafty, and coolheaded. What could we not have achieved if we too had a few Havelocks among us—Havelocks as well as the new rifles and limitless supplies of unpolluted cartridges so that we could have fought on equal terms.

Then our men saw something else: a village being sacked with military thoroughness and its women dishonoured. Fattepur, by being in the vicinity of the place where our troops had offered battle, had had its fate sealed. They saw it being cordoned off and set on fire. Those who tried to escape, even women and children, were thrown back into the fire or shot while escaping. Even as they were retreating, our sepoys looked back in horror and swore vengeance. If that was what the white man did to his victims, it was up to them to wreak a similar vengeance.

So ended the first battle for Kanpur, a battle which was not a battle at all but a walkover, a shooting down of people from a range at which they could not shoot back. So also ended a village called Fattepur.

It was not till late on the following night, the thirteenth, that I first heard of our defeat. I immediately sent Balarao with two more battalions to reinforce Jwala Prasad and then busied myself preparing for the defence of Kanpur.

All through the following day Tantya Topi and I went up and down the Allahabad road like rabid jackals, trying to determine the best piece of ground for making a stand. Behind us, in the opposite direction, radiated long lines of fleeing refugees. A city was being emptied; its people abandoning it before the fate of Fattepur overtook it.

Seven miles from Kanpur the road from the cantonment joins the main Delhi-Allahabad road near the village of Maharajpur. This was the place we selected. We placed the last of our guns and men astride the two converging roads. Our left flank rested on the river, our right in a labyrinth of mud walls surrounding a village whose name I have long forgotten.

"We have to concentrate our strength on our right," Tantya pronounced. "Mother Ganges will shield us from the left."

It was not till daybreak of the fifteenth that Balarao succeeded in linking with Jwala Prasad's force, which had regrouped near the village of Aung, thirty miles from Kanpur. Almost at the same time, at daybreak on the fifteenth, Havelock, who had marched all night from the opposite direction, caught up with them and opened his attack. Here our infantry was able to repel the first British onslaught, but once again the more accurate and longer-ranged weapons of the enemy took a heavy toll of our sepoys, and after a while our ranks broke up. Balarao and Jwala Prasad pulled back a further seven miles, to the Pandu River.

Pandu is a tiny little stream. Except during the four months of the monsoon, it is easily fordable at any point. Now, with the first onrush of the rains, it was a swollen, swirling torrent of muddy water and therefore a formidable military obstacle. Here Jwala Prasad and Balarao decided that the only bridge over the Pandu must be defended at all costs or, as a last resort, blown up. But their intention must have been plain to Havelock, who was equally determined to capture the bridge intact. He launched a feint frontal attack against their position beyond the bridge and, at the same time, sent a force to attack the left flank. As this fierce, two-pronged attack developed, our sepoys left their positions and began to run, making for the bridge. Everyone thus converged on the bridge while those who were detailed to blow it up waited with impatience for the very last company to cross over.

By that time it was already too late. Havelock's Highlanders came screaming on the heels of the retreating troops and seized the bridge before it could be demolished.

As he was supervising the crossing of the bridge, trying to maintain some sort of order among the fleeing troops, Balarao was struck by a bullet, which went right through his shoulder. Late at night he was brought back on a litter to Maharajpur, where Tantya and I were anxiously waiting for news of the battle. We did not know it then, but it was in this battle that Major Renaud too was hit. He died of gangrene a week later.

The Pandu bridge is twenty-three miles from Kanpur, and thus sixteen miles from our position at Maharajpur. As the retreating troops reached us, Tantya and I allotted them new positions. All night they kept coming, spent and demoralized. We gave them food and water and brave words, and then exhorted them to make yet another stand.

And hard on their heels, as though impervious to hunger and thirst or physical exhaustion, came the irreversible column of ants; two victories had only whetted their appetite for more blood.

I have described our position, with our left flank protected by the river and the right by a mud wall. Tantya and I had walked along the riverside and decided that the terrain, broken and knee-deep in gluey mud, was quite impossible for a military force to negotiate. We confidently expected the attack to come from the right, and were prepared for it, having sighted our guns to cover all the likely approaches.

We were proved wrong. Havelock kept away from our right as though he knew exactly what we had laid on for him. Instead, he pushed a thin line of Highlanders along the crevices and through the mud and water on our left. And Mother Ganges, instead of rising and sweeping them away like termites, opened her arms and conveyed them undetected to a point where our defences were thin. It was only when the redcoats were right in our midst, screaming and charging with the bayonet, that we realized that we had been attacked from the left.

Havelock had resorted to a desperate gamble, pinning everything on the success of his quite audacious manoeuvre. For, in order to sneak his Highlanders along the riverbed, he was compelled to leave behind all his heavy equipment. If the attack had not come off or our defence at the point of attack had been stronger, the bulk of his infantry would have been cut off from its food and ammunition and its camp followers. Even the medium and heavy guns had been left behind.

But the gamble paid off—paid off, I am convinced, only because the Indian coolies organized a human chain to bring up the rifles and ammunition needed for the attack, and even the food and the cases of rum. The Highlanders swept clean through our lines so that Tantya, who was guarding the right flank, and I were separated. Seeing what was happening, I rounded up the only remaining twenty-four-pounder and some of the smaller guns and ordered a point-blank cannonade into our own left flank. Admittedly, some of our own men were killed by our guns, but the attack suddenly lost its fury, and at last the enemy troops gave in to exhaustion, lying down wherever they were, panting, while British officers rode up and down yelling at them to get up and carry on the fight "in England's name!" No one stirred, until they began to pass round bottles of rum. That made them get up and surge forward towards our few guns still firing.

One by one, our guns fell silent. English curses and obscenities drowned our own war cries and the names of our gods. By nightfall we were fleeing in all directions, leaving the Kanpur road wide open.

The next morning, Friday, July 17, the British flag once more flew over Kanpur.

In describing the main features of the three battles for Kanpur, I have skipped over the most talked-of event of the week and possibly of the entire revolt: the slaughter of the women and children held captive in Bibighar. This took place on the evening of the fifteenth, while I was camping in Maharajpur, frantically preparing for a battle, and while the first of our troops retreating from the Pandu River battle had already begun to arrive. And, as I shall relate, the days that followed were so crowded with events and I was so cut off from Kanpur, that it was not till a week or so afterwards that I heard the first garbled versions of the massacre.

And before I had heard about Bibighar, I was told about the hanging of Azijan by Havelock. "So they don't even spare women," I remember saying to my nephew, Raosaheb. "Even Nadir Shah did not kill women."

"They say it is because she helped us actively. She incited the sepoys."

"In that case, shouldn't we have killed all the white women in our hands?" I screamed at him. "After all, it is their boast that their women too fight beside their men—as the equals of men!"

I did not know that someone had done just that, killed the women, and even the children as well, at Bibighar.

On the night of July 15 Bibighar, the love nest, became the house of massacre: the hundred and seventy white women and children held prisoners there were slaughtered. The horrifying details of the manner of their death, of how they were hacked to death by professional butchers because no one else could be persuaded to do the killing, and how the dead and wounded were all flung into the same well may or may not be true. But, of course, even granting that the details have been exaggerated, the fact remains that every single woman and child in the place was killed.

I know that at Satichaura it was the sepoys of the disbanded regiments who were responsible for the massacre. But the sepoys had nothing to do with Bibighar; if only out of religious scruples, no Indian soldier would bring himself to murder captive women and children, no matter who ordered him to do so. As such, it may well be true that the killing was done by butchers who were led by a woman.

What woman? Many people believe that it might have been Hussainy Begam.

The name conjures a witchlike creature, withered and permanently bent under a dripping dungbasket, her hair standing like wire. She was shrieking wildly and beating her breast when I last saw her. She had just been told that her daughter had been burned alive in the burning of Daryaganj.

Some have even suggested that she was my mistress, on the principle, it would seem, that any woman who did something particularly horrifying in Kanpur just had to be one of my supposedly numerous mistresses. No, Hussainy was not my mistress. As a young woman, she had been a lavatory maid in Bajirao's harem, and in Kanpur we had pressed her into service as a sweeper in the artillery bullock sheds.

A woman who had grown up on the periphery of a packed harem, like a dungworm beside a cesspool, a dumb witness to unspeakable orgies, herself defenceless against the assaults of the palace menials, and who had gone on piling grievance upon grievance all her life, had she found an outlet for the accumulated venom of a lifetime?

While in Kanpur I had often noticed her, almost as one notices a scarecrow. But, try as I might, I cannot credit such a creature with possessing a mind, let alone the power to influence men to do her bidding, even at a moment of mass hysteria. Or had her daughter's death caused some deeply buried impulses to erupt? Who can say?

And yet I know that something very much like this must have happened. Only a combination of panic and rage could have caused it; panic and rage were the twin serpents released by the savagery of the Company's column. I cannot think of anyone in Kanpur—and certainly not myself, who was looked upon as a white-lover and as such distrusted—who could have controlled the men and women whose families had perished in the acts of prophylactic village burnings; and the destruction of Fattepur on July 12 was the last straw. Three days later someone quite like Hussainy Begam must have led the butchers into Bibighar.

Satichaura and Bibighar are monuments to our brutality. "Look and be ashamed," the world will forever admonish us. "This is what you have done; this is what you are capable of." So long as the sun and the moon go round, our noses will be rubbed in their dregs.

One can find excuses, but excuses cannot make facts vanish. They will remain with us forever, like spectres, jeering at us and tormenting us.

And yet the point must be made that both were a form of primitive retaliation against the savagery of the advancing column and have to be viewed in the same frame, as composite pictures. If Daryaganj and the other villages had not been burned down as guilty villages, Satichaura might never have happened; and if Fattepur had not been destroyed merely as a followthrough to a victorious military action, Bibighar might never have happened.

Military defeat often breaks out in violence in the most unpredictable ways, and the irrefutable example of this that, perhaps naturally, occurs to me is the wanton destruction by a British battalion of their unfortunate camp followers before the walls of Delhi, which also took place at about this time. They were massacred for no other reason than to assuage an unquenched blood lust. The British attack had been repelled by the defenders of Delhi, and so the fury that was to be unleashed on the citizens of Delhi was directed upon the camp followers—the water-carriers, sweepers, porters, grooms, cooks, bearers, and bootblacks, all neatly huddled up for convenient slaughter like a herd of sightless sheep.

And Bibighar too was avenged measure for measure within two days, and in Kanpur itself. Here Neill, now promoted to brigadier, showed that he had nothing to learn from Hussainy Begam. He rounded up Kanpur's most prominent and respectable citizens and ordered them to be hanged. But, before being hanged, they were made to atone for the sin of Bibighar by cleaning its floors.

And under Neill's orders, the task of cleaning was to be made "as revolting as possible," which meant that men of the highest learning and lineage, who could not conceivably have had anything to do with the massacre, were made to crawl on all fours and lick off the mess of clotted blood and urine and faeces. It was Neill who transformed the ancient banyan trees of Kanpur into a "hanging garden," using the trees for gibbets and elephants for drops, and, as a lesson to the natives, left the bodies dangling from the branches, to be pecked at by scavenger birds till the limbs rotted and fell to the waiting dogs.

PART III
GONE AWAY

Chapter 20

The spirits of darkness hid my shame. The streets of Bithoor were empty, the houses shuttered. That night no lamps were lit.

How much time did I have? Would my enemies go on to Kanpur or would they come galloping after me with cries of "Gone away!"? I did not then know that I had all but beaten back Havelock's attack; that, having drawn upon the very last reserves of physical resources, the redcoats had lain down wherever they happened to be and curled into rum-sodden sleep. Not even the lure of plunder could make them get up and take another step.

Hurry, hurry, I kept telling myself, there is much to do. And yet there was no confusion in my mind. I did everything as though I had thought it all out beforehand and was putting into operation a plan previously prepared.

I told my nephew Raosaheb what I was going to do and sent him off to make the necessary preparations, and I also sent the wounded Balarao with him. I deputed my other brother, Baba, to try to save as much of the family gold as possible. The only hiding place we could think of at the moment was the well behind the animal park. It was thirty feet wide and sixty deep, and always held plenty of water. Now the monsoon rains had filled it to the brim. Into this well went the Portuguese candlestands that had been made for some church, the Mogul wine pitchers that needed a strong man to carry them, the hundreds of sets of platters and dishes and goblets which the Peshwas had used for their ceremonial feasts, and box after box of gold mohurs.

While Baba was getting all the gold pieces together, I opened the two strongboxes in the underground vault and told Champa and Gangamala to bring out their contents and pile them on the bedroom carpet. From this lot I began to separate the pieces I believed were the most valuable and put them on a shawl spread on the floor. The two piles grew—one on the carpet and the other on the shawl. The big pile on the carpet I transferred into a camphorwood chest, which I sent down to the well. I have always wondered who appropriated it. There is no mention of such a box in the list of objects recovered from the well by the prize agents.

Champa and Gangamala brought up the last of the ornaments. Now we were alone, a family: man, woman, and offspring, standing around a pile of jewellery like nomads around a campfire. Seven generations of Peshwas had acquired the jewels. The green flame that glowered like the blazing eye on Shiva's forehead was the emerald called Shiromani, believed to be the largest in the world, although it was an awkward shape—more than three inches long but less than an inch broad. My ancestor Nana Saheb, for whom I was named, had had it set into a turban clasp. The Naulakha necklace reared its head like a cobra that had been stepped on; it was called Naulakha because the first Peshwa, Balaji, had paid nine lakhs of rupees for it. Since then, at the time of the installation of every succeeding Peshwa, more and more stones of matching lustre had been added to it, so that now, in the impoverished India of the Company, it was believed to be literally priceless because there was no one rich enough to buy it. The two red spots that were like the bleeding hearts of tiny birds were the rubies with which the first Nizam had placated the first Bajirao after the battle of Palkhed. This most illustrious of my ancestors had shocked his family and court when he had had the rubies set into eardrops and presented them to his mistress, Mastani. The clamour set up by Bajirao's enemies and friends had forced Mastani to decline the gift, and Bajirao in disgust had put them away in the vault and pronounced that no one who was not as beautiful as his Mastani might wear them. For a hundred and fifty years they had lain unused. Neither Gopika nor Rama, who were wives of later peshwas and reputed to be very beautiful and very conceited, had coveted them.

Other nameless diamonds and emeralds and rubies twinkled

like coloured fireflies from bracelets and belt buckles and rings of the seven Peshwas and their wives and mistresses, and clusters of pearls dimmed by disuse looked like wax beads in the candlelight.

The clocks in the hall below chimed. A whole hour had already passed. "Please hurry," Champa said. Her face was bloodless and her voice dry, and the thought crossed my mind that she looked like a sati, a widow about to burn herself.

"You and Ganga take something," I invited, "in case you too have to go into hiding for a time."

Without a word, Champa walked to the side of my bed and picked up my slippers. "These are all I want."

This was no time for sentiment. I shut my eyes and plunged both hands into the pile. I handed a fistful of jewels each to Champa and to my daughter. "Go and put these away," I told them.

Obediently they went in. I tied up the remaining jewels in a bundle and tried it for weight. The bundle was the size of a man's head but surprisingly light.

The big emerald and the jewels from the Naulakha today adorn a king's crown. The other bits and pieces I sold to buy the necessities of life or for bribing my way out of awkward predicaments— once I gave an amethyst the size of an almond to a fisherman who merely ferried me across the Ganges. And Mastani's eardrops went to a woman every bit as beautiful as Mastani, just as the first Bajirao had willed.

I untied the bundle again as Champa and my daughter came back. There were other things I wanted to take away. The saffron breechclout of Ramdas, the two tattered bits of bark bearing some of the verses from the Geeta copied down by Bajirao I, which he had always carried in battle, the single earclip of cheap coral that was given as a good-luck charm by Brahmendra Swami to Balaji I, and the thin gold toe rings worn by my grandmother Anandi. Revered as objects of worship, these had all been kept in the prayer-room.

Then Champa darted in again and came out with a sword in a faded purple scabbard and placed it beside the folded flag.

"Not her! Not Jayanti!" I cried out in shocked protest. A sword to us is a woman, even a goddess, to be referred to as "she"; and all famous swords bear names, feminine names. This one was Jayanti, "The Victorious," the most famous sword in my land after Shivaji's Bhavani. It was Bajirao's sword—the first Bajirao's, that is—and none of his successors, valiant though some were, had dared to strap it on. How could I, defeated, hunted, a failure, commit this desecration?

"They will slaughter cows with her," Champa pointed out.

"Then we'll bury her, somewhere safe."

"Swords are not meant to be buried; they're meant to be used."

It was not an admonition; it was the voice of reason—a sati dispensing wisdom. Meekly I picked up Jayanti, touched my forehead to it, and strapped it on. The harness fitted snugly, as though it had been made for me.

I tied up the bundle again, now increased to the size of a small pumpkin but hardly heavier. The clocks ticked away the seconds. The moment I was dreading was upon me.

I held my daughter's thin, trembling body tight against my chest and said a quick prayer. Then I pushed her away, and sternly, as though to leave no doubt in her mind that I had more important things to attend to, ordered her to bed. The time had come for a young girl to be sent to bed to cry herself to sleep so that her father could accomplish his vanishing trick without complications. Gangamala was my illegitimate daughter and her mother my senior concubine, and, however much I might love them both, they had no place in what was to be made to look convincingly ritualistic.

So I sent my daughter to bed and explained my plan to her mother. I was, to all appearances, taking the *jal-samadhi,* which meant that I was going to drown myself publicly, in a ritualistic act. For this I had to be accompanied only by the members of my family; it was their right to be with me while I went to my death and their obligation to perform the last rites over my body. Champa understood the position perfectly.

"The British will keep you under house arrest," I said. "They might even take you and Ganga to Kanpur and keep you under a guard for a while. But they're not going to do either of you any bodily harm, if only because you are not of my family."

"Why should they?" Champa asked confidently. "You didn't kill their women."

"I didn't kill even their men," I told her. (Neither of us knew what had happened in the Bibighar the previous night.) "They might get drunk and loot the wada, but their officers are bound to keep them in check."

"Of course they won't harm us," Champa said as though trying to reassure me. "Now, please hurry."

"In a few days I hope to be able to make another stand. Meanwhile, I shall try to get a message across to you. You and Ganga keep in readiness. I'll send Azim or someone to bring you."

"I shall pray for it."

"If you can slip away, we should be together again in a week."

"Nothing can part us, not even death." She was dry-eyed and actually smiling, and I had the feeling that courage was flowing from her into me.

I slung the bundle over my shoulder and busied myself tying the knots and adjusting the straps. My hands fumbled and my eyes misted. How was I ever going to face it, this moment of parting from this woman who had been closer to me than anyone else? I tried to remember a suitable prayer but couldn't. Helplessly, like an animal waiting for a word of forgiveness, I looked up.

Champa had gone—gone so that I should not linger, so as to make it easy for me to go without fuss. "Champa!" I called out, but no answer came. And suddenly I was grateful, conscious that a barrier had been lifted, an area of pain bypassed.

I ran down the stairs as fast as I could, and then was brought to a halt as though jerked by wire, my feet rooted to different steps. I heard a roar, a terrifying jungle cry of anguish and protest, and recognized the call of Sheru, my favourite tiger. And as though on cue, there was a mighty cacophony of animal calls as the bears and the hyenas and the jackals and the monkeys joined in. The inmates of the zoo were complaining that no one had given them food or water that day.

I cursed and turned about, livid with rage, ready to blast whomever I saw for this criminal neglect and to order that the animals be fed and watered at once. And then I remembered that it was too late for such an order. I fled, pressing my hands against my ears to shut out the reproach of the animals, whom I had loved as my children.

The way to the ghat had never seemed so long. Now there were people in the streets, but still no lights. No one jeered or cursed; instead they were invoking their gods and offering me their blessings. *"Har-har! Shiva-shiva!"* they moaned, and some, I would have sworn, were sobbing.

On the top step of the ghat stood Kashi, dressed in green and wearing glass bangles up to her elbows. In her hands she had a tray with five tiny *divas,* or butter lamps. She circled the tray around my head and with a finger placed a red dot on my forehead.

She too was going through a ritual, the ritual prescribed for a wife about to become a widow because her husband was committing suicide. I was struck by her poise and, even more, by the tears flowing freely from her eyes. How could anyone distrust so convincing a performance?

Kashi flung down the tray and it went clanging down the steps. Then, bending down, she broke her bangles against the stone embankment. Thus declaring that she had accepted widowhood, she went down the steps with bowed head and shaking shoulders and took her place in the waiting boat. The other women of my family were already there, and so were the men—Balarao, swathed in bandages, Baba, and Raosaheb. I stood on the lowest step, the water lapping my feet, and offered a prayer: "Mother Ganges, your son comes to you. Cradled in your lap all his life, it is by your wish that he now ends it. On this, his very last journey in this world, what more can he ask than that he go into the next with your blessings!"

"Nana Saheb is preparing for the jal-samadhi!" the whisper went through the small crowd that had gathered on the ghat steps. "Ending his life by giving it to Mother Ganges."

My intention thus sufficiently impressed on the minds of the onlookers, I got into the boat. All the women now began to sob. Baba, in a choked voice, said farewell to the crowd on my behalf. "We were defeated in Kanpur and have been separated from Tantya Topi and others. Now the yellow-faced ones are on their way to Bithoor, and my brother, whom you have all these years held to your bosoms, has decided to remove himself from this world so that their wrath might be tempered. He seeks your blessings. He goes happily, knowing that mortal man can seek no better death than to commit his body to Ganga-mayi."

As we pulled away, a thin wail rose from the bank, and, as though affected by it, the animals in the park once again broke into their heart-rending chorus.

We were nineteen in the boat, and, on the pretext of lightening the load, Raosaheb ordered the three boatmen to leave us. And they, as though relieved not to have anything more to do with the condemned, scrambled over the sides and ran splashing through the water without so much as a backward glance. We now lit all the candles we had brought with us—perhaps a hundred in all—and Raosaheb and Baba took the oars. We made progress in slow jerks. The skyline of Bithoor receded, and the cries of the animals became fainter. I took off my slippers and my turban and my outer robe and, one by one, threw them overboard. Then, dressed only in a pilgrim's knee-length robe and clutching my bundle and sword, I clambered over the side and swam back towards the bank till my feet touched bottom.

I looked back. The boat had merged into the surrounding gloom, and I knew where it was only by the cluster of lights gliding away as though carried by the current. As soon as I had regained my breath, I began to wade, making for a spot about half a mile above the Bithoor ghat. On reaching dry sand, I took off my gown and squeezed it dry and put it on again.

The boat was now only a speck of light above the flat black expanse of water and scarcely moving. Even as I watched, the lights suddenly went out and a piercing ululation arose, exactly as when a death occurs. Within seconds, the people waiting on the ghat got the message, for lights suddenly began to appear among them, like darting fireflies, and then I could hear the rhythmic chanting of the death service as more and more voices joined in: "*Wasansi jeernani yatha vihaya.* . . . Even as we cast off worn-out garments, so does the immortal soul abandon this body. . . ."

My teeth chattered and my knees wobbled. It was my death that they were bewailing. The wet gown clinging tightly against my skin was like a shroud pinning me down, inducing paralysis. And then somewhere a shot was fired and its report went rolling over the silent water. So the looting had begun. I ran, trying to prevent myself from thinking of the woman I loved, of my daughter who had so obediently gone to bed. I kept reminding myself of all my failures in order to prod myself onwards, stumbling in the sand and falling and rising again. I had a long way to walk and no time to lose.

It was too much to expect that Havelock and Neill would be taken in by my ruse. They were bound to make the most searching inquiries and disbelieve witnesses as a matter of principle—unless, of course, they happened to be European. Then someone would bring a slipper or turban and that might make them waver. They would then wait the extra day for the body to float and would announce a reward for its recovery. The British would never believe that a death had occurred until they had seen the body. To them, the putting out of lights, the death wail of women, or the priests reciting the funeral service meant nothing. After a couple of days of waiting, they would proceed to hang all those who had come forward to tell them I had taken the jal-samadhi and energetically resume the chase.

And yet my plan was very sound and very practical. I knew that for at least three days I would be immune from pursuit. During the coming day, I was going to hide in Nizam Ali's house in Akbarpur, and I had arranged that in the evening a boat should come there to ferry me across the river. I was heading for a place called Chaurasi, where the members of my family would have already gone and where I proposed to live for a few days before deciding on my next move. To be sure, I had not sent word to Nizam Ali that I was going to be his guest for the day, but in his house I was sure of a welcome. A man who had won a reputation as being the exterminator of white men was not likely to betray me to the enemy.

Everything was not yet lost, I kept trying to convince myself. The dragons of wrong had reached Kanpur, but they still had a long way to go. Tantya had escaped, taking away the bulk of his force; Mani, who was now the Rani of Jhansi, was carrying on the fight with the utmost determination; and Begam Hazrat Mahal, the Queen of Oudh, had gathered a large force and was daily offering provocations to the enemy. There was still a good chance of the tide's turning—it might turn today, if the Scindia so willed. Then I would join forces with Mani or with the Begam, and one day I would return to Bithoor riding on a white charger. Ganga-mayi would welcome back the child she had so callously abandoned.

The house loomed in the darkness, looking like a Mogul tomb, ghostly and oddly luminous, its outlines obscured by the ancient tamarind grove. The big wrought-iron gates were closed, but a wicket to the side swung open as I pushed it. My bare feet scuffed softly over the gravel of the long curving drive. Beyond the house the river emerged, and beyond the river the orange bar that was the edge of the rising sun.

I was still about thirty paces away from the front porch when I heard a shrill scream such as might have been emitted by a mortally wounded wild animal, and over the jolt of panic it caused, I heard the words cried out in English: "No! Oh, please . . . not that! No-ooo!"

I ran towards the house. The porch was empty and the front door shut. Knowing the layout of British bungalows, I looked for a bathroom door bolted from the outside for letting in the sweeper and discovered one at the back. I darted in, my feet making hollow thumping sounds like magnified heartbeats. A figure swathed in bedclothes shot up from a mattress on the floor and a terrified, boyish voice jabbered in alarm. I brushed past, making for a room from which I could now hear loud moaning, and came up against an arch covered over with heavy *chic* curtains. I slashed at the ropes that held the curtains in place and only then realized that I had drawn my sword.

A rope snapped and the bamboo curtain swung to one side, showing a gap just wide enough for me to squeeze through. I tumbled into a large, high, bare room with wooden floorboards which must have been the dining-room. The early-morning light seeped through the darkened skylights like a monsoon fog, and there was a foul smell, as in a neglected zoo, the stench of excrement and urine and stale sweat in a tightly shuttered room. Something moved on the floor, a grotesque, many-limbed form that writhed and slithered in the wetness.

But almost at once things took clear shape. On the floor were two women, one bending over the other. The one lying on the floor was naked and her hands and feet were tied by ropes to nails driven into the woodwork. At her side was a widening pool, which

I knew was blood, and the blood was oozing in a thin trickle, from the palm of her hand, through which a long black nail stood out like a dagger. The other woman was bending over. Dressed in a voluminous black *kamis* and pyjamas gathered at the ankles, she looked like an obese vulture. She had one foot planted on the prone woman's wrist and she was driving a nail through her other hand, the nail held securely in position in the centre of the palm, a mallet raised high as she took careful aim.

"Oh, no! Please . . . I beg . . . I'll do anything—yes, anything. Oh-oo!"

It began as a shriek that penetrated your eardrums like needles and ended in a shuddering whimper. But before it had ended, I had brought the sword down across the fat, arching back, cutting the woman in two. With a loud plop, like a jack fruit splitting, the two halves fell on either side of the other woman, in the foulness of faeces and urine, and blood shot out from great red holes in spasmodic jets, drenching my ankles.

Now I was bending over the naked woman. Her eyes stared at me unblinkingly and her body kept squirming as though from some inner rigour. Abruptly the squirming stopped and the eyes closed. I did not know whether she had died or fainted. But I had recognized her: Eliza Wheeler.

The shuffle of bare feet and a sharp, snakelike hiss of alarm followed by a guttural gasp made me spin round. In the archway, peeping through the slit I had cut into the curtain, were two faces: a beardless youth and a withered, toothless woman. "Hi-Allah!" the woman gasped and her mouth fell open. For a moment no words came, just a series of lizardlike clucks, and then, after a sharp release of breath like a bark, she completed her sentence: "Hi-Allah! He's killed the mistress—cut her in two pieces!"

The boy's eyes rolled and he cried out in a whine, "*Toba!* You know who he is? The King! Nana Saheb!"

They both stood as though looking at a ghost, staring stupidly but absolutely frozen and soundless. I raised my sword and made a dash at them. "*Jao!*" I yelled. "Go away! *Bhago! Ekdum*—quick!"

The woman screamed and the boy recoiled as if I had hit him. Both withdrew their heads and scuttled away like spiders into a chink in the wall.

Chapter 21

Eliza had been fished out of the river after the Satichaura shooting and Nizam Ali had taken her away. In the three weeks she had been in his house she had suffered much. He had forcibly converted her to Islam and married her, but in the end she had managed to kill him. After that Nizam Ali's wife had sworn to torture her to death. She was the woman I had killed.

"I don't think she was sane," Eliza told me weeks later. "As a couple, they formed a team, though she was years older. Both were religious fanatics and prayed several times a day. At first they merely kept me locked up, but there were no other privations. I was given food and water regularly and left to myself. Then a bearded man came to the house and went through some sort of a ceremony. After that the wife told me I had become a Muslim."

A man would have been circumcised, I thought to myself.

"She was a horribly perverse woman: all she wanted was for her husband to have a child, which she herself could not give. It was she who ruled the house. The servants hated her. The next day there was another ceremony. The woman gave me some sweets and told me I had become her sister—that I was married. That night it began. The wife and the old lavatory maid held me down. The man raped me. The next night too the same thing, and the next."

"You don't have to tell me," I assured her.

"Who am I to tell, then, how I became pregnant? There is no one left. I'll go mad if I don't tell someone."

This was after I told her that her family had perished at Satichaura, and at the moment I could not think of anyone she had ever known who might still be in Kanpur. All the same, I said, "They'll be happy to know you're alive. Many of your father's friends must be among those who are now in Kanpur."

She was silent for a long time and then shook her head. "There is no one—not one single person that I care for. What am I to go back for? To be jeered at because I am going to be a mother, carrying a child implanted by numerous acts of rape, knowing that I couldn't even say for certain who the father was?"

"It might have happened to anyone," I said soothingly.

"It happened to me. And that is not how I would ever go back cringing, an object of pity."

"This sort of thing is soon forgotten."

"The women never forget. They never forgot who my mother was. She was a general's wife, but she remained a robber's mistress. How often did she tell me that she wished she had stayed on in the Pindari camp! Am I to go before the same women, showing a big stomach and begging to be accepted?"

She didn't have a big stomach, and for myself I could not understand how she could be so sure that she was pregnant, only six weeks or so after she had been made Nizam Ali's wife. And what did she mean "the same women"? At least the Kanpur ones had all been killed. "I'm sure that when things settle down you will think differently," I tried to soothe her. "I'll arrange to have you sent back any time you wish to go. You just have to say when."

"Only if you send me away, I shall go," she answered very evenly, "but never because I wanted to go."

God knows I did not want her to go, but at the same time I did not want her to stay merely because she had nowhere else to go, and above all I wanted to make it clear to her that the choice was hers.

I should have realized that the die was already cast. Fate had brought us together at a time when the sensible course for us to take was to remain together. A hunted man had saved an abused woman from death; their separate pasts had gone up in flames. How else could they face whatever years were still left to them except by clinging together, by giving and taking warmth and comfort and strength and companionship?

This was, as I said, the sensible course. What made me fight it was an attitude of mind. I did not want Eliza to accept the situation merely because she had been forced into it.

Her thoughts were far away. The blue eyes looked into the distance and their pupils dilated as though they were seeing things which were not there. The look on her face was Janaki's, rebellious, defiant.

"But you killed the man," I pointed out. "No one can ever forget that."

"I killed him, yes, but only after it had gone on for many days. The same thing every night. The two women swearing obscenely and admonishing me to be complaisant, and then holding me down and cleaning me up, preparing me for the man to come tearing into me like a crazed bull. I would scream—scream as loud as I could, hoping some passer-by or even the servants would come rushing in. I thought I would lose my mind when the woman came at me with a stick or whip. And then I remembered what my mother had done under similar circumstances. She had pretended to give in and then waited for her chance. So that night I said yes—to everything I said yes. I bathed myself and later the two women did not have to hold me down. They merely watched—it was horrible."

Even hearing about it made me squirm with disgust. "And was he too taken in?"

"Not that first night, nor the second. The women would be crouching on either side, waiting to pounce. But I was allowed a little more freedom. At least I was permitted to go to the bathroom unattended. One afternoon I got up and went into the bathroom and picked up the stone slab on which the big vessel of water rested. I crept into his room. He was sleeping on the floor because of the heat. He was snoring and his mouth was wide open. I raised the slab as high as I could and brought it down . . . on the head. It broke like an eggshell."

"You killed a man with a stone!"

"Like a cobra, by crushing his head." Her nostrils flared and her eyes glinted. "The crash must have been heard all over the house, and I remember he also made a sound, a sort of aah!—but very loud. Everyone came rushing in, the wife and the other woman, her son the groom and the servants. They jumped on me and held me down. All I could do was to laugh, like a mad woman. After that the wife had me dragged to the dining-room and tethered my hands and feet to nails driven into the floor."

That was three days before I found her.

"They gave me neither food nor water, and once that woman urinated in my mouth."

"You speak of servants. Where did they go?" I asked.

"They buried the man within hours—it was so hot. Then they came back to the house and I heard the wife ranting at them and heard them answering back. It seems they all wanted to run away because the British were coming. Soon they were quarrelling and the woman came running into the dining-room screaming. They threw her down and tore away her clothes and raped her in turns. Then they let her go and fell on me. After that they went through the house smashing things and taking whatever they wanted, while the woman kept shrieking abuse at them. That night they must have run away. After that there were only two of them in the house, the lavatory woman and her son the groom."

"And the wife."

Eliza shuddered. "Maybe she had lost her mind altogether. She put on those mourning clothes and never removed them. She would go about mumbling words of prayer and chuckling softly to herself, and every so often bending over me to tell me of the tortures she had devised. She was going to pierce my eyes with heated needles, but only one at a time. She was going to pour honey all over me and bring in a swarm of lion ants, brand me with faggots, pour spoonfuls of sizzling oil over my nipples. And when I said, 'Oh, God,' or 'Oh, Christ,' or something, she thought of the idea of driving nails through my hands and feet. I was in the right position. And she and the other woman kept egging that horrible boy to take liberties. I cried for water. She said she would give me some, and then squatted over my face."

All this Eliza told me many weeks later in our hideout in the fort of Chaurasi, after she had partially recovered her health, and when there could be no doubt that she had become pregnant. But the morning I had burst in upon her she was hardly conscious of what was happening. She would only moan and mumble incoherent things and go limp and rigid by turns. I gave her water, only spoonfuls at a time, and fanned her to sleep, and, after she had rested a bit, removed her to another room and sponged her body. I found some clothes and put them on her and then made her lie down on the mattress that the groom had slept on. She kept dozing off but waking up with a start every few minutes, and several times she gave out stifled screams.

I went from door to door, putting my ear against the panes. How long would it be before the redcoats came? Had they already surrounded the house? Why had I not killed the boy and the old woman? They must even now be telling some patrol commander where to find me.

The house had been picked clean by the servants. Only some heavy pieces of furniture remained, tossed in corners because the carpets from under them had been removed. The smell of putrefying flesh came in waves from the room where the woman lay where I had killed her, and bright-green insects banged against the glass panes for admittance. Were they, I kept wondering, attracted by the smell, or was there some other way by which they discovered where bodies lay decomposing?

The hours dragged on as though the time machine had been filled with molasses instead of sand. But at last the light began to fade. Eliza was sitting up now, leaning against a wall, but she was not able to do much more. I picked her up and hoisted her onto my back, hooking my arms under her knees, and walked out of the house.

I lay back on the sand, oddly comforted by the presence of the woman for whose protection I had suddenly become responsible. The smudged line that was the opposite bank had merged with the darkness before I heard the faint slap of oars. But the boat slid into view almost immediately after. Even in the darkness, I recognized the two figures: the one tall and athletic, Azim, the other squat and with the immense shoulders of the professional wrestler, my manservant Waghu. Even as the prow of the boat crunched softly against the sand, I could see them both looking fixedly at the inert bundle lying beside me. And then at a gesture from me, Waghu came and lifted Eliza and carried her tenderly into the boat.

Kashi took charge of Eliza. She prepared special food for her and coaxed her to eat. She washed her hair, changed her clothes, and cleaned and bandaged her wounds. She scolded her and pampered her and sang songs for her. Eliza, whose only wish was to be left to die in peace, was slowly brought back to life.

How little have I written about Kashi? But then what was there to write? She was married to me, but she was no more than a piece of furniture in the wada—something to be put on display on public occasions. My adversity had, as it were, infused life into her. By some right I never remember conceding, she had become the mistress of my household, such as it was now. To be sure, I was grateful to her for taking over the running of my house in exile, but I must confess I never expressed my gratitude to her. To me she was like a serpent in the closet, the superlatively beautiful curse that I had to guard against taking to bed. It has never been easy for me to think of Kashi as a woman. When she ceased being a curse she became a goddess, and you cannot really show kindness to a goddess. You might set her up in a shrine and deck her with flowers; certainly you cannot go to bed with her.

Our new perch, the village of Chaurasi, was about five miles from the river and a good thirty from Bithoor. The very next day after our arrival there I sent Azim back to Bithoor to get in touch with Champa and to make arrangements for her and Gangamala to be brought to Chaurasi. Three days later, when he had still not returned, my mind was full of forebodings, and I began to feel that something terrible had happened to them.

That day I learned about the sack of Kanpur and about what happened to Azijan. She was declared an active rebel, and Neill had ordered her to be hanged with the very first lot of captives in Kanpur. But his superior, Havelock, had intervened. The British knew that Azijan had been my mistress and that I had visited her several times while I was in Kanpur. At the time, Havelock was investigating the reports of my death by drowning, and he offered to spare her life if she would assist in his inquiries. Instead, Azijan had hurled brothel obscenities at her captors and declined to cooperate, and left Havelock no option but to agree to the death sentence. She was the first woman to be hanged from the Kanpur banyans.

For a few hours grief for the dead had pushed back my anxiety for the living, but as the day progressed all my fears came snapping back. Unable to bear the suspense of waiting for news, I rode over to the river and kept a vigil by the bank for Azim's return. I was squatting in the sand, reciting prayers to myself, when some villagers came and told me that Bithoor too had been plundered and my house burned.

Something burst inside my head, but there was no pain, only a numbness. "What about Ganga?" I asked meekly. "And Champa? Where did they go?"

They did not know. They had only heard some people saying that they had seen the wada burning and had heard the soldiers yelling in jubilation.

By nightfall Azim had still not returned, so I rode back to Chaurasi. Early the next morning, when I was again setting out for the riverbank, he came in, bowing very low. He was wearing a plain white turban, the headdress of mourning.

If you put your worst fears into words, sometimes they act as a charm. "So they're dead?" I asked, and I had to sit down because my legs folded.

"No one can say for certain, Malik. Some women were hiding in the tykhana when the wada was set on fire, but whether Champabai or Gangamala was among them no one can say."

"Then why are you wearing a white turban?"

Azim did not say anything, but hung his head.

"What did they do to the animals?"

"The same thing they did to Wajid Ali's park. Slaughtered the deer for meat, the tiger and leopards for their pelts. The elephants they sold for the price of ivory. Nothing was spared."

Like a whipped dog crawling into a familiar corner, I rushed to the back of the house where we had set up the prayer-room and knelt down.

Champa, my mistress and the mistress of my house, though not married to me was yet the woman who was closest to me. Once she had told me that even though she was not my wife she considered herself to be entitled to perform sati if I happened to die before her. In all seriousness she had implored me to leave instructions to my descendants that she should not be prevented from doing so on the grounds that she was not married to me. I had then reminded her that neither she nor my wife could be cremated with my body because the British had banned the practice of sati. In the event, she had performed her act of self-immolation while I was still alive.

And my daughter, who was the gift of the Ganges, had vanished as though she had been claimed back by the Ganges. Whether she too was trapped in the tykhana, or underground chamber, of the wada when they burned it down, or whether, as several people have told me since, she was abducted by the Gujars, I myself never saw her afterwards. "Where are you, Ganga?" I would often call out in my sleep and find myself awake, sweating and shivering at the same time.

This was the only time in my life that I toyed with the idea of death. There was nothing left to live for, neither person nor cause. I thought out different ways of killing myself till my brain felt unable to function. In the end I decided to take the easiest way out. I would give myself up. The first white soldiers who came upon me were sure to put an end to my troubles.

I would die, but not as a fugitive. I would put on the Peshwa's robes and stand glittering in their path, and in my hand I would hold the sword of Bajirao I. I would laugh in their faces and die with God's name on my lips. My countrymen would at least approve the way I had chosen to end my life.

I was fast asleep one afternoon when the call came. Outside in the street was the tramp of marching feet. I jumped up and put on my robes and my *pagri,* or turban, and tied the purple sword belt around my waist. Then I darted out and stood in the hot dust of the village square, reciting the gayatri mantra to give me courage.

But the troops belonged to the 43rd Infantry. They had crossed over into Oudh and were making tracks for the Terai jungles, where they hoped to go into hiding. In the state of mind I was in, it took me a long time to size up this situation. And then it dawned on me that they had misunderstood my dramatic gesture.

For suddenly they were marching in step, their shoulders pulled straighter and their heads held rigid. Someone gave a curt word of command and the whole column crashed to a halt. Several men snapped into immaculate salutes and someone from the back gave out a loud cheer: "Nana Saheb *ki jai!* Victory to Nana Saheb!"

Deserting soldiers had bumped into a runaway king. Their separate shames frogmarched both back into the conflict. It was all I could do to prevent myself from collapsing in the dust, in full view of the sepoys.

After that, they began to arrive from all over Oudh in small and large batches. They sorted themselves out into their original squadrons and companies and a sort of order gradually came back. We decided to move into the adjoining fort and make a proper camp. A flagpost was put up. By the end of July I was no longer a fugitive but the commander of an army five thousand strong.

It was a heady feeling to see the soldiers gathering together for yet another campaign, headier still that they had accepted me as their leader. It showed that they still believed in the cause, that they still believed in me. With such men around you, you cannot go on thinking of ending your life.

From them I discovered that the British had been completely taken in by my ruse. Indeed for a time they had believed that I had killed all the members of my family as well, because a Eurasian clerk who happened to be in Bithoor at the time told them that he had seen me taking my family out into the Ganges and that afterwards everyone had seen the boat going down.

But with troops by the thousand gathering around me, I could no longer remain in hiding, nor was there reason to do so. We were strong again and eager to take the offensive. I sent a battalion across to set up camp within sight of Bithoor, and for a long time no British patrol dared to venture within miles of our headquarters at Charausi.

How often, during the months that followed, did we sense the nearness of victory? And yet the pattern remained unbroken: at the last moment, something would happen and victory would slip out of our grasp. Slowly I began to think to myself that we were just not fated to win; that it was in pursuance of some divine purpose unfathomable to us that Mother India would go on being postituted by an alien breed; that her sons and daughters, for some forgotten sins, would go on remaining slaves.

"The new rifle, the Enfield, is winning the war for them," was Azim's comment. The Enfield gave them the advantage of overwhelmingly superior fire power. And they also had the contingent of diseased minds formed by the "loyal" sepoys.

And yet, even with these immense advantages, they were jittery and diffident, for now they were on the borders of Oudh, the heart of enemy territory. Here they and their rule were regarded with unrelieved hatred and horror; here they knew that every single Indian was their enemy at heart and that there were no "loyal" sepoys or other kinds of vermin among us; here even they could not camouflage and degrade the revolt by calling it a "mutiny," for their opponents were not restricted to their ex-sepoys. And as though they were reluctant to proceed to a final showdown, their movements now became marked by a degree of caution they themselves would have derided in others as cowardly.

The weeks that followed brought us heartening reports of the enemy's disquietude. Havelock had set out with his force to relieve Lucknow but had thought it prudent to retreat and go back towards Kanpur. He and Neill had quarrelled. Havelock had been superseded by a new general, Outram. After that, even though Outram and Havelock had gone on to Lucknow and succeeded in breaking through to the besieged residency, the sepoys had quickly closed the ring again, bottling up the relieving force together with the relieved.

The galling part was that even this hollow victory of the enemy was made possible by the berserk fury with which the Sikhs had stormed the defences, vying with the Highlanders for the honour of being the first to break into the Residency and, in the process, dying like locusts caught in a grass fire. But by now we had become inured to this particular degradation—to see our own countrymen shedding their blood in order to assist in the mechanics of Mother India's ravishment.

"We need to win just one battle," Azim said fervently, as though he was saying a prayer. "If Allah gives us just one victory, that will turn the tide."

How often did we not pray for that single victory that we needed to reverse the current of the war, for, as much as to the enemy's superior arms, our defeats were attributable to an attitude of mind: the inner conviction that the white man was unbeatable.

"Just one battle won," Azim went on in that same religious voice. "Even an accidental victory—in Kanpur, in Lucknow, Delhi, anywhere."

Then the wavering troops would have stampeded from all sides to join us and "loyal" sepoys would have deserted their masters overnight; then the princes waiting for just such a signal from the skies would have jostled each other to display their national spirit.

The re-emergence of Tantya Topi gave shape and sinew to our visions of that victory. From Maharajpur he had fled to Gwalior, where, in my name, he had appealed to Jayaji Scindia to declare for us openly. The Scindia had rebuked him and ordered him to leave his presence. Yet, incredibly, Tantya was able to win over nearly half of the Scindia's army. Whether that superlatively wily man, Jayaji Scindia, had himself engineered this orderly defection, I shall never know, nor, I fear, will anyone else, for that is the sort of thing that a man like the Scindia never talks about. But the whole affair is typical of Jayaji's tortuous mind and of his amazing propensity to play both sides of the house.

So Tantya was back, with his own force almost intact and with a half of the Scindia's army as well. His contingent now numbered six thousand, and it was camped at Kalpi, barely forty miles from Kanpur.

Kanpur trembled; trembled · for all that reinforcements were daily arriving. The British held anxious conferences and got busy shoring up the defences and laying in stores and pulling back their troops from their missions, and they even prepared a new Entrenchment. Their caution made us bolder. Soon, the territory west of Nawabganj which is a part of Kanpur was dominated by us. I crossed the Ganges at will and spent nights at Bithoor, and I even visited Tantya at Kalpi.

We were waiting for a part of the Kanpur force to be moved across the Ganges to the relief of Lucknow, where, as I have related, the original enemy force as well as the relieving contingent had been besieged by the sepoys. That was when we would strike, so as to make quite sure of the single victory we so desperately needed.

But the British hung on in Kanpur, almost as though they had written off Lucknow, which was a welcome development to us. If they waited long enough, Havelock and Outram would have no option but to surrender, as Wheeler had. Then the Lucknow sepoys would join us. Together, we would make short work of Kanpur.

Everything thus looked poised for that single victory. Then came the unmistakable tap of fate. In late September we heard the first rumours of the fall of Delhi. And suddenly all around me I could see demoralization setting in like some form of paralysis. For us the rumour was confirmed when the British in Kanpur celebrated with drink and with the ringing of church bells. Again, as usual, the shock was barbed with the poison of infidelity: of the eleven thousand troops that had taken Delhi by assault, as many as eight thousand had been "loyal" sepoys, our kith and kin, and so were all the camp followers.

And even so it had been touch and go, for we soon heard how one of the senior generals, Wilson, had actually advised retreat. All of us were convinced that if these eight thousand had fought on our side the British would have been driven back from the walls of Delhi, as we were convinced later that if the Ferozpore contingent had not fought on Havelock's side and if the Indian camp followers had not vied with each other to tow his guns through the mud or to bring his ammunition and food in headloads I, not Havelock, would have come out the victor in the battle for Kanpur.

Disgust filled my mind: slaves were assisting their masters to conquer their own motherland and thus perpetuate their slavery. No country could live down such degradation of its people—we deserved our fate.

In the wake of this catastrophe, the barbarities of the victors were like pinpricks on a gaping wound. Numbly we heard how a subaltern called Hodson had suddenly become a hero by murdering three of the Emperor's sons, who had surrendered to him. Hodson ordered them to undress, made them get into a bullock cart, and then shot them and sent their heads on a platter to the bereaved Emperor. Then Metcalfe, who had been the Company's ambassador at the Mogul court, appointed himself the Company's executioner. As though to ensure that not a single Mogul heir should be left to act as a focus of loyalty, he organized a hunt for them and hanged them in batches. Those who saw the hangings told me that a smile played on his lips and that he chewed a black cigar messily as he watched their death throes.

With Delhi behind them, the conquerors set out in packs, to burn villages and to spear Pandies for sport. Hodson and others had plenty of sport: they killed farmers and tradesmen with schoolboyish wantonness. They were in no mood for tame solutions; battles fought and won were not enough. The people must be punished, their houses destroyed, their women dishonoured.

Women were dragged out screaming and pounced upon in bazaars, so that the word "rape" itself acquired plurality, a collective connotation, and people spoke of villages and townships raped, not of single women.

Chapter 22

The monsoon passed. The days became bright and cool. The British, to all appearances, were in the grip of a heartening torpor. Despite the provocation daily offered by our patrols, they would not be drawn out of Kanpur; meanwhile, their Lucknow garrison was being diminished by disease and starvation. Our hopes again began to soar.

Then we heard that Jung Bahadur, the Maharaja of Nepal, had declared war on us and had sent Gurkha troops to aid the British. The Gurkhas were already in the field, safeguarding an entire flank for their allies just as the Sikhs had done for the British column besieging Delhi.

"Any day now our enemies will resume the offensive," Tantya wrote from Kalpi. "This was what they have been waiting for."

And right enough, Sir Colin Campbell, who had replaced Grant as the Commander-in-Chief, arrived in Kanpur to take personal charge of the operations. The very next week he crossed the Ganges into Oudh—and then the sepoy resistance in Lucknow ended.

This day, November 17, shall ever be observed in Oudh as a day of mourning. What the British did to Lucknow cannot be balanced against a hundred Satichauras, cannot be washed away by banning all mention of it from history books, cannot be atoned for by a hundred years of the most unblemished administration. It was as though every single soldier was wreaking a personal vendetta against the men, women, and children of the city, and even against its bricks and mortar; the orgy of killing, rape, and vandalism did not abate for weeks.

And it was in this gloom, brought about by the emergence of a new enemy and the fall and rape of a splendid city, that we set out for our held-over attack against Kanpur. All things considered, we made a creditable showing. We forced General Wyndham, who was now in charge of Kanpur, to withdraw into his new Entrenchment. With the exception of this stronghold, the city was ours for a week. Admittedly, there was some sporadic looting by the city's habitual criminals, but we did not indulge in senseless destruction or carnage.

And then, flushed with his Lucknow victory and with the Gurkhas holding the northern approaches securely, the C.-in-C. came charging back to Kanpur to the aid of its beleaguered garrison. On December 6, after a bombardment that lasted all morning, he attacked. The relentless concentration of fire by the latest in weapons was too much for us. Our line broke and once again we were in full retreat. Kanpur fell to the British for the second time.

Sir Colin then personally charged one of his subordinates, Brigadier Hope Grant, to destroy Bithoor as thoroughly as he himself had destroyed Lucknow. Stevenson, who had carried out the first sack of Bithoor, the British general felt, had left behind little evidence that the place had been visited by an avenging force.

So Hope Grant set out to emulate the thoroughness of his chief. Like machines of destruction, his soldiers ripped up and dug out and toppled, broke glass and burned anything that would burn. Not even a single stone might have remained standing on another to reveal that a neat little township had once stood there, had not a grotesque, gnomelike creature quite unintentionally obstructed the process of the sack. Like some diseased rat coming out of a sewer, he stood in the path of the soldiers and saved Bithoor from the fate of Lucknow. He also gave me three weeks of respite from pursuit.

It was Nanak Chand, stepping forward to reveal to the British the place where I had secreted my gold. The Company's paid informer and temporarily ours, the man I had so thoroughly disgraced, had now returned to duty. He also offered to give his masters the fullest information about the happenings in Kanpur during their absence, for he had kept a most detailed diary. But his masters had no time to listen to him just then or to bother about his diary, for they had scented gold. Nanak's diary had to wait.

In midstride, the destruction ceased. Hope Grant pitched his tent right in the grounds of the animal park and ordered his engineers to empty the well. For twelve days continuous chains of buckets drew water over four pulleys before the well was emptied. On the thirteenth day they began to bring up the boxes of species and plate. After that it took another week to divide the prize money according to established practice.

"Established practice" is an officially recognized phrase; every battle from Plassey onwards had helped to establish it more and more firmly, with a set of carefully drawn rules to fit all contingencies. The higher your rank, the more you received. The commanders made fortunes, the privates got the price of a few bottles of grog. How many country estates in England and Scotland had begun life as a covetous gleam in some prize agent's eye? How many hundreds of bazaar women had been stood up against walls and trees by drunken redcoats as the consequence of "established practice"?

It was not till the middle of December, till the last trinket had been retrieved and weighed and claimed and ticked off, that the prize agents were withdrawn. But the destruction of Bithoor was not resumed. Hope Grant, Mansfield, Sir Colin himself, several colonels, and "the pack" of hard-riding, ambitious young officers out to win their spurs—such as Hodson, Grant, and Gough—took after me in full cry. There was a price on my head.

"If only we had unlimited gold to throw in their paths," Azim lamented. "Then they would never go on campaigns. They'd just sit, holding committees over prize money and doing each other down."

Their lust for gold gave us time to make plans for the future. The revolt had failed; that was now clear even to us. All we could do was to harass the enemy by resorting to what were known as "mountain rat" tactics. So we broke up our remaining troops into several independent bands, each to operate on its own as long as possible and then vanish into Nepal, which was the only foreign country near at hand to which we could escape.

To suit our hit-and-run tactics, I decided to increase my mobility by sending the women in my entourage to a place of greater safety. Queen Hazrat Mahal now came to my rescue. After the fall of Lucknow, she had fled to the fort of Baunda, which she hoped to defend for a long time. She offered to keep the women of my family with her and proposed that when she could no longer hold on in Baunda she also would make her way into Nepal and take them with her.

The night before we were to leave for Baunda Kashi came to see me. "What are we to do with the child when it is born?" she asked. "Eliza says she will have nothing to do with it."

This was a complication I had not given a thought to. Eliza's child was expected in March. "Begam Hazrat Mahal will do whatever is necessary," I said.

"Cannot I adopt the child?"

"But it was conceived in an act of rape!"

"And for that the little thing is to be sacrificed—smothered before it utters its first cry?"

"There must be several excellent homes for foundlings."

Her eyes brimmed and her voice cracked. "This is the only favour I have ever asked of you," she reminded me. "Please let me adopt this child. I can never bear my own. . . . Please. I shall never ask for anything again."

Kashi, consigned by her peculiar union with me to the fate of never having a child of her own, was begging to become a mother. Those whom you have wronged must hold some hypnotic power over you, for I hung my head in shame. It was true that this woman who had become my wife while still a child had never once asked me for anything. Now her pride, spirit, whatever it was, had broken and she was begging with tears in her eyes. "Yes," I told her, and in sudden gratitude, she bent down and touched my feet with both hands.

I was a hunted man, an outlaw with a price on his head, whose likeness, so I had heard, had been recently posted on trees and street corners all over Oudh. All the same, previously I had had little to fear since I always had thousands of devoted followers around me. There was no question of the British capturing me without a major battle.

But now that I was going to Baunda to deposit the women of my family there, I would have to pass through country which was wholly under British control and quartered ceaselessly by their patrols. Three large columns were known to be camped between Chaurasi and Baunda, a distance of roughly a hundred miles. My best chance was to sneak through as inconspicuously as possible, unhampered by an escort, which, in any case, would have been quite useless if we were to stumble into one of the main enemy columns. So I cut down the size of our party to the minimum. There were Eliza, Kashi, my sister Kusuma, the wives of my brothers, Baba and Balarao, and of my nephew Raosaheb, and their six maids. Then there were myself, Azim, and Waghu, and about half a dozen servants.

It was only after we had set out that I realized how vulnerable we were, a party in which the women outnumbered the men. Whenever some villager spied us from a distance, he would come closer to investigate, and soon there would be a small crowd. One or two of them would recognize me and then there would be much shaking of heads and startled faces jerking in all directions. Some would fall at my feet and some scuttle away in fear; some would bring us food and water, some brought money. No one wanted us around for long. They knew that any village known to have sheltered my party would be burned down as a matter of course, that anyone suspected of helping me would be speared to death. They would beg us to go away.

And among their number there would always be one or two who would quietly slip away and make for the nearest British outpost to report our presence. Luckily however, whenever this happened, the other villagers would warn us and we would make a run for it and try to get across the river, to put the Ganges between us and our pursuers.

We quailed, expecting capture by the hour, dreading the sound of hoofbeats, darting from hole to hole like rabbits at the baying of hounds. Hunger and thirst were our inseparable companions and fear sat like a cold lump under the ribs.

I had hoped to finish the journey there and back in two weeks. In the event, what with the detours we were forced to make, it took nearer six.

And during this journey I made a startling discovery: that there was someone who towered far above the villains of my imaginings, such as Renaud and Neill and Hodson; someone far more brutal, vindictive, malevolent—I, Nana Saheb.

I discovered that, all unknown to me, I had become the "villain of the century," replacing Napoleon Bonaparte as the hate object of a large section of the world. Azim, who was familiar with the country, would stray into the wayside villages and bring back gossip and old newspapers and handbills distributed by the Company's officials. And from these I learned many things: for instance, that housewives in England had taken to invoking curses upon me and sticking pins into my portrait, which they had carefully cut out from copies of the *Illustrated London News*.

I have since become reconciled to this invective. At the time, however, I felt that my mind was becoming unhinged, that I was losing the power of reason. It was so easy to believe what they were saying about me, if only because so many of them were saying it so often; so easy to think of myself as some kind of a freak, an object to frighten children with. How could I go on hiding, when they had blown me up to the size of a mountain? How could I escape detection, when those who were hunting me had been taught hatred as though it were a drill movement or a set of prayers to be memorized by repetition?

From the few issues of the Calcutta weekly *Friend of India* that came into my hands, I gathered that the paper had been running instalments of Nanak Chand's "Mutiny Diary" as well as a special column of letters from its readers suggesting the most fitting punishment for me. The punishment was unvaryingly death, but the manner in which I was to be tormented before death left a lot of scope for individual ingenuity. A man called Edward Harris had suggested that I should be put into beggar's garb, complete with belled cap, put astride a camel face-to-tail, and thus led through the Kanpur bazaar for the people to fling abuse and dirt at—before being shot like a dog; I wondered if it was the same Edward Harris who had been a frequent guest at my house. And a woman who signed herself "Sylvia Military Wife," and who, I believe, was none other than the Sylvia Bolten who had come to Kanpur to marry Azim, had suggested that I should be put into a cage so constructed that I would be unable either to stand up or stretch out fully while lying down, and thus taken through the principal towns of India and then exhibited in London so that the public should get a chance to see what the century's greatest villain looked like.

"Tally-ho, the packs," Sylvia ended her letter, "and good hunting!"

The few extracts from Nanak Chand's "Mutiny Diary" that I read made me glad that I had once humiliated him. The fabrications in the diary were cunningly dovetailed into a handful of incontrovertible facts to make the whole thing look convincing. Nanak was, of course, trying desperately to ingratiate himself with the British and wrote the sort of things they wanted to read. Here he revealed that it was he who had told Hope Grant where to find my family gold. Not that the gold would have remained hidden for long: the Company's officers would have discovered it on their own in any case, for they can scent out gold as a frog scents out water under a rock. But with this bit of favour to his masters, Nanak Chand had instantly become a man to be trusted, and nothing that he told them could be wrong. After all, he did happen to be in Kanpur in those days.

Separated from my followers, my ego bruised by the acclaim with which the British were being welcomed back by their erstwhile subjects, my self-confidence shot to pieces by the readiness with which everyone seemed to accept the evidence of my villainy, I began to lose faith in myself. I was defeated. Therefore whatever I had believed in was wrong. This distorted logic would shroud my vision and doubts would come from all sides like vultures converging around a carcass.

And then I would wonder if this perversion of values was not the effect of witchcraft. If thousands of housewives stuck pins into your picture every evening at the same time, muttering curses, you were bound to be afflicted by some sort of an evil spell.

But a brahmin's religion equips him against sorcery. I would fold my hands and recite the gayatri mantra, the short prayer whispered into your ear at the time of the thread ceremony. Its words seek strength from the inexhaustible refulgence of the sun— strength of mind, that is, to enable you to maintain clarity of thought in emergencies. And, right enough, the shroud would lift and shadows flit away. I would lie back, exhausted as though after a fever but with a clear brain. I had plenty of time to think.

And after that I was able to work out the answer. It was that my being blown up into a "monster of ferocity" was a deliberate act. Our revolt had thrown up a surfeit of British heroes but no villains to balance them against, and they needed villainy of the requisite magnitude to serve as a backdrop for heroism. How hollow would Havelock's victories have seemed if I, Nana Saheb, had not been their principal objective!

So they magnified the horrors that were already there and invented some, and a hundred zealous servants of the Company were ready to testify that I was responsible for everything that had happened in Kanpur. And the new monster was held before the public at large in a portrait purported to have been painted by Beechy. What puzzled me was that I had never sat for a painting by anyone called Beechy.

We were perhaps midway between Chaurasi and Baunda. An unmusical clapping sound awakened me from the depths of sleep. The afternoon sun picked out the members of my party huddled among the piles of stones of some nameless fort. All were looking at Waghu, who was red in the face from blowing into the fire of sodden logs with which he was trying to heat the water to boil the lumps of jaggery which we carried as emergency rations. How many meals did we make of mildewed jaggery stewed in water?

Dhak-dhak-dhak! The curt beats came closer and closer as though nosing us out, and through the man-high sugar cane emerged the village crier, dressed in the sleeveless red singlet that was his badge of office, his limbs grimed with sweat and dust, hands expertly banging away at the leather stretched over the mouth of an earthenware jar that was his *dholak*. Standing a few paces from us, he put up his head and bellowed like a bull challenging his rival, and the lump in my chest suddenly expanded and froze and my eyes blurred.

"A lakh of rupees—a hund-red thousand! To any person who delivers Dhondu Pant Nana Saheb of Bithoor into British custody —or to any person who gives information that will lead to his arrest. A hund-red thousand!" The proclamation was rounded off with a hard thumping of the dholak.

The professional village crier, the beater of drums and proclaimer of announcements, was, by ancient custom, a *maang,* the lowest among the untouchables. He stood raven-black in the afternoon glare, surveying our cringing group, his passport to wealth. Then, very self-consciously, he strode up to a pile of stones and fastened a bit of paper to it. I saw Waghu pick up a large stone and Azim reach under the folds of his robe for his *jambia,* the curved dagger.

The crier turned, gave a quick look all round, and came towards me. Carefully depositing his drum on a tuft of grass, he fell at my feet, gasping, "Malik! Malik!" His shoulders shook.

The fear that had ballooned within me made me react as I did, for I stepped back as though to ward off a blow. Only when I saw him cringe away and slap his own face in repentance did I realize how much I must have hurt him.

"I know I have no right to pollute you with my touch," he stammered. "I—a maang—the lowest. Forgive me, but I was so overcome."

I had recovered by then. I clasped his hand with mine and said, "Don't be a fool! It's just that . . . that the days for anyone to throw himself at my feet are gone. And you don't want to tell the world who I am, do you? Unless you want to claim the lakh of rupees?"

He sprang to his feet and his eyes narrowed in defiance. "Have I been bitten by a mad dog that I should betray my own master? My sons will spit in my face, my wife hang up her sari at the village entrance and stand naked to all comers to shame me."

"But there are others who may be watching, someone from your own village who might stray here. If he saw you touching my feet, would he not be tempted? A hundred thousand is a lot of money."

He withdrew his hands gently from mine and a dazed look came over his face. He shook his head several times before he pronounced, "It is said in Lucknow that no one can give you away and live to claim the reward."

I knew that this was not an index of my popularity but of the new wave of hatred against the British that was sweeping the country. Everyone had been so horrified by the severity of their vengeance that perhaps what the maang was telling me was literally true. Anyone giving me away would have been stoned to death and not even his brother would have come to his rescue.

"And to think that hardly six months ago I had proclaimed you king, told everyone, 'The land has returned to God; the rule has returned to the Peshwa.' "

Was it only six months ago that the land had returned to God? How briefly had it remained in his hands.

"Here, Malik, I hope you will not say no to these." From the depths of a bulging shoulder bag he pulled out a dozen or so brinjals, fat and glossy, and then an enormous scented melon the colour of gold.

These munificent gifts, almost certainly filched from some wayside garden, made my mouth water and I was instantly ashamed of my weakness. Barely six months earlier I had been proclaimed king and had distributed gold bangles. A few months before that I had given lavish entertainments and served trout and champagne. Now I was grateful for the charity of the village maang, the pariah of the Hindu social order. Did he detect the gleam in my eye? For he said, "I shall bring more, when the sun goes down."

"We won't be here in the evening."

"Malik, it is safe here. No one knows, except me."

"The white sahibs too are out, hunting," I explained. "And they are skilled hunters."

He stared blankly and nodded. "The gods are on their side."

Now that I felt that I was relatively safe from betrayal by my own people, my main anxiety was what "Military Wife" had called the "packs"—batches of hunters out for sport. Any moment one of them might stumble into our little group, and I knew perfectly well that none of them would trouble to deliver me into official custody. I would be hanged from the nearest tree or torn limb from limb. On-the-spot justice was their greatest boast. Also there was the keenest rivalry among the column commanders to possess my skull as a table ornament, as an inkstand or an ash tray.

After I had got rid of the maang, I went to take a look at the notice he had stuck on the broken fort wall. It showed a picture with a lot of writing underneath it. And as I stood, a laugh came out, right from the belly, involuntary as a belch. My eyes blurred and I sank to the ground in a surge of relief. The portrait was not mine. What was more, I knew whose it was. The housewives had been sticking pins into the wrong man; invoking curses to strike down a Meerut banker.

So this was the picture they had circulated all over India. So this was the reason why I was still not run to earth. Of course the picture would not have deceived anyone who had known me well, but then so few of those who had known me well were still alive.

Only lately have I been able to resolve the mystery. No doubt the portrait was by the famous artist Beechy, but its subject was Ajodhya Prasad, the Meerut banker. It was he who had given it as a present to the London barrister John Lang, whom he had called to plead his case against the Company when it withheld payments of his bills amounting to millions of rupees. Lang had won the case, and among the many gifts his grateful client had showered on him when he left for England was the portrait.

As it happened, Lang knew me well enough not to have mistaken the portrait as mine. He had visited Bithoor three or four times and has even written about these visits. A boisterous, fun-loving, and, at the same time a highly cultivated man, Lang had always tended to look upon the Company's servants as uncouth and pompous tradesmen, and I have not the least doubt that passing off his client's portrait to the *Illustrated London News* as mine was his idea of an excellent prank.*

The portrait served a specific need. A new hate object had been discovered somewhere in the wilds of India, and the public had to be shown what it looked like. And Ajodhya Prasad, looking rakishly affluent, wearing flowing robes and a perfectly circular *chakri* pagri on his head, smoking a hookah, his eyes puckered in a sensuous leer, must have filled the bill admirably. The merchant prince needed only a sword to give him a martial air. It must have been painted in in a matter of minutes.

But to return to the time of my first look at this portrait: for a minute or two I must have sat down before it, shivering with relief, and then managed to prop myself into a standing position to con-

---

* Oddly enough, this portrait is still being used to show what Nana Saheb looked like, as for instance in Michael Edwardes's *Battles of the Indian Mutiny* (London, Batsford), published in 1963. —M.M.

front it again. I peered at it a long time before I read the notice. It was in two languages, English and Hindi, and below the announcement of the reward was my description:

> The Nana is thirty-three years of age, hair black, complexion wheat-coloured, large eyes, and oval face. He is understood to have grown a beard. Height about five feet ten inches. He wears his hair very short (or at least did so), leaving only as much as a small skullcap could cover. He is full in person and of powerful frame. He has not the Maratha hooked nose with broad nostrils but a straight, well-shaped nose. There is a small mark on his forehead, shaped like a new moon. He has regular teeth and black hair. His ears are pierced and bear ring marks. He has a servant with a cut ear who never leaves his side.

I glanced at Waghu. The torn ear was covered by flowing locks of hair. There was no reference to a white woman in the notice, which meant that they had no idea that Eliza had gone with me.

Thus, from stray villagers we ran into I learnt that my own people would not have readily given me away, and from the notice I learnt that the white men and their "loyal" followers were looking for the wrong man. And there was something more. As I have indicated, my main danger was not from the British army columns so much as the smaller hunting "packs." Now from the newspapers I had been able to read and from Azim's mysterious visits to wayside villages, I gathered that the packs too had given me up because I was considered to be too strongly protected and gone after easier pickings. There were mansions to be looted, fat, panicky bankers to be held for ransom, villages to be burned, and above all traitors on the run to be speared. Clearly marked swaths of burntout crops showed the progress of British hunting parties. On the Grand Trunk road from Allahabad to Kalpi, so everyone said, there was not a single tree within sight which did not have a human body dangling, but even though our party kept away from the main roads, we too saw plenty of skeletons hanging from trees.

It was this evidence of their greed, and possibly even more than greed, their lust for blood, that made me realize that the danger was not as great as I had imagined. But, of course, there was always the chance that someone who had known me or Eliza before might blunder into us by accident and recognize us. And that would be the end.

The worst that could have happened did happen: the patrol commander who caught up with us was someone who knew both Eliza and me well. And yet it was not the end.

We saw a thin plume of dust over the skyline and soon heard the hoofbeats. Then the patrol emerged over the crest of the low hill.

"There are about a dozen horsemen," Azim whispered. "One redcoat. The rest are sepoys."

We saw them rein their horses abruptly and every head turned in our direction. "The white man has jumped off his horse now— he is looking at us through a telescope. Please turn your head away."

I could see the gleam of the telescope. "I don't want to arouse suspicion," I said under my breath. "In any case, they're looking for someone who looks like Ajodhya Prasad." But fear was already making my lips gum and my heart thump. For, even at that distance, there was something oddly familiar about the officer. Did he have the same feeling about me?

The officer had mounted again and was saying something to the others. Obviously he had ordered them to stay where they were and was coming up to investigate. He was still about a hundred yards away when I recognized him: Michael Palmer.

He came at a slow canter, a messenger of death. Instinctively I began to recite the gayatri mantra, praying for strength to be able to think clearly, but this time it failed me and my thoughts broke up into incoherent fragments. He had reached us, he had dismounted, he was saying something in that singsong voice of his— and long before his message registered, my eyes were smarting.

For the gift of life is a very big thing; it is the proper function of gods, and it was difficult to imagine a creature less godlike than this bloodless, sharp-witted half-caste who was despised by both the races that had thrown him up. And yet it was true. The small kindness that I had once shown him had grown to monstrous proportions in his keeping and was now being hurled at me camouflaged in swear words.

"Thank you," was all I could say.

He flung a curse at me and held out his flask of brandy. Then, in a tone that he might have used to talk about the weather, he proceeded to explain where the troops were and what I should do to evade capture.

"Hope Grant has discovered your hiding place. He is waiting to attack Chaurasi the moment he gets confirmation that you are there."

"Thank you."

"He's like a terrier, that Hope Grant. Keep out of his way."

"I will. And Sir Colin?"

"Fudge, sir! You're way out of date. 'Sir' no longer, but Lord, no less. The Queen has made him Lord Clyde. But to his troops he's still known as Old Khabardari—Old Overcaution!" He rounded off with a conventional Hindi obscenity.

"But where is he?"

"You don't have to worry about Old Khabardari. He won't attack a rabbit hutch without twenty-four-pounders to open the attack. You'll hear him coming from miles away—banging away at everything in sight."

"I'll remember."

"His Lordship is in Barriely. But Hodson and Gough are sticking to the river. You watch out! They're going to divide forces and beat both banks of the Ganges simultaneously."

Hodson's name made my skin crawl and dried up the saliva in my mouth. Before I could work my tongue loose, Palmer had emptied his purse into my hands. Then he swung himself into his saddle and cantered away, suddenly elegant the moment he was mounted.

Not once did his eyes stray towards the other members of my party. He did not even look at Eliza, whom he had used so unscrupulously even though he knew that she had fallen in love with him and whom he had so callously abandoned to marry his plantation widow.

Was he, I wondered, repaying his debt to me or was he paying back whatever he owed to Eliza? She was sitting a little apart from the others, keeping her eyes lowered as though either ashamed of the censure of the world at her pregnancy, which was now sufficiently advanced to be obvious, or too proud to favour Michael Palmer with a glance of recognition.

By this time, six months after Satichaura, the British had been able to establish that the only person from the Entrenchment who could not be accounted for was Eliza. All they had to go on were vague and garbled rumours that some sepoy had been seen carrying her away. Now Palmer had seen her with his own eyes, but he did not give her away. In letting me go he was as good as throwing away a lakh of rupees. I was quite sure that his marriage to Bellamy's widow had not made him so rich that he could have casually given up that kind of money.

With his coins clutched in my hands, I prayed to my gods to accept this new god as their peer and to make him prosperous and respected and to unite him with a multitude of fecund women so that his seed should proliferate.

Chapter 23

So they were only waiting for my return to Chaurasi to attack it. I had no place to go back to. For a hit-and-run raider it was an ideal state to be in—a hit-and-run raider unhampered by his *kabila,* or family women.

After returning from Baunda, I was hardly in the same place for two successive nights. Our bands roamed only in the hours of darkness, like bandits, but at that we caused a lot of damage and confusion among our enemies. Even though three major British columns were ceaselessly on the prowl, they never once caught us in the open. This was a phase of the war I enjoyed and will always remember with fondness and a little pride, for our casualties were always light and we could see the mounting anger and nervousness in the ranks of the enemy.

In some ways the very success of our new tactics caused us a good deal of trouble. Thousands of the ex-sepoys of the Company who had escaped and gone into hiding now came clamouring to join us. Many were without weapons and thus of no use to us, but, instead of turning them away, I sent them off to a camp we set up near Kandakote, which was conveniently close to the Nepal border. This camp I placed in the charge of Balarao, who had now recovered from his bullet wound.

For the moment the British were taking things lightly. All the same, we knew that they would never rest till they had snuffed out all the centers of resistance. Meanwhile, for us there were odd flickers in the gloom. A valued friend, Raja Beni Madhav, had wiped out an entire British squadron, and the Mad Mullah's raids were making the British look clumsy and amateurish. He sent me his blessings and asked for hookah tobacco, which I was happy to send.

Then for a time a star flashed. My boyhood companion, Mani, who was now the widowed Rani of Jhansi, had joined forces with Tantya Topi's band and together they had marched to Gwalior to force the Scindia to join us. But by now Jayaji Scindia must have seen the writing on the wall. Confronted by Tantya and Mani, he took the quite astonishing step of running away from his capital to put himself under the protection of the nearest British garrison.

Like the excellent billiards player he was, Jayaji Scindia always thought two moves ahead and knew that the British would soon be looking into evidence to determine who had remained loyal to them and who hadn't, and that so far the Scindia's actions had been hardly above suspicion. Now he had turned the confrontation into an opportunity to polish up his credentials. He gave a creditable imitation of a frightened man running to a friend and crying, "Help!" for he had even left his womenfolk behind. Needless to say, the women of his family were never for a moment in any danger—after all, they were among their own people.

In Gwalior, on June 3, 1858, the Rani of Jhansi and Tantya held an investiture to proclaim that the Maratha confederacy had been reborn and that, in my absence, my nephew Raosaheb, who was with them, had been installed to act as the Peshwa.

Bugles blew and guns were fired in salute to the acting Peshwa. Alas, no one outside the fort was taken in by this fanfare. Gwalior was looking south, at a cloud of dust in the distance that was a British column approaching—a column with a new commander in search of victories, Sir Hugh Rose.

Within days, Sir Hugh attacked this provisional capital of the new Maratha confederacy. We lost the battle and Mani died fighting. At about the same time that this evil news was brought to me, I also heard that the Mad Mullah was murdered by a petty Raja anxious to establish proof of his loyalty to the winning side, and that Beni Madhav had been put to flight by Hope Grant.

Now only Tantya Topi remained, a lone figure striding the horizon, the last bull elephant in a burnt-out forest, dying of his wounds but still trumpeting and beating the earth with his trunk. If

I emerged as the greatest villain thrown up by the "mutiny," Tantya Topi just as surely was the greatest hero of the "revolt."

The ship was going down, even if the flag at the masthead still fluttered. Nepal loomed before me, dark and mysterious like some nether world from which no one ever returned. We called it "The Abode of the Sightless Gods." My ancestors and the kings of Nepal had sent each other elephants and shawls and swords on the days of our common festivals. Now Nepal was ruled not by a king but by its so-called Prime Minister, Jung Bahadur, who was popularly known as the King of Kings. Ten years earlier he had massacred most of Nepal's leading noblemen as they were gathered for a court function and thereby eliminated most of his rivals, deposed the reigning king and externed him, and placed the heir apparent, a mere boy, on the throne. Now, even though the boy-king had come of age, Jung Bahadur still ruled Nepal as though it were a personal estate and was accepted by the world as its master. He had openly sided with the British in our revolt and had sent troops to put it down. What would he do when I suddenly appeared at his doorstep?

"The Ranas are Rajputs," Tika Singh, himself a Rajput, announced with visible pride. "They claim descent from the Chittore clan. They can never refuse asylum to someone who had placed his turban at their feet. Chittore tradition forbids it."

"What is tradition to a usurper?" Azim asked, "to a man who has driven his own king and queen into exile. And how many rivals has he not put to death? He has exiled even his own brother. . . ."

"Tradition is always most precious to those who have the least claim to it," Tika Singh said gravely. "But that apart, no one in Nepal will risk causing a brahmin's death. Never! It's the greatest sin. It is laid down in the *shastras* that whoever kills a brahmin consigns forty-two generations to hell."

The fact that I happened to be a brahmin, combined with the certainty that the British, once they caught me, would have hanged me without much ado, was my strongest guarantee of finding asylum in Nepal. No cow was ever killed in Nepal, a truly Hindu oligarchy; killing a brahmin, or even causing his death by accident, was the greatest sin a man could commit.

"Even if a brahmin were to kill a cow, or indeed the king himself, there would still be no question of executing him," Tika Singh said.

And yet the reports I had heard about this man made me diffident. He was callous and calculating, and above all had identified himself with British interests in India. He emulated their mode of living and dressed like a British general, and he made no secret of his admiration for them. He had risked excommunication, to say nothing of an inevitable palace revolution to make a trip to England, and the English, on their part, had feted him as though he were the King of Nepal and not its Prime Minister. Queen Victoria had received him and the stately homes of England held entertainments in his honour. At a more practical level, as a reward for running to their aid during our revolt, the British had already given back to him a large portion of the Terais, the Himalayan foothills, which Nepal had always longed to repossess. Would such a man risk breaking his alliance with the greatest military power on earth for the sake of a fugitive merely because he happened to be a brahmin?

Azim, for one, did not think so. "He's a hard-headed realist, far too worldly to bother about either chivalry or religion," he pronounced. "He'll see who offers more, the Peshwa or the British, and if the British offer more, he'll sell you. Let's have no illusions. But, of course, if he can get what he wants and still take credit for saving a brahmin's life, he would most certainly prefer that."

In the monsoon of 1858 I made camp at a place called Bankee, in the crook of the river Rapti. How Lord Clyde discovered this somewhat inaccessible hideout I shall never know. Luckily, as Michael Palmer had predicted, Old Overcaution preceded his attack by a deafening cannonade on one of our outlying pickets. My bodyguard and I had ample time to load our pack elephants with everything we wanted to take away. When the British troops ultimately swarmed in, screaming bloodcurdling war cries, we were already across the river. For a while they kept up a brisk fire in the direction we had gone and then, I have no doubt, got busy looting our camp.

We made tracks for our base camp at Kandakote. The first thing

Balarao told me when we arrived was that the Company's rule had ended and that the British Queen had taken the running of India into her own hands. He showed me a copy of the Queen's proclamation, which someone had brought into the camp.

The proclamation bristled with pompous words and noble sentiments, but it left us exactly where we were. India had ceased to be a trading company's private property and would from now on be a Queen's dominion. But the very men who had run the country as a private enterprise were now to govern it as a dominion. Canning remained as the Queen's Viceroy and the Company's officials, both civil and military, were, by the terms of the proclamation, "confirmed in their offices." Smothered in the sauce of royal self-righteousness was the same old mercantile toughness and arrogance:

> We deeply lament the evils and miseries which have been brought upon India by the acts of ambitious men who have deceived their countrymen and led them into open rebellion. Our power has been shown by the suppression of that rebellion.

"So we must not even have ambition," Balarao commented. "It is a privilege reserved for those who are appointed to govern us."

Nor did we have any delusions that the Queen's desire to show mercy by "pardoning the offences of those who had been misled" applied to people like myself. In any event, the men on the spot who were to dispense that mercy were none other than the Company's servants against whom we had risen in arms: the Hodsons and the Coopers and the Metcalfes were now waiting with pinched nostrils and bared teeth for the rebel leaders to throw themselves at their feet so that they could fleece them to the bone and then hang them from the nearest tree. The roadside trees all over Oudh bore witness to their proneness for mercy.

And right enough, from her refuge in the fort of Baunda, Queen Hazrat Mahal issued a counterproclamation calling upon her erstwhile subjects not to be taken in by the promises of Queen Victoria:

> It is the unvarying custom of the British never to condone a fault, be it great or small. No one has ever seen, not even in a dream, that the English forgave an offence.

Galvanized into action by this ultimate impropriety, Lord Clyde once again trundled his heavy artillery, this time in the direction of Baunda, Hazrat Mahal's stronghold. But, as though to demonstrate that the British Queen's proclamation had meant exactly what it said, he sent a messenger to tell Hazrat Mahal that if she gave herself up she would be pardoned and a handsome allowance given to her. Many of Hazrat's advisers now implored her to accept this offer, but her hatred for those who had usurped her husband's kingdom was too pure and too deep-seated for compromises. Realizing that her courtiers were anxious for peace on British terms and that her fort would fall to the enemy without a fight, she escaped from Baunda with barely a hundred of her most devoted followers, taking her son, Brijis Kadar, as well as the women of my family with her. In the beginning of January she sent me word that she was holed up in a place called Baharich, only a short march through the hills from the Nepalese frontier.

On January 4, 1859, Hope Grant attacked our Kandakote base. As it happened, however, we were prepared for this attack because our spies had forewarned us about his movements. While Balarao and I, guarding the two extreme wings, which were anchored on hilltops, maintained a steady fire on the advancing column, the bulk of our force fell back from the centre. Two hours later Hope Grant stormed a camp that had been vacated before even his advance guard had approached within sight of it. I was told that he cursed us loudly for our cowardice.

All the commanders of our separate bands had orders to take their troops immediately to Baharich, where Hazrat and her followers were marking time. Here Balarao and I joined them and we all set out on our pilgrimage to Nepal, the Abode of the Sightless Gods.

The time had come to see what the King of Kings was going to do.

Chapter 24

The Nepalese seemed to know our plans in advance. A Gurkha officer met me on the forward slope of Triveni Ghat and told me he had orders to bring me and my family and Queen Hazrat Mahal and her family to a shooting lodge about a mile away. The remainder of our people were to camp where they were.

The shooting lodge was tall and narrow, like an upended book. Its tower had several openings to observe game, but these were now shuttered with chic curtains. After the hundred or so people who formed our cavalcade had circled past this building in single file, we were made to halt.

All of us kept glancing at the chic curtains, knowing that behind them sat a man who had become a legend: Jung Bahadur. A whole hour passed before an apelike creature, wearing the gaudiest uniform I have ever seen, made for a much bigger man than its wearer, came out of the lodge and gave me a stiff, British-type salute. Speaking excellent Hindi, he announced that his name was Balbhadra Singh and that he was a colonel. He had, he revealed, been commanded to "serve" an order on me.

I read the order. In effect it said that Queen Hazrat Mahal, her son, Brijis Kadar, and their followers were welcome to Nepal. As to the others, while a spirit of chivalry alone forbade the Nepalese government from turning away my wife and the other ladies of my family, I and my brothers and followers would have to leave Nepalese territory immediately, since "Nepal was a sworn ally of the British government."

Jung Bahadur was quite safe in admitting Hazrat Mahal and her son, who, in any case, had been offered a pardon by the British themselves. But even at the time I remember thinking that this was not the order originally intended to be served on me. Admittedly, it did not have a single correction or erasure, but the ink still seemed moist. Later, I discovered that Jung Bahadur who had heard reports of Kashi's beauty had been peering at her through a telescope and had made up his mind to possess her. The "other ladies of my family" had been lumped in merely to preserve an appearance of decorum.

I wrote my reply on the spot. Considering the circumstances, perhaps I was a little too forthright, my language too explicit. But, then, I wanted to make it clear to Jung that even though I needed his help badly, it did not mean that I was prepared to place my turban at his feet.

For, after pointing out how unfailingly perfidious the British had shown themselves to be towards their sworn allies and how they were plotting to destroy our common religion, I admonished Jung for running to the aid of those against whom his forebears had fought so valiantly:

> Such enemies Your Majesty clasps to his bosom, while you turn away a family friend, the descendant of the Peshwas! Your incivility surpasses all that I had been warned to guard against.

Was it my postscript that saved me from instant banishment? For, in all innocence, I told Jung Bahadur how relieved I felt that he had agreed to give shelter to Hazrat Mahal and her son and to my wife Kashi and to the other ladies of my family.

Late in the evening Balbhadra came loping back. He explained that Jung Bahadur himself could never have a talk with me because he wanted to go on maintaining that he had no knowledge of my whereabouts. But otherwise there was no reason why ordinary courtesies should be waived. "Her Highness the Senior Maharani is in camp," he said, "and would be delighted to make the acquaintance of Rani Kashi-bai, to whom she has sent a most pressing invitation to dinner."

I readily agreed. After Kashi had been escorted to the shooting lodge Balbhadra seemed much more relaxed. He drank half a bottle of brandy and shared my meal and we sat over hookahs. He had, I discovered, a quite disconcerting habit of changing his voice to suit the topic of conversation and a laugh that sounded like a cascade of hisses. "I am deputed to . . . to settle everything." He bared his teeth and hissed. "My master must go on maintaining he knows nothing. But how long can one go on pretending ignorance when as many as twenty thousand of Your Highness's followers have come into our land—like locusts."

I took him at his figure. "That just shows how they must hate your friends the British," I retorted, "if twenty thousand men are willing to leave their homes and families to escape from them."

We were like wrestlers going through the conventional preliminaries: crouching, making intimidating gestures and striking attitudes, dancing and flexing our muscles before actually coming to grips. Half the night we wrangled, both sides gaining ground imperceptibly and giving in just a little. In the process, we agreed that if Jung Bahadur would secure from the British a general pardon for my followers, I would not stand in the way of their being sent back to India. In return, Jung Bahadur on his part would connive at my staying in Nepal, provided I lived in disguise and also provided I never set foot within the Kathmandu Valley.

Since it was unlikely that I would want to venture into the Kathmandu Valley in any case, the stipulation made me uneasy. "But my wife will be there, won't she?" I said.

Balbhadra laughed—or emitted a hiss—and his voice abruptly changed to a conspiratorial whisper. "The Maharaja will no doubt arrange for one or two female companions of the right ages to be made available to you."

"That's not what I had in mind," I said acidly. "What I meant was why can't my wife and I live together?"

His frankness was utterly deflating. "The other women, yes. Oh, yes, that can be arranged."

"But not Kashi-bai?"

"No."

"For God's sake, why ever not?"

The voice was almost inaudible now. "That my master did not confide in me."

A sudden suspicion jolted me. "Is the Senior Maharani really there in the lodge?" I asked.

"Her Highness was there when I brought the message."

"You mean she isn't there now and that lecherous swine has my wife at his mercy?"

"No woman could be in better hands."

I jumped to my feet and uttered a foul oath and ordered Balbhadra to get out of my sight. He stood up and bowed, muttering, "I cannot understand. The world knows that Your Highness has abandoned your wife—that Kashi-bai is still a virgin."

A helpless rage gripped me. "That doesn't mean I would sell her to that lout!"

He shrugged and hissed. "One has to take the rational view. I'm sure that my master would be quite willing to . . . to make generous concessions in other respects."

"Bugger your master."

"What shall I tell him?"

"Tell him that he is no gentleman, that he is a body servant of the British before whom he grovels. Tell him rather than accept his insulting conditions, I'd try and seek accommodation with the British."

"That is impossible. The British have announced that they will hang Your Highness."

I ran at him with upraised hands. He turned and fled.

It was nearly an hour before Kashi returned from the lodge and, instead of going to the tent at the back where the other women were staying, as she would have normally done, she came straight to where I was sitting under a tree. Did she, I wondered, look somehow different? Was there a fresh glow on her face, a new swing in her walk? I burned with jealousy. "A good dinner?" I asked, trying to control my voice.

"It was strange food."

"How many were there for dinner?"

"Just the two of us."

"You and the senior wife?"

"Me and Jung Bahadur."

"What is he like?"

"What his pictures look like: a lion in uniform."

"What did he have to say?"

Did her breath suddenly quicken as she answered? "Exactly what he had sent his man to say to you."

"He certainly took a long time saying it."

Kashi did not answer, but neither did she look flustered. "He offered to keep you as his mistress?" I asked.

"Yes."

"And what did you tell him?"

She did not say anything, but her face reddened and her eyes glinted.

"You bitch!"

My wife, who had been trained to look haughty, flinched instead. This was the first time I had insulted her.

"God! For twelve years now you've been brought up to be a princess, and the first man who asks you to lift your sari . . ."

"He wasn't the first man," Kashi said very evenly.

"Oho, so he wasn't the first."

"No. That Englishman who slept with Azijan, he too had asked me. But that time I said no."

"Meaning this time you said yes?"

"That time I wasn't trying to save my husband's life—and also . . ."

"Yes? Also?"

"Also I still clung to the hope that someday *you* would."

"You have disgraced every single one of the Peshwa wives!"

"I was never a Peshwa wife—I was a child widow."

"Oh, you evil woman, why did you have to go and do this?" I wailed.

"Because this is the best thing that could have happened—to you, to me, to all of us. Why can you not see what stares you in the face? The British will kill you, and here is your only chance. How long are you going to run like a rabbit? And I too will get my release from widowhood—I too will get what I want."

"What do you want?"

"I want to be a woman, not merely a repressed freak. I want to live, to become a mother, to experience physical love, violent, abandoned. I want to be in the glitter of a great king's court, not in a hermitage. I'm past twenty and what else was there for me but the prospect of lifelong abstinence, to die before I ever learned to live? And, above all, I did not want to be the cause of my husband's death. Don't you see, my lord, that I am doing this as much for you as for myself? . . ."

"I could kill you," I said.

"It is only because you did not want to kill me that you have driven me to these solutions. Killing me now will not solve anything. By rejecting me as your wife, you saved my life. God has given it to me to do you the same service, by rejecting you as my husband."

She had been brought up to say things like a queen, and there was nothing I could do but to shake my fists and shut my eyes and to yell at her to go away. But there was her bell-like voice again, controlled and without a tinge of passion. "And may I say how grateful I am to you for letting me live!"

Later that night, when I thought the whole thing over more calmly, I came to the conclusion that this was perhaps as neat a solution of my marital tangle as I could ever expect. After all, I could not keep Kashi girded in an imaginary chastity belt all her life. Early the next morning I sent word for Balbhadra to come and see me again. He came just after sunset.

"Supposing—just supposing—I were to agree to your master's conditions," I said, "what exactly is my fate going to be?"

"As I said, Your Highness goes into hiding in some inaccessible place, like our Terai jungles. There is no reason why anyone should give you any further trouble."

"Except that the British are bound to find out eventually. Nepal is a small country. People are bound to talk. There is a reward."

"Oh, I agree that the British will come to know—almost at once they will know. The point is that the Maharaja Jung Bahadur will not know. And in Nepal, that is all that matters." He blinked several times and added, "The Commissioner of Daang, Colonel Sidhiman, has orders not to show any interest in a band of sadhus of the Mouni sect who might be coming to his district—sometime this week."

"Mouni sect?"

He nodded, almost from the waist. "The silent sect—they never speak to anyone. They also have women disciples."

"Your Maharaja thinks of everything, doesn't he?"

"His Highness is a very wise man."

"But this is absurd, don't you see? How long can Jung Bahadur go on pretending that he doesn't know anything about me? The British, once they're on the scent, will send their own agents. They'll then confront him with first-hand evidence."

Balbhadra stared at me for a full minute and then said something which had the effect of an icy mist enveloping my body. "How long," he asked dramatically, "till you're dead?" Then he began to chuckle, hissing and shaking his head from side to side. His stomach wobbled and saliva bubbled in his mouth.

"How long?" he said again. "Perhaps a few months—not more. Only till someone—anyone—from among your followers dies. There will be a cremation. Then Maharaja Jung Bahadur himself will send your ashes to be immersed in the Ganges—in a golden urn. After that you can live happily ever after."

The British had once been taken in by that trick; it was not likely that they would fall for it twice. "They'll never believe it," I protested. "They'll demand proof—convincing proof."

"There can be no stronger proof than Maharaja Jung Bahadur's word," he said very flatly. "In Nepal if His Highness says a man is dead, he is dead. No proof is necessary."

The words were like spiders running over my skin. For a long time neither of us said anything. Was there anything more to say, I wondered?

"So I go to the Terais, and the women of my family go to Kathmandu," I said. "Is that right?"

"Please!" Balbhadra said in an alarmed voice. "Not all the women. I carry special instructions for the white lady. She must not go to Kathmandu."

"What's that?"

"Quite unthinkable. The only white woman in Kathmandu is Mrs. Ramsay, the Resident's wife. The presence of another will be instantly noticed. The British Resident will create no end of trouble. And my master wants no trouble with the British."

"Then what does he want me to do with her?"

"She must be sent back—to her own people."

"But she doesn't want to go back. I offered several times to send her back."

"Then she must be—made to vanish. It can be arranged." He snapped his fingers, making a metallic sound. "Tonight, if you wish."

"Look," I said, "if anything happens to Miss . . . to the white lady, the whole thing is off," I said in a voice which I hoped carried the hint of a threat.

He shrugged. "All that I must ensure is that she does not go to Kathmandu."

"There is another little detail I would like to settle," I said.

"Yes?" His voice was suddenly alert, his little nose twitching as though to detect a scent.

"It's about my sister."

"Kusuma-bai?"

"Yes. I am worried about her. She is not of my family any longer, she is married. Her husband lives in Gwalior—Baba Apte's son. Because she was only a child, she had gone on living in Bithoor, and then she got caught up in all this." To myself I sounded diffident, ingratiating, and I was glad to see the relief reflected in his face. His slitty eyes positively glinted. For some reason, he too was anxious that our talks should not fail.

"And you wish to send her to her husband's house?"

"I am most anxious that she should not become embroiled in all this."

"But naturally. Oh, I'm sure it can be arranged. Certainly," he promised with alacrity.

Perhaps it was a blessing that Kusuma was what she was, plain and pudgy and demure, a girl not likely to arouse the lust of a man like Jung Bahadur. Then and there we settled the details of her journey to Gwalior.

Of course that night, sitting before a log fire under the Terai sky, I had no idea that, in arranging for my young sister to be sent to her husband's house, I was doing anything more than sparing her the hardships and privations of exile. All I was conscious of was that another awkward problem had been settled without the customary bargaining. I was about to say something to indicate that there was nothing more to settle when I heard Balbhadra clearing his throat as though he had something important to reveal.

"It will cost you a thousand a day."

If he had thrust a pistol into my ribs he could not have startled me more. In a hoarse whisper that must have betrayed my agitation I asked, "What's that?"

"A thousand—every day. Rupees."

"What on earth for?"

"For Your Highness to live in Nepal. The British have offered a reward of a hundred thousand. We could easily get them to double it."

"A thousand a day?" I squawked.

"Irrespective of how many followers choose to remain with you."

"And where does your Maharaja imagine I'm going to get the money?"

He bared his teeth and screwed his eyes tight, but this time did not emit a hiss. "His Highness is a collector of jewels—a connoisseur. And always he pays for what he fancies—pays handsomely."

"Not for virgins," I could not help retorting. "Virgins he just appropriates."

"Oh, but diamonds are different. They carry curses—ill luck. In Nepal you can steal a woman, but never a diamond. Even a robber will take gold but leave the precious stones behind."

This was a time for silence. Now I knew why this grotesque creature was equally anxious that our negotiations should not fail. I had something else besides Kashi which Jung Bahadur coveted and which some peculiar prohibition of Nepalese tradition prevented him from stealing.

"I have been charged to make an offer for the Naulakha necklace."

"No one in the world is rich enough to buy the Naulakha," I told him. "I thought that was well known."

"Maharaja Jung is an extremely wealthy man. And besides . . ." His voice was now like an insect crawling under your pillow. "Besides, the price of an object depends on circumstances. How the buyer is placed, how the seller."

"And which one holds the gun in his hand."

He shook with mirth. "Yes, and who holds the gun. But, of course, among friends there is no question of anyone holding a gun, no? Fair is fair. For the Naulakha, I am authorized to make an offer that will ensure you three months of undisturbed residence in the Terais. Ninety thousand rupees."

I was too furious to say anything. He was offering exactly a tenth part of what Balaji had paid for it a hundred and forty years earlier; since then, what with the additions made by his successors, the necklace had grown enormously in value. Now it would be worth at least fifty lakhs.

The rustle of the insect crawling through dry leaves was there again. "What shall I tell my master?"

"I must have time to think," I told him. "Shall we continue our talk tomorrow?"

He jumped to his feet and into a position of attention. "Certainly," he said. "Tomorrow I shall come again. Tomorrow is more auspicious." He bowed as though doing a drill movement and turned about.

I went on sitting where I was, hunched over a bolster and staring at the heap of embers that was all that was left of the log fire, trying to make sense of the situation I had found myself in, overcome by a feeling of utter loneliness. I was a man who had left behind everything that was familiar and was now disposing of precious heirlooms to be able to buy himself a few months of respite in a strange land.

Did I doze off for a few moments? I don't know. But on the other side of the fire, where Balbhadra had crouched like an emissary from the world of demons, appeared a face that belonged to a remembered past, a face calm and chiselled and made beautiful through an ordeal. I stared at it as in a trance. Only after she spoke did I realize that it was Eliza.

"Kashi tells me that the Begam and all of us are to proceed to Kathmandu," Eliza said.

"Kashi knows far more about this than I do," I said bitterly. "So far as I know, there is nothing decided yet. We still have to settle the price."

She was looking straight at me and her face glowed from the

light of the embers. "I came to say that I don't want to go to Kathmandu," she said.

"Oh, but you won't. They want to have you sent back to Kanpur."

"What have I left in Kanpur—or anywhere else? No one—nothing." She shook her head and paused as though to brace herself. Then, in a voice that had become suddenly thick, she added, "I want to remain here."

"Here?" I repeated foolishly.

"Wherever they let you live."

I laughed. "The only life left for me is that of a hermit, a sadhu who has taken a vow of silence—someone who has left the world behind."

"I too have left my world. Two can make a new world."

I hesitated a long time before I could bring myself to ask, "Why do you want to do this? Because you have nowhere else to go?"

How defiantly she shook her head, and her voice was clear and earnest as she answered, "No. Because there is nowhere else I wish to go."

A gust of wind came and rustled the embers and set up a screen of smoke between us. Then the smoke blew away, revealing Eliza's face with the firelight playing over it. Her eyes were closed and at their corners were tears. And suddenly my loneliness vanished.

Balbhadra and I resumed our wrestling match the next afternoon, beginning where we had left off. As he had said, the day must have been propitious, for, by the end of it, we had reached complete agreement on all points, as they say.

I had made up my mind not to protest about the rate of my daily fine but to concentrate on getting a better price for the jewels. In any event, it was clear that I was not going to be paid anything at all. The amount due to me was going to be held in deposit and worked off against the payments to be made by me.

But we bargained hard. Slowly, almost imperceptibly, the price of my necklace advanced, at times only by a few hundred rupees. Finally, when it hovered just below four hundred thousand and I was about to give in from sheer physical incapacity to go on, Balbhadra raised it to four hundred thousand. We thereupon shook hands and closed the deal. For a time Balbhadra stretched himself on the carpet and lay panting. I had bought myself thirteen months of life. What had Balbhadra got out of it?

Chapter 25

And I shall say this of Jung Bahadur: he was selfish, stubborn, vain, and quite ruthless. But he never broke his word. What he said he would do he did. The difficulty was to get him to give his word, and this he never did lightly.

Once I had parted with the necklace, things began to happen. Kashi, with her adopted son, Eliza's baby, went to Kathmandu; and Kusuma went there with them for the time being. But Eliza and the wives and children of my followers were allowed to remain with us. I made camp near Butwal in the Terais, and Balarao and Baba and Azim busied themselves putting up shelters for the coming monsoon. There were about three hundred of us still left, the others had gone back to India under the general pardon which Jung Bahadur had secured from the British.

From Butwal, on April 20, 1859, I sent off my Open Letter, to Queen Victoria and to her Government in India. After explaining that I was not responsible for either Satichaura or Bibighar, I declared my resolve to continue the struggle. "All I want you to understand is that I am not a murderer," I wrote, "but at the same time you have no enemy more determined than myself. So long as I live, I shall fight."

I sent a copy of this letter to the nearest British official, a Major Richardson in Gorakhpur. Richardson must have been new to India and thus ignorant of the special rules of behaviour incumbent upon white men in the East. He sent me an immediate reply enclosing a copy of his Queen's proclamation and calling upon me to give myself up since, as he put it, if I had not murdered women and children, I had nothing to fear.

"You would be a fool to give yourself up," Jung Bahadur warned me through Balbhadra. "And, besides, you would ruin all my carefully laid plans for your future."

I had, of course, no intention of giving myself up, but I found out that, for his routine assurance of pardon if I had not "murdered women and children," Richardson was severely rebuked by his superiors. The new lieutenant-governor of Oudh then made a public announcement that even if it was proved that I was not guilty of murder I could never escape punishment because of my "persistence in rebellion." He went on to declare me an outlaw.

Was this what the gods had willed—that black should parade as white, wrong as right? Indignantly I wrote back to General Hope Grant, who was still hovering near Kandakote, questioning the right of the British to judge me because their rule itself was unjust, their *Pax Britannica* a fraud committed on our people. "What right have you to occupy India?" I demanded. "How can we accept the argument that you firanghis are the masters and we 'outlaws' in our own country?"

That, as it turned out, was my very last letter to the British authorities.

Sometime in June Balbhadra came again specially to tell me that Kusuma had been sent to Gwalior, and in time a letter arrived from Baba Apte, Kusuma's father-in-law, assuring me that she had arrived safely. The messenger who brought the letter also brought the news of Tantya Topi's capture and execution. The very last drum in the forest had stopped beating; the silence of defeat engulfed us.

Was there some secret conspiracy in Nepal not to warn me about the perils of the Terai monsoon? And did Jung Bahadur deliberately guide my steps to these jungles hoping that the monsoon would rid him of an unwanted obligation?

It nearly did. The Terais have been likened to a slice of paradise from October to April; they are just as surely a segment of hell during the months of monsoon. The ground becomes a bog alive with frogs and leeches and the air is thick with insects exuding sharp, medicinal smells. For four months the millions of frogs bellow ceaselessly and a vapour envelops the land, creating mysterious shapes all around you like shadows upon smoke. I would swear that all the birds and all the other animals except one migrate or are suddenly struck dumb. The exception is the rhinoceros, a nightmarish creature, an amalgam of a turtle, an elephant, and a hog. This armour-plated, congenitally blind monster waddles and sleeps and noisily mates in the ooze. Everything—clothes, shoes, furniture, the barks of trees, and the walls of houses—acquires a coating of green slime, and to the rattle of the incessant rain and the booming chorus of frogs, death in the form of Terai fever comes searching you out, riding, as the Nepalese insist, not on a buffalo but on a rhino.

The Terai fever has a terrifyingly precise, unalterable cycle. A man goes down with shivers, which, the next day, give place to a raging fever. On the third day he goes into a coma. On the fifth he dies.

At first they fell in ones and twos, and then by the dozen. In late August at least fifty of my men were already dead and twenty or so were in the grip of the disease. That was the time when, as though on cue, Sidhiman, the Commissioner of Daang, came to make inquiries about our well-being. He seemed almost disappointed that my brothers and I were still alive.

Then, on September 19, Balarao came down with fever. I sat by his side, praying endlessly. On the third day, as he lost consciousness, he was clutching my hand tightly and there were tears in his eyes. On the sixth day he died.

Sidhiman came to attend to the cremation, which was just as well, for I was too dazed to go through whatever was needed to be done. Bala's death had a paralysing effect on me, as though a limb had been severed. It was Sidhiman who rounded up the priests and supervised the ritual. I merely ignited the fire, wondering how long it would be before we were all carried away. The fog pressed from all sides like some garment of death.

We did not know it then, but with the passing of the heavy rains the disease too was to leave the Terais, but only to come back with the next monsoon, and the next.

On the thirteenth day after the cremation, Sidhiman came again.

He collected Balarao's ashes and took them to Kathmandu, where Jung Bahadur himself received them with a good deal of fanfare and then deputed a team of priests to carry them in a golden urn for their final journey to the Ganges at Benares. Then he wrote to the British Resident, Colonel Ramsay, that Nana Saheb of Bithoor, who, all unknown to his officials, had been residing in Butwal, had succumbed to Terai fever on September 23, and that he, Jung Bahadur, was making arrangements for the ashes to be taken to Benares to be immersed in the Ganges.

"In Nepal if Jung Bahadur says a man is dead, he is dead," Balbhadra had told me—and it was precisely as he had said. I just ceased to be. Suddenly we found ourselves isolated. A sadhu, a holy man, appeared in Nepal, but the sadhu belonged to the silent sect. He and all his disciples had taken vows of lifelong silence. Eliza, her hair cut short to suit her role as the principal disciple, lived with me openly. The fact that she bore me a daughter on March 13 of the following year caused absolutely no comment for the simple reason that by then the pattern of our segregation had become firmly set. The villagers watched us from a distance as one might watch some strange animals, and they brought us their produce, but they respected our vows of silence and spoke only to the two or three servants. I named my daughter Mani, after the Rani of Jhansi.

Colonel Ramsay, conditioned by his years in Nepal never to question Jung Bahadur's word, sent a report to Lord Canning that I had died, and Canning passed on the good news to the British Government.

It was, I subsequently discovered, left to the Secretary of State for India, Sir Charles Wood, to raise doubts. He directed the Viceroy to send him more positive information so that my death could be established beyond all doubt.

Back went Colonel Ramsay to Jung Bahadur, who, after chiding his visitor and his Government for doubting the word of an ally whose friendship had been so amply demonstrated, offered to make what he called a sporting bet. Balbhadra was present at this meeting and told me what happened.

"All right," His Highness told the Resident. "I am quite prepared to admit a British force into Nepal to look for Nana Saheb.

But if this force does not find him within three months, will your Government undertake to hand me back the strip along your border which is now known as the British Terais?"

This "sporting bet" Ramsay prudently declined. It was, he has recorded, "a wager Jung Bahadur could not lose. He could, with the utmost facility, keep Nana or any other party out of the way of any cavalcade of persons."

That the British remained unconvinced they made amply clear. "His wife still wears the mark of marriage," Colonel Ramsay pointed out to Jung Bahadur, "a thing no brahmin lady would ever do if she were a widow."

"I have not seen the lady," Jung Bahadur answered, "but if, as Your Excellency asserts, she flouts custom, it is not for me to correct her."

Meanwhile, in India itself, officials everywhere were exhorted to carry the search into every town and village. A description and a copy of my "portrait by Beechy" were supplied to every public office. Hundreds of vagrants were rounded up and marched to police stations and subjected to agonizing interrogations. And, right enough, several Nanas were discovered.

In 1862 a vigilant customs clerk in Karachi caught two men whom he believed to be myself and Waghu, just as they stepped off a coastal boat. After a protracted trial, for which the pair was taken to Kanpur and put through endless identification tests, it was discovered that this Nana was a man called Hirji and the Waghu was his cousin. They were goldsmiths from Marwar.

But by this time another "Nana" had been arrested in Ajmere by the Deputy Commissioner himself, a Major Davidson, after a somewhat dramatic·midnight raid on a pilgrim resthouse. He too was taken to Kanpur and "inspected" by almost anyone who professed to have known me or even seen me. This man too turned out to have been who he said he was right from the start, a bangle vendor named Apparam.

Undeterred by these false scents, the search had gone on with proverbial British relentlessness, and in the proceedings against Apparam it came out that the Government had employed a large number of paid agents solely to help in their search for me. The agents dressed themselves as sadhus and mingled with groups of pilgrims and listened to their gossip. Several more "Nanas" were dug up but, before long, I ceased taking further interest in these goings on in India. Already India was a foreign country, another planet.

In Nepal itself it was the proud boast of Jung Bahadur that "an ass could not fart without my coming to hear about it." Alerted by the British efforts to run me to earth, he gave orders that no stranger was to be permitted to penetrate into the districts where we were camping. After one or two men who might have been genuine pilgrims had been shot on the mountain paths leading to our camps, the paid agents must have got the message. No political refugee was ever given better protection, for I had now become a point of honour. The King of Kings himself had declared that I was dead; it was up to him to see that no British agent succeeded in proving him a liar.

But never again did we spend a monsoon in the Terais. From April to September, we moved to Taklakote, on the Tibetan border, and when the cold weather arrived we returned to Butwal. Migrating with the seasons, we yet lived in a segregated world of our own, like a herd of deer, at a purely animal level. Our life became circumscribed by food, sex, primitive comforts, and herd discipline. Desires did not diminish but adjusted themselves to the scope for fulfilment. The ability to find pleasure in the simpler things of life heightened, the horizons of the mind contracted, and ambition shrivelled and died, unmourned. Eliza and I were like some symbolic couple, like Rama and Sita during their exile, finding total fulfilment in one another and hankering for nothing which we could not find in our own surroundings.

This surely was nirvana, a state of being freed from the coils of life. Once again there was a woman to love and a child to address me as father. As the leader of this small herd, I led a richer, more satisfying life than I had as the master of the wada at Bithoor or as the Emperor's short-lived Peshwa.

The seasons came and went. Only occasionally, when death struck one of our party, would I be reminded of the passage of time. And then my mind would be filled with a vague uneasiness.

But in nirvana thoughts of the future were unrealistic; the present was all. "Baba!" I would hear my daughter's shrill call, demanding my instant attention, and cares would fly away like truant children.

Admittedly, Balbhadra appeared like a creditor every few months. I quickly got rid of him by selling him whatever he was after and buying for myself another two or three months in paradise. Never were precious stones put to better use.

These are not afterthoughts, a wet-eyed look back at a period of subnormal living. My exile really had become my dream world.

So when Jayaji Scindia, as though I were somehow on his conscience, sent a message in the winter of 1871 inviting me to live in Gwalior, I very firmly declined. The following summer, on the pretext of going on a pilgrimage to Badrinath, Baba Apte came from Gwalior to explain what the Scindia had in mind.

"My master gives his word that no harm will come to Your Highness. He has great influence with the Viceroy and the Resident is his personal friend. He is confident of getting you a pardon. But even if the British prove obdurate, a ship can be hired to take you to some country where you can live openly."

"But I have never been happier," I said.

"He said something about gold—I was to tell you that it could be sent anywhere you wanted it sent."

"What use is gold to a sadhu?"

Baba Apte gave me a pitying look. "No man can be happy away from his own country, his own people," he mumbled.

How could I explain to him what had happened to me—or that a citizen of paradise did not think in terms either of people or country?

Soon after Kashi had reached Kathmandu, Jung Bahadur had set her up as his principal concubine and had installed her in a house conveniently close to Thapatali, his palace. He engaged a staff of servants for her and put her on a handsome allowance. In Nepal Kashi blossomed like a vine transplanted in soil ideally suited to its growth, and she scandalized the court by taking other lovers. I must confess that, even in nirvana, it gave me a peculiar sense of satisfaction that she should not have remained true to Jung Bahadur. Her promiscuity was a kind of vicarious revenge.

We were never husband and wife, and yet a kind of fondness

must have grown between us, even though, on my part, it was never more than the fondness for an animal that has strayed into your yard and has gone on living there. Now the animal had found another good home. Only the bonds of our wedding service remained, everything else had perished. On my part there were no regrets, I only wished her well.

On the fourth and last day of Diwali, Hindu wives worship their husbands. They put on ceremonial garments and wear jewellery and flowers and circulate a tray containing butter-oil lamps before the husband. Into this tray the husband drops his anniversary gift. In Bithoor Kashi had performed this ceremony every year and, much to my surprise, had continued doing it even in Nepal. What she sought to gain by these annual visits to me I never tried to discover. Perhaps she wanted to establish for herself that I was still alive, that she could go on wearing the red dot on her forehead in token of a husband living and indulge her taste for gold saris and expensive jewellery. In Nepal, as in India, widows are consigned to wear plain white garments of the coarsest cotton, and no jewellery, not even glass bangles, are permitted. Anyway, I had never dropped a gift in the tray with the oil lamps.

Her visits were not surreptitious. She brought me greetings from Jung Bahadur and, occasionally, messages which he would not even entrust to Balbhadra. I never questioned Kashi about her life in Kathmandu, about her relationship with Jung or, later, with the court painter, Gaganrai, or, later still, with about half a dozen of the more prominent Ranas who were striving for Jung's downfall. She was living a life of her own, and had I not, long ago, surrendered my right to be a part of it? To be fair, I cannot imagine how, in a country such as Nepal where heads rolled with each change of ruler, the favourite concubine of a king-maker could have made some sort of provision for herself and her adopted son without ingratiating herself with the potential king-makers.

While Gaganrai made her immortal by making her the model for his pictures of Hindu goddesses, the Gurkha soldiers adopted her as the sex image of their bawdy songs. These songs are sung in groups, one man asking the leading questions and the others clapping and answering in chorus. Something like:

"And the colour of her breasts, O the colour of those breasts?"
"Like wheat, O, like ripe wheat."
"Who threshes the wheat, O, who threshes it?"
"They thresh it in turns, O, it is turn by turn."
"On Mondays, on Mondays?"
"The King of Kings, O, the King of Kings."
"On Tuesdays, on Tuesdays?"
"The painter of kings, O, the painter of gods."
"On Wednesdays, on Wednesdays?"
"Who knows, who knows?"
"And who is the father of her son, O, the father of our captain?"
"What a question, what a question."

The vulgarity mounts as the cups of arrack pass. The son they referred to as "our captain" was not Kashi's, of course, but Eliza's. Kashi had looked after him well and furthered his interests. Already, at sixteen, he was a captain in the Nepalese army.

Model for goddesses or the butt of soldiers' bawdiness, Kashi wielded great influence in the Nepal court. And how hard she worked to preserve that little dot on her forehead—the dot that I alone could qualify her to wear by the simple act of going on living. Kashi turned out to have been a far more valuable asset than either the Naulakha necklace or the Shiromani emerald.

Chapter 26

In both our great religious epics, the *Ramayana* and the *Maha-bharata,* the duration of *vanawasa,* or jungle living, that the princi-pal characters have to undergo is the same: fourteen years. And, curiously enough, when I had been in Nepal for nearly fourteen years, the omens began to appear.

Waghu died. A snake bit him while he was asleep and he never regained consciousness. It was difficult to imagine that someone so big and tough could be so easily killed. Waghu had been with me as long as I could remember, so that by now he had become a part of my life. His dying must have killed something within me too, leaving a cold, empty feeling which comes back whenever I think of him. The grief I felt at his death must also have dulled my mind to the other warnings that soon followed.

First, even though the money at my credit had run out, Jung Bahadur's man did not turn up to buy more jewellery. Hitherto, Balbhadra's visits had been so regular that you could tell the dates by them. The break in the pattern could only mean that something had gone wrong.

And then Azim fell ill and began to talk of his desire to end his days in Mecca—but, as he kept insisting, "only if Malik will permit." As soon as he recovered, he went. This man who was not even of my religion had been closer to me than my own brothers. I did not come out of my prayer-room to say good-bye; sorrow is so much easier to bear when you are by yourself.

A few days after Azim had gone we heard that Jung Bahadur

was planning another trip to England. Hundreds of porters carried his baggage to the railhead, and teams of priests camped in Benares to oversee the dispatch of sealed vessels of Ganges water to the ship in Bombay.

"He must be quite mad," I said.

By now we were no more than a dozen. Instead of advisers and ministers, I was reduced to a cook and a clerk and a priest and a few personal servants. It was the priest who commented, "When the time for destruction comes, thoughts become distorted."

"Badri will grab power," my clerk pronounced with complete conviction, for that was what had happened on the last occasion when Jung Bahadur had gone to England. Jung's brother, Badri Narsing, had seized power and declared himself to be the Prime Minister. Jung had to resort to an appeal to the army and a drastic confrontation to win back his position. After that he had publicly dishonoured his brother and exiled him. Now Badri was believed to be back in Nepal and living in the Terais not far from us.

"They say that ex-King Rajendra has sent Badri," the priest repeated the latest rumor. "Rajendra too has been biding his time to get his throne back—now he is merely a mouse under his own son's cradle."

"How can Jung Bahadur think of leaving Nepal at a time like this?" the clerk questioned. "He'll be away for at least a year."

"It doesn't take much more than two months to reach England nowadays," I told them. "They have dug a canal to join two seas."

"But even a year—even a few months! Once he leaves he will never be suffered to return. It is death he is seeking."

Within a few days, I discovered that nothing could have been further from Jung's mind than a trip to England. The much-publicized plan and the dispatching of thousands of boxes and sealed vessels of Ganges water to Bombay were all a part of Jung Bahadur's move to throw his adversaries off balance. On the very day he was due to start an announcement was issued from the Thapatali that the trip was cancelled because the Maharaja had fallen off his horse and suffered serious injuries. He wanted to be where he was, in Kathmandu, to deal with his enemies in his own way and on his own ground.

And I also discovered that somehow I had become a material factor in the struggle between Jung on one side and the deposed king and Badri Narsing on the other.

That was when the fourteen years of my exile ended. The walls of nirvana suddenly collapsed and I was shot back into the stream of life.

My new manservant, unused to emergencies, came to me looking dazed and mumbling something about a Maharani, and there behind him stood Kashi, hands folded and head bent as though in the presence of a temple idol. As always at the sight of this stunningly lovely woman, my breath quickened and my blood raced. I stared at her without longing, as one might at a famous statue, and I studied her as one might a slave offered for sale, feature by feature and limb by limb. I remembered a Nepalese proverb that a woman was like a lichi tree, no use to anyone after she was thirty. And yet, here was this woman, now in her mid-thirties who was still the favourite concubine of the King of Kings and the part-time mistress of Gaganrai and one or two others.

And again, as always, even though I had examined her all over, I could not bring myself to look this woman in the eye. "How is the Maharaja?" I asked. "I hope the injuries are not really serious."

"There are no injuries," Kashi said. "He did not even go riding that day."

Fear was building up within me. I sensed the imminence of bad news. I swallowed and said, "But there were public prayers at his escape, sweets distributed to the poor. And he cancelled the trip."

Kashi was shaking her head. "All put on. He never meant to go. He wanted to draw them out—the ex-king and the others—to come into the open. Begin acting instead of plotting."

How many times in his life had Jung Bahadur escaped assassination, how many times foiled the plots of his rivals by the most daring and ruthless means? Once again, he was drawing them into the open so that he could hit back and crush them.

"And have they begun to act?" I asked.

"They have killed Balbhadra—poisoned him within two days of the Maharaja's accident."

So Jung's tactics were already bearing fruit. Believing him to be bedridden, they had killed Balbhadra, his right-hand man. Big bulls were about to lock horns. How many would perish before their bout was over? But Kashi was saying something.

"The Maharaja sent me to tell you that your presence is a threat to his position. He is very sorry but he can no longer offer you protection. That is why he has not bought any more jewels."

I should have fathomed this before. It was an odd facet of this astounding man's character that he would never take on an obligation he could not expect to fulfill. "But do I still need protection," I asked naïvely, "after all these years?"

"You are one of the more important targets. They're going to kidnap your daughter or Eliza and hold her for ransom: the ransom being that you must publicly own up to being Nana Saheb. Jung Bahadur will be denounced as a liar by the ex-king. Then Badri will hand you over to the British for as much of the Terais as he can make them give back. He will instantly be acclaimed as the man who won back Nepal's lost territory."

It was somewhat involved, and yet it was Nepal all over. To win back the whole of the Terais which had been appropriated by the British was every man's dream, and murder and kidnappings were the normal ingredients of political bargaining.

"What does he want me to do?" I asked.

"I am to take Eliza and Mani back to Kathmandu. They will be kept right in the Thapatali. Later, they will be sent wherever you want."

I remembered the time when Jung Bahadur himself had forbidden Eliza to enter Kathmandu. Now that particular objection had gone. Perhaps his agents had told him that no one was likely to take Eliza for an Englishwoman.

And then a shiver passed through me as I recollected that this was something I had gone through before, become suddenly parted from those I most loved. Did this too mean that I would never see Eliza or Mani again? And, before my eyes, the Thapatali, a building I had never seen, was going up in flames and red-faced soldiers were laughing and dancing all around.

I was aroused from my abstraction. "What did you say?" I asked.

"He has said that you must leave Nepal right away—today."

Panic gripped me. "Right away!" I gasped. "But why the hurry?"

"He believes that even a day's delay would be fatal," Kashi said breathlessly. "They're quite desperate."

Thus was I thrown out of my nirvana and into the coils of *sansar*, worldly life. My first look at life showed me a lovely woman dissolved in tears.

Why was Kashi crying? What was I to her—to this woman whom I had married but never loved or honoured, merely used? Why should she waste tears on me? Would I, if I had heard that Kashi had died, have felt a moment's grief? Hardly. And here was Kashi crying bitterly because I was going out of her life forever.

Fear and panic gave way to an awareness of guilt. I went up to her and raised her chin and, for the first time in my life, kissed her —chastely, as one might a sister.

"I was fated to bring you bad news," she apologized. "Forgive me."

I dried her tears with the end of her sari and then went into the small courtyard at the back of the house. From under a paving stone, I took out the brass box in which I had kept the last few bits of my family jewels. I took out Mastani's eardrops.

Her face was composed, but her eyes were still unnaturally bright. "I want to give you something," I said. Like a beggar woman preparing to receive a piece of stale bread, she spread out the corner of her sari. When she saw what I had dropped in it, she recoiled in disbelief.

"But how can I?" she gasped.

"They're mine to give," I said.

"But—but I have heard of them. They're Mastani's."

"A very beautiful woman's."

She shook her head several times and her eyes again filled with tears.

"Her lover would have wanted them to go to someone like you —someone as breathtakingly lovely as his own Mastani."

She closed her eyes and tears rolled down her cheeks. "He would have deserved you, too," I said. "Lived with you as a wife even if there had been a thousand curses."

I swear she blushed, blushed while she was still crying. And, in an effort to hide her face from me, she bent down and touched my feet in gratitude, gratitude for what I had said even more than for what I had given her. I offered her my blessings, as a father might bless his daughter.

Perhaps a man who has known defeats as often as I have cannot help making something of a ritual of them, which may be the reason why I made up my mind to go back to my country without a single servant or companion. I would be a pilgrim returning from the Himalayas, carrying all his belongings in a rolled blanket, a pilgrim-crutch filled with the tiniest of gold coins to see me through emergencies. I distributed the rest of my money, gold and silver, equally among my servants. Bajirao I's sword I sent as my parting present to Jung Bahadur, for I knew that, in his court, it would always find a place of honour. I still had a few of the family jewels left. These I handed to Eliza.

"This is all I have to give you," I told her. "But some of them are valuable. You can live comfortably, and there should be enough left over for Mani's dowry." The catch in my voice made me stop.

At such moments Eliza's English side comes to the fore, in the ability to give courage by appearing to be unruffled. She smiled brightly and put away the jewels in a cloth bag without so much as a glance at them. "I've still not finished packing," she said and went in.

I crept into my prayer-room, quite overwhelmed with self-pity, bemoaning my fate that even the hermit shell that I had wormed myself into had been cracked open; that, after fourteen years of sheltered living which had made me soft and flabby, I was again being thrown to the wolves. I was nearly forty-nine years old.

How could I, a man whose prayers had been so rarely answered, still have any faith left in the power of prayer? I had, I knew, run to my pooja room as another man might have run to a tavern, invoking my gods not because I believed that they would somehow resolve my problems but because, being a brahmin, prayer had become a habit with me.

I did not know what I was praying for; what specific favour I was seeking, what specific evil I was trying to ward off. The metal gods gleamed coldly, making geometric patterns of light. I shut my eyes and folded my hands and tried to concentrate. It was no use.

I heard Eliza's step. "Mani and I are ready," she said.

I did not say anything, because there was nothing to say. For a while we stood in silence, a man and woman whom fate had thrown together and was now wrenching apart. Then Mani came in and stood on my other side. I clasped their hands and walked with them to the waiting palanquin. The moment they got in, I turned and fled, back to my shrine, my escape hole.

As I said, by then I had little enough faith left in the power of prayer. But that day some god must have been listening. All that I had in mind and had been unable to put in my prayer was given to me.

Chapter 27

It was like being pulled by some invisible line. I could never have kept away from Kanpur and Bithoor for a last look even if these towns had been hundreds of miles out of my way. As it happened, they were right in my path to Gwalior, the direction in which I had decided to head. I crossed the Ganges barely ten miles below Kanpur.

And since this visit coincided with my adoptive father's *sraddha,* or death anniversary, I seized the opportunity of having the prescribed pooja performed on the bank of the Ganges. The presence of the river enhances the merit of a pooja.

Admittedly, I have never felt anything but deep contempt for my adoptive father. But, just as I never showed the slightest disrespect to him while he lived, I never failed to perform the religious ceremonies for the peace of his soul after he died. A son has duties, and these have always been sacred to me. While I was still at Bithoor I had, of course, performed Bajirao's sraddha in a manner befitting the last Peshwa. Sehnais played from dawn and priests came all the way from Gaya and Benares to participate in the prayers. I gave away eleven cows to the poor and fed a hundred and one brahmins before breaking my own fast. Such lavishness was not possible while I was in Nepal, but I never neglected the basic ritual. I always had my priest read the *sarvapitri,* the prayer for the dead, and gave him food and a gold coin and myself observed a fast.

Thus, on the morning of January 28, 1873, I was squatting before a *Gangaputra,* or a son of the Ganges, as these priests are known, dipping tulsi leaves in a copper vessel containing a mixture of milk and honey and sprinkling the mixture on a coconut resting on a mound of rice, while the priest chanted the sarvapitri. He was, I remember thinking, an exceptionally competent priest, for he knew the somewhat intricate service by heart and did not once have to open his book.

Before me stretched Mother Ganges, its waters overlaid with a thin mist. The sun came up and suddenly the mist was a sheet of hammered copper and, beyond the bright-yellow fields of mustard, the spires of the riverside temples stood out like polished spear-heads.

"Your name?" the priest was asking.

"Dhondu," I told him, still uplifted by the spectacle of the Ganges at sunrise.

He incorporated the name into the invocation and asked me my father's name.

"Bajirao."

"*Kailasaprati jati Baji-sonurayam . . . ,*" he began, and then suddenly stopped in the middle of his recital. The break in the religious, humming voice sent a shiver through my body—unless it was a gust of wind.

"And what was his father's name?" Now his voice was sharp and high-pitched, no longer sanctimonious.

I should have anticipated this difficulty, for the ritual requires the names of four generations to be included in the prayer. "It is not necessary," I said peevishly.

"It is necessary."

I shrugged, trying to make light of it. "Raghunath," I told him. "And his father's?"

"Again Bajirao."

Suddenly he keeled over and stretched himself on the sand, folding his hands to the rising sun and the river. "Holy Mother Ganga," he said softly, "you have shown me my master. They said he had died long ago."

"I am nobody's master," I told him sternly. "One rupee is all I can pay for your services."

He was not listening. In the mist-wet sand, his thin body

stretched rigid as a pole, his threadbare shawl flapped in the morning breeze.

Somehow we got through the pooja. The priest, whose name was Kashiram Pande, insisted that I should be his guest. He told me with visible pride that Mangal Pande, the first man to be shot by the British as a rebel, was a cousin of his, but this I did not believe. Almost anyone whose surname happened to be Pande had begun to claim relationship with Mangal Pande.

He took me to his house behind Sirsaya ghat and brought a *charpoy* onto the veranda for me to sleep on. In the evening, as I lay in bed, he told me what had happened in Kanpur after I had gone away: first-hand details of the plunder and the burning and the wanton ferocity, of the carnage that had gone on for weeks in the spirit of some barbaric carnival. My throat muscles constricted and harsh yellow specks of anger danced before my eyes.

"I'll take you around and show you," he offered. "There are restrictions on movements still, and some places are forbidden for Indians. You might do something that might give you away. Let me come with you—I have a little influence too."

I gladly accepted his offer. He was still droning away when I fell asleep.

Kanpur, a town without history, a bastard of British parentage dropped at the feet of the Ganges, a military encampment grown into a city, now had both history and geography. The British had created it, and it had become the scene of their humiliation and of their revenge.

They had levied a fine on the city, and with the money they had laid out a pretentious garden, forty acres of it, called the Memorial Garden. The memorial was for the British dead, the garden for the British living. The Indian dead had no memorial, nor the living Indians a garden; in fact, they were forbidden entry into the Memorial Garden, even though, of course, the gardeners and other menials were Indian.

After Kashiram Pande had whispered a few words into the ears of a near-by paan-shop owner, it was arranged that, if we approached from the riverside, we would find a small wicket gate left unlocked. "We shall see the well first," said Pande.

"The well" was no longer a hole in the ground; it had been filled up and a platform built on its site. A marble angel stood on the platform, looking, because of the wings sprouting from its back, like some minor Hindu god; and around this desexed figure was a marble screen such as one might find in a Mogul harem, which was said to be the gift of Lady Canning. Set into the arch of the enclosure was a white tablet with the following inscription:

SACRED TO THE PERPETUAL MEMORY
OF A GREAT COMPANY OF CHRISTIAN PEOPLE
CHIEFLY WOMEN AND CHILDREN
WHO, NEAR THIS SPOT
WERE CRUELLY MURDERED BY THE FOLLOWERS
OF THE REBEL DHONDU PANT OF BITHOOR
AND CAST, THE DYING WITH THE DEAD
INTO THE WELL BELOW
ON THE 15TH DAY OF JULY 1857

I was not responsible for this slaughter and had never condoned it. Inwardly I felt a spasm of gratefulness towards whoever had composed the inscription, for had he not at least refrained from saying what so many others swore to: that it was I who had ordered the massacre?

Or had he? A slow anger built up as I stared at my own name on the cold marble In its sly, indirect way, it pointed an accusing finger. Even assuming that those who had murdered the women and children were my followers, was that enough reason to link my name with their crime?

And the British knew that they were not my followers. If they had been, they would have obeyed my orders that women and children were not to be harmed. That I had given such orders was, I believe, established beyond doubt in the inquiry they had instituted after their return to Kanpur.

It was a mean, spiteful thing to have put my name on this plaque, implying that I was somehow at the back of it all. On the same principle, should not Queen Victoria's name be inscribed on a thousand monuments in India to suggest that she instigated the

atrocities perpetrated by her subjects? A tablet at the site of Daryaganj, for instance, paid for by some Indian Lady Canning, would
proclaim to the world:

> A VILLAGE STOOD HERE.
> IT WAS BURNED DOWN BY THE MEN OF
> QUEEN VICTORIA'S ARMY
> ON THE 12TH DAY OF JUNE 1857.
> THE MEN, WOMEN, AND CHILDREN WHO RAN OUT
> WERE THROWN BACK INTO THE FIRE.

It hurts because it is not true. Despite the most exhaustive inquiries, no one has been able to establish that I was anywhere near
the Bibighar or even that anyone had seen me in Kanpur when the
slaughter occurred, as hundreds had seen Hodson shooting the
heirs of the Mogul emperor or as thousands had witnessed the
public hangings of the remaining princes by Metcalfe and Boyd.

This, I felt, was exactly how another victim of the concentrated
calumny of the East India Company's thugs must have felt more
than a hundred years earlier: Siraj-ud-Dowla. After his capture of
Calcutta, he had ordered his prisoners to be securely guarded. The
man in charge of the prisoners had decided that the best place to
keep them would be the guard-room in which the British had kept
their prisoners. Here, during the night, many died—but not a hundred and twenty-three, as one of the survivors, a Mr. Holwell, reported. Earlier, Holwell had been denounced by his own compatriots as a habitual liar, but this time everything he had to say was
implicitly believed. A monster was needed, and Mr. Holwell had
dug him up. Siraj, whose greatest crime had been that he had made
a feeble attempt to drive out the white traders from Bengal, became the Black Hole Monster.

How many people realize that the man who qualifies best for that
particular infamy was Fredric Cooper, the British Commissioner
of Amritsar who, during our revolt, locked up his prisoners in a
windowless room in a village called Ajnala? By the next morning,
forty-five had died of suffocation. The total tally of Cooper's victims is nearer five hundred, but the others were shot in batches of
ten, tethered hand to hand. But no one has called Mr. Cooper any
kind of a monster, and many speak of him as the Hero of Ajnala.

Bibighar needed another monster, and there were many who were willing to point the finger. I, Nana Saheb, became the Bibighar Monster.

I was still thinking of Siraj-ud-Dowla, whose real crime had been that he had allowed a man like Clive to defeat him. If Siràj had won at Plassey, there would have been monuments erected in his honour in every village in Bengal and ballads sung to his glory, and he would have gone down in history as the man who saved his country from enslavement.

"Come on," I heard an urgent whisper. "We must slip out before they close the gate."

It was like coming out of a dream. Siraj-ud-Dowla vanished. An anxious priest stood by my side. "I never did this," I said to him.

He smirked and shrugged. "It doesn't matter. They have done far worse things."

I knew that even he would not believe that I was altogether blameless.

Stealthily, as untouchables who had strayed into a temple yard, we crept out. The little gate was still open.

At the Satichaura ghat, which was now called the Satichaura Massacre Ghat, there was no tablet, only a chunky stone cross inscribed:

IN MEMORIAM
27TH JUNE 1857

How peaceful it was, this scene of madness and carnage. It was cold in the shade of the trees and warm on the sunlit bank, and in the air was the nose-tickling scent of mustard blossom. The river was shot with colours like a mallard's wing, and along its edges stood grey-and-white cranes like penitents meditating upon their own reflections. I shut my eyes and filled my lungs again and again with the clean, winter smells.

And suddenly it was summer. A searing wind came over the white-hot desert, the wind that we call the loo, but a loo which had the special, abrasive rasp of the Devil's Wind.

The smell of sulphur arose in the air, and the riverbed was strewn with cinders and ashes, and the water was like dark oil and the boats were lying on their sides or locked together in groups and burning.

The silence had the quality of silence that falls after an uproar. Heads bobbed up from the water and someone raised a hand to me. "I am sorry," I was saying. "Sorry, sorry . . ."

I screwed my eyes tight and dug my nails into the palms of my hands to force my mind back to the present. I concentrated on the bloodless wraith in the snow-white dhoti who was blinking anxiously at my face. Kashiram Pande, my priest and guide for the day, grinned reassuringly.

"Nothing to see here," he said. "Only the cross."

This was my land. My mind would forever be chained to it, my spirit haunt it everlastingly. Wherever I might go, I would never get away from Kanpur.

Again we crept away. I was racked by a feeling of guilt, an awareness that this was sacred ground and that we were committing sacrilege by treading on it. But then this feeling of being an intruder, of polluting something by your mere presence, was altogether unavoidable in Kanpur for the simple reason that most of the available space had been cordoned off and signposted as constituting hallowed ground, and memorials were everywhere.

Close to the site of Wheeler's Entrenchment there was another covered well with a stone cross over it. Against my companion's whispered entreaties, I ventured close enough to read the inscription:

IN A WELL UNDER THIS CROSS WERE LAID
BY THE HANDS OF THEIR FELLOWS IN SUFFERING
THE BODIES OF MEN, WOMEN, AND CHILDREN
WHO DIED HARD IN THEIR HEROIC DEFENCE
OF WHEELER'S ENTRENCHMENT
WHEN BELEAGUERED BY THE REBEL NANA

I might have myself written this one. I myself professed to be what it declared me to be, a rebel. The deaths were regrettable, particularly those of the women and children, but they were the casualties of war, inevitable in a conflict. It was just unfortunate that they were caught up in the front line.

After that we wandered among the ruins. Savda Kothi, where I had held court, was razed to the ground and even the earth ploughed over to erase all signs of its existence, but Noor Mohamad's hotel, where I had lived for the last few days, still had some of the walls standing. We went down to the Golaghat bazaar and walked through the infamous Hanging Gardens, where the banyans had been festooned with human bodies dangling in figures of eight and figures of nine.

It was cool under the banyans, so ancient that once the Lord Krishna himself is said to have rested under them. "Do you know where poor Azijan was hanged?" I asked. Kashiram Pande did not.

I walked round the empty space enclosed by spiked railings where once the Bibighar had stood. Now the tablet pronounced it to have been the House of Massacre. Whether you were British or Indian, this was a shrine that could not fail to make you burn with hatred for the other race. To the British, this was a place where the women and children held prisoners in Kanpur had been done to death only a few hours before they retook the city. How many Englishmen must have stood before this railing and sworn vengeance? How many more would do so in the years to come? And who can blame them?

To Indians, the House of Massacre will always remain a shrine to offer prayers of anger and swear oaths of vengeance, for it was a memorial as much to British atrocities as to our own. In our minds, Bibighar can never be separated from its causes or its consequences; to us, Bibighar, Fattepur, Daryaganj are interrelated, and the massacre of July 15 is only a part of its gruesome backlash. The monument to this crime is a denunciation not only of the butchers who hacked the British women and children to pieces but also of Neill and his subordinates who avenged the crime with matching ferocity.

My skin prickled as I stood before this shrine to racial hatred. I tried to imagine what kind of a man this Neill could have been to have compressed so much violence and hatred within him. And then I remembered reading that the British citizens of Calcutta had paid a public tribute to him and said something to the effect that he had filled a page in the annals of history and that he was an honour to his country.

"Here in India, his name will never be remembered without a shudder," I said almost to myself.

My guide must have known what I was thinking about, for he said, "He was the most hated man, Neill Saheb."

"I am the most hated."

"With him the hatred still lives." His words came as an icy whisper charged with meaning.

"But he's dead, didn't you know?" I said. "He died soon after Kanpur."

"But the feud is not dead," he answered in the same icy voice.

"What do you mean 'not dead'?"

"I will show you in the evening. Come on, it is not good to stand here too long. Englishmen too come here—stand for hours."

We went back to his house, and after the evening meal I told him that I was going on to Bithoor the next morning.

"You want me to come and show you round?"

"No, I shan't need a guide for Bithoor."

He gave me a hard look and nodded. "Just as you like."

That was when I reminded him about Neill. "Why did you say that the feud still lives?"

"Because Neill Saheb made Dafedar Zaffar Ali lick the blood from the floor of the Bibighar."

"But Zaffar Ali . . . I know the name well. He never joined us. He was in the Entrenchment, on their side, till he was driven out."

"All the same, he was one of the hostages."

"And he was hanged?"

"No, burned, being a Muslim. But before dying he left orders to his son to avenge his death by killing Neill Saheb's son."

"It is sixteen years since the revolt," I pointed out.

"What is sixteen years?" the brahmin asked. Then he darted into an inner room and brought out a crumbly sheet of paper. "Read this," he said. "The original was in blood, but many copies were made—to be distributed."

The writing was in Urdu, faded and blotchy but quite legible. It said:

O, Mohamad Prophet, be pleased to receive into paradise the soul of your slave, Zaffar Ali, whose body was cut open by flogging and who was made to lick the blood on the floor of the Bibighar as ordered by General Neill and who, before this day is out, will die. And O, Prophet, in due time, give strength to my infant son, Mahzar Ali of Rohtak, that he may avenge this desecration on the General's descendants.

For a moment we were both silent. In the distance a bugle sounded the last post. "It is wrong," I mumbled.

"What is wrong?" Pande asked in an affronted tone.

"Hatred should not be passed from father to son."

He shook his head. "Great wrongs must be avenged," he said very sternly, "however long it takes."

"The son may turn out to be a kind and good man. Why should he be made a party to this—fettered to a father's deathbed ravings?"

"Deathbed ravings! These are the sacred embers from the fire, to be preserved and fanned again." Almost angrily he snatched the paper from my hands. "What would you have done if your father had left that to you as his last wish?" he demanded.

That night I could not sleep. Thoughts raced through my head and the ghosts of Kanpur against my lids fluttered. I saw the monuments and their tablets and wandered among the ruins of buildings and the dark groves of the banyans furred with age and draped with hanging white roots that resembled human forms. I heard the *thumrie* played by Azijan's girls as a background to the screams of the white children and the brown children, and I saw Eliza being carried away by Nizam Ali and held down by his wife and servants while he raped her, and I saw General Neill riding at full gallop with a burning torch, setting fire to temple and mosque and house and laughing . . . laughing.

And in my own mind I knew that, no matter how long it took, Mahzar Ali would go on fanning the sacred ember till he had honoured his father's command—honoured it, or passed on the ember to his descendants.*

---

* General Neill's son, A. H. S. Neill, joined the Indian cavalry and by 1887 had risen to the command of the 2nd Central India Horse, in which Mahzar Ali, Zaffar Ali's son, was a trooper. On March 14, 1887, Mahzar Ali shot his commanding officer while on parade, in full view of the regiment, and then gave himself up. —M.M.

The mother of rivers flowed serenely past the ruins, as though nothing had happened. But Bithoor had gone; of the old Bithoor that had been the vestigial kingdom of the Peshwa, nothing remained. The wada stood like a skeleton of an elephant on a hillock, picked clean by vultures but somehow still on its legs. Thornbushes grew in Bajirao's hall of mirrors, and the masonry around the gaping holes where the doors and windows had been was still charred. Fragments of broken glass glinted among the boulders.

For a moment I stood beside the well in which I had concealed the plate, the cash, and some jewellery. How much was there? I hardly remember. Certainly much, much more than what the Prize Agents reported. They speak of a gold bowl weighing forty pounds; it was one of a set of six. They don't mention either the Portuguese candlestands or the Mogul wine jars. They found eight ammunition boxes packed with gold mohurs worth three and a half million rupees. I remember Bajirao's telling me that the coins numbered three and a half million—but of course I never had occasion to count them.

In Bithoor there were no gardens, no memorials, no hallowed ground forbidden entry to either black or white. Every vestige of the ex-Peshwa had been obliterated. Now Bithoor was an insignificant huddle of huts beside the Ganges, just as it had been before the last Peshwa chose it as his place of exile. The house he built, the menagerie, the serais, the ghats, the exquisite set of white marble temples, all had been reduced to rubble as though a gigantic plough had been drawn over everything. A partridge called from the bushes in the hall of mirrors. Fifty chiming clocks had once stood in that hall, clanging incessantly because their timings had been kept deliberately staggered.

I turned to look at the dead elephant that had once been my home. I stood watching, determined not to see what was not there, trying to concentrate on the cock partridge calling from where the clocks had chimed. Perhaps someday some rich man will erect a memorial here, I thought, complete with a white marble plaque to remind my countrymen that this too was consecrated ground— consecrated not because of those who had lived in it but because of those who had died in it when it had gone up in flames.

And, in spite of my resolve to keep my mind from wandering, I saw before me an arch, complete with a white plaque of virgin marble, waiting for some craftsman with a chisel to carve out its message:

BEHIND THIS ARCH STOOD SHANWAR-WADA
THE HOME OF THE LAST PESHWA
IT WAS BURNED DOWN BY THE BRITISH
ON JULY 19, 1857
WHILE THE WOMENFOLK WERE STILL INSIDE

Perhaps my wording lacked the dignity of the Kanpur plaques, but it happened to be far more true than any of them. They did burn the house and Champa and the other women who were hiding in the tykhana were burned alive.

Around the burning wada, I could see the soldiers, their haversacks bulging with loot, their faces carroty and shining from the wine in my cellar, milling around and roaring with laughter and making obscene onomatopoetic sounds as though the screams of women and the howls of animals trapped inside were sounds of revelry. And I could see their commander, Major Stevenson, sitting on a roan charger that had been mine, horrified at what was happening and yet unable to halt the process as I myself had been at Satichaura. I had never met Stevenson but I had heard many stories about him and knew him to be a kind and warm-hearted man who did everything in his power to curb the excesses of his men. They can tell me what they like, but I shall never believe that he had known that the womenfolk were still indoors when his men set fire to the wada. Was he not actually censured by his commander, Lord Clyde, for not being sufficiently vindictive in destroying Bithoor?

Served-them-right! Served-them-right! Served-them-right! someone was shouting in a chirpy, schoolgirl voice. My reverie broke. It was the partridge, of course, challenging an imaginary rival. There was no Major Stevenson on horseback and no memorial arch. Memorials are only for the victors.

Chapter 28

His face might have been carved out of weathered teak—inexpertly carved, with slits for eyes and a jutting jaw where the wood had a knot. He had put on a good deal of weight, and his shoulders were massive and his stomach bulged like that of a wrestler who had given up exercise. Standing up, he reminded one of some prehistoric man-figure dug out from a buried civilization.

At the moment, however, he was sitting down, all hunched up, his brow puckered in a scowl, his lips moving as though to assist in some complex thought process or in muttering curses. For his mood was dark. He had been trying to extract a promise from the Resident that if he persuaded me to give myself up, the British would let me live in the country in quiet retirement. He had failed.

"They never relent," I told him. "Don't tell me you were taken in by that bit in Queen Victoria's proclamation. No one else was. In fact, when Major Richardson wrote to me in Nepal to give myself up, Jung Bahadur warned me not to be a fool." I had brought in Jung Bahadur's name because I had a feeling that Jayaji Scindia fancied himself to be more astute than Jung Bahadur.

"But after sixteen years!" Jayaji moaned. "And mind you, it's not as though everyone were still all that bloodthirsty. Osborne himself has several times told me that it would be best to let bygones be bygones."

Colonel Willoughby Osborne, the British Resident at Gwalior, was a close friend of the Scindia's. Jayaji had revealed to him that I was his guest in Gwalior. Osborne had thereupon rushed to consult General Daly, the commander of the nearest British garrison, and between them they had decided to make the Scindia deliver me into their custody.

Again I resorted to sarcasm. "I just cannot imagine Jung Bahadur letting himself be pushed into a situation like this."

And again the Scindia ignored my taunt. He said, "The Viceroy seems determined to extract whatever milk is still left in the mutiny; he just won't let the old cow die."

Was he too trying to rile me? If so, he was succeeding. I said, quite sharply, "I'm sorry Your Highness chooses to call our revolt 'the mutiny.' "

His immense shoulders flexed and contracted. "One gets so used to—to saying things in the approved way. And I for one must never make a slip; I can't afford to talk in any language but the one laid down by the British. Don't forget, I'm their ever-trusted ally—ever-trusted. Even in my sleep, I have to live up to that trust." He gave a hearty laugh as though something had amused him. "That's the whole point: the British must never cease to trust me."

"But there is no danger of that, ever, is there?" I said.

Was this man, cast in the mouldings of some primitive god, quite immune to sarcasm? Jayaji went on chuckling to himself and tapping his bare foot rhythmically on the floor. Then, turning his whole frame toward the door, he called, "*Aao!* Enter!"

A man came in, his presence an affront to the gleaming marble floor, to the mosaic of Kashan prayer rugs, to the delicately carved lotus-patterned grille of the windows—through which, like a giant displaying his oiled torso, reared the great yellow fort of Gwalior which housed a strong British garrison. His dhoti, which barely covered his knees, was torn and dirty, his tattered gown had been made for a smaller man. He had a full face with many wrinkles and a week's growth of greying beard.

"Stand facing the window," Jayaji ordered. For perhaps two minutes he studied the man from head to foot, as a buyer might examine a horse, and then curtly ordered him to go and put on some decent clothes. "Come back when you are ready!"

Then Jayaji had pen and ink and paper brought in and dictated to me the letter which I was supposed to have written to him on arrival:

I have come to Gwalior after long and continuous suffering. Your ancestors were always obedient to and well-wishers of my ancestors. Relying on this, and also taking you to be of my family, I, without the least hesitation, place my head in your lap. I am helpless and friendless and leave you to do as you think fit. I pray for your increased prosperity.

I signed the letter and said, "No one will believe I wrote it. It is not my language at all."

"By the time the translators have done with it, the language will be that of all other translated documents," the Scindia commented. "Besides, all they'll bother about is the signature. If that's genuine, you are you." And he smirked as though pleased with his own thoughts.

"Tell me," I said. "You're not going to show this letter to the Resident, are you?"

"Oh, yes, I'm sending it to him right away."

"And you think it will make them take a more charitable view?"

"I don't know. We must first convince Osborne," Jayaji said blandly. "Ah, here's our friend again, all clean and dressed up."

The man came back now shaved and bathed. He wore a white, knee-length robe over a gold-bordered dhoti, and on his head perched the tasselled red Pagri of the Poona brahmin. He no longer looked destitute, and yet his face was shadowed by some inner sorrow, as though he suffered from an incurable disease.

"Take a good look at this man," Jayaji told me. "Who does he remind you of?"

"No one."

"Look carefully. Is there or is there not a mark on the forehead?"

"Well, there is a faint nick."

"And the lobes of the ears?"

"What about them?"

"They are pierced."

"So they are."

"Surely he has worn a *bhik-bali?* There are marks."

"Now that you say so, yes, there are faint grooves such as might be made by earrings."

"So, now, who does he remind you of?"

I shook my head. "Sorry, but should I know? Who is he, anyway?"

I got the impression that the Scindia had been waiting for me to ask that question. He waved both hands as though whisking off an insect and said, "You ask him. Who he is, where he comes from. All that."

The man in the scarlet pagri stood breathing hard and nervously shifting his horny feet and blinking at the Scindia, and I felt sorry for whatever he was being made to go through. "What is your name?" I asked.

He turned to face me squarely and, taking a deep breath as though to brace himself for some ordeal, said, "Dhondu Pant. I am also called Nana Saheb—Nana Saheb of Bithoor."

And suddenly I knew what Jayaji Scindia was going to do.

The man's name was Jamna Das. The Scindia had discovered him in a *serai,* or traveller's resthouse, at Morar months earlier.

As if to give me time to compose myself, the Scindia was smoking his hookah with great concentration. "You don't really believe they'll be taken in, do you?" I asked him after Jamna Das had been dismissed.

He closed his eyes and filled his great chest with smoke. His words came mixed with a gust of smoke. "The British have never doubted my word."

"But they'll soon prove he's not me."

"Not soon. Only after they've gone through a trial. It takes years."

"But this is so—so juvenile! It'll never work."

"Do you know how many Nana Sahebs they've discovered so far?"

"Two."

"I know of at least six, and no doubt there were many more," he said between gurgles. "All six were taken to Kanpur and kept there on show for months. All turned out to be false. And yet you'd be surprised how many people swore that one or the other of them was you."

I was still diffident. "But this wretched man. Who's going to testify that he is me?"

"Who will testify?" the Scindia asked dramatically. "Those who know you most intimately will testify. Your sister Kusuma, her father-in-law, Baba Apte, I, Jayaji Scindia."

"But this man is not going to go on saying he's me once he discovers he's going to be hanged?"

"Hanged? No one's going to hang him once he's proved to be an impostor! Oh, he's safe. A few months in jail, that's all. And he knows he'll be compensated. Now I must rush off, hundreds of things to do."

"How long have you been keeping him?"

"For about six months. I had another man before him, but he died."

His confidence was altogether infectious and drew from me a spontaneous compliment. "Even Jung Bahadur would not have dared to put across anything quite so audacious."

The Scindia bowed as gracefully as his bulging stomach would permit. "Well, you have exactly four hours in which to coach your double," he told me. "Now it's up to you."

"Four hours!"

"That's all. I'm going to get the Resident here at midnight. These little touches heighten the effect."

Jamna Das made a good pupil. Colonel Osborne, the Resident, was summoned to the palace at midnight to take charge of him. "He confessed to all your crimes and explained all the particulars about your whereabouts over the last sixteen years most convincingly," the Scindia told me.

And the next day, my sister Kusuma, haughty, matronly, and the picture of unquestionable probity, identified Jamna Das as her brother Nana Saheb and, in the presence of the Resident and General Daly, shed dutiful tears over his fate. After that they called in her father-in-law.

"Baba Apte was even more dramatic," the Scindia told me. "The old man coolly put on his spectacles and gazed at Jamna Das intently. And then, in a charged voice, pointed his finger at the man and said, 'You are Nana!' "

The festival of Dassara came two days later. That evening, when Jayaji Scindia dropped in to see me, he was in a jubilant mood.

Obviously everything had gone well. He was dressed in his magnificent ceremonial durbar robes, glittering with chains of pearls and diamonds and an imposing array of British decorations. He had just attended a public function where he had delivered an important speech. "What do you think of this bit?" he asked, and in a completely different, public-platform voice, continued, "This man was concerned with wholesale massacre. He is the enemy of this government as much as of the British Government, for he was the real originator of the mutiny. I therefore considered it my duty—my sacred duty—to hand him over to the Resident at Gwalior. This I did on the twenty-second of October."

"And what did they say?"

"They applauded, and the Resident congratulated me on my English," he answered, dropping back to his natural voice and purring like a kitten. "And you know what they're doing? You'll never believe it. The Resident announced publicly that the British Government is making me a present of the temple you had built in Benares."

"Aren't you carrying this deception to unnecessary lengths?" I asked. "Once they discover what you've been up to, they will come down on you like an elephant's foot."

I am afraid that this most circumspect of men uttered an unprintable word and accompanied it with a disgracefully obscene gesture. "I shall let you know what happens," he promised. "Meanwhile, the Viceroy is sending two men all the way to Gwalior to identify our man: some doctor who was in Kanpur and another man. . . ."

A wave of panic came over me. "Not Dr. Tessider?"

"That's right, Tessider, and another man, a Colonel Mowbray Thomson, one of the survivors of the Entrenchment. They're to make a report to the Viceroy, and after that they will send Jamna Das to Kanpur."

"Look," I said, trying to gulp down my fear. "Tessider was my doctor. A doctor knows his patient better even than his wife. He is never going to certify that that mendicant is me."

Jayaji shot out his arm straight at me and squinted over it as though it were a gun barrel. "Tell you what," he offered. "I'll take a bet with you that this Tessider will say neither yes nor no. In the end the man will be taken to Kanpur for a detailed examination by other experts. Any bet." He lowered his hand and held it out to me.

I laughed with relief and shook my head. "In Nepal no one ever took a bet with Jung Bahadur. In Gwalior I am not so foolish as to take a bet with the Scindia. Now I know that the man will go to Kanpur."

"Come on, I'll give you odds," the Scindia tried to tempt me, still holding out his hand. "Big odds." And he circled round me as though daring me to touch his hand and accept the wager. Then he broke into a jig, bouncing up and down and turning round and round in an outburst of sheer animal spirits. It was like seeing an elephant trying to trample a mosquito, and that is the last impression I carry of Jayaji Scindia.

Before Tessider and Mowbray Thomson arrived, I was whisked off from Gwalior. It was only later that I learned that Tessider did not think that Jamna Das was me, that to him he appeared "a most disreputable fellow, cringing and humble, and utterly different" from the man he remembered as Nana Saheb "in his glory at Bithoor." But Mowbray Thomson overruled him. I don't know when Mowbray Thomson had ever seen me; he had certainly never come to my house. But, after seeing Jamna Das in the clothes I normally wore at Bithoor, he gave it as his opinion that the prisoner before him was Nana Saheb.

While all this was taking place in Gwalior, I was on my way to Malwan, a port in the heart of Maratha territory. I reached Malwan nearly a month later. Here a ship manned entirely by Arabs, hired by some rich Muslim merchant for a haaj pilgrimage, waited to set sail. I didn't realize till the ship's master, in flowing robes, received me on deck that I was the Mecca-bound pilgrim. Very ceremoniously and communicating with gestures since we had no common language, I was conducted to my cabin.

It was dim in the cabin, even though the evening light filtered through two small round holes. Two Muslim women, draped from head to foot in burquas, sat huddled on a bunk on the far side. They both whipped round in alarm as the door opened and I entered, the meshed slits in their veils aimed towards me. And then one of them shot up like a bird and flung herself into my arms squealing, "Baba! Baba!" And my eyes suddenly misted.

Many months later, while I was still in Mecca, someone sent me two cuttings from the London *Times,* and I would have taken a bet even with the Scindia himself that it was he who had sent them. One, dated November 30, 1874, after quoting General Daly as saying, "The probabilities are with the Scindia. If he has been deceived, the deception is remarkable," laments that "public opinion grows daily more skeptical." And the other item, dated December 5, 1874, is a dispatch from the *Times*'s Calcutta correspondent: "The Government is satisfied that the prisoner is not Nana Saheb. Scindia admits he was mistaken."

Azim, who had already been in Mecca for some months, joined me soon after my arrival and, without a word from either of us, resumed his duties as my secretary. Mecca has little to recommend it other than its holiness; it was certainly no place for a non-Muslim to live. Luckily, Azim too had had enough of holiness by now and was eager to leave. He had already made many influential friends in the Shareef's court and through them was able to arrange that, by paying for the privilege instead of receiving a salary, I would be appointed the Shareef's agent to the Sultan of the Ottoman Empire.

So here I am in Constantinople. Here the seasons have a tameness. From my bedroom, I look into a shelving forest. The trees are cypresses, dark and melancholy; they look like fat nuns mourning. And the patches of blue I see through their foliage are the Bosporus, a noisy, boisterous juvenile sea. Here it is always cold and the summer is a fraud; if you can sleep with your windows open, it is a Turkish summer. Even the quality of light is different, as though given by a different sun, or as though there is a gauze curtain stretched over the sky.

Here there is no danger for me and mine. We want for nothing that money can buy, for the Scindia, who has financial interests all over the world, has arranged for Mr. Soloman's counting house here to give me credit for the elephant-load of gold I had entrusted to him in 1856.

This pale world is not mine. The vivid colours of my land and the profound silence of the Ganges are somehow closer to me than my surroundings. And yet I do not yearn to go back. I have crossed the Ganges for the last time. The embers I carry are for warmth on this oasis halt, not for fanning into another sacred fire, but I know they will last me through the night.

MORE ABOUT PENGUINS

For further information about books available from Penguins in India write to Penguin Books (India) Ltd, Room 2-4, 1st Floor, PTI Building, Parliament Street, New Delhi-110 001.

In the UK : For a complete list of books available from Penguins in the United Kingdom write to Dept. EP, Penguin Books Ltd, Harmondsworth, Middlesex UB 7 ODA.

In the U.S.A. : For a complete list of books available from Penguins in the United States write to Dept. DG, Penguin Books, 299 Murray Hill Parkway, East Rutherford, New Jersey 07073.

In Canada : For a complete list of books available from Penguins in Canada write to Penguin Books Canada Ltd, 2801 John Street, Markham, Ontario L3R IB4.

In Australia : For a complete list of books available from Penguins in Australia write to the Marketing Department, Penguin Books Australia Ltd, P.O. Box 257, Ringwood, Victoria 3134.

In New Zealand : For a complete list of books available from Penguins in New Zealand write to the Marketing Department, Penguin Books (N.Z.) Ltd, Private Bag, Takapuna, Auckland 9.

FOWL-FILCHER
Ranga Rao

While the British still rule India, a son is born to a hunter who works for a minor maharaja. From the time of his birth, the boy, who is known only by his nickname Fowl-filcher (which has its origins in a crime of which he is wrongly accused), gets into a series of increasingly hazardous and hilarious scrapes with, among others, tigers, dogs, nymphomaniacs, ghosts and mundane municipal councillors. Eventually this wildly comic romp turns sombre as *Fowl-filcher* gets involved with a crooked politician and comes to grief.

Apart from being a wonderfully funny first novel, *Fowl-filcher* paints a fascinating picture of India after the Raj.

A DEATH IN DELHI :
Modern Hindi Short Stories
Translated & Edited by
Gordon C. Roadarmel

A collection of brilliant new stories from the
writers who have revolutionized Hindi liter-
ature over the past forty years. The short
stories in this volume take up from where
Premchand (the greatest writer Hindi has
ever produced) and his immediate successors left off and offer the reader an excellent
and entertaining introduction to the diversi-
ty and richness that the modern short story
at its best can offer. Among the writers
represented are Nirmal Verma, Krishna
Baldev Vaid, Shekhar Joshi Phanishwar-
nath 'Renu', Gyanranjan and Mohan
Rakesh.

'By far the best collection of recent Hindi
short stories to have appeared in English'.
—*David Rubin*

THE ROOM ON THE ROOF
Ruskin Bond

Rusty, a sixteen-year-old Anglo-Indian boy, is dissatisfied with life in the declining European community at Dehra Dun. So he runs away from home to live with Indian friends who introduce him, much to his delight, to the dream bright world of *bazaar* life, Hindu festivals and a way of being that seems utterly enchanting. Rusty is hooked at once by all this and is forever lost to the prim proprieties of the European community.

'Mr Bond is a writer of great gifts'
—*The New Statesman*

'Like an Indian bazaar itself, the book is filled with the smells, sights, sounds, confusion and subtle organization of ordinary Indian life'
—'Santha Rama Rau in the *New York Times Book Review*

Winner of the John Llewellyn Rhys Memorial Prize